Rena

Shelley Munro

Munro Press

Rena

Print ISBN: 978-1-99-106368-7
Ebook ISBN: 978-0-9951395-2-7

Editor: Evil Eye Editing
Cover: Kim Killion, The Killion Group, Inc.

Munro Press, New Zealand.

First Munro Press electronic publication October 2020
First Munro Press print publication November 2024

DEDICATION

For Paul, my husband, partner in crime, and fellow adventurer.
Every day is a good day.

Introduction

A mysterious robed man is haunting Rena Carrington's dreams. He's chatting each night, giving her details of the future. Worse, he's seducing her with his fiery kisses and silken caresses. Her dream man is spoiling her for other men since none of them measure up to Mr. Tall and Mysterious. During this, Rena's sister disappears, presumed dead, and Rena struggles to protect her niece from her sister's eye-on-the-chance ex.

After losing his wife and child, guilt has David seeking refuge with the druids at the monastery on Smoking Isle. Discovering Rena on the dreamscape yanks him from his quiet, scholarly life. He's thrust into a dangerous adventure where he and Rena must keep the Dragon Isles residents safe from ambitious dragons intent on change.

Rena might clutch her skepticism, but her eyes do not deceive her. Her mystery dream man is no mirage, and he insists they're stronger together. A former soldier, David is no stranger to war, but now the stakes are higher than they've ever been. His heart is on the line, a child is in danger, and his newfound dragon friends need his help.

Rena and David—no turning back. No second chances. It's do or die.

You will love this final book in the Dragon Isles trilogy because it's full of dragons—both menacing and benevolent. There's a courageous military hero who kicks butt and saves the weak, a human woman strong enough to tame him, and a world full of mystery, magic, and mayhem. Plus one or two dragon-caused infernos when good butts against evil.

Author Note

Welcome to David's and Rena's romance and the third book in the Dragon Isles trilogy. You'll also get reacquainted with the couples from the first two books—Liza and Leo plus Cherry and Martinos—as they continue to get to the bottom of the trouble in the Dragon Isles. No cliffhangers in this one, and only one plot thread still open—that of Blaze's missing sister. Sasha has her own standalone book where she'd let you know what she's been up to all this time. A little mischief, for sure!

Don't want to miss Sasha, Dragon Isles 4? Or the next book after that? Sign up for my entertaining newsletter at my website. (https://shelleymunro.com/newsletter/)

Happy reading!
Shelley

CHAPTER 1

My Dream Lover

Despite the drooping of her eyes and fatigue tugging at her limbs, Rena Carrington resisted the siren lure of sleep. She blinked and stood before directing her legs onto a carpeted area large enough to do star-jumps.

"One. Two. Three." Rena counted them off, legs pumping, arms flapping, and brown curls bouncing. The late-night television movie played in the background.

She would not sleep.

She. Would. Not.

The horror movie continued, the strident music warning the viewer the heroine was doing something stupid. *Again.*

"Don't do it!" Rena shouted at the red-haired woman, hoping verbal interaction might warn the heroine away from the creepy cornfield. The heroine ignored her and crept forward to commit further acts of stupidity.

Rena's jaw opened in a full and inelegant yawn. Thankfully, no one sat in her tiny flat to view her tonsils.

"I refuse to go to sleep!" Rena shouted. A shudder worked down her spine, and she yawned again. *Popsicles*, she was so tired. Exhausted, actually, and she admitted it wouldn't be long before her body revolted.

She'd drop off to sleep from sheer necessity, and the black-haired, brown-eyed hunk with the weird blue tattoos would saunter into her dreams. *Again.*

Rena strode through her compact open-plan lounge to her galley kitchen. She checked the water level in her kettle and pushed the power button. A cup of strong coffee should do the trick.

Her hand trembled as she sloshed the boiling water into a cup. Instead of adding milk as was her standard practice, Rena forced herself to take the caffeine straight and unadulterated.

"Ugh! That's disgusting." She surrendered and added a dash of milk.

She sat at her minuscule breakfast bar and stared into space, sipping the hot beverage. A scream rippled from the TV, and Rena jumped. Coffee splattered over her fake marble countertop, and a pithy curse escaped.

It wasn't fair.

She hadn't asked for this burden.

She yawned again, her eyes heavy and uncomfortable. Without volition, she bowed her head. Her eyes fluttered closed. She jerked herself awake, and a hearty sigh of disgust escaped.

If she didn't sleep, she'd never get through the coming day. Her father had asked her to check in at his office and collect his mail plus she had errands. Calls to return. Busy. *Busy.*

While sleep might be a necessity, she could do it without dreaming.

She *would* do it without entering the dreamworld that shook her to the core. She swallowed hard and forced herself to her feet. Like a zombie, she shuffled from her kitchen, down the passage to the sole bedroom. She adored this flat, housed in an old converted Georgian mansion. She'd fallen in love with the space—one of six flats for sale—the moment the real estate agent had opened the elegant door and ushered her inside. It had always been her haven, but right now, her home smothered her like a prison.

She flicked on the light, illuminating her ultra-feminine bedroom with cream-and-lavender sheers at the windows—a side she hid from the outside world of her casual job with her father and her university studies.

Rena pushed her legs to function, directing them toward her double bed covered with a blueberry-and-silver duvet. Sluggish with fatigue, she toed off her leather slip-on shoes and socks and left them where they fell on her thick slate-gray rug. She tugged off her jeans and shirt and crawled onto the bed in a tank top and panties. In deference to a fall in the temperature, she fought her way under the covers to the violet sheets. Before she even turned off the light, her eyes slid shut.

I will not dream.

I. Will. Not.

She repeated the mantra in her mind. Once. Twice. Three times before she sank deep into sleep and nothing else registered.

David McKenzie paced the grove of oak trees at the rear of the monastery, his cowl drawn over his black hair to screen his face and his black robe blending with the shadows. The rest of his fellow druids were relaxing in the solarium, reading, chatting to others, and two senior druids plied their needles, repairing the druid tapestry that told the history of their order. No one would miss him, at least not until morning.

The woman was so obstinate. She was fighting him when he was attempting to help the dragon. He needed her assistance because the dragon was more dead than alive. It was the druid way to offer help, to live a simple life, and give service to others who required aid.

The dragon screamed his anger, his fear, and David heard his suffering in the dreamworld. David ached to free him from his agony. He'd tried, and when nothing he'd done had released the creature, he'd searched for answers during his waking hours.

He'd sensed the invasive rot for some time, so he'd watched, asked questions, and skulked in corners. Now, he embraced the dreamworld he'd ignored because of his wife's disapproval of the ungodly talent inherited from his mother. Until he'd taken an unexpected dreamwalk several months ago, he'd focused on his magic studies with Brother Jasper and his study of herbs and their various properties.

Once he'd discovered the trapped dragon, the beast he suspected one of his fellow druids had banished to the other world, he'd embraced every one of his talents. While he could enter the dreamworld via anyone on the Dragon Isles, he'd traveled farther to the mainland. Following his instincts, it had taken time to find the right person, but once he'd forged the path, he could slide into her dreams without expending much energy. With each successive journey, he honed his skill.

Rena Carrington was fighting him.

Stubborn wench.

He needed her to submit, to allow him to slide into her mind so he could pass on messages.

Whatever the druids and their cohorts had in mind for the Dragon Isles and those humans who lived on the mainland, they'd set their plan in motion. Destiny had snared a human for him to communicate with, and from what he'd learned while reading Rena's dreams, she was part of the puzzle.

"Come on, Rena," he urged. "I want to help, but I can't until you sleep." David paced another circuit of the oak grove. The dampness of the ground beneath the leaf litter rose with each determined step, the scent pungent and ripe. A hint of green herbs wafted from the gardens, the breeze drifting in his direction.

"Please, my sweet cynamone," he whispered.

He sensed the instant slumber took her. His breath hissed out with relief.

David strode over to a sheltered spot where he allowed himself to rest and prepare to enter the dreamworld. He sank onto the thick leaf litter and reached over to drag a handy branch into place. He chanted a swift concealment spell, his fingers forming a rune until a faint vibration filled the air. Any of his fellow druids going for an evening walk would see nothing out of the ordinary unless they were searching for him. Only then, his camouflage rune might fail, and he'd need to do some quick talking, depending on the questions he received.

With his protections in place, David let himself sink into sleep. Once he entered deep slumber, he allowed his dreamself to step from his solid body and enter the world of imaginings. Rainbow colors flashed in front of his eyes, with paths leading in myriad directions. Ribbons grew from a series of clumps. The nearest was full of black, red, and blue streamers—those of sleeping druids—while others were the dreams of those who lived on Smoking Isle. Each colored path led to a sleeping being, his or her head full of fantasy images.

David strolled farther into the dreamscape, searching for a particular turquoise strand. *Ah!* There it was. He tugged at it with his mind, his body floating as he drifted closer to Rena. A sense of peace fell over him—the certainty he was following the right path.

The turquoise strand ended at a shimmering doorway. At his arrival, the entrance slid open to reveal the pretty purple and gray room beyond, which held a plush bed with a single occupant. Excitement raced through him. The first time they'd met, Rena had been walking through a garden full of flowers and vegetables. Mature trees and sculptures from the Renaissance period had created visual interest while a bubbling brook ran down the edge of the garden. Their meeting had gone well, but the sizzling physical attraction between them had startled David. He'd thought his heart had died with his wife hundreds of years ago when Vikings had sacked the monastery and small farms on Iona Island off the coast of Scotland.

His second meeting with Rena had taken place in a plain, narrow bedroom where their passion had exploded, running out of control.

They'd touched. They'd kissed. They'd made love, and the exceptional desire had blindsided them both. David had tried to resist Rena's lure, but his willpower had disappeared on a lengthy journey the moment he'd walked into her dreams. Their meetings since had gone the same way, their mutual lust boiling over into the physical act, albeit occurring on the dreamscape.

David stepped into the bedroom, curiosity taking in the details. While the bed was familiar, the other items were foreign. A flashing clock. The fabrics of the bedclothes. The style of the wardrobe. Rena's garments, which she'd tossed on the floor.

"You're here." Rena scrutinized him with big, brown eyes. Her brown tresses were in disarray, the curls a mass of confusion and disorder. She wore a bright pink sleeveless top that clung to her breasts and hid nothing from his avid gaze. Her long legs were bare, and the way her knee crooked offered him a glimpse of her matching pink panties.

"I have information." He trained his gaze on her gorgeous face, her stubborn red mouth, and the fascinating beauty mark to the left of her upper lip. "Why did you linger?"

"This is not normal," Rena snapped. "We've had sex. More than once."

"Yes." His gaze sought hers, and he winged reassurance her way. It didn't work. If anything, her agitation increased.

"Most women don't have dream lovers. You're spoiling me for other men. No one of my acquaintances can compete with a muscled hottie like you." She snorted. "Even your scars are sexy."

He grinned, his inner male delighted by her words. The scars on his back and hip tingled. "That's not the reason I waited for you to fall asleep. You have a friend called Cherry."

"Yes," she agreed, wary now.

"She will meet a stranger on the beach. She needs to help him."

"Why?"

"Because the druids have set a plan into motion. Whatever they've done has disturbed the natural pattern of life. I need to right the wrong."

Her head jerked up. "Is Cherry in danger? Joanna?"

David hesitated. "I don't believe so. The man, your Cherry, finds will not hurt her. He will do his best to protect her and Joanna. He will fight for her."

"S-should I tell Cherry? Warn her."

"Yes," David said. "She must do everything possible to help him."

"Where did he come from?"

"That is not important."

"You can't enter my dreams and withhold information from me," she snapped.

He beamed, her feistiness thrilling him. He'd never have believed he'd enjoy a woman of an independent nature. A woman who challenged him instead of acquiescing to his every wish or request. A woman who wasn't afraid to express her opinions.

"Why are you smiling?"

"You make me smile. You're feisty and exciting. Delightful."

"Huh! I'm ordinary. My nose is too big, and my hair is a mess. I have a temper, and I can be mean if someone pisses me off. Sarcasm is my middle name."

"We each have our faults. The senior druids say I am too curious. They'd prefer me to carry out my duties and not show independent thinking. To them, questions are inappropriate, but I require mental stimulation. I prefer to keep busy and enjoy learning. If it weren't for the library, I'd have turned crazy many moons ago."

"Intelligent men are sexy," Rena blurted.

"Then we are of one accord." David winked at her and took pleasure in the way her brown eyes narrowed. "Intelligent and prickly women are turn-ons for me. You look tired."

"Someone is keeping me awake."

"You tempt me, my cynamone, like a bee to a bright flower."

"But you're not real, and what's a cynamone?"

David chuckled at her grumpiness because it was so her. *So his cynamone.* "You are my sweet cynamone. It's an endearment from my time after the cinnamon spice. It suits you because you're sweet and piquant. And I am a flesh and blood man who lusts for you," he whispered, sauntering closer. "Soon, you'll understand."

"You burst into my dreams, turning my world topsy-turvy. This...whatever we have is crazy."

David sat on the edge of the soft bed, heartened she didn't retreat or display fear. His courageous lady.

Her brown eyes held the same wonder he experienced, and excitement tumbled through him. "I'm asking a lot from you. I'm demanding your acceptance when this is new to you. Strange, but I mean you no harm. You can trust me."

"Can I? Should I accept the word of a stranger? You *would* tell me to trust you. It's in your best interest to acquire whatever you need from me."

Her logic drew another grin from him. "You're right, but I'm speaking the truth. Make sure you inform Cherry. Tell her not to let his appearance scare her. I believe he will not harm Cherry or Joanna."

"An assumption?" Rena asked. "Liza...Liza..." She broke off and swallowed hard as if a lump filled her throat. "My sister is missing, and the police suspect she is dead. Drowned. T-they can't locate her body. Cherry and I haven't told Joanna yet." She broke off again, this time with a sob.

David frowned, wanting to reassure Rena. He closed his eyes and focused, allowing information to drift willy-nilly. An answer firmed, and his eyes popped open again. "Your sister is alive. That's all I can tell you. Sorry."

"My father and I recently made contact with her and Joanna. It doesn't seem fair she's gone so soon. I hate keeping the truth from Joanna, but she's a child. The one thing we are certain of is hiding Joanna from her bastard father. He uses her as a pawn and cares nothing for his daughter. She's a means to an end."

Unable to help himself, David slid across the bed and drew Rena into his arms. She fit him with the perfection of an interlocking puzzle piece, her body even softer than in his memories. "You've told me nothing is official yet. I believe she is alive. Have faith."

Instead of pushing him away, Rena leaned into him. He wrapped his arms around her and rested his head on top of hers. Her scent suggested herbs and lemons instead of flowers as he expected. Nice. He drew in the fragrance and pressed his lips to her temple.

"Kiss me," she said.

Their gazes met, and something electric passed between them.

"Are you certain?"

"Is it against your monk laws?"

"Druid. I'm not a monk."

"What's the difference?"

"A druid is capable of magic." David went with the simplest explanation. "And I can walk through dreams."

She angled her head back. "Why did you choose my dreams?"

"Instinct," he said, recalling the strand of bright turquoise that had shimmered in the light and called to him. "Your dream tether is stunning in its beauty."

"Tether?"

"I see dreams in ribbons, each one a different color. A variation. Once I go to sleep myself, I can follow any of the ribbons and enter the dream of the one I've chosen."

Her brow furrowed. "That's not creepy or anything."

"Do you still want me to kiss you?"

Her gaze darted to his mouth, and the frown marks on her forehead faded. "I can feel your arms around me, so I guess I don't need one."

David chuckled. "Now you've put the idea into my head, I'm of a mind to steal a kiss."

She stared at him, and he noticed the flecks of amber in her brown eyes. "What happens if you stay with me and don't return?"

His gaze lowered to her red mouth, and he studied the curve of her lips. Her tongue darted out to moisten her bottom one, and a groan built in his chest. He thought he might burst if he couldn't kiss her soon.

"David?"

"My mother told me I'd die if I don't return to my body. Once the sun rises, I'd weaken. If I haven't returned by the second sunrise, I'll never awaken. Don't worry. I'm careful."

He smiled at her wide-eyed expression. David placed one hand on her shoulder and lifted the other to cup her chin. She sucked in a deep breath, diverting his gaze to her breasts. More to explore later. He lowered his head and touched his lips to hers—a slight press of mouths. Her gasp and her lack of retreat enticed him to deepen the caress. *Heaven*. She trembled and pressed those luscious breasts against his chest.

David wished his robe away, and as always in the dreamscape, the black fabric dissolved, leaving nothing but skin. He stretched out beside Rena and drew her close.

"We're doing the beast with two backs, aren't we?"

David's grin appeared without conscious effort on his part. "Ah, I thought you'd pretend I was your fertile imagination again. It's why I'm acting with caution."

She sighed. "I've discussed Liza and Joanna with you before. I keep pretending my memories of our time together aren't real, that stress is sending me bonkers. Guess it's time to yank my head from the sand."

"Hallelujah."

"Now you're laughing at me."

"Never," he said, but he suspected his eyes made him a liar. "Let's make this easier. We've kissed in our dreams and made love." He paused and sent her what he expected was a wicked, wolfish grin. "The best sex of my life." He hid his wince of disloyalty to his wife, reminding himself she'd died hundreds of years ago.

Rena huffed. "Do you make a habit of seducing women in their dreams?"

His smile wiped free. "No! That'd be creepy. You're the only woman I've wanted on the dreamscape."

"How did you choose me?"

"I told you. Your turquoise tether called to me. You are my key." That grin curled his lips again. Yep, it sure felt wolfish to him. "Once I glimpsed you, the last thing I wanted was to retreat. You're beautiful, Rena. I adore your brown curls. Your tawny skin. Your golden-brown eyes. These full red lips." He traced his finger over her cheek.

"Oh," she said.

He waggled his eyebrows at her. "Can I take your clothes off now?"

"If you must."

Now she was teasing him. He willed away her clothes. When she awoke in the morning, she'd find them twisted around her body as if she'd had a restless night.

David took in her body, the dips and curves, the sensual shape that called to him. Would always call him, he suspected, even when they grew older. "You are exceptional. Stunning."

She rolled her eyes. "Laying it on thick. Where do you live? I don't understand why this is happening. I'm the sensible, level-headed one in the family. The details person grounded in reality," Rena wailed. "That's why I study science. Yet, instead of embracing truth, all I want to do is trace your tattoos with my tongue. It's not normal, I tell you."

"Shush, my sweet one. The working details aren't important. Just accept we're connected, and we adore each other. A lot."

"The sex is exceptional," she said, yet she sounded glum about the magical sparks between them. "No one else could measure up."

"There you go then," David murmured, trying to hide his satisfaction. He slid his hands over her collarbone and kissed her. He captured and plundered. It was a claiming. An acknowledgment and the passion flared between them, shining hot and bright until they both burned.

Flashes of turquoise twined over their bodies, caressing and brightening their skin. He dipped his head to suck her nipple. She bucked beneath him and groaned.

"David, yes. So good. It's a bungee of pleasure that arcs downward and gathers into arousal. More," she pleaded.

"My pleasure." He used his mouth on one nipple and his fingers to stimulate the other. His hands wandered her hips and her upper thighs while she cried out encouragement. Her hands ran over his back and cupped his buttocks.

When he lifted his head, they were both breathing hard.

"Turn over," she ordered. "Let me play."

"Not too much touching," he said. "When I explode, I want it to be inside you."

Her chuckle veered into evil. "Use every ounce of your willpower. It feels as if you've never given me a chance to explore your body. I want to lick your tattoos so badly. I've never seen bright blue tattoos like yours."

"The tattoos are natural and form on some druids. I think of them as a symbol of my druidism. And you have touched me. Last time we made love, you sucked my cock. I came in your mouth, and it was amazing."

She blushed—a charming wash of color against her olive cheeks and gave an expressive huff that made him grin. Her fingers glided over his hip, setting a long-ago sword wound tingling again. She stroked his length until he gritted his teeth with the effort to hold back his release.

"Rena," he warned.

"This is a dream. I'm certain you'll recover fast enough to do this again." Without giving him the right of reply, she took his cock deep into her mouth. Her tongue swept over his tip and dipped under to caress the sensitive underside. All the time, she worked him with her mouth, her hands pumped and teased. His balls drew tight, his body tense with excitement and anticipation.

"Rena." He gritted his teeth against his impending climax. "Please, let me come inside you. Please."

To his relief, she heeded his warning and backed off.

"Spread your legs," he barked.

"So romantic," she taunted even as she followed his order. She splayed her legs, flashing her sex at him. Her folds glistened with arousal, but David stroked her, wanting to make sure she was ready for him.

"David, please. What happens if I wake up and we haven't finished? A waste of a perfect erection." She gave him a sly squeeze.

He laughed with genuine amusement. Despite her impatience, he took the time to kiss her. Their tongues stroked together, and the vibration of a groan rippled through Rena. She clutched his shoulders, twisting beneath him, restless and eager. He allowed her to turn their bodies, so he lay on the bottom.

Her gaze held daring and challenge, and he just laughed as she positioned his shaft and sank down. Their collective moan echoed in her bedroom. She rose upward and dropped back down, falling into a rhythm that had his toes curling and his orgasm pulsing in his balls.

"Touch yourself," he said on a groan. "Please, Rena. I want to see you come."

This time, she obeyed his request and stroked between her legs while rising and falling. David shuddered, the pleasure swelling inside him. Tendrils of sensation raced up and down his spine. Rena gasped, her moan music to his ears. He'd learned her body, her reactions to his touch, her touch, and sensed she'd almost caught her orgasm. David waited for a heartbeat, concentrating on Rena's pleasure. The faint intake of air. The tiny spasms of her channel—a warning she was about to shatter.

Ah! There were the ripples.

David released the reins of restraint as Rena increased her rocking motion. The tremors increased in speed and intensity. Rena threw back her head and closed her eyes, her entire body twitching with her pleasure.

David watched for mere seconds before he crashed into climax, and his seed spurted. Incredible. So, so fine.

Gradually, they came back to themselves. Rena stretched on top of his body, and he wrapped his arms around her. David kissed the tip of her nose, and they lay at peace, awash in the afterglow and togetherness.

He had to meet her in person. Happily, his foresight told him this was a forgone conclusion with so much at stake in his world. All his recent hours of practicing dreamwalking had led him to this moment, led him to meet Rena. The odd things at the monastery and the strange behavior of the senior druids had started this journey.

David had used his available weapons and talent to discover the source of his suspicion. He'd noticed the meetings with dragons, and while that wasn't unusual, the frequency of the encounters was higher than usual. There was the sizeable building the druids had allowed the dragons to construct, ostensibly for monastery use.

He'd watched people coming and going—humans, dragons, and druids.

Senior druids.

So far, he hadn't entered the warehouse to learn the building's purpose.

The activity continued day and night.

He'd grown weary of remaining awake, and his dreams had offered unforeseen information. Somehow, he wasn't sure how he'd followed a tether to a fisherman. He'd seen a rogue wave sweep the dragon overboard. The humans aboard the boat had tried to save the dragon, but the swell had ripped him away, tossing him to the mercy of the sea.

Rena fell quiet, and as she sank deeper into her sleep, a barrier grew between them and the dreamscape. David kissed her forehead and slipped away while praying she'd recall the details he'd related to her. She needed to pass them on to her friend.

It was a matter of life or death for the dragon.

CHAPTER 2

Sneaking and Skullduggery

Rena slept late, only the phone pulling her from her bed because she'd left it on the other side of her room. Forgotten to set the alarm. *Again.* Luckily, this was a day when lateness didn't matter since she was on a break from her studies.

"Hello."

"Where is my daughter?" her caller gritted out. A familiar voice.

Rena hung up without speaking and blocked the number. Her fourth blocked number since Tony made a habit of borrowing phones to trick her into answering.

Liza had made a rotten choice in Tony—a bully who expected

everything to go his way. Rena and her father adored their newfound family and intended to protect Liza and Joanna who had moved from New Zealand to England to escape her ex. Her lost sister and niece filled a gap for Rena and her father after her mother had died from cancer. Liza had given them a new purpose.

Her phone rang yet again, and Rena eyed it with trepidation. If that were Tony, she'd give him an earful even though it was better not to engage.

But Rena recognized this number. The police. Her heart beat faster, her trepidation morphing to panic. Had they found Liza's car? Her body?

God, she couldn't lose her sister now. It wasn't fair.

"Rena C-Carrington." While she aimed for poised and polite, her voice broke. She closed her eyes and winged a prayer skyward.

"Ms. Carrington, it's Sergeant Basingstoke from the Bamburgh police station. I have more information for you about your sister." He hesitated, driving her stress levels even higher.

She loathed that pregnant pause.

"Normally, we'd visit in person. Is there someone there with you?"

"I have a friend," Rena lied. "Go ahead."

"Your sister's car went over the edge of the cliff. Divers discovered the vehicle on the seabed a few hours ago. We have not located your sister."

"I see," Rena said in understatement because she didn't

comprehend any of this. "Maybe she swam to shore?"

"Although conditions were decent yesterday, the currents are strong in that area. Our divers will continue to search today, but our assumption is the current has swept her out to sea."

Tears formed in Rena's eyes and dripped down her cheeks and over her chin. One by one, they plopped to the floor. "You—you don't think the outcome will be favorable."

The sergeant hesitated again. "I'm sorry," he said in a calm, emotionless voice. "It's possible the divers might locate her before dark."

But he had doubts. They lurked in the careful way he considered his words before he spoke.

"I'm sorry, Ms. Carrington. If you have questions, please contact the station."

"Thank you." The phone dropped away from Rena's ear, and her tears dripped from her chin and onto the floor. This... Liza gone. David had told her Liza was still alive. Who did she believe?

She set her phone on the counter and lumbered into her compact bathroom to shower. Once she was calmer, she'd phone Cherry. But after she made herself a coffee and called, she discovered her friend had already heard the dreadful news. Rena grabbed clothes at random, dressed, and brushed her rat's nest of curls. When that didn't help, she slapped on a cap to hide the wayward locks before hustling to visit Cherry in person. She found Joanna ready for school and held a whispered conversation with

Cherry.

"Cherry, you told me Liza talked about visiting Holy Island. Lindisfarne. It occurred to me this might be an excellent place to hide Joanna from Tony. The full tide cuts the island off from the mainland. Strangers stick out, and if we sneak away without Tony spotting us, we should be safe enough. None of us have prior contacts to the island, so he'd never search for Joanna there."

"That's a marvelous idea, but what about my bookstore?" Cherry asked.

"We need to stall until Liza returns."

Cherry gaped at Rena. "Are you listening to yourself?" She glanced toward the kitchen where Joanna was eating breakfast. "It looks as if Liza drove over a cliff. How can she still be alive?"

"She was alive in my dream."

"It was a dream, Rena."

"I know it sounds crazy, but it was so real. Look, give it two or three days. By that time, we'll have more info. If things don't turn out the way my dream showed, we'll come up with another plan. Dad should be back in England by then."

"Maybe." Cherry didn't sound convinced.

Rena forged onward with her plan. "Since it's a school day, why don't I volunteer to drop off my neighbor's daughter? From a distance, she resembles Joanna."

"Will that work?" Cherry asked.

"It's worth a try. I'll call you once I get home."

There was no way she'd let Tony have custody of Joanna. They were lucky that at the last moment, Tony had decided he wanted to take his young girlfriend to London for a fancy dinner and a visit to the theater. If he'd had physical charge of Joanna on the day Liza had gone missing, he'd have won.

"I'm not sure if Tony knows Liza has vanished since the press hasn't reported the accident. It might be on the news later this afternoon, though."

"Okay," Cherry agreed. "I'll pack and organize for Mum to mind the bookstore."

"Will she agree to do that? I thought your mother didn't approve of your store."

Cherry sighed. "She wants me to find a man, get married, and produce the requisite grandchildren."

"She considers your books an unnecessary tie that takes up your spare time," Rena finished.

"Yes, but she'll do it because her friends enjoy visiting and browsing the books. I'll get a lecture or two, but she'll help. If the worst happens, and she closes the store, it doesn't matter."

It *did* concern her, though, since Cherry worked on a tight budget. Rena made a mental note to visit the store. If Cherry's mother wasn't keen, Rena would arrange alternative cover and pay the wages out of her pocket. Thanks to her generous father, she could afford this. Cherry would argue, but she was helping to protect Joanna.

"Contact me if you have any problems. I'm trying to stay positive and trust my dream man is right, but it's so hard. Oh, wait! Let me tell you about my dream last night."

"Your sexy druid," Cherry teased.

Heat converged in Rena's cheeks. Since Cherry knew her well, she'd notice Rena's discomfort.

"He told me you'd meet a man on the beach. Please help him. He means you no harm."

"That's what your druid said?"

"He's not my druid."

"But you are having steamy passionate sex with him," Cherry teased again. "Where will this mystery man come from?"

"David didn't say but assured me he'd help you and Joanna and protect rather than harm."

"Sounds intriguing, but I won't hold my breath," Cherry replied with a smile in her voice. "We're talking about a dream man. I'll book a cottage for two weeks and talk to you once we arrive on the island."

"Two weeks should do it. Talk to you later."

Once Rena arrived back at her flat, she ran through her plan. Satisfied, she picked up her wallet, hurried from her apartment, and locked up before she knocked on her neighbor's door.

"Hey, Susan. I'm heading out for bread and milk. If you want, I can drop Fiona at school on my way."

Susan jiggled her six-month-old baby on her hip. She'd tied her hair back in an untidy ponytail, which did nothing to hide her reddened eyes and fatigue. "You're a lifesaver! Adam cried all night, and I'm running behind schedule. Fiona, are you ready to go to school?"

Fiona ran from the kitchen with her pigtails bouncing. She dragged her red school bag with her. "Ready!" she shouted.

"Have you got your sunhat?" Rena asked.

"*Ooh*, yes! Here it is." Susan slapped it on top of her daughter's head. "Leave it there," she instructed her daughter. "You won't lose it if it's on your head."

"See you later." Rena paused. "Do you need milk or bread?"

"Yes! Both, please. I'll get you money."

"Pay me when I get back." *Perfect.* With the hat in place, Tony would assume Rena was taking Joanna to school, especially if he remained at a distance. Rena grinned and ushered Fiona out the door and toward her mini.

The school drop went without a hitch, and although she didn't spot Tony, the itching sensation at the back of her neck told her he was skulking in the background. If it wasn't him, it was one of his evil minions. At least the school administration and the teachers knew not to release Joanna to anyone except Liza, Rena, or Cherry.

After doing a few things at the office for her father, Rena stopped at the local supermarket to grab milk, bread, and a packet of tea. At the last minute, she tossed in a package of chocolate digestive biscuits. Her stomach rumbled with the force of a volcano, and after checking the time, she treated herself to a full English breakfast. She'd run in the afternoon to make up for the extra calories. Two hours later, she delivered a bottle of milk and a loaf of sandwich bread to Susan. Her neighbor took a while to hunt out the correct change.

"Pay me tomorrow," Rena said.

"No, you've done me a favor. I'd hate you to think I don't pay my debts, or that I take you for granted. You were a lifesaver this morning."

A flash of shame shot through Rena. If Susan suspected the reasons for her generous act, she might have second thoughts.

"Ah! Here you are." Susan handed over the correct change. "Bless you for taking Fiona to school. Adam stopped crying and went to sleep, which allowed me to have a quick nap. Thank you!"

"No problem. Any time." Rena waved goodbye and hurried back to her apartment. By now, Cherry should've reached Holy Island. She juggled her shopping bags and her keys while she unlocked the door. The door opened before she inserted the key.

Rena halted, her brow furrowing because she'd locked up when she left.

With her heart banging her ribs, she nudged the door wider.

From the doorway, it was easy to see someone had entered her home. Her belongings littered the floor of the lounge. A purple pot lay on its side, the dirt mashed into the carpet and the plant sitting several feet away. The intruder had swept her favorite books off her wooden shelves and ripped pages from their bindings. Her kitchen cupboards and the pantry doors hung open, and someone had picked up her stacks of dishes and dropped them on the floor.

Interestingly, her television and her one indulgence, her expensive sound system, remained undisturbed. The change she tossed in the bowl on the counter was still in plain sight.

Rena cocked her ear and heard no foreign sounds coming from her bedroom. She picked up her phone and rang the local police station.

"Yes, this is Rena Carrington. I'd like to report a break-in."

The police receptionist took details and promised someone would drop by to take a report in person.

While she waited for the police to arrive, she entered her flat, pausing to listen for out-of-place noises. When she heard nothing to cause alarm, she did a quick search. As far as she could see nothing was missing, not even her favorite handbag, which she took *everywhere*. Her sister and friend would be shocked if they'd learned in her haste and fatigue this morning she'd left it behind. They often wondered aloud if the leather handles were stitched to her hand. Rena scowled, thankful the intruder had left her bag since it had belonged to her mother. She'd thought her flat secure from burglaries because visitors needed to ring the doorbell at the front for entry.

Susan hadn't heard the intruder's presence or an unexpected commotion. The flat on her other side was empty during the day, the couple who occupied it leaving for work at seven every morning. She returned to her front door and studied the lock.

Not a scrape or scratch marred the brass. The culprit was careful or...

Her eyes narrowed.

Or they had a key.

Both Cherry and Liza had a key to her flat. Her father too.

Rena sighed. She'd get the locks changed and go from there.

She sat around for almost four hours before the police arrived. She spoke with the constables—one male and one female—and took them through her flat.

"Are you certain you locked your door, Ms. Carrington?"

"Positive." Rena was almost one hundred percent certain, but she'd tossed and turned so much the night before, and what sleep she'd had hadn't left her rested. The druid's fault. The drift of her mind and memories of her lovemaking sent a blush to her cheeks.

"Have you given your key to a boyfriend? Perhaps an ex who you parted from on unpleasant terms?" the female constable asked. "This is personal rather than an opportunist crime since you've stated nothing appears to be missing."

Rena barked out a laugh. "No time for a boyfriend. My studies take up most of my free time." Tony was her best bet, but she didn't want to draw attention to the situation with Joanna.

"What are you studying?"

"Forensic science," Rena said. "It's holidays at the moment. I popped out to pick up a few groceries and to take my neighbor's daughter to school. I was away for two hours."

"Did your neighbor hear anything?" the male constable asked.

"She was up all night with her baby, and she sneaked in a nap when the baby went to sleep. I doubt she heard a thing."

He nodded and scanned the disordered room again. "We'll check with your neighbors and ask if any of them saw anything suspicious."

The female constable jotted a last note on her report before she signed it and handed Rena a copy. "For your insurance claim."

"Thank you. Can I clean up the mess now?"

"Yes," the male constable said.

The two constables left, and Rena scanned the mess and sighed. Before she started, she snapped photos of the property damage to go in her insurance claim.

Cleanup took ages, and she muttered several curses under her breath. When she spotted Tony next, she might kick his arse.

Although she didn't tell the police, her gut told her Tony had committed the crime.

Once she'd finished her cleaning, she took stock of her remaining food supplies and went out for dinner at her local Indian restaurant. She locked her door and hoped Tony didn't make more trouble. He hadn't attempted to ring her again, but he'd receive an earful if he did.

When she rang Cherry, it was late.

"We're here, and everything went well," Cherry said, her tone chirpy. "The cottage is gorgeous, and Joanna has settled down well. Um..."

"Yes?"

"I met your mystery man."

Astonishment bloomed in Rena because she'd harbored the same doubts as Cherry. "What is he like?"

"He's nice."

"Nice? That's a nothing word. It doesn't tell me anything. How did you find him? Where did he come from?"

"He says he comes from the Dragon Isles."

Rena scrunched her forehead. She'd never heard of the place. "Where?"

"He's a dragon shifter, Rena, and Joanna and I stumbled across him on the beach."

Rena's mouth dropped open. "Say what?"

"A dragon shifter."

"You let a dragon move into the cottage."

"Don't be silly, Rena. A dragon wouldn't fit inside the cottage. Martinos is in his human form."

Rena spluttered, her mouth working like a goldfish. Luckily, Cherry didn't witness her reaction because teasing would've ensued. "Are you sure about this? You haven't seen his dragon form. Is he on drugs or drunk?"

"Credit me with sense. He's sane and normal, albeit bruised and battered," Cherry said. "I might be quiet and less adventurous than you, but I have an excellent bullshit meter. I would never place Joanna in harm's way. You told me your dream man said he was safe."

"Sorry, I know you'd never endanger Joanna, and David assured me he was harmless." And she couldn't keep fooling herself. David wasn't her imagination, and she wasn't losing her marbles.

"Joanna likes Martinos. For a child, she's an excellent judge of character."

"How long is the dragon staying? When is he going home?"

"He's trapped here. The protective barrier between his world and ours has snapped back into place. He ended up tossed into the sea and almost drowned. He's here until he works out a way to return home. I promised I'd help him."

Rena scowled, worried despite Cherry's assurances and those of her dream man. "Did you see Tony?"

"No, I took my time driving to Holy Island. We saw nothing suspicious before or after I called you from the teashop."

"Good. That's good. Someone broke into my house."

"Rena! Why didn't you lead with that?"

"You distracted me with talk of sexy druids."

CHAPTER 3

The Mysterious Warehouse

E xiting the dreamscape always left David exhausted, his temper less certain. The irritability was a character flaw, according to Brother Jasper, the senior druid in charge of his training. His mentor. Brother Jasper either knew or suspected David was underplaying his magical strengths. Yet, the older druid had never chastised him for his lack of ambition, as the more senior druids often did.

Instinct had driven David to keep his dreamwalking talent a secret since those he'd told in his previous life had never reacted well. Given his suspicions the druids were part of the imbalance on the Dragon Isles, he was glad he'd hesitated.

Part of his irritation was that he yearned for more time with Rena.

A fact that still bemused him since he'd never looked at another woman after the death of Helena, his wife, and Brianna, his daughter, during the Viking raid on Iona. He'd been away in service of his lord's army at the Crusades. His arrival home to death and destruction had gutted him, knocking him off his path and shoving him onto a different one. He'd followed his mother's advice and studied the druid arts as penance. He shook himself away from the past, impatient with himself for lapsing and pushing into the locked memories.

Rena's fault.

His presence might confuse her, spook and scare her, but the shock of their meeting reverberated within him too.

He'd assumed his path would be a solitary one.

It appeared he'd been wrong.

The bell tolled for the morning meal, and David forced his fatigued limbs to swing over the edge of his narrow bed. The chill of the tiles beneath his feet jolted him awake. A short-term fix. David padded barefoot across the frigid floor. His cell contained a bed, a dresser, and a wooden wardrobe. Before he'd retired for the night, he'd filled an ewer with water, and now he poured a few inches into a pottery bowl. He washed his face with a cloth, and the chill shocked more exhaustion from his weary muscles. A quick wash of the rest of his body had him standing straighter, his sluggish brain more alert. David pulled a clean black robe—the color symbolizing his student status—from his wardrobe and pulled it over his head.

Time to begin his day and attend to breakfast for the senior druids.

After that, he'd complete his daily tasks in the garden. Only then could he skulk around the complex and attempt to gather information on the mystery warehouse several strangers had built close to the druid's vegetable plot. So far, the vigilant senior druids—the red robes in particular, who had trained for years in the art of magic—had foiled his attempts to explore more. It was the red robes who powered the barrier that kept humans on the mainland of Britain from spotting the Dragon Isles.

Curious and intrigued by the new building, he'd asked questions. The red robes had run him off while Brother Jasper hadn't known and had muttered about asking Brother Matthew—the head druid in charge of the monastery—what the devil he was up to by spending their money without consultation.

David ran a comb through his overlong hair and tied it at his nape before thrusting his feet into leather sandals. Dressed, he hurried to join the juniors in the dining room. He prayed he didn't fall asleep in his porridge.

As usual, Brother Jasper marked him present and sent him off with his fellow black robes to serve the senior druids their early meal. David yawned, earning himself a rebuke from one of the more senior druids. He wore a white robe, signifying he was of the religious division, and looked after the brothers' spiritual needs. Two druids at the same table wore the blue of the artistic sector. The druid to the right of him wore a red robe. Brother Matthew, the head druid who sat at the top table, wore a golden robe to show his importance to the order.

David forced himself to concentrate on spooning out porridge. Other black robes dispersed bowls of fresh yogurt, berries from their garden, and jugs of milk.

As usual, he eavesdropped on the various conversations, the older druids speaking freely and treating him and the other black robes like pieces of furniture. Nothing of interest grabbed his attention. Brother Henry had gout in his big toe from overindulging on red wine last night. Brother Stephen was discussing his upcoming lectures on spiritualism and, in particular, reincarnation and sins committed in the previous life. The red robe at David's table kept his head down and spoke to no one. He shoveled plain porridge into his mouth, intent on finishing his meal.

David took a mental note to learn where the red robe went once he left the dining room. He suspected the magical sector was part of whatever had thrown their world out of sync. It was the dissonant vibration in the air—the same one he'd heard for the first time almost four months ago.

What he didn't understand was why no one else sensed the disturbance or felt the changes in the air. A question that plagued him.

David finished serving the porridge. "Excuse me." He bowed his head in deference, willing to play the game to fix the wrongs in his world. "Would anyone like seconds of porridge?"

"Bread," the red robe barked. Unlike most of the other red robes, he didn't possess a stomach paunch.

"I'll bring the bread and honey straightaway." David hurried to the kitchen to collect two baskets of bread. On his second trip, he carried out a tray bearing two jars of honey and another two of fresh butter.

Before his senior charges could make the request, he told them he would be back with a pot of ale. His sector of the dining room kept him busy for longer than the others. By the time he finished, the porridge had disappeared. Muttering under his breath, David reached for two pieces of bread.

"One per person," the druid in charge of the juniors barked.

David replaced one portion of bread and gritted his teeth. Several of the juniors sent him a sympathetic glance since they'd eaten a bowl of porridge before the supply ended. The senior druids treated the juniors as glorified servants and grew plump from excess food while the juniors often missed their meals.

David shrugged away the angry words that tickled the tip of his tongue. If he drank two cups of sweet tea, his empty belly might forgive him for the lack of food.

While he ate, he pondered why the barrier suddenly allowed travel between the worlds. He had no clue how many dragons or humans had passed through the opening. Foresight had told him of the one who'd traveled to Holy Island, but the chances were high that others had made the journey. A mystery for sure.

He disliked ambiguities.

David claimed the teapot before everyone else thought about a second cup. He spooned in extra sugar and stirred it while he studied the other juniors. Not one of them owned the intelligence to cause the disturbance in the air. It *had* to be the magical sector.

But was Brother Matthew part of the plot? David snorted into his teacup. What if the disruption was his imagination? He'd speak with his mentor, Brother Jasper, this morning. Learning more regarding the man who'd traveled through the barrier might help. Somehow, he must find the energy to enter the dreamscape tonight. He limited his visits, but meeting Rena had changed everything.

Perhaps the myths Brother Jasper spun him about David's position as lock held a smidgeon of truth. Perhaps Rena was his mythical key.

David stacked his dishes with the others and tromped off to the library, where he took private lessons with Brother Jasper. Both he and Brother Jasper knew David no longer required the extra tuition since his magical skills had progressed to the red robe level, but they kept up the pretense. Brother Jasper drilled him in advanced magic along with other subjects such as reincarnation. David also helped Brother Jasper with his duties as monastery librarian.

"Ah, David. There you are," Brother Jasper said. "Can you shelve these books for me while we go over your knowledge of herbs? My arthritis is playing up today. Once you've done that, we'll have a jam tart and a touch of rosehip tea to ease my pain."

"Ginger tea is better for your arthritis." David picked up several books on herb craft and another on magic lore and strode to the stuffed wooden shelves to replace the reference books used by the druids who'd visited the library.

"Ah, I thought I might fool you today." Brother Jasper was missing one front tooth, but his smile still lit his round face, and David felt a surge of affection for the man who'd helped him to dig free of his misery.

David continued returning books to shelves while Brother Jasper quizzed him about various herbal recipes, poisonous herbs, and those with medicinal uses.

"Excellent, David," Brother Jasper announced almost two hours later. He scratched his shaggy gray hair then patted his generous belly. "I think it's time for our break. Stir the fire and put the kettle on to boil."

When they sat and cupped their hands around their steaming mugs, David asked his burning question.

"Have you learned the purpose of the warehouse?"

"No." Brother Jasper released a huff. "Brother Matthew told me to mind my business and stick to the library and my students. I questioned the brothers, but they're in the dark too."

"Something is off with the monastery. I can't explain it, but the air is wrong. There's a weird vibe." David scowled. "Do you sense it too?"

"I am not the lock," Brother Jasper said in a mild tone.

"Not that again." David ran a hand through his long, black hair. "I'm nothing special."

"Untrue. You're a rare talent and the brightest student I've ever taught. You could advance to red robe without difficulty."

"No, I'm happy continuing with my studies and spending time with the other black robes."

"Most would've advanced by now." Brother Jasper's eyebrows pinched together. "You're drawing attention whether or not you want it."

David rose and took their empty mugs to wash outside in the well. As he returned to the library, the bell rang for lunch.

Later that afternoon, they assigned David to work in the vegetable garden. Impatience filled him as he followed the senior druid in charge. Of all the rotten luck. He'd hoped to end up with the juniors tasked with picking grapes since the vines were closer to the warehouse.

He'd have to sneak out after dinner and skulk then. David

yawned and slapped his hand over his mouth.

Brother Allen drilled him with a steely glare. "Are we keeping you awake, Brother David?"

"I apologize, but I didn't sleep well last night."

"Eat more vegetables and take stewed prunes with your porridge," Brother Allen snapped.

Several of his fellow druids sniggered like small boys, but David ignored their amusement. He'd have to eat a serving of porridge first, not that he required the roughage. David stood impassive while he received his assignment. Weeding and thinning six rows of carrots. Gritting his teeth, he squatted by the first row and started work. The tedious labor let his mind drift, the voices of the other juniors floating through the air.

Three of his fellow druids chatted about their favorite food and what they intended to do on their next half day. One druid sang as he plucked beans off the vine for their evening meal. Over to his right, two of the druids discussed a female dragon they'd seen visiting the monastery.

David's ears pricked at the mention of a visitor. He hadn't seen strangers since the dragons had built the warehouse.

"I missed it," he murmured to Brothers Jason and Paul. "Let me live vicariously through you," he pleaded. "Describe her to me, so my dreams are colorful." As he'd hoped, they turned into their juvenile selves, their laughter close to giggles.

"She was taller than any human female I've seen." Brother Jason smacked his lips and made motions with his hands. "Her blue dress barely contained her breasts."

"Did she have blonde hair?" David whispered. "I'm partial to blonde hair."

"Black as a raven," Druid Paul said. "A straight, shiny black, and it was long enough to reach the top of her round bottom." He issued a hearty sigh. "A toothsome wench." He glanced over to check the senior druid's vicinity and chuckled when he spotted him leaning against a tree trunk, his mouth wide as he snored. "I got hard just looking at her. Imagine a woman like that on your arm."

The two druids sighed, and David joined in, letting them think he was as interested as they. Any woman they were describing wouldn't compare with his lovely Rena. His lover. Rena would scare these imbeciles with her intelligence.

"I wonder why the dragon woman was visiting," David mused.

"She carried a box with her. She must've left it with the senior because her hands were empty when she left," Druid Paul said.

David glanced at their supervisor and saw he was still snoring. "Do you think she'll visit again? I'm curious now and would love to see this bodacious dragon in person."

Brother Jason scratched his face and left a smear of dirt on his pale Roman nose. "I described her to Brother Chester, and he told me she's a regular visitor. He thought it was a dragon from the ruling clan on Smoking Isle."

"Not Nandag, The Strongminded?"

"He didn't tell me her name."

David considered. "How often does she visit?"

"About once a month. I haven't seen her for a while," Brother Jason said.

"I suppose she met with Brother Matthew to pay the clan's tithe." David scratched his itchy chin, contemplating the woman's visit. He'd need to renew his grooming spell soon to keep his beard at bay. Tithe payment was the most logical reason for her visit.

Brother Paul stroked his wispy beard. "Normally they send a senior courtier. Besides, Brother Roger told me Brother Matthew took her to view the mystery building."

The out-of-bounds one. Not that any of the senior druids had given a reason for the forbidden area. A thought occurred. If he could find someone on the dreamscape—a person inside the warehouse who had fallen asleep, he might gain information that way.

Except if he expended his energy on inserting himself into someone else's dream, he couldn't visit Rena. "What do you think they're doing with the new warehouse?" David murmured.

Brother Paul and Brother Jason exchanged a glance. "We have a bet running. The first one to discover what is happening over there misses a month on the cleaning roster. You want in?"

"How many have taken the bet?"

"Six so far," Druid Paul said. "The others are too scared of getting caught by the senior druids."

"Can I let you know tomorrow?" David asked. "I need to think because if only the senior druids and leading dragons are visiting and entering the warehouse, perhaps it'd be safer if we didn't know."

"*Pfff!*" Brother Jason snorted. "You're frightened."

"I value my position here," David replied.

"You're old." Brother Paul wrinkled his nose. "You're still a junior despite your years here. I heard one of the seniors say you have no ambition."

David bit back his reply, the one that burned on his tongue. It was true he'd spent many years healing after he'd discovered his wife and child had died. Monastery life had suited him when he had no reason to live. Lately, though, that had changed, and he craved more, resenting the hours of labor, although he enjoyed his time with Brother Jasper. He'd signed up for life when he'd first entered the monastery, positive nothing would alter his mind.

Rena had changed everything.

"Lack of ambition isn't a crime. There are worse things," David commented. Such as lack of integrity. Dishonesty. Bullying. The younger men had joined at least one hundred years after him. Once men entered the monastery, life passed with less haste, and aging slowed. David wasn't sure how this happened, but like many of the others, he accepted the boon and continued his work.

David frowned. Several of the senior druids had seemed older and more irascible than usual. The disturbance he sensed, could it be upsetting the balance at the monastery in a more significant way than he realized? He needed to consider this and discuss the matter with Brother Jasper.

"Are you willing to bet you'll discover the purpose of the warehouse before the others?" Brother Jason persisted.

"Stop that lollygagging and finish your chores," the senior druid ordered.

David resumed his task, his mind busy, and his hands moving methodically along the row of carrots. Somehow, he needed to investigate whatever the senior druids and the dragons were storing there.

As he moved down his row of carrots, one corner of the warehouse came into view. A red-robe approached with Brother Matthew. The men had a quick discussion before the red robe nodded.

Brother Matthew disappeared into the trees bordering the warehouse while the red robe eyed the warehouse. The magic druid lifted his hands, and the faint prickle of David's skin indicated the construction of a magical spell. David scanned his fellow brothers, yet none of them hesitated in their chores. None of them paid a scant bit of attention to the druid's presence. David frowned, keeping his head down while he continued thinning carrots.

He found it strange no one else sensed the dissonance in the air.

It was like a constant itch on his skin, and only investigating and fixing the wrong would repair the irritation and make it cease.

David's fingers continued moving, tugging at crowded seedlings until only the most vigorous plants remained. Once he worked down the row to the spot where he could see the corner of the warehouse, he blinked. The building was no longer visible. The prickles danced across his skin again. A barrier to screen the warehouse from curious eyes? That made sense, and he wondered why they hadn't done that earlier. He sorted through the feasible reasons and came up with only one. Whatever they intended to store inside the warehouse hadn't arrived until now.

David sucked in a deep breath, his chest expanding at the realization he needed to study the dream strands as often as his energy allowed. He'd already pushed himself to the limit staying with Rena for so long each night. While his ability to remain had increased in length, he couldn't visit her if he needed to investigate the other strands in search of clues.

"Aren't you finished yet?"

David jerked, lifting his head and shoving back the burst of temper that simmered through him. No, he'd not accomplished his set task. The druid had given David responsibility for more rows than the others.

David shook his head. "No, brother."

The druid pursed his lips. "Please continue until you complete your rows." His voice rose to carry to the other junior druids.

"Those who have concluded may have free time until the noon meal."

Most of his fellow workers left, leaving four brothers along with him still working. David continued along the row, working on automatic while he formulated a plan. He needed to discover what was in that warehouse.

Chapter 4

Sexy Dreamwalker

Rena disconnected from yet another call to Cherry. Cherry and Joanna were safe. The dragon with them wasn't causing trouble—at least as far as Cherry had admitted to Rena. Joanna was amusing them by pretending to be a boy instead of a girl, although what Liza would think of her daughter's short hair was anyone's guess.

Sudden tears burned Rena's eyes, and she blinked hard. Liza and Joanna had spent just over a year in England, and they'd become a valuable part of her family. She loved the pair, and her father adored his granddaughter. Liza couldn't be gone. Rena declined to believe the stupid police report until she saw Liza's body with her own eyes.

Besides, David thought Liza was still alive.

Rena sniffed and swiped at the moisture shrouding her sight. She'd pack a bag to prepare for the move to join Cherry and Joanna on Holy Island. Keep busy to limit the worry time and tire out her brain, so she slept without dreaming.

Not that exhausting herself had worked so far. David kept popping into her dreams like a magical genie. At first, she'd blamed the spicy Thai meal she'd eaten for dinner, but when she'd made her bed the next morning, the head imprint on her second pillow had changed her mind. It was as if two people had slept in her bed, which made no sense since she'd met David in her dreams. Heck, if anyone could read her thoughts, they'd edge away to escape her craziness.

Rena rolled three of her favorite T-shirts and placed them inside her weekend bag. She added two pairs of leggings and five sets of underwear. Toiletries. What did she need? She padded into her bathroom and rifled in her cupboard under the hand basin. She tossed items into her toilet bag, checked the contents, and added a deodorant. Done.

She returned to her bedroom and scanned her mental list again. Two candy bars and a packet of crisps in case she had a snack food craving. Her Kindle and phone were in her handbag. A hat and casual clothes. Old ones she intended to change into at the shopping center. If Tony had eyes on her, she'd make his life difficult. She would not be the one who led him to his daughter.

With her bag packed, she could no longer delay her need for sleep. She stripped off her clothes and slipped into bed naked. After setting the alarm on her phone, she switched off the light.

She must've fallen asleep fast because David arrived straightaway.

"You're here," she said.

"I've been waiting for you." He strode the distance between them and took her into his arms. Giving in to temptation, Rena leaned into his muscular chest, as always impressed by the solidness of him when this was a mere dream.

She tipped back her head. "Is something wrong?"

"First, how is everything on your end? Has there been word of your sister?"

"No." Rena pulled away a fraction. "The police have scaled down the search. They believe her body was swept out to sea."

"I'm sorry. Death of a loved one is never easy. Don't give up hope yet because my gut says your sister is alive."

Something in the way he commiserated with her told Rena he had personal experience.

"Cherry found the man on the beach. He's a dragon."

Rena watched David's expression as she uttered the words. He didn't blink or react as if this was unexpected. *Huh*. Who knew dragons existed? "Cherry told me the druids placed an armband on him to suppress his dragon. He can't remove it by himself. He needs a druid to do a spell." She wasn't sure she believed a word of this either.

"*God's bones*. The dragon part doesn't surprise me, and I sensed he was in trouble, but I did not foresee the armband. This explains the terror I experienced." He pursed his lips. "I've never heard of anyone binding a dragon."

"Cherry said he was in a dungeon and escaped. Do you have a spell to help him remove the armband?"

"I'll research in the monastery library," David said after an interminable pause. "It's hard to believe any druid might do this."

"Perhaps they did it for money."

"Possibly. Anything else I need to know?"

"I'm leaving home tomorrow. I'll travel to Edinburgh in Scotland on the bus to avoid Tony. Once I'm certain he or one of his minions isn't following me, I'll travel to Holy Island to join Cherry and Joanna."

"You'll be closer to me," David murmured. He ran a gentle finger down her nose, the corners of his eyes crinkling.

Heat bloomed on Rena's chest and swelled up her neck. She seldom flushed. Rena met David's gaze, witnessed his amusement, and everything inside her softened. Lord, she liked this man, which was all kinds of weird because who fell in love with the man of their dreams?

"What will you do? What should I do?" she asked.

David ran his hand over her head and cupped her neck, his

expression full of tenderness. She sighed and leaned against him.

"Keep your head down and your eyes open," David murmured. "Once you arrive on Holy Island, watch for strangers."

Rena pulled back to study his face. Despite the dark, she saw him without difficulty. "Tons of tourists visit the island each day. How will I recognize a stranger?"

"Dragons, both male and female, are larger and more muscular than humans. They're tall and act as if they own the world," David added, his tone wry.

"The voice of experience?"

"I've met a dragon or two in my time."

"When?"

"During the crusades. The tourists return to the mainland once the tide is low. Correct?"

"The crusades?" Rena's mouth dropped open enough to attract daredevil bugs. "The ones with knights and castles and holy places?"

David tapped her chin, laughter lines digging into his features. "Yes."

She continued to stare at him, her mind working at warp speed. "But that was hundreds of years ago. Many hundreds. How old are you?"

The corners of his eyes crinkled further. "Older than you, my sweet cynamone."

"But...but..." She shook her head. "You're not old and wrinkly."

He chuckled, his brown eyes twinkling. "Druids age slower. Dragons too. I believe the humans who live on the Dragon Isles also age less, but they do not live to over one-hundred-and-fifty-years-old."

"One-hundred-and-fifty?" She didn't hide her astonishment.

"Yes, I think that's right. Back to the topic at hand. You need to watch for strangers who loiter on the island after the sea covers the causeway. You'll recognize a dragon in their human form. They wear their arrogance like a warm cloak during a cold snap."

"Right." Rena nodded, still intrigued by the age thing. She needed to discuss this with Cherry. David didn't look or act old. His face sported a tan, and the lines garnered by experience and life were absent on his face. If anyone had asked her, she would've guessed his age at around thirty. She shook herself. "What will you do?"

"I'll be investigating on my side," David said.

"Will you be in danger?"

His smile widened into pleased. "Will you worry about the old man who fought in the Crusades?"

"You're not old," she snapped.

"You care." He kissed the tip of her nose and released her, stepping back. "I'm glad because I care for you too. Be careful. Tell the dragon I'll locate a spell to remove the obstruction binding his dragon." With a wave, he retreated farther until his form faded.

A sense of loss filled Rena. The man of her dreams was an

enigma, a mystery she wanted to solve, and that told her she was in bigger trouble than she'd admitted.

David left Rena and forced himself to retrace his steps and follow the dream leash back to its source. Warmth softened his apprehension regarding his next task. Rena was tough with sharp edges, but she amused him, drew his laughter, and the memories of how pleasant life was with the right woman.

As always, leaving Rena's dream left him off balance. He dragged in a deep breath and studied the other tethers and their winding streamers stretching toward the horizon of the dreamscape.

Ribbons of black and red and blue lay before him. The same colors as the robes he and his fellow druids wore. He searched for other colors and spied one gold strand. The head druid. Although tempted, David left his explorations of that leash. The head druid was old and looked it, meaning he had hundreds, perhaps thousands of years on David. More experience. Wilier.

No, it was best not to conduct his experiments on that tether.

He studied the others. Green. Yellow. Purple. Pink.

He noticed something else he hadn't earlier because Rena's turquoise tether had drawn him, and he'd ignored the rest. The ribbons bloomed from central clumps. Rena's tether lay in a stump with an enormous array of colors—shades of the rainbows that sometimes curved across the mountains of Smoking Isle. A host of black tethers with a smattering of red, blue, and the one gold came from another clump.

The monastery, he realized with excitement.

This could make things easier. If there were strangers inside the warehouse, the tethers should sit near or within the monastery clump. The largest cluster that included Rena's was presumably the mainland. It made sense since it was so much bigger than the others.

If his hypothesis held, the other clumps should be from each of the Dragon Isles—except if that was the case, he didn't understand why the monastery had their own grouping. He strode over to the nearest cluster and picked a red leash at random. He needed to determine which group belonged to which island. Before he grasped the tether in his hand, he tugged the cowl of his robe over his face.

The last thing he wanted was to meet an acquaintance who recognized him, one who might create difficulties during his waking hours. David hesitated. He could will his robe off when he was with Rena. Could he will his clothes to change?

David closed his eyes and pictured black trews and a matching black shirt—something to blend. When he opened his eyes, his robe remained. He gave a mental shrug. So be it. He centered his mind and followed the red tether. Once he'd almost reached the end, he slowed his pace, every one of his instincts advising caution. He kept his left hand on the ribbon and pushed through the dreambarrier. Once inside, he studied his surroundings.

A battalion of dragons flew overhead with a red dragon flying in advance.

David frowned, not recognizing the area. Without warning, the battalion dived downward toward a village. David glimpsed children playing on a grassy field, his lips curling up in a half-smile at the innocent pleasure and the high-pitched laughter. It reminded him of happier times.

The dragons kept plunging lower, and horror flooded him. Before he could react, shout a warning, do something, flames erupted from the lead dragons.

Once they'd released their dragon's breath on their hapless victims, they rose into the air, to allow the next row of dragons to fire their flames.

Soon, the entire village was burning, and the grassy field where the children were playing was a fiery mass of flames. The red dragon in the lead bugled in triumph, not a shred of guilt in his gaze as he wheeled around and led away his battalion.

David gaped in disbelief at the devastation. This didn't feel like a nightmare. For this dragon, the dream was pleasant. A reverie where his deepest desires played out, and he won. Every time.

Perturbed, David drew back and pulled from the dream, his entire being shaken by what he'd seen. Did all dragons dream in this manner? David must learn for peace of mind.

He chose a green, and with a sick lurch of his stomach, followed it until he could view the inner workings of this dreamscape.

He steeled himself as he entered. This one was more recognizable. He heard the hissing of the stones before he saw them through the dream vision. At least that answered his question. This clump belonged to the residents of Hissing Isle. A tall, muscular man strode toward a woman where she sat on a large rock, watching the waves rush to shore.

Tension slid through David as he waited to learn what might happen next. His anxiety slid from him with a whoosh when the woman waved and called out. The man started running, and when he reached her, he lifted her into his arms and spun her around. The woman shrieked with laughter, and David relaxed even further. A pair of lovers.

David checked his internal clock and decided he had time to enter at least two more dreams tonight before he left the dreamscape and rested for the following day. He couldn't afford to fall asleep at his tasks or draw the senior druids' wrath. Although he knew part of their silent censure and attitude toward him was because they perceived him as a man of no ambition, he hated to draw more of their ill-will.

The next two tethers gave him no concern. This process would be laborious. He'd need to check other dreams to learn if the warlike vision of the first was widespread. Sighing, David retreated and followed his strand back to his physical body. As he settled, he acknowledged he was spending more and more time on the dreamscape. He'd never pushed his strange power so hard or used it so extensively. Concern that he might become trapped flickered to mind now and then. In the past, the risk hadn't mattered, but now that he'd met Rena, he must exercise caution.

With Rena traveling to Holy Island, he wondered if they could meet in person. Running his hands over her silky skin in the actual world appealed to him on every level.

Perhaps his dream woman could turn flesh and blood, and he'd caress her glorious breasts and *feel* her satin skin beneath his fingertips.

CHAPTER 5

A Fountain of Library Books

David dragged his weary body from his narrow bed around half an hour before the bell to signal breakfast resonated through the grounds. As a junior the druid in charge expected him to arrive five minutes early to set the tables in his assigned section. This morning, he needed extra time to wake and function.

He hustled to get to the bathing pools before the other juniors. Bypassing the warm ones, he plunged into the coldest, the frigid water doing a decent job of pulling him to full alertness. He burst above the surface, water streaming from his hair and upper torso. David forced himself to linger for a few minutes before he lifted from the pool using his upper body strength instead of the steps at the far end.

Naked, he walked over to where he'd left his towel and robe. Two of the newest juniors rushed into the bathing room, slowing when they spotted him. He knew what they saw. A strong body covered with the scars of battle. Funny, the lesions never bothered Rena. She'd asked during the first days of their dreamscape meeting, and he'd told her he was an ex-soldier. The truth as far as it went. He had been a soldier. His mouth twisted since he figured she'd have a dozen questions for him during their next visit.

Helena had never asked.

In the past, thoughts of his long-dead wife would've invoked arrows of pain. Since meeting Rena, his distress had eased, his guilt at leaving Helena and his child defenseless. People healed with time. It seemed he was one of their number, although at first, he'd thought the loss might kill him too. For a while, he'd barely functioned. Gloomy days. Long, endless days of toiling, the brothers issuing order after order. Assigning chore after chore. Brother Jasper had come across him one day and informed David he required help in the library. Over the years, the man had aided his mental recovery.

David ignored the pair, heads together, whispering about his scars. No doubt his lack of ambition too. Something—David was never sure what—had stopped him from progressing through the ranks and taking his final vows where he'd pledge his absolute loyalty.

"You should hurry if you want to get to the dining room before the peel of the morning bell," he warned.

Both juniors jolted as if his words surprised them. Yes, he was a loner. Solitary, but he hadn't always stood alone. Rena had wrought changes, made him want to improve and become a better man. But the niggle of trouble at the monastery had grabbed his interest first. Rena was a fortunate offshoot of his investigation—the one he'd started to quench his curiosity.

David pulled on his robe and placed his towel in the washing basket. He prayed he didn't get laundry duty because that would keep him busy for the entire day. He'd never get to the library.

Laundry service. David forced his expression to remain blank and returned the senior druid's gaze. Brother Sefton loathed what he called David's laziness. Whenever he was in charge of the work distribution, he assigned David the worst chores.

"Brother Paul and Brother Allen, you are also on laundry duties."

One of them groaned in displeasure while Brother Sefton was peering through his glasses at his list of assignments.

"Who protested?" Brother Sefton's irritation rose, as evidenced by his unruly eyebrows. When not one of them replied, he studied each of the brothers. "You're tasked with laundry for the entire month. What do you say to that?" Brother Sefton peered over the top of his eyeglasses. "Right." His expression betrayed his pleasure, the cleverness he experienced in inflicting the punishment.

"I will make certain my fellow druids understand I've assigned the three of you to laundry duties. Now, for the other task assignments."

David blanked out while Brother Sefton allocated chores to the other juniors.

The day passed with the back-breaking work of operating the massive wringers and stirring the robes in tubs of boiling water. They received brief meal breaks when other brothers relieved them, but other than that, the physical work took the entire day. The sole benefit of laundry duty was they didn't need to wait tables during the meal service.

That night, David fell into bed and dreamless sleep. He didn't wake until the morning bell. Thank the gods and goddesses laundry day only occurred once a week. Today, although he'd suffer punishment for his tardiness, he'd receive an easier task.

After breakfast, David waited with the other junior druids for the chores assignment. Brother Sefton again. David stood waiting and watchful for the worst task to fall on him. Gardening. *Not him.* Deep cleaning the dining room. *Not him.* Pruning the hedges. Now, he wouldn't mind that job given it would place him near the now invisible warehouse. *No, not him.* Mowing the lawns. Still not him.

Library duties for the entire day.

"Brother David," Brother Sefton called. "Brother Jasper has

requested your services in the library. He told me he has several dusty chores for you."

David inclined his head and waited for Brother Sefton to dispense the remaining tasks. Happy with his stint with his favorite brother, David hustled to the library building.

The main door was locked.

Puzzled, he strode to the rear, which was closer to the main complex and found that barred too, which surprised him. Brother Jasper left at least one door open if he was expecting David.

Brother Jasper had grown deaf during the last year, so gaining admittance would take time. He pounded on the door, winning the censure of two senior druids strolling past.

David trotted over to them and inclined his head with politeness. "I beg your pardon. Brother Sefton told me to help Brother Jasper in the library. Both doors are locked, and Brother Jasper isn't answering."

The tallest of the two druids snorted. "Jasper is as deaf as a dining table. I can let you into the library with my key."

"Thank you," David said. "I don't wish to disturb Brother Sefton."

The other senior barked out a laugh. "I've heard the druid doesn't approve of you, young man. We will save you this once. Come."

They bustled to the front door, and one produced an oversized brass key. The senior twisted it in the lock and shoved at the door.

It opened six inches before it came to an abrupt halt. The two seniors shared a perplexed glance. The first shoved, and the door budged a scant inch more.

"Can we try the rear?" David asked.

"I don't have the rear door key." The senior placed his face against the gap. "Good morning, Jasper. Are you there?"

When no one replied, and the door remained impassible, one brother turned to him. "Please run and inform the head druid of the problem. Tell him we require his presence and his key for the rear door."

"Yes, sir." With worry riding low in his gut, David hustled through the commonroom until he reached the staircase leading to Brother Matthew's private office. He bounded up the stairs, expecting to find the second-in-command at his desk. The desk was empty, but voices drifted to David from the office beyond.

David hesitated at the door. He hated this, drawing the senior druids' attention. Instinct had him keeping his head down, and his actions covert. It was the reason he hadn't shared his unease with his fellow druids.

David rapped on the door. The voices beyond ceased. A lengthy pause occurred, and David wondered if he should knock again. He lifted his knuckles, but the door flew open before he could.

"Yes?" Brother Matthew barked.

David glimpsed the man sitting in the seat opposite the senior druid's chair before Brother Matthew stepped into the outer office, closing the door behind him. Slightly taller than David and rangy, the druid's jaw was smooth without a hint of whiskers.

He glowered daggers down his bulbous nose. "Why are you here? This area is out of bounds to junior druids. Why are you interrupting my meeting?"

"My assignment today was to aid Brother Jasper in the library," David began.

"Yes. Yes," the senior druid snapped. "Get on with it."

"Something is blocking the front door, and the senior druids sent me to ask you for a key to the rear entrance," David said, keeping his tone even.

Brother Matthew's face had turned scarlet, and a vein ticked at his temple. "Why did they send a junior druid?"

"It was Brother Pierre and Brother Kelvinos."

Some of the *oomph* faded from Brother Matthew's anger. "Very well. Wait here while I get you the key. Once you have gained entrance, give the key to Brother Kelvinos. Do you understand?"

"Yes, sir."

Brother Matthew opened his door, and David sneaked another glance at the visitor. A dragon. An older one who was familiar, but David couldn't recall when he'd seen him. He committed the dragon's features to memory and, for one uncomfortable moment, connected gazes with the visitor. David dipped his head, allowing his cowl to hide his features, but not before he'd witnessed the authority stamped on the dragon's face. The hint of cruelty. The arrogance of one who possessed power and the unlimited ability to wield it.

Hopefully, the head druid's visitor would see him as being below his interest, given that David was a junior druid. David, however, would remember this man. He needed to learn where he'd come from, his purpose, and why he seemed familiar.

"Here you go," Brother Matthew said. "Remember, once you have used the key, give it to Brother Kelvinos. Tell him I will see him during the midday meal."

"Yes, sir." David accepted the key.

David clomped down the stairs. He met Brother Colin, the second-in-command, on his way outside.

"Can I help you with something, young brother?" he asked, his brown eyes kind.

"Brother Matthew gave me a library key. Brother Jasper isn't answering the door, and I can't get inside."

Surprise tightened Brother Colin's droopy face. "That sounds serious. I'll come with you."

David didn't answer but increased his pace. The second-in-charge kept up, despite his ample girth and shorter legs. When they reached the library, Brother Pierre and Brother Kelvinos stood at the front door. As David reached them, Brother Kelvinos shouted.

"Jasper! Are you there, Jasper?"

"No reply?" the second-in-command asked.

"Not a peep. Brother Colin, this is most irregular," Brother Pierre said.

David brushed past them and strode to the rear of the building. The seniors trotted after him. He inserted and twisted the key, yanked on the door, and stumbled back as several boxes of books tumbled through the doorway.

"What the devil?" Brother Colin muttered, his rosy cheeks standing out against his pale features.

David righted the boxes and stuffed the books back inside to create a path for the senior druids.

"Oh, my," Brother Pierre whispered after peering inside. "Where did these books come from?"

"I heard we had a library delivery," Brother Colin said. "No one mentioned the quantity. Brother David, can you find a way past this barricade and locate Brother Jasper?"

"Yes, sir," David said.

David stepped across the threshold, and magic teased at his feet and bare legs. It held a playful tickle and was unexpected. He squeezed against the wall to bypass a tower of boxes. Once David cleared the obstacle, even more boxes barricaded his exploration. It was as if the library had caught a stomach ailment and had regurgitated books by the hundreds.

"Can you see Brother Jasper?" Brother Kelvinos called.

"Not yet." Astonishment filled him on seeing the sheer number of books in the room. Myriad colors and sizes sat in haphazard piles while yet more boxes forced him to scramble over and around.

"Brother Jasper? Are you here?" When no response was forthcoming, David made his way toward the small office that occupied one corner of the square library.

It was an obstacle course, and he was out of breath by the time he reached the office. It was every bit as messy as the rest of the library. David squinted into the dark corner and fumbled for illumination. When he failed to find a lantern, he formed runes with his hands and mumbled a hasty spell. Four floating lamps appeared at ceiling height, their light allowing him to see.

"Brother Jasper," he called. "Where are you?"

Several books tumbled off a stack behind David.

"Have you found him?" Brother Colin demanded as he attempted to squeeze past a fallen shelf. His ample girth hindered his passage.

"Be careful, Brother Colin," David called. "The books are unstable, and magic fills the air."

"I don't understand," Brother Colin said in bewilderment. "Jasper never mentioned a problem at the library. He has maintained our collection for years without difficulty."

David shaped his fingers into a different rune, and the lights he'd created bobbed above him as he pushed deeper into the library. "Brother Jasper must be here somewhere. I was trying to recall when I'd seen him last. Last night, I believe. I didn't see him at breakfast."

"Now that I think on it, I haven't spoken to Jasper today." Brother Colin's voice held deep regret. "We need to search the library to establish if he's here."

"Yes, sir. I'll search in a grid pattern, so I miss nothing."

A fountain of books bubbled up from the floor, taking them both by surprise. Brother Colin stumbled and fell on his arse while David squeezed against a set of bookshelves to avoid the flying books.

"Well, I never," Brother Colin spluttered.

"Sir, might I suggest you stop the books coming, while I search for Brother Jasper."

"Of course, my boy. Go ahead."

David was thankful his suggestion had steadied the druid's shock, and as he maneuvered his way through the stacks of books, he heard Brother Colin's steady chanting. Waves of potent magic caressed his back. The constant fall of volumes reduced to occasional thumps, letting David focus on his search.

He poked between boxes and shelves. "Brother Jasper. Can you hear me?"

He squeezed past a large stack and stared at the bottom of a sandal before he registered he'd located his mentor. David swallowed, sorrow filling him as he removed the boxes burying Brother Jasper. No one could survive the weight of the mountainous pile.

"Sir," David shouted, his heart heavy. "I've found Brother

Jasper."

"Wait there," Brother Colin ordered. "I'll come to you. Keep talking to guide me, Brother David."

"Be careful, sir. The piles are unsteady. It's dangerous."

"I need to care for Jasper," Brother Colin stated in a voice that brooked no refusal.

After a few minutes, Brother Colin came into sight.

"Brother Colin, watch the boxes in front of you. They're unstable."

No sooner had he uttered the words than the upper boxes on the stack toppled. Brother Colin released a muffled shout.

"Brother Colin!" When he didn't receive a reply, David retraced his steps. He discovered a dazed Brother Colin once again sitting on his arse.

"You're right," Brother Colin said in a muffled tone. "The boxes are wobbly. I think I've twisted my ankle."

David glanced around and saw they were near the front door, which was close to the office. "I'll help you stand, sir."

"What about Jasper?"

David shook his head. "I'm afraid he's past help. Let me help you from the library, and then we can remove Brother Jasper."

Brother Colin inclined his head. "Thank you, Brother David. You have a wealth of commonsense that the younger druids lack."

"Brother Colin, were you able to stop the books?"

"Yes. I managed a temporary fix, but once we clear space,

we'll better understand what we're facing. If Jasper couldn't deal with the influx of books, I doubt my spell will work either. The place stinks of magic." His sharp blade of a nose wrinkled in confusion. "The magic feels mischievous, like a child. Almost like an inexperienced druid experimenting with his power."

David gaped at him. "You think one of us is responsible for this?"

"Yes," Brother Colin said. "An unfortunate accident has had unforeseen consequences."

Given the weird sensation at the monastery, David thought this was worse than a prank.

"Please don't discuss this with the other brothers. Restrict your conversation regarding the matter to me or Brother Matthew. You will receive your directions straight from us."

"Yes, sir."

"I will deal with Brothers Pierre and Kelvinos. Once you help me outside, I want you to wait here with Jasper. I don't want him to be alone."

"Yes, sir."

"Once the medical druids tend my injury, I will return with Brother Matthew."

"Brother Colin, what if the books arrive again?"

"You have my permission to wait at the side door. Do not let anyone inside."

"No, sir." He assisted Brother Colin past the stacks of books barring their way to the front door. Brother Colin's bulky middle pressed against David, making him stagger. He lurched before correcting his path. They were both breathless when David maneuvered Brother Colin outside.

"Brother Colin, if you wait there, I will summon Brothers Kelvinos and Pierre to help you to the sickbay."

"As soon as the medical department works their magic on my ankle, I'll return," Brother Colin promised.

A few minutes later, David made his way into the library. Deciding to make himself useful, he returned to the area where he'd discovered Brother Jasper. He could remove the boxes and books from around his body and study the titles to see if he could find something to aid the bound dragon.

Digging Brother Jasper's body free took physical effort. And strangest of all, each of the titles burying him was identical. *Magical Spells for the Beginner.* David laughed, his humor overloud in the quiet room. He flipped the book open and stared at the title page that acknowledged Brother Jasper as the author. Acting by instinct, David cast a rapid reducing spell on the manuscript. Once it fit on the palm of his hand, he shoved the book into the depths of his robe pockets.

The magic still shimmering across his skin, dug in harder for an instant, before relaxing and fading from the room. When he turned back to the pile of books that covered Brother Jasper's upper torso, each of the titles was different. He stared in confusion and unease. Aware of the passing time, David worked to free Brother Jasper from the prison of books. He stacked them in a structured pile that wouldn't endanger anyone else.

Five minutes later, a shout told him Brother Colin and Brother Matthew had arrived. David went to greet them. Both men wore worried expressions.

"My apologies for making you wait." David dipped his head in a respectful bow. "I locked the door and used the time to remove the books from around Brother Jasper."

"Good thinking, Brother David." Brother Matthew scanned the jumble of books and scratched his bald patch, his countenance befuddled. "That will save us time. Is Jasper dead?"

"Yes, sir. He hasn't been dead for long. Full rigor has not set in yet. My best guess is that this happened earlier this morning or late last night."

"You have experience with bodies?" Brother Matthew asked.

More than David cared to remember. "Yes."

"Is it safe for us to enter?" Brother Matthew asked.

"If you're careful. Follow me." David noted Brother Colin was walking on his ankle again, the druid medics' magic offering rapid healing for injuries. Unfortunately, they couldn't revive a dead brother. David entered the library again and shifted boxes and piles of books as he went to create a clearer path for the senior druids.

When he reached the spot where Brother Jasper had fallen, he stood aside to let the seniors gaze down at their fallen brother.

"Jasper," Brother Colin murmured. "What were you doing? Why didn't you ask for help?"

Brother Matthew remained silent, and David stole a glance at him to catalog his reaction. His features were stoic. "Brother David, please finish uncovering Brother Jasper's body so we can remove him for the proper ceremonial sendoff."

David nodded his agreement and restarted his task.

The senior druids chatted, and David eavesdropped as best he could.

"The books bubbled out of the floor, you say?"

"Yes, I placed a temporary spell to stop the increase of books, but I believe we need a stronger force to stamp out this magic," Brother Colin said. "Last night, Jasper told me he was busy, and he asked for Brother David's aid today. I agreed to the labor request and added it to our daily list."

"I don't like this," Brother Matthew growled. "You stay and supervise, Colin. I'll get the magical team to quash the original spell. Perhaps we'll discover a signature to point us to the culprit."

Brother Colin nodded his approval of the order.

David cleared the last of the books from Brother Jasper's still form. He pushed to his feet and bowed his head in a show of respect. A brief prayer fell from his lips.

"Well done, Brother David," Brother Matthew said.

The midday bell rang for luncheon.

"You may go to the dining room. Do not discuss this with

anyone. Not the junior druids, nor the senior druids who ask questions of you. Do you understand?" Brother Matthew pierced David with his gaze, and David felt the rush of magical compulsion writhing over his face and creeping down his body.

Pressure built inside David, a force that told him to agree. With this came a slash of fear at the faintest notion of disobeying Brother Matthew.

"Yes, sir. I will keep my counsel on this subject and will not answer questions posed to me."

"See you follow my instructions, or else," Brother Matthew added with a grim glare.

David nodded, not keen to learn the head druid's version of punishment. Not only did he feel compelled, but a healthy dose of fear accompanied the emotions brought on by the spell. He'd never had much to do with Brother Matthew, apart from the regular assembly meetings and during mealtimes when he'd waited on the senior druid's table. Now, he decided his lack of interaction boded well, and a wise man wouldn't underestimate this druid.

Brother Matthew stalked away without looking back. David shook himself and prayed the man didn't have the power to read his mind. The miniature book in his pocket weighed a ton, and the secrets he held close to his chest burdened David. This quagmire he'd found himself in the middle of had far-reaching tentacles, and right now, it felt as if one curled around his neck and was strangling him to death.

CHAPTER 6

Holy Island, Here I Come

R ena checked into a backpacker hostel in Edinburgh, near the Royal Mile. While most of the residents were younger, she wouldn't stand out as an imposter if she dressed in jeans and a T-shirt. Tension slid through her as she exited the hostel to find a cafe. She found one a few streets away and, identifying it as a local hangout for the nearby businesses, she pushed through the double doors and entered. She took possession of a table in the corner with a view of incoming customers and set her handbag on the floor between her feet.

A time-worn woman with deep lines on her face but kind blue eyes took her order and promised to return with a pot of tea.

Rena plucked out the pre-paid phone she'd purchased and fired a text off to Cherry. She rang Cherry after waiting five minutes.

"Where are you?" Cherry asked.

"Just arrived in Edinburgh. If Tony has followed me, I want to make certain he thinks I'm visiting friends, so I'm catching up with two university buddies." She pushed away her worry at David's last message. He'd stepped into her dreams and asked her to get to Holy Island as soon as possible because he needed her help.

While she trusted David and anticipated their interactions, she refused to place Joanna in danger. After her machinations, beating Tony was still at the top of her list. The man was a scab on humanity and sought to use Joanna to bleed Liza dry. He didn't possess a conscience, and she refused to let him win.

"We're doing the tourist thing and searching for a druid to help Martinos with his problem."

"Are you *sure* you can trust him?"

"He's helped with Joanna and has done nothing to make me doubt him." Cherry's tone told Rena her friend had lifted her chin in that stubborn way she had when she intended to stand her ground. It didn't happen often, and that was telling.

Cherry's mother belittled her daughter about everything from the lack of a boyfriend to her chosen occupation. If Martinos bolstered Cherry's courage and made her see herself for the incredible woman she was, Rena would suspend her judgment. If he hurt Cherry, all bets were off. Rena would ninja his butt.

"Does Joanna like him?" Curiosity led her to voice this question since Joanna saw more than most children.

"She enjoys his company." Cherry chuckled. "He's her go-to person for boy questions. She's so funny." Her breath emerged in an audible rush. "I miss Liza. Joanna reminds me of her in so many little ways."

"I know," Rena said. "She can't be dead. I prefer to believe David's version that she's safe. The police still haven't found her body."

"I rang them this morning. They're calling off the search. If the divers don't find Liza today, they're giving up."

Rena heard the thickness in Cherry's voice and then overheard the whispers of masculine comfort from the other end of the line. She mentally cheered and gave the dragon dude brownie points.

"I'm hanging around Edinburgh today. I might come to Holy Island tomorrow. If not tomorrow, the next day," Rena said. "I have a friend who might help your dragon."

"Really?" Cherry sounded excited.

"I can't promise anything, okay?"

"Anything to help Martinos. His dragon is dying," Cherry said, sobering. "I-I want to help him."

"I'll call you tomorrow. If I have time, I'll visit the library. There's an outside chance I'll discover something to help him."

"Thank you. We both appreciate it. Have you spotted Tony?"

"No, thank goodness. If I see the creep, I'm liable to smack him."

"There's a law against that," Cherry chirped.

Rena gaped and snapped her teeth together. Cherry never made jokes. Her lack of confidence held her back. Rena's lips curled in amusement and approval. "Are you sleeping with him?"

"None of your business."

"You are! That was quick. You never jump into bed with a man this soon. You told Liza and me, it was the reason your dates never hung around for long. They hated waiting for the sex reward."

Rena waited, counting the seconds. Cherry would break soon and blurt out everything. *One. Two. Three. Hmm*, still nothing. Rena waited a fraction longer, then she grinned. Wow, this dragon was having an impressive effect on Cherry. Rena approved.

"Okay then." Rena's lips quivered in silent laughter. "Since you won't follow the girlfriend code and give me deets, I'll get on with my day."

Her grin widened on hearing Cherry's swift intake of air. Rena held back her laughter with difficulty. She couldn't wait to meet the dragon.

Rena filled in her day with a combo of sightseeing and a visit to the library. She researched Holy Island and dragons and also other nearby islands. She couldn't find any reference to the Dragon Isles.

On her return, she tagged along with hostel guests and hit the local pub for dinner and drinks. She figured she'd blend better if she stayed with a group. Two glasses of red wine, along with a chicken pot pie, eased her stress, and by the time she returned to the hostel, she had a pleasant buzz.

She cuddled into her narrow bed and closed her eyes, falling into sleep. David joined her almost immediately.

"What's wrong?" she asked, taking in the tension in his shoulders.

"I mentioned the weird things happening here."

"Yes."

"They've increased. My mentor, Brother Jasper, is dead."

"I'm so sorry. How did he die?"

"He's the librarian. *Was* the librarian," he amended. "I found his body this morning, crushed under the weight of hundreds of books. The library was full to the brim with books. Stacks everywhere. Boxes. So many books." His eyebrows furrowed, and he shook his head.

"Where did the books come from?"

"It was the strangest thing. Dozens and dozens bubbled up through the floor while I was there. Imagine a fountain of books. That's what I witnessed this morning."

Rena frowned. "Are you saying someone murdered him?"

"It's suspicious since Brother Jasper had magical skills. The head druid told me not to discuss the matter with anyone. He threatened me, but Rena, I don't think it was an accident. Brother Matthew told me to wait with Brother Jasper while he sought a red robe."

"They're the ones skilled at magic, right?"

"Yes. While I waited, I cleared the books from Brother Jasper's body. Every book bore the same title—*Magical Spells for the Beginner*. I picked up one, and it was full of Brother Jasper's writing. When I heard the senior druid returning, I shrank a copy and placed it in my pocket. As soon as I did that, the titles on the other books changed. It was the strangest thing."

"Have you read any of the book?"

"I've only had time to read the first chapter. We stopped work to commemorate Brother Jasper."

"And?" Rena prompted. "What did the diary say?"

"Brother Jasper has been spying on Brother Matthew, our head druid. They used to be friends, but it seems they had a falling out around six months ago."

"Over what?"

"Brother Jasper doesn't say." Frustration crept into David's voice. "I've felt something was off and mentioned it to Brother Jasper, but he didn't comment, and now he's dead. It's a weird sensation as if someone is rubbing my skin the wrong way. An irritant I can't scratch."

"Do the others sense this disturbance?"

"Everyone is continuing in the usual way."

"You need to be careful," Rena said. "If someone murdered your Brother Jasper, you're in danger too."

David scowled but offered her a curt nod. "I'm trying to keep my head down. They have assigned me to clean the library. Brother

Matthew gave me the task himself. My suspicion is he doesn't want other brothers speculating."

"But if you know, won't that make him watch you more closely?"

"Yes." Evident unhappiness followed this admission. "When will you come to Holy Island? My gut is telling me the situation here has links with the dragon turning up on your side."

"Couldn't it be a coincidence?"

"My intuition says otherwise. I've learned to note my hunches. It's helped to keep me alive."

Rena nodded, understanding this since she listened to her gut too.

"There's something else. I interrupted Brother Matthew's meeting with a dragon when I rushed to get the key for the library rear door. Two of the junior druids mentioned an older dragon visited the monastery."

"Do you think it's the same one?"

David shrugged, his brown eyes full of concern. "The one I saw was older. I swear I've seen him before, but I can't remember where. Despite his age, his posture was erect, so he's still strong and healthy. Brother Matthew treated the dragon with polite wariness. He was angry when I burst into his office."

"Does it sound like the same dragon the other druids mentioned to you?"

David's brows rose. "Maybe that's why he seemed familiar.

They told me the senior druid showed a dragon around the new warehouse. The one that's now invisible. The other brothers don't recall the building."

"A compulsion spell?" Rena asked. "Is that possible?"

"When I was working in the garden, there was a sense of wrongness each time I glanced at the spot. I sense it's there but the others—not so much."

"Interesting," Rena said. "Do the other druids dreamwalk?"

David hesitated. "The talent seems rare. I don't discuss it because the idea scares some. Helena forbade me to mention it and pleaded with me never to dreamwalk again. She insisted my ability was the work of the devil."

"Who's Helena?"

"My wife." David held up a hand just as Rena was about to let loose with her temper, because she was *not* an affair kind of woman. But something in his expression stilled her protests, and she waited for him to say more. "She died. Helena and my daughter lost their lives during a Viking raid."

"Oh. I'm so sorry." Her gaze flitted from his, and self-loathing filled her because she'd assumed he was playing her. She swallowed and forced herself to meet his gaze again. "Really sorry. Losing your wife and daughter must've been incredibly painful."

"After their deaths, I went to the monastery. I've been there ever since."

She nodded, unsure of what to say. Finally, she swallowed.

"D-did anyone in your family dreamwalk?"

"My mother. She found me on the dreamscape one night, and after that, she'd come and collect me, and we'd go off on tiny adventures. It was our secret."

"Your father didn't know?"

"No. Mother told me I shouldn't tell anyone."

Rena thought over what he'd told her, relieved at the shift of topic. "You haven't met other people on the dreamscape?"

"No."

"Which means your talent is rare, and you're wise to remain silent."

David's mouth pressed into a grim line. "I skim most dreams. You're the only one I've interacted with since I couldn't resist."

"I am pretty unforgettable."

He rewarded her with a grin, and his entire demeanor lightened. "Bighead."

Rena cocked her head. "Do I get a kiss tonight?"

"Every night." David prowled closer.

Rena breathed in his familiar scent, a masculine fragrance with hints of the wild and greenery. Her heart pumped out a few extra beats as she sank into his kiss. This dream man understood her unlike any other, and his kisses took her out at the knees. She clung, drifting in the warmth of his strength and the pleasure his touch stirred to life.

When David drew back, they were both breathing hard. "You've bewitched me."

"You've stolen my words." Rena worried her bottom lip. "Will we meet in person one day, or is this all we'll ever have?"

"I don't know," he said with a heavy sigh.

"Am I in danger? Cherry and Joanna? I mean, if I keep hanging around you."

"I've taken steps to ensure secrecy, but I can't be certain no one is spying on me."

Rena stiffened, her mouth falling open as she scowled at him. "You mean someone else can enter my dreams?"

David shrugged. "I've told you I've never spotted anyone on the dreamscape, but I can't be the only one with the power to dreamwalk."

Reassuring. *Not.* "What about dragons? What should I do if I spot one?"

"Don't approach them," David ordered. "If they're on Holy Island, they're not meant to be there. Don't speak with them or follow them, but give me a description when you can."

What about the dragon with Cherry? "Have you met Martinos? The dragon staying with Cherry and Joanna? I mean, Cherry is safe, isn't she? You wouldn't have told me to tell her to save him if he was dangerous. If he hurts Cherry or Joanna, I'll never forgive you."

"As far as I can ascertain, your friend is safe." David finished his sentence with a wide yawn.

"David, you're exhausted. As much as I enjoy your company, return to your bed and sleep. You can't help anyone if you're fatigued."

Deep lines formed on his forehead and bracketed his pinched mouth. "Things are happening fast. I need to jump into more dreams and search for clues."

"My point stands," Rena said. "Sleep tonight and investigate tomorrow. Please, David. Do it for me."

His expression softened. He still looked tired, but he took Rena in his arms. He kissed her cheek and just held her. She pressed against him, savoring the closeness and the sense of security his touch brought.

"Finding you has changed my life," David murmured. "I'm eager to start my day and get to you instead of endless hours, blending into each other."

"Wow, you smooth talker, you," she teased.

"It's nothing less than the truth."

Rena pushed away, far enough to see his face. "You're the first man to interest me in a long time."

"You're not seeing anyone in your world?"

Interesting. David bore the same insecurities. "There's no one in my life except you." She met his gaze and made sure he understood she spoke with honesty, that she spoke from the heart. The truth—she couldn't imagine finding a man who attracted her more than David.

"Please try to sleep. You're haggard, and I'm certain your brain will function better if you rest."

He stared at her for a long moment, then a smile marched across his face, stealing her breath. "You care for me."

"I do." She never hesitated. "Which is why you should listen."

"You win. I'll try to visit you tomorrow night. Hopefully, I'll have more news to share with you. Take care, sweet cynamone."

David released her. Instantly, she missed the physical connection, and she fought her instinct to call him back. No, he needed rest. She repressed her selfish reaction and forced a smile.

"Tomorrow," she promised.

David faded away, leaving her experiencing loneliness, which was silly.

The next morning, Rena slept late. She'd shared a dormitory room with three other women, and only one still remained when Rena finally stirred.

"Have a pleasant dream?" the woman asked, her accent Antipodean. The blonde sported a tan, which brought out her blue eyes.

"Why?"

"You were moaning in your sleep."

But they hadn't had sex. Why would she moan? "I had a

91

nightmare," she lied without a blink.

"It sounded as if you were in the middle of a sex dream." The woman winked. "I was kinda envious."

"I'm sorry I woke you."

The woman shrugged. "No problem. You going down to breakfast?"

"I thought I might." Rena's suspicions rose. She didn't know this woman, but she'd never underestimate Tony. The man held a mean grudge and was vindictive enough to hire a tourist to cause difficulties.

"I flew in last night. My name is Kylie."

"Rena."

"Do you know of a cheap cafe for breakfast?"

"Sure," Rena said. "Ten minutes, okay for you?"

The woman bounded out of bed and scrambled into her clothes. "I'm ready. You realize I have an ulterior motive for the breakfast question."

"Oh?"

"I'm hoping for hints of places to visit here in Edinburgh."

Rena cocked her head and searched Kylie's earnest face. "I can do that."

"Right, let's go."

Rena enjoyed Kylie's company. She described the free walking tour she'd done and recommended it for orientation within the city.

"How long are you staying in Edinburgh?"

"I'm leaving tomorrow or the next day at the latest," Rena said. "I've already been here for two days."

"Where are you heading next? Maybe we'll meet up again."

"I'm playing it by ear," Rena said. "If the first bus goes to Inverness, I'll head in that direction, or if it's easier to get to Glasgow and travel up the west side of Scotland, I'll go that way."

"Ah. I admire your uncomplicated way of choosing your adventure. I'm a planner and did an itinerary of my trip before I left Australia. Just thinking about your method gives me hives."

"Different strokes for different folks." Rena ate her last mouthful of toast and marmalade. "And on that note, I'd better hustle."

Rena paid for her breakfast and hastened to the nearest office to purchase bus tickets. Even so, she took a roundabout route, watching for anyone suspicious. By the time she reached the ticket office, she was certain no one was following her.

She took her place in the line and pulled out her phone to study the timetables for Holy Island. Not tomorrow morning, but the bus was running the following day.

Rena booked her ticket and spent the rest of the day visiting a friend, wandering the Royal Mile, and grabbing a few essentials. She found another library and researched dragons. Most of what she discovered was hearsay, and she was no wiser by the time she ended her search.

Since it was early afternoon, Rena found a quiet corner in the hostel community lounge and picked up an old magazine.

She must've fallen asleep, and somehow, David found her.

"How are you here?" she asked.

"Afternoon nap. It's Sunday, and our routine is different." He waggled his brows, his expression dopey yet charming.

"You sound better."

"I can't stay long," he said. "But I think I have discovered a spell to free the dragon. Brother Jasper had the perfect one in a research book. Tell your friend and the dragon to search for magic trees."

"Magic, in what way?"

"Ones that yield their leaves, bark, and flowers for spells. Practitioners use several of the old tree varieties to aid their magic."

Rena pulled a face at the obscure clue. "I'll arrive on Holy Island tomorrow. The Edinburgh bus makes stops in other places, but I assume we'll be on time because the driver needs to reach the causeway at low tide. How will you do the spell if you're at the monastery and the dragon is on Holy Island?"

"Another spell I've found should pop me through the barrier at the point of the magical trees. My theory is it'll act like a portal."

Spells and portals? The entire subject was a bit *woo-woo* for Rena's scientist's mind, but given the man had walked right into her dreams and seduced her, she figured she should suspend her disbelief. "Right," she said. "Is there anything else I should do?"

"Find the magical trees. You should meet me there."

"I'll do an internet search for the info."

David paused as if he wanted to ask questions. He'd queried many things during their acquaintance and appeared to enjoy learning about modern technology. "The yew grove here is best for me. Yews are a powerful tree, and our magic druids revere them."

"Didn't you tell me you were spending most of your time in the library now? To sort out the mess Brother Jasper left?"

David snorted. "The convenient scapegoat. The more I read of Brother Jasper's journal, the more I'm convinced of wrongdoing at the monastery. Brother Matthew asked me to set aside any private papers I found. That makes me suspect he's searching for something."

"What?"

"Maybe it's the book I've already found and have concealed. The head druid hasn't told me what he's expecting me to discover. If he's specific, he'll raise my suspicions. The druids don't respect independent thinking. They expect us to follow orders without question."

"You sound disillusioned."

"Maybe," David said. "Things have altered here. An insidious transformation I barely noticed."

"Perhaps it's you who's changed," Rena suggested.

"Meeting you?"

"That and the changes you're experiencing with your fellow druids. We're dragging you into the twenty-first-century kicking and screaming," she teased.

"I should go," David said. "It was sheer luck I found you sleeping."

"Bye." An instant later, Rena was awake, and she went to work, doing an internet search on English trees and Holy Island. When nothing came up in her search, she plugged in yew trees, since David had mentioned them and read of their history. One interesting fact—they often grew near old churches. Once again, she searched for churches and yew trees plus Holy Island.

The church lacked trees in their grounds, the buildings near to the coast and the town center—a mere dot on the map. There weren't many trees on the island full stop. Rena paused, pondering her next move. A walk and something to eat.

Kylie intercepted Rena at the hostel door with a broad grin worthy of a toothpaste ad. "Dinner at the pub?"

"Sure." It was nice to have company for a change, although the Australian girl asked a lot of questions.

Rena answered some and deflected others, her suspicions rising. "What did you do today?"

"I took the walking tour you suggested," Kylie said. "The guide was excellent, and it was no hardship listening to his gorgeous accent for an hour."

Rena grinned. "True. There is something about a Scottish accent. And on that note, I'm heading back to the hostel."

"Stay for another drink," Kylie suggested.

"You can, but I've had enough. The budget is tight."

"All right. I'll see you later."

Once she returned to the hostel, she rang Cherry and mentioned the magical trees. Cherry said they'd look for trees during their sightseeing. Kylie arrived back, and in frustration, Rena cut their chat short.

The next morning, after a dreamless night, she walked to the depot and boarded the bus heading to Holy Island. The entire time, nerves jostled her mid-region, and she jumped at shadows, positive that Tony or a hireling would follow her to Holy Island and place Joanna in danger.

On reaching the outskirts of Edinburgh, her anxiety dispersed, and her mind turned back to yews since she'd decided they were the most likely candidate for magical trees, given the research she'd done online. She let her mind drift then straightened.

An obvious next move.

Ring the minister at the Holy Island church. If yew trees are typically near churches, then he might have spotted the trees on the island or know of the closest ones on the mainland.

Decision made, she dialed the minister of Saint Mary's church.

"Hello," she said when a male answered the phone, telling her he was Rev. Whiteson. Well, at least she was speaking with the correct person. She introduced herself and posed her question.

"Yew trees?" Interest sparked in his voice. "Why does a youngster have questions about yew trees?"

"I read about their mystical properties, and I wondered since Holy Island was so important in its time if the monks had planted yew trees. If I don't view any here, I'll visit churches on the mainland." Not bad for an explanation, given it was spur-of-the-moment babble.

Rev. Whiteson laughed. "A little test, my dear. Our ancestors indeed planted yew trees near churches. Because the trees live for hundreds of years, we're uncertain if they planted the trees first or the churches came before the trees. While there are no trees around my church, there is a grove farther inland. Do you have a vehicle?"

"No, I'm arriving on the local bus. Is the yew grove a simple walk from the center of town?"

"It will take you an enjoyable hour to walk there and another hour back. If you intend to visit the castle and the abbey, you might run short of time to catch the return bus."

Rena smiled, relief rippling through her. "My friend has rented a cottage. I'm staying with her for a few days, so timing isn't an issue."

"Excellent. Pass through the town and take the walking path to the nature reserve. Keep walking for an hour—signposts mark the way—and you'll see a path on the left with a sign pointing to the yew grove."

"Thank you very much." Rena resisted her powerful urge to pump her fist into the air. No need to attract attention.

"I hope you'll pop in and see me at the church during your visit.

I'd love to hear your impressions of the trees. Oh, and remember not to touch them. The leaves and seeds and even the wood are toxic."

"Yes, I read that. It made me wonder how our ancestors crafted their bows from the wood."

"A lot of trial and error, I'd say."

"Thank you, Rev. Whiteson."

"You're welcome, my dear."

Rena hung up, pleased with her afternoon's work. She called Cherry, but her friend didn't answer. Cherry had told her she, Martinos, and Joanna intended to drive around the island and search for trees. It was possible Cherry's mobile was out of range. She'd try again later.

Rena settled back to enjoy the coastal view, her mind shifting to David and the spell he intended to create to help free this dragon. Her life was a made-for-television movie, and even then, it'd stretch the viewer's imagination.

Kylie rang the number Tony had given her and waited for his reply. He'd paid her well to cozy up to his sister-in-law, and her lack of information wouldn't please him.

"Kylie," Tony's smooth voice crooned down the line.

She pulled a face. The gods had blessed the arsehole in the looks department, and he knew it. He had an over-inflated opinion of himself and an entitlement that irritated the hell out of her. If she hadn't been desperate and dead broke, she would've told him to go to hell.

"Did you speak with her?" he asked.

"Yes."

"Did she have the kid with her?"

"No. Rena never mentioned a child and appeared to be traveling alone."

"Blast it," he muttered. "She's as big a bitch as her sister."

Kylie bit back the retort that came to mind, not wanting to antagonize him. He thought nothing of physical and mental cruelty and plain meanness, as she'd learned when she'd first met him in the pub on Kensington High Street in London.

He sighed, and Kylie heard the *tap-tap-tapping* of his fingers on a desktop.

"She still in Edinburgh?"

"She left this morning. She told me she wasn't certain if she'd go to Inverness or travel to the west coast via Glasgow."

"Does she have a car? Did you get the registration number?"

"She was traveling by bus. I followed her to the station. It looks as if she headed to Glasgow."

"She have much luggage?"

"A backpack and a black handbag."

"Ah!" he said, the sound gloating. "At least she's stuck to type.

Anything else?"

"Are you certain she isn't on holiday? Because she'd been sightseeing. I followed her when she took a walking tour. She visited the castle and walked along the Royal Mile."

"The bitch is trying to keep my daughter from me," Tony snarled. "She won't win this battle."

Kylie refrained from commenting and waited.

"Anything else?"

"You promised me another five hundred pounds."

"And you believed me. Stupid bitch." Tony disconnected the call.

Kylie stared at her mobile, the stinging pressure of tears pushing at her eyes. She'd suspected the man might screw her over, but at least she'd received travel money to get to Edinburgh, two night's accommodation, and two hundred pounds. She'd economized as much as possible and had enough money for a week if she was frugal.

Once she finished her soup, she'd do a round of the pubs and search for a job.

At least one agreeable thing had come from this debacle. Kylie was in Scotland, the land of her forebears, and she was way out of Tony's orbit.

Safe.

She prayed Rena stayed out of his clutches. No one deserved an arsehole like Tony in their lives.

CHAPTER 7

Reunion

Driving over the causeway fascinated Rena. The road was still damp, and the sea licked at the sides of the thoroughfare in parts. The receding tide exposed mudflats, and Rena wondered what it'd be like to walk the Pilgrim's Way from the mainland to the island as the locals had many years ago. This visit, she didn't have the luxury of time to struggle through the mud on foot.

Once the bus reached the tiny town, the driver gave everyone strict instructions to return to the bus on time.

"I will leave behind any latecomers," the bus driver spoke in a gruff voice. "The tide waits for no man and certainly not for tardy sightseers who can't stick to a schedule."

Rena hid a grin at his stern, earnest features, glad she didn't need to worry about timekeeping.

The passengers collected their belongings and exited the bus. Rena pulled up a map on her phone and scowled when she couldn't get service. Lucky for her, she'd studied the directions to the rental the previous night. She hurried, excited to see Cherry and Joanna, but the cottage was empty when Rena reached it. She left her backpack on the deck out of visible sight and slung her handbag strap over her shoulder.

Time to find these yew trees. David had told her he'd attempt to use the trees during the late afternoon since many of the senior druids rested in their quarters before they emerged for dinner.

Rena found the marked path and set out, enjoying the sea tang and the peppery-green fragrance wafting from the plants on one side of the trail. Her thoughts wandered, and doubts crept into her mind.

If she told any of her casual acquaintances, she was having dream sex with a gorgeous druid, and it was the best sex of her life, they'd give her a side-eye and ring a friend to gossip about Rena's warped mind. Yet, David seemed so real, and sometimes when she woke in the morning, she spotted his head imprint on her spare pillow. And each morning, her body felt loose and limber and well-used, as if she'd enjoyed passionate sex during the night.

Okay, those things, no matter how weird, sort of made sense since the brain was a powerful organ.

But magical trees and time portals? Heck, add dragons to the equation. Rena prided herself on her rational mind, but this...believing in David pushed her from her comfort zone.

With her mind churning, Rena kept walking while scanning the scenery. Flat stretches of land. Views over the water. The path wound inland, and she listened to a thrush singing in the thicket. The photos she'd glimpsed during her computer search had shown a distinct lack of trees. She followed a bend in the path and tipped her head back. She sucked in a herb-scented breath and released it.

The massive yew trees grew in a tight clump, and excitement and enthusiasm had Rena jogging closer, and circling the trees. The larger ones drooped downward and had grown new roots from branches and multiplied. The ruby-red berries glowed with jewel-like intensity in the sun.

"This must be the place," she murmured.

A vehicle pulled up in a parking lot to her left, and Rena tensed. It couldn't be Tony. She'd taken such care.

Not that she wouldn't put it past him to pop out of the woodwork and give her a heart attack. Rena hadn't liked the man the first time she'd met the pompous cheat. According to him, Liza was the culprit in this scenario. Rena whipped around, ready to flee.

She took two strides before her brain caught up and went online again, and she recognized the red-haired woman.

"Cherry!" Rena started running and threw herself at her best friend. She hugged her hard, and tears formed at her eyes. Although it hadn't been long, so much had happened since they'd parted.

"Aunt Rena," Joanna piped up, looking so much like Liza, Rena's breath caught.

"Joanna."

"Jo!" Joanna shouted in a loud voice.

Rena stared at her niece, not comprehending why Cherry and the large male beside her were laughing.

"Long story," Cherry said, her brown eyes glittering with mirth. "Rena, this is Martinos."

Rena sized up the tall and muscular man at Cherry's side. He had long, curly black hair and stubble defined his jaw. She noted Joanna's complete absence of fear, and she reserved judgment. The man hovered next to Cherry, a protective vibe coming from him, which Rena found reassuring. Sweet. This man was a dragon.

The dragon-man froze, his gaze lighting on something behind her.

"Who is that?" he gritted with suspicion.

Rena whipped around, her breaths coming in hard pumps. "David?"

It was David. *In the flesh.* A tall man in a concealing black robe. As she spotted him, he let the cowl drop away from his face to reveal his long black hair. His familiar clean-shaven features held the same lazy grin he offered whenever they met in the dreamscape.

She dropped her black bag, took two steps and found herself running.

He caught her in his strong arms, and then they were kissing.

"Who is that man?" Joanna hollered.

Rena loosened her grip on David and pulled away a fraction. "This is David."

Cherry's brows rose. "*The* David?"

Unexpected heat coasted to Rena's cheeks, and she was confident the olive skin she'd inherited from her mother didn't hide a shred of her embarrassment. "Yes."

David's low chuckle had her jumping away, but he snared her arm and tucked her back against his side. "I see Rena has mentioned me."

"A few times," Cherry teased.

"I can't stay long." He nodded at Martinos. "Show me the cuff."

Martinos peeled off his shirt, and Rena winked at Cherry when she caught her friend's gaze. "Nice," Rena mouthed.

"I'm not sure if the spell will work," David said, meeting Martinos's gaze with honesty. "I had limited time to study the various spells."

"Do your best," Martinos said. "I appreciate your help."

David approached Martinos and placed his big scarred hands on top of the decorative cuff that encircled Martinos's beefy biceps. "Ladies, please stand back. The spell might turn explosive."

"I'm a boy," Joanna informed him, shouting once again.

"Jo," Cherry chided. "Remember, we discussed the magic trees. Rena's friend needs to do a special spell to remove Martinos's armband. Please stand with me and Aunt Rena. We'll watch from over there."

"Good luck," Rena murmured.

David flashed her a smile, but she knew him well enough to see the strain at the edges. Something about the armband perturbed him. A wealth of questions tugged at Rena, but she held her tongue as she retrieved her bag and joined Cherry and Jo by the car.

"He's handsome." Rena stowed her handbag in Cherry's car. "Are you sure you can trust him?"

"You're sleeping with a man you met in your dreams," Cherry retorted. "Pot. Kettle."

Surprised at Cherry's feistiness, Rena barked out a laugh. An insight into the man...uh...dragon.

David started chanting, a low stream of foreign-sounding words. Rena couldn't hear clearly since his back was to her, but she caught the strain on Martinos's face. His features went tight, and his jaw worked as he ground his molars.

"Martinos," Cherry whispered, the color bleeding from her cheeks. She took half a step before Rena's arm shot out to stop Cherry's interference with the spell.

"I trust David. He's a decent man with good intentions, and I believe in him."

Cherry jerked her head back and placed her palm against the middle of her chest. "You? The practical woman who only believes what she sees in her microscope? Did I hear right? You'd better repeat that for me so I can tell Liza."

At the mention of Liza, both women froze. Desolation passed over Cherry, and Rena wrapped her friend in a tight hug.

"I know," Rena said. *"I know."*

They clutched each other, seeking comfort. Rena screwed her eyes tight and blinked when she saw a burst of bright color. A dull thump sounded, then a savage roar.

"A dragon," Joanna whispered, her mouth slack with wonder.

Rena and Cherry relaxed their hold on each other and stared at David and the red dragon towering over him. The dragon threw back his head and roared, a wall of flames spurting from its giant mouth. David backed away toward a yew tree, and the dragon's stirring wings barely missed him. The dragon sprang upward, taking to the air. He flew a tight circle of the yew trees before heading straight for Cherry and Rena. Rena grabbed Joanna and dived for cover behind the car.

"Cherry!" Rena shouted.

Her friend gaped at the approaching dragon. "Wow."

"Cherry! Get out of the way. He'll—" Before Rena finished, the dragon plucked Cherry off the ground, and with a flap of his giant wings, lifted higher into the air.

Cherry's shriek rippled back as Rena scrambled to her feet. But there was nothing she could do. The dragon was a mere speck in the sky.

"David, will Cherry be all right?" She sought his gaze, and it didn't reassure her.

"I think Martinos cares for her."

"How do you know that?" Rena demanded. "You've seen Martinos for all of ten minutes. First, Liza, and now Cherry. Holy—" She glanced at Joanna. "Holy frogs, this is not happening."

"I watched your friend and the dragon before I showed myself. They care for one another." David touched his fingers to her cheek.

The caress packed a bigger punch than any on the dreamscape. His touch had satisfied her, but now she yearned for more. Joanna's small hand on her arm grounded her. Rena scanned the spot where she'd last seen the dragon. She couldn't see anything except the sky and a few puffy clouds. Some of them held a tinge of darker gray. "Are you sure he won't hurt her?"

"My gut says no, but Martinos's dragon was suppressed for years. He burst free as soon as the armband dropped. From what I've heard, the dragon can control the human and refuse to yield if pushed hard enough."

Not fantastic news for Cherry.

"Why did he take her?"

"It's possible the dragon likes Cherry and wanted her with him. He trusts her."

"An excellent courtship plan," Rena snapped. "What if he drops her?"

"It's impossible to predict his behavior."

Rena paced to release her edginess and fear. "You could've warned us before you started the spell."

"I'm sorry, cynamone."

"Is Aunt Cherry coming back?" Joanna shouted. "I wanna ride with the dragon."

"Is it necessary to shout?" Rena demanded.

"I'm pretending to be a boy. Boys are noisy. They yell," Joanna explained, also at a shout.

David chuckled and held out his hand. "Hello. My name is David. I think your Aunt Cherry will be fine with the dragon, but it might be a while before she returns."

"Oh. Okay. I'm Jo." Joanna glanced around before whipping off her hat and beaming at them. "Do I look like a boy?"

"You cut your hair," Rena said.

"The boys at school pull my ponytail," Joanna said. "It's annoying. Aunt Cherry let me get my hair cut. Uncle Martinos got his hair cut too."

"Uncle Martinos," Rena repeated.

"Yes," Joanna said. "He's nice. He showed me how to draw dragons. Aunt Cherry says he has talent at art stuff."

Rena had guessed right. Cherry and Martinos were closer than Cherry had confessed. And it appeared Joanna had thrived with the pair watching her.

"Uncle Martinos turned into a dragon," Joanna said. "He's cool. We should go home. I'm hungry. Uncle Martinos and Aunt Cherry will come back when they're tired of flying."

"I... Okay." Rena glanced at David. "Are you coming to the cottage with us?"

"A short visit. The spell worked quicker than I'd planned." David sidled closer to Rena. "On my next visit, I'll know where to find you."

"Aunt Cherry said we're having fish and chips for dinner at the pub," Joanna said. "Can we still do that?"

"Uh, I guess so." Rena opened the driver's side of the car and let out a relieved breath on seeing the keys. Joanna piled into the rear of the vehicle and fastened her seat belt.

David hovered, more diffident than usual. "Where should I sit? What do I do?"

"Do you not have motor vehicles in your world?"

"This box is a motor vehicle?"

"Or a car." Rena rounded the hood of the car and opened the door for him. "Sit on the seat here." She gestured him to get in. Once he sat, she reached over to fasten the seat belt. "This is a safety feature, and our laws make it compulsory for us to wear them when we're driving." He nodded, and once he tightened his robe around him, she shut the door.

Rena jumped into the driver's seat. She started the car, and

David tensed.

"Driving in a vehicle is safe," she said. "We've never discussed the technology at your home. Other things distract us."

"True." David leaned forward in his seat, taking in his surroundings with interest as she pulled onto the road and started the drive toward the village. "It goes so fast. You must save many hours of walking."

"Most people drive these days. People don't walk often and have weight issues because of lack of exercise and surplus food."

David nodded, but the scenery captured his attention. A few houses. Men and women dressed in unusual clothing showing skin.

Rena indicated a right turn, and she pulled off the road. She halted in front of the cottage, and once she'd switched off the engine, Joanna exited and ran toward the entrance.

"Would you like to come inside?"

"Yes, please. I want to see some of your world."

"I guess I thought our worlds were similar."

"I live in a cell in a dormitory. Druids at the monastery have few possessions. The people we traveled past had clothes and belongings with them."

"Don't the dragons and the humans who live on your islands have things?"

"I suppose they do," David said. "I've never visited the towns on the Dragon Isles."

"Come inside. I'll make a cup of tea. Knowing Cherry, she'll have something yummy to eat. When it's time for you to return, I'll give you a ride to the yew grove."

David followed her into the cottage. Joanna clattered into the kitchen to join them. While David was busy checking his surroundings, Rena filled the kettle and put it on to boil.

"This world is fascinating. So many unfamiliar things. I wish we had more time."

"Save your questions for later. We need a plan. How do we rescue Cherry?"

"I'm hoping Martinos's dragon will come to his senses and let Martinos gain enough control to shift to his human form."

"What if he injures Cherry?"

David rubbed his chin, his brows drawing together as he considered her query. "It's impossible to predict the dragon's reaction. You told me you thought Cherry and Martinos were close. We have to hope that whatever Martinos feels for Cherry will have bled through to his dragon."

"Even though the armband suppressed his dragon for years?"

"I'm hungry, Aunt Rena," Joanna announced, interrupting their murmured conversation. "Breakfast was a long time ago."

Rena opened the fridge to peer at the contents. Beside her, David gaped at the variety of foods. She squeezed his arm in understanding. "How about toasted sandwiches and tomato soup?"

"Yay!" Joanna shouted.

"Hat off," Rena told Joanna. She couldn't get used to her niece's shorter hair and shook her head. "Do you enjoy pretending to be a boy?"

"Yes, it's fun." Joanna beamed. "Can I help? Boys cook. Aunt Cherry said so." She didn't wait for Rena to reply but ran off to wash her hands without being asked.

David stared after the girl, amusement tugging at his lips. "She's bright and funny."

"She resembles Liza, her mother." Her voice wobbled, and David wrapped his arm around her shoulders.

Joanna clattered back into the kitchen and skidded to a halt. "Are you Aunt Rena's boyfriend?"

"Yes," David said.

"No," Rena said at the same time.

David turned her to face him and leaned closer to kiss the tip of her nose. "Yes. You and I are involved. I don't intend that to end."

"B-but we're from different worlds. How can we continue? The dreamscape... It doesn't feel real." She hesitated. "No, that's not what I mean." She gave an irritable shrug. "I want to turn to the man I'm with and speak with him. Hug or kiss. Argue face-to-face."

"Shush, cynamone. Neither of us can read the future—my foresight can be tricky—but we'll work together. We'll take one day at a time. I promise we'll find a way. Now that I've found you,

I'd hate to lose you, Rena."

They cooked together, David helping along with Joanna. Once they'd finished cooking, they sat at the dining room table and ate.

"I'd love to stay, but better leave. I don't want the brothers to miss me."

"What will they do if they notice your absence?" Rena asked.

"I don't want to invite questions or get removed from library duty. It gives me access to research books and an excuse to closet myself away for lengthy periods. I've been working extra hours, and Brother Matthew approves of my diligence. That's a wonderful thing. He's less likely to suspect me of spying on him."

"Understandable. Joanna and I will give you a lift back to the yew grove."

"Thank you." David rose from the table and collected the dirty plates.

"You're house-trained," Rena teased.

He frowned, and she wondered if it was wrong to mention his wife.

David caught her expression and shook his head. "I helped Helena around our home when she was pregnant. She found it difficult during the final months."

"I appreciate your help. In my world, men are helpful and enjoy cooking while others leave everything to their wives and girlfriends."

"I can't wait to question you further," David whispered.

With the dirty dishes stacked in the dishwasher, the three of them jumped into Cherry's car. With everyone buckled up—David learned fast—Rena drove toward the yew grove.

She entered the small town and drove along the main street.

"That's a big man," Joanna said without warning. She pointed at the tall man with long black hair who stood near a gift shop. He was watching the passersby.

"Keep driving," David spoke fast, his tone urgent as soon as he spotted the stranger.

Rena motored through the village without slowing, her gaze going to her rear-vision mirror once they were almost out of town. "Is that a dragon?"

"Yes," David said. "We must hurry. I'm unsure of how the dragon traveled here. Whether he used the yew grove or disappeared as Martinos had with Cherry..." He trailed off with a grimace. "He can't catch me here."

Rena nodded, and once she was clear of a loitering group of tourists, she put her foot down. As soon as they reached the yew grove, David leaped from the car. "I'll try to visit tonight. You and Joanna should leave. Can you drive in a different direction?"

"Yes. Later." Every part of her wanted to kiss him goodbye, but she forced herself to remain behind the wheel. "I loved meeting you in person."

"We will make this work," David said, reading her doubt and vulnerability with ease.

Rena watched David jog into the trees before she pulled out of the gravel parking area. She drove home a different way, but given the island was small her choices were limited. They had to pass through the town again.

"Can you still see the dragon-man?" she asked Joanna once she'd turned onto the main street.

"No. Wait. Yes," Joanna whispered.

Rena continued driving, her pulse racing as she headed in the direction of the castle that stood on the coast like a sentry.

"David," she whispered. "I hope you stay safe. Now that I've met you once, I want to see you again."

CHAPTER 8

Danger Hovers

"Aunt Cherry, Uncle Martinos, and I saw the same dragon before," Joanna announced.

"What? When?"

"When we visited the pub for a drink. I don't think Uncle Martinos liked him. I drank a soda and burped loud."

"Oh," Rena said in total understatement.

Joanna pressed her face to the window and blew out a breath to mist the glass. Rena couldn't find it in her to growl at her niece. First Liza and now Cherry. The dragon had seized her so fast. Neither she nor David could have prevented the dragon from stealing her away. Cherry's scream replayed in Rena's mind. Terror might've had Cherry in its grip, but she hadn't flailed or struggled. She hadn't fought the dragon's hold.

Rena shook her head, an unwilling smile curving her lips.

"Is the dragon-man following us?" Joanna asked.

"Where?" Rena barked. She'd taken a circular route and thought he'd have vanished by the time they reached the town again. "Where is he?"

"He's eating ice cream. Oh, he's seen us. He's waving." Joanna returned the wave.

Rena accelerated to hustle the hell away. She sneaked a glance out the window and caught a second wave for her benefit. As she disappeared around the bend, he laughed. The massive black-haired lout was enjoying her terror. "Have you seen the man near the cottage?"

"No," Joanna trilled, and tension eased from Rena.

"That's good," Rena whispered. "Perhaps we'll have dinner at home. We-we should stay out of sight of that man."

Joanna's eyes rounded. "Is he dangerous?"

"I'm not sure," Rena said, striving for honesty. "We're best to stay away from him because David says he's dodgy."

"Is David really your boyfriend?"

"Ah..." What the hell. "Yes. David is my boyfriend."

Joanna grasped the seat with her small hand. "Mummy says I'll like boys one day. I don't think so."

"Right." Rena suppressed her laugh and pulled up in front of the cottage. What was the dragon doing here? She ran through a list of possible reasons. Life in the Dragon Isles might've bored him, and he wanted a change, or he'd craved ice cream or a human girlfriend. *Yeah, right.*

Whatever the reason, his presence made the hair at the back of her neck prickle. She scanned the area around the cottage and saw nothing out of the ordinary, but unease still had her stomach churning.

"Aren't you getting out of the car?" Joanna asked.

"Yes, of course." Rena grabbed her handbag and exited the vehicle. "How does pizza sound for dinner instead of fish and chips?"

"Yes!"

"Excellent. You can help me make the dough and cut up the toppings."

"Okay. Do you think I can ride on a dragon? It looked like fun. Aunt Cherry is so lucky."

"Right. So lucky," Rena echoed, wondering if Cherry felt blessed. "Wash your hands, and we'll start the pizza."

Later that night, after Joanna went to bed, Rena stared at the television screen, her mind working on explanations for the dragon's presence on Holy Island. She came up with three reasons, none of which pleased her. One: they wanted to expand their territory and were checking the possibilities. Two: they wanted revenge on humans for hunting them. Three: they were sightseeing or starting a new business offering tours for tourists.

"Huh!" Now she was really stretching.

Rena yawned. Time to retire for the night.

Sleep came with difficulty. Her brain refused to let go of the fact both Liza and Cherry had vanished, and at least one dragon was wandering Holy Island. Tony was the least of her problems.

When she fell asleep, her rest was fitful, and she kept waking. For one moment, she glimpsed David, but his image blurred, and he faded as she jolted awake.

She lay frozen in position, her pulse pounding. Her senses screamed something was wrong, but she couldn't hear an out-of-place sound. Rena pushed upright. When she heard nothing, she crawled from bed and wandered to the kitchen to make a cup of tea.

She stared out the kitchen window while waiting for the kettle to boil. A shadow flitted between two trees.

Was someone out there?

Anxiety sent a prickle of chill bumps down her spine. When not a thing moved, she gave a shaky laugh. This cottage was way too isolated for her liking. She glanced at her watch and wished she could sleep. Right now, she could use an adult to drive the silliness from her head. They were safe here, and Tony was miles away on the mainland with not the slightest clue of their location.

Tony sat in front of his computer, his gaze on the blip on the map he'd pulled up on the screen. The tracker had been expensive but worth every penny since his wife thought to hide his daughter from him.

He'd informed Liza he'd leave if she paid him off. Simple for her, given her daddy's wealth. She'd refused, ordering him to rot in hell.

Silly bitch.

She didn't know the meaning of hell.

Once he'd finished dicking around with her, she might get a clue. Now that he knew where she'd hidden his daughter, he could reclaim Joanna and apply pressure on Liza.

He should've done that from the start, but he'd enjoyed the cat-and-mouse game he'd started.

Holy Island.

He did another internet search to check out the island. *Hmm,* interesting. If they thought the tide would keep him away, they were mistaken.

His phone played a few lines of a Queen classic, and he picked it up. Fear twisted his gut on seeing the ID. *Fuck.* He needed that money. If the bitch had given him the cash when he asked for it, this problem wouldn't have escalated.

The phone rang twice more while he decided if he should answer. His hand trembled as he accepted the call, and that irked him.

"Tony speaking."

"Why didn't you answer?"

"I was on the toilet," Tony lied.

"The money is due at the end of this week."

"Got it covered."

"Make sure you do. You promised the last time the payment fell due. If it'd been up to me, I wouldn't have been as forgiving as the boss."

Tony scowled. The man's boss had doubled the interest rate. He'd hardly call that forgiving or generous. "You'll receive your payment on time. No worries."

"Fantastic. That's all I wanted to confirm. Catch ya."

Tony swallowed hard, the blast of dizziness making him glad of his chair. The clock was ticking, and he'd need to hustle to pull together a plan.

The tide cut off Holy Island each day, so he'd have to time his visit.

He needed that money. Hell, it was his to take. He'd earned it by putting up with the silly bitch. He hadn't wanted a kid, but it turned out their daughter was the very weapon he required to shove the knife deeper into his wife's chest. Yeah, he'd get the money and the kid. He'd have a means to target his wife for as long as he needed one.

CHAPTER 9

A Faulty Memory

David had discovered a cache of papers Brother Jasper had hidden beneath the bookshelves and was busy skimming them. He didn't hear Brother Matthew until it was too late.

"Ah, what have you found there?" Brother Matthew asked, his gaze sharp and full of suspicion.

"I found them under a pile of books," David said.

"Give them to me." Brother Matthew held out an imperious hand. "You carry on clearing this mess. You've made excellent progress, but the other brothers wish to know when they can enter the library to peruse their areas of interest."

David handed over the papers while cursing inwardly. Of all

the rotten timing. With so much happening, he found himself stretched thin. Last night, he'd been so tired that holding onto the dreamscape had been impossible. And even more worrying, he'd thought for another moment he'd spotted a robed silhouette in the distance. When he'd tried to return, the figure had disappeared, and he wondered if fatigue was making him see things. He'd tossed and turned for the rest of the night.

"I want you to concentrate on clearing the area around the research tables so we can at least open part of the library."

"Yes, I'll start straight away." David bowed his head in a show of respect while thoughts tumbled through his mind. The senior druid's presence put a stop to his investigation. Not that he'd discovered anything apart from the book and the papers, now tucked in Brother Matthew's robe pocket.

"How long before the library is functional?"

"If I start now, the study area should be ready by tomorrow morning."

"Excellent." Brother Matthew rubbed his hands together. "I'll send you two helpers."

David nodded. "Thank you."

Brother Matthew bustled from the library, and when David could no longer see or hear him, he bit out a sharp curse. Damn and blast.

Whatever had been in those papers had satisfied Brother Matthew. He'd had no compunction in letting other brothers into the library. David wandered over to the research location and started picking up books and sorting them into piles. What could've been in those papers? And why the devil hadn't he heard Brother Matthew's arrival in time?

A spell?

It was an obvious answer, which meant David needed to be extra careful in his actions. He stacked the books on the study tables he'd unearthed, and normality returned to the area. He righted bookshelves, muscles straining to yank the weighty wooden frames up from where they lay on the floor. After a furtive glance at the door, he searched beneath the shelves. Yes! David shoved the papers he found deep into his pockets, not taking the time to peruse them.

Footsteps had his heart racing, but instead of turning his head, he checked on the shelf's stability. Confident it wouldn't fall on anyone, he sorted the books and shelved several medical tomes.

"Brother David," a junior druid hailed him.

David turned to spot Brother Peter and Brother Allen.

"We've come to help," Brother Allen boomed.

"The place is a mess." Brother Peter planted his hands on his hips, his slight figure dwarfed by the mountain of books.

"It is," David agreed. "You should've seen it before I started work."

"But you've cleaned for three days," Brother Allen stated, his freckled expression aghast, even though he didn't come out and accuse David of slacking.

"I welcome the help. Brother Matthew wants to reopen the library tomorrow."

"What do you want us to do?" Brother Allen asked.

David indicated the toppled shelves with a sweep of his hand. "We should pick up all the shelves and make certain they are stable. Once we do that, it will be easier to tidy the books."

"But the books will be out of order," Brother Peter said, his young face earnest.

"We'll put the books in their proper places once the floor is clear and we have the tables and chairs in place," David said.

"A workable plan." Brother Allen nodded in approval. "Let's start."

David, with the two brothers' help, made quick work of placing the shelves in their former positions. A few had broken, so Brother Peter left to ask Brother Felix to help repair them. Soon the four druids worked in concert, setting the library to rights. David scanned books but discovered nothing out of the ordinary.

While he worked, he listened to the younger druids for useful tidbits of gossip. Nothing helpful. Not one mention of the warehouse, now hidden by a magical spell. Not one mention of monastery visitors. Not one mention of Brother Jasper and his funeral, which had taken place the previous day.

The lack of funeral discussion struck David as sad. "Who is taking over from Brother Jasper?"

"Who?" Brother Allen asked.

Each of the younger brothers stared at him.

"You're getting old." Brother Peter tittered. "Brother James is in charge of the library. He'll be back at work here as soon as we finish. Remember, he's been sick and on bed rest for two weeks."

David shook his head. The others took his action as one to clear his noggin when it was an expression of dismay. What game was Brother Matthew playing? He had to be part of the conspiracy because he'd been supervising David. David wondered if Brother Matthew might try a spell on him to make him think his memories were faulty.

He made a mental note to write himself a reminder in case he forgot his mentor. The spell they'd used to hide the warehouse hadn't zapped him. He needed to record what was happening each day and conceal this diary. And he had to finish reading the last of Brother Jasper's book and his new discovery.

After late supper that night, David retired earlier than his fellow brothers. Several of them shouted easy insults about his advanced age and his requiring a nap, which David shrugged off. If only they knew.

He scanned the papers he found first and was glad he had. Excitement raced through him as he read Brother Jasper's scrawl.

I have learned the dragon who visits Brother Matthew every week has something over him. Blackmail is a nasty word, but I believe this relates to the strangers at the sacred yew grove, and it is the only thing that makes sense. I hid behind a bush and watched three dragon shifters walk into the yew grove and disappear. Unfortunately, I think Brother Matthew is the instigator of this illegal use of the grove's magic. He heard me asking questions, and the next day I fell ill after my evening meal. Someone tampered with my food since I ate the same bread, soup, and cheese the others ate. None of them were sick. The more I witness, the more I fear something is afoot.

The rulers of Hissing Isle, Perfume Isle, and Smoking Isle agreed to pay the tithe to the druids for keeping the Dragon Isles safe from human prying eyes. I can't fathom the reasons Brother Matthew is allowing dragons to pass through the barrier to the other side. He risks our peaceful way of life. He risks everything, and for what?

Try as I might, I can't understand the reasoning behind Brother Matthew's acquiescence. He hasn't visited his sister and her two boys, which I find strange. Instead, he lurks around the monastery, popping up in the oddest places.

Dragons terrified the human race, so I don't know why they'd wish to venture into the human world. I think it would be a foreign place—different from when we last walked the mainland shores. Our way of life has changed little over hundreds of years.

That was close. Brother Matthew almost caught me. I hope if something happens to me, that someone will find my notes and put a stop to the unlawful activities here at the monastery. Our job is to ascertain the correct running of the barrier. The dragons pay us a tithe to do this. Chosen dragons shouldn't benefit from exclusive use.

Only good should come from its utilization, but I fear corruption is loose.

I will split my notes and hide them. I find my memory is fading when it used to be excellent, despite my age. These notes will serve a dual purpose. It will keep the information safe and will also refresh my memory when I forget things.

David reread the note. "A spell to make the brothers forget what they shouldn't see," he whispered. That made jotting down his memories important, although David hated to think of someone searching his cell when he was busy elsewhere.

Rena.

The obvious solution to his dilemma.

He'd find Rena on the dreamscape and tell her everything he'd learned. That way, if the spell forced his memories to retreat, he'd have a backup in a safe place.

David reached for the hot milk and honey he'd poured himself and took a sip. The strange taste had him spitting the mouthful back into his cup. A senior druid had handed it to him, told him he didn't mind making another. Suspicion rose in David.

Right. That did it. He must take care of what he ate and drank, and now, it was imperative to connect with Rena tonight.

David prepared for bed and doused the lantern. His cell went dark, the area in the main dormitory quiet since the other brothers—most of them—were still in the community hall. He closed his eyes and commenced the breathing exercises an older brother had taught him when he first entered the monastery. In those days, he'd wake with nightmares of battles and trying to save his wife and daughter from the Vikings. The brother had died in an accident during the wheat harvest, but David remembered him fondly and still practiced the breathing exercises the druid had taught him.

He sucked in air and held it for a count of seven before exhaling to another count of seven. At first, he'd thought the breathing exercises were a stupid waste of time. He'd soon discovered the simple act of breathing held terrific power. Conscious breathing doused his panic and made him feel in control. Correct breathing helped him to relax and fall asleep faster than usual.

Besides, once he reached Rena, he could relax and be himself. He pictured the young child he'd seen with Rena. Although she'd been older than his daughter, she'd reminded him of Brianna. He smiled, the memory of his daughter running through a field no longer holding the power to hurt. Instead, he embraced the recollection with joy. A moment of his life when innocence had touched him and made him feel clean.

David popped onto the dreamscape and studied the clusters of ribbons twirling in a faint breeze. No turquoise one for him to follow. Not yet. Disappointment seared through him. If Rena wasn't here, he must use the time to dip into someone else's dreams. One of the brothers?

No, the clump held a mere three ribbons. He moved further into the dreamscape and followed his instincts. A stunning violet ribbon attracted him, so he followed that one to the end.

He popped into a child's bedroom, surprise freezing him. Wait. He knew this child. Joanna. Rena's niece, and the one who was pretending she was a boy, despite her pretty brown eyes giving her away.

"Uncle David," she said in her sweet voice. "What are you doing here?"

"I wanted to visit your Aunt Rena," he replied, his chest tightening on hearing her refer to him as an uncle. "But she isn't asleep yet."

"Oh."

"Can you remember things?" David asked. Alarm filled him because his lips had turned numb. He needed to pass on the information before he forgot it. "Do you have a good memory?"

"Yes." Joanna tugged the bedcovers into place. "I'm excellent at secrets too. Aunt Cherry said."

David suppressed his smile. "I need you to give a message to your Aunt Rena, but you can't tell anyone else. Can you do that for me?"

"Yes." Her eyes remained solemn as she awaited further instructions.

"Tell your aunt Brother Matthew is involved. He has added something to the food that makes the brothers forget things they see but shouldn't. Can you remember that?"

"Yes." Joanna repeated it back to him.

"There is more." David hoped he wasn't putting too much pressure on the girl. "Brother Matthew is allowing dragons to pass through the yew grove. Please take care."

Joanna nodded and repeated their entire conversation to him.

"One more thing. Brother Jasper died because he discovered something he shouldn't have, and Brother Mathew caught him." David wondered if he should've told the girl this, but she nodded again.

"I'll tell Aunt Rena as soon as I can."

"All right. Tell Aunt Rena I told you. If I forget, she needs to remind me."

"I will, Uncle David."

David nodded and prayed he didn't cause nightmares for the child. "Sweet dreams, Joanna."

"Are you going to marry Aunt Rena?"

"I'd like to." David meant every word, although he had no inkling of the practicalities to ensure this. He'd committed himself to the monastery so long ago, and his contact with the other brothers and his daily tasks had pulled him from his depression. These days, his memories of his wife and daughter were more bittersweet. He recalled the better times, even if sadness edged the recollections.

"I can't wait to tell Mummy about my new uncles. Can you

draw pictures?"

He thought of the interest he'd found in herbs and other medicinal plants. He'd kept a notebook with scrawled details and illustrations of the plants, their flowers, seeds, and berries. "I draw plants and flowers."

"Will you show me?"

"Not now, little one. Another night, *hmm*?" He hesitated. "Can you remember what I told you?" He sought the information, frowning. He'd told the girl something. Joanna. Why could he recall her name and not what he'd told her?

"I remember everything."

"That's good." An understatement since fear had replaced his memories. He lingered, wondering what to do for the best. If he asked further questions, he might confuse her. No, he'd return home and pray for a favorable outcome. He turned away.

"Goodnight, Uncle David."

"Sweet dreams, little one." David scuttled along the dream ribbon with less poise than usual. He popped out of Joanna's dream, his mind in turmoil. The message's importance filled him with urgency, yet frustration filled him, too, because his mind was an empty slate.

Rena awoke tired, grumpy, and perturbed. David hadn't visited, and that left her out of sorts. A noise jerked her upright, her pulse galloping.

"Bother," Joanna said in a loud voice. She let out a loud burp, and Rena's brows rose at her niece's delighted giggle.

"Joanna," Rena called as she slid out of bed. The chilly wooden floor had her scrambling for a pair of socks. She pulled on jeans and a blouse, dragged a comb through her hair, and hurried to the kitchen.

"What is going on here?"

"Uncle Martinos isn't here to help me with my rice bubbles. I dropped them. Sorry!" she added.

Rena observed the pile of rice bubbles covering the floor. "I didn't realize the box held that amount."

"It was new," Joanna said helpfully.

Rena sighed. "Let me put on the kettle, then I'll find the broom and sweep up this mess. How do you feel about scrambled eggs for breakfast?"

"Yay!" Joanna shouted. "That's my favorite."

"I know." Rena grinned because her niece was shouting again. "Did I hear you burp?"

"Yes! It was a perfect one. Nice and loud."

"Well, if your mother heard that, she'd expect you to say pardon me."

Joanna nodded. "Pardon me, Aunt Rena."

Rena filled the kettle and got to work on the rice bubble

explosion. They'd need to risk going to the mainland to replenish their food stocks today, so she pulled out her phone to check on the tide. Later this afternoon. If they went then, they'd have to hustle to get back again before the sea cut them off from Holy Island.

Once the floor was clean, Rena cracked four eggs in a bowl, added milk, herbs, and seasonings, and tipped the entire mix into a heated pan.

"We'll drive into town this afternoon and stock up on our food supplies. Is there anything you want? We need to write a list."

"A new notebook, so I'm ready to draw plants and flowers with Uncle David."

Rena frowned at Joanna. "When did you talk to David about drawing plants?"

"Last night, while I was asleep." Joanna clapped her hand on the side of her head, her action dramatic and worthy of an Oscar. "I'm meant to tell you stuff."

Rena's brows rose as Joanna told her about Brother Matthew and spells and Brother Jasper dying. "Ah, anything else?"

"He told me to tell you because he couldn't. He told me it was a secret."

"Why didn't he visit me?"

"You weren't in bed."

Rena buttered two pieces of toast. She served the eggs and handed one plate to Joanna. "Anything else?"

"Dragons are visiting here, Uncle David said. I'd like to draw another dragon. Will we see one flying today?"

Hopefully not. "I'm not sure," Rena said. "Finish your eggs, and we'll write a shopping list."

Later that afternoon, she and Joanna set off for the mainland. Rena had dressed in clothing she wouldn't normally wear, taking advantage of Cherry's wardrobe. Joanna had dressed in her boy disguise, and if Rena hadn't known Jo was her niece, she'd have walked past her in the street.

"We're just going to the supermarket," Rena explained. "I want you to stay right beside me and not wander off."

"Will we get my new notebook?"

"Yes," Rena said. "And if you're extra good and stay beside me for the entire shopping trip, I'll buy you a pack of coloring pencils."

Joanna's eyes shone with excitement. "Yes, please. I promise I'll be well-behaved."

Rena flicked Joanna's hat. "You're always good, son."

They giggled in charity.

The supermarket visit ran without a hitch, and Rena didn't spot anything to alarm her until they drove back over the causeway in a line of traffic. A huge mountain of a man loitered near the road. To a casual bystander, he'd appear like a husband waiting for his wife or perhaps a traveling companion. Rena's rapid glimpse had her mind screaming *dragon*. She glanced into her rear-vision mirror and noticed he'd straightened after spotting her.

"That man looks like a dragon."

Rena's gaze followed in the direction Joanna had pointed. Her niece was right, but this man was older with shorn gray hair, and he held himself with dignity. Despite his additional years, he strode without hesitation, his shoulders square, and his gaze intent. Although he wasn't as large as the first man/dragon Rena had spotted, his attitude screamed in charge.

Rena flicked her gaze away to the traffic on the road. The number of vehicles always increased during the hours the causeway opened. When she could recheck her mirror, she spotted the two men together.

Dragons.

One spoke to the other, then they glanced in her direction. Not a casual scan of their surroundings, but one dragon was pointing her out to another.

This wasn't good. Not good at all.

CHAPTER 10

Between a Rock and a Hard Place

The morning bell rang loud and insistent, ratcheting up David's aching head from bearable to pounding. He blinked and dragged himself out of bed. He had a rapid wash with water from a bowl, the icy temperature shaking away his fuzziness. The last time he'd had a morning-after headache like this was during his early years as a soldier before he'd married and grown responsible.

David scowled and reached for his robe. He recalled nothing of the previous evening.

A booming knock jerked him to speed.

"You're late, Brother David. Hurry, or I will add punishment to your existing tasks."

"I apologize." David thrust his feet into his sandals and forced his legs to speed. His head thumped with every step, and his stomach stirred with an ominous rumble. Aware of the red robe glaring after him, David breathed with care and headed for the kitchen and the dining room. Whatever he'd drunk—or perhaps it was something he'd eaten—it had affected his stomach and his head.

On reaching the kitchen, he noted several junior druids were in a similar situation. To his right, he heard retching, and seconds later, a vomit stench filled the air. Two other brothers lost their fight.

The kitchen druid—a senior—shouted, "Get out of my kitchen! I don't want the food contaminated. You." He pointed at David. "Get a bucket and clear that mess. You. Start serving the porridge. You, take out the teapots. Move it."

David jumped to attention, finding a cloth. He cleaned up as best he could before mopping the area with the soapy water the kitchen druid used to maintain cleanliness. By the time he finished and escorted the stricken brothers to their rooms, the breakfast service had ended.

David trudged back to the kitchen to help with dishes, his stomach less tender, but his head still aching. At the outreaches of his mind, a memory flittered. Something important. Try as he might, the recollection eluded him.

With the dishes done and an enticing bread aroma filling the kitchen, he gave his section a final wipe.

The kitchen-druid entered as David was leaving to go to the library. "Did you eat, lad?"

"No, brother. Meal service had ended by the time I returned."

"I'm about to take the dinner rolls out of the oven. Cut yourself some cheese and take two of the rolls with you."

"Thank you." David hid his surprise.

Although his stomach protested against food, he took the rolls for later. With his meal wrapped in a cloth, he hurried to the library. Several senior druids stopped him to ask when they could use the library. He opened the door and stood aside.

"You can come in and use the study area now. We are still sorting the books, but the tables are clear."

Their faces brightened as he let them inside, although they soon started grumbling when they couldn't locate their desired research books. The druids kept him and Brothers Allen and Peter running with orders to find particular titles.

He and Brothers Peter and Allen missed lunch because the senior druids complained to Brother Matthew that the library was appalling and the juniors must set it to rights. An hour later, Brother Peter and Allen moaned over their empty stomachs, and for the sake of peace, David gave them a dinner roll and cheese each. He filled his complaining belly with two mugs of water from the well.

The chilled water burned away the last of his headache, and his energy returned while the food ceased the other brothers' bellyaching. The senior druids had them racing around for the rest of the afternoon. Books on specific herbs and medicinal recipes were missing or sorted on the wrong shelves. When dinnertime came, David continued working in the library after completing his kitchen chores. Brother Peter and Allen went to dinner, leaving David in the peaceful and empty library.

Something tickled his mind—a memory or perhaps something he'd forgotten to do. David continued puttering around the library, picking up books and placing them on the correct shelves. During the task, he let his thoughts drift, not attempting to grasp the wisp of memory hovering in the background.

David worked for two hours until brothers wandered past the library for a short constitutional after dinner. He held his breath, hoping none tried to enter or berated him for missing dinner service. The older druids loved their routine, and anything out of the norm upset them.

Luckily, no one entered the library or even glanced in his direction. David picked up a book of beginner spells, his eyes catching on the title. *The druid armband.* No sooner had the thought solidified in his brain than a rush of other information rushed him. Brother Jasper. The bewitched dragon on Holy Island. Rena.

Ah, Rena.

How could he have forgotten her?

Why had he forgotten her? David thought back. The senior druid had given him food. The bread rolls. Another had given him a drink. The obvious conclusion—one of the druids was adding an extra ingredient to the food and/or the drinking water. No, not the water because he'd pulled some from the well and drank it.

The cold liquid had helped to clear his head. So not the water, but perhaps the tea the brothers drank at the end of their meals.

Along with the surge of memories came the knowledge of Brother Jasper's book and sorrow at his mentor's passing. He hadn't finished reading what the brother had written and needed to do that in case he uncovered more information to help him and Rena learn what was going on in his world.

He spent another hour shelving books, trying to fill the time before he could retire for the evening without inviting comment. Had he recalled everything that had faded from his memory? He couldn't say with certainty. But the knowledge of someone authorizing additions to the food served in the dining hall told him not every senior druid was in collusion.

David wondered if he should try to gain entrance to the mystery warehouse and decided now wasn't the right time. He needed others to help him puzzle out the clues.

One thing was certain—life at the monastery had become complicated and dangerous. An image of Rena squeezed into his mind, and a smile curved his lips.

Perhaps he should base himself on Holy Island and skulk around the monastery when the need arose. Alternatively, he could leave the monastery and seek help at the mansion at the other end of Smoking Isle. If he was lucky, Martinos or another dragon of his acquaintance might be there and aid him.

David frowned, tossing one alternative against the other.

Both dictated he burn his bridges. The place had been his haven when he most needed one. It was only recently things had changed.

After checking the way was clear, David left the library and slinked through the shadows. Whatever he decided, he'd need to keep his manner natural and pretend to eat as usual. He could grab vegetables fresh from the garden and pocket raw ingredients while he labored in the kitchen. That would work for now.

David detoured to the garden, keeping to the shadows. Although it wasn't against the rules to wander the monastery grounds, he preferred not to invite nosey questions and attention. Once he reached the garden, he picked a bunch of grapes and plucked three apples. He also discovered late strawberries and a handful of raspberries to take the edge off his hunger.

The flicker of light caught his attention, and he noticed something he hadn't earlier. He could see part of the building. Was it because he hadn't eaten the food? No. He'd seen Brother Matthew instruct one of the red robes to create a spell to turn the building invisible.

So why was it visible now?

David ghosted closer, taking care of his footfalls. Two figures. One held a lantern in his hand while the other trailed the first. It was the same dragon he'd seen in Brother Matthew's office. The lantern light offered a better view of the first figure too, and he committed his features to memory. The pair entered the warehouse and didn't return.

David hesitated. Did he risk going closer and coming face-to-face with the dragons or one of the senior druids, or should he wait for longer?

Judging by the rising moon, the hour grew late. He'd wanted to discuss what he'd learned with Rena. He'd explore the area later.

As David retreated and sought the shadows, he spotted the bob of a second lantern. He crouched against the trunk of an apple tree and prayed it concealed his presence.

The light swayed as it came nearer. David was certain of imminent discovery, but the druid carrying the lantern detoured through the grapevines. David huffed out a silent breath. Once the druid passed him, he followed at a discreet distance. For a brief instant, the light shone in the brother's face—a rangy male with a bulbous nose and protruding ears. Brother Matthew. The man meandered to the building and disappeared inside. David lingered in the hope he might discover more. He sought a closer hiding place and sank to the ground to wait. The minutes ticked past. His legs cramped from remaining in position for too long. He fidgeted to get his blood flowing. With his gaze on the building entrance, he rose and stretched his limbs.

Without warning, the door opened, and Brother Matthew emerged. The head druid paused to scan his surroundings. David froze too, his breath catching in his throat. *Please don't notice me.* Eventually, the druid moved, and David saw he was carrying something in a bag. It was a bag, unlike any David had seen before. One from Rena's world.

The dragons had brought supplies from the humans back to Smoking Isle.

That posed the question—what type of supplies?

David waited for another half an hour, but no one emerged from the building, and Brother Matthew seemed to have returned to his quarters.

It might be an idea for David to explore the senior druid's rooms if the opportunity arose. Improbable, he concluded, although the junior druids kept the common room clean. He could volunteer for the chore. But no. That would draw attention to himself.

It took another three-quarters of an hour before David reached his cell. The other juniors were asleep, judging by the loud snoring coming from several cells. David kicked off his sandals and placed the three apples he'd kept in a safe hiding place before reclining on his bed, still dressed in his robe. He closed his eyes and focused on deep breathing as he drifted closer to sleep.

Relieved to find himself on the dreamscape, he located Rena's turquoise ribbon. As always, it glittered, outdoing the others in its vicinity with its vibrancy. He placed his left hand on the tether and followed it to the end, bursting into Rena's dream.

"David," she cried on seeing him. "Where have you been?"

David took her in his arms, admitting to himself he'd been as anxious as her. "The last time I visited the dreamscape, I couldn't locate you. I followed another pretty ribbon and found Joanna."

"She told me. Are you all right?"

"I believe the head druid has authorized the use of a magical potion added to our food. It makes one forget things they've seen. Something went wrong, and many of the juniors were sick, including me. The weird thing is they've recovered, and none recall being sick."

Rena pulled back to stare, apprehension shading her beautiful eyes. "How come you can remember?"

"I've restricted my diet to fresh fruit and vegetables straight from the garden. I've drunk only water that I drew from the well. Once I did that, the fog in my mind receded."

"Won't the others notice you're not eating or drinking in the dining room?"

"Yes," David said, pleased with her understanding of his dilemma. "I'm unsure of my next action."

"What are your alternatives?"

"I can leave the monastery and join you on Holy Island, or I can travel to the mansion farther south to find Martinos and Cherry."

"I'm worried about Cherry."

"What does your gut say?"

Rena closed her eyes, and when she opened them again, she smiled. "My intuition says Cherry and Liza are safe in the Dragon Isles."

"We have the same opinion. So what do I do? Once I leave the monastery, I won't be able to return. Brother Matthew will notice my absence."

Rena pursed her lips. "Your Brother Jasper died under suspicious circumstances. What is to stop another death if someone catches you skulking where you shouldn't be?"

"You think I should leave?"

"This afternoon, Joanna and I spotted two dragons. At least, I know one of them was a dragon because Joanna saw him when she was with Cherry and Martinos."

David tensed, every protective instinct in him roaring to life. "Did they see you?"

"Yes."

"Can you describe them to me?" His pulse raced, his hands clenching to fists while he waited for her reply.

"One was younger, around your age, I guess. He had long black hair, but he had it in a man bun. He's big like Martinos with a similar build." She paused. "The man is arrogant. He caught us watching him and let us know it."

"And the other one?"

"He was older with short, gray hair and with a healthy

appearance. This one acted as superior as the younger one, but he held an air of command." Rena paused again. "If I had to guess, I'd say he was the one in charge."

David hissed. "The dragon I saw in the head druid's office. I got the impression the dragon scared Brother Matthew. Brother Jasper thought there was blackmail involved."

"Who is he? What do you think he wants?"

"Not a clue," David said. "I saw Brother Matthew carrying a bag that looked as if it might come from your world. They may be bringing in goods from the mainland to sell for profit."

"I wondered if the dragons want access to the territories they lost when they retreated."

"It's possible a sector of dragons has decided they're tired of confinement to the Dragon Isles." David issued a heavy sigh from the bottom of his lungs. "It might be something else. Do you have any ideas?"

Rena shook her head. "Whatever it is, the dragons are confident of success."

Fear rose in David, fear that the dragons might hurt Rena or Joanna. "It makes me uneasy knowing the dragons observed you." At that moment, David decided. He'd leave the monastery and join Rena. At least that way, he could offer protection. Possessiveness flooded him. He needed Rena and wanted her safe.

If he had to return to the Dragon Isles, he could attempt a dreamwalk or, as an alternative, travel through the yew portal.

"What if I follow them?" Rena asked. "Learn where they're going."

"No! Dragons have a better sense of smell than humans. They'd notice you trailing them and lead you into a trap or worse. No, I forbid it." The instant the words left his lips, he wanted to groan in frustration.

Hadn't he already learned Rena was a modern woman? Independent and used to acting of her own volition. She'd explained that in her world, women earned their money and lived in houses without men. Sometimes women lived with their children, and other families were two men with children. Rena had told him this, and he should've known better to forbid her to do anything.

"I didn't know that." Rena hesitated. "That makes things tricky."

David's breath whooshed out, relief uppermost. "I'm sorry. I didn't mean to issue orders. My wife took direction from me. She looked for me to protect her and our daughter."

"You didn't fail," Rena stated before his thoughts could drift in that direction. "You were fighting in a war, doing the right thing. We have horrific problems in our world too. Last week a man in America walked around a shopping center carrying a gun. He shot everyone he could see. Men, women, and children. The news report said fifty-seven people died before the police shot the man. Bad things happen to good people, David. You can't continue blaming yourself."

David listened, listened to her words, appalled at the security breach. "That does it."

"Huh? What does it?" Rena asked.

A sharp tug yanked at his shoulders. Before David could reply, his contact with Rena dissolved, and he toppled arse over teapot. His right foot caught on a red ribbon, and he sprawled forward, thunking his head on a ribbon clump. A hooded figure in black stalked him, faceless in the shadows.

Panic roared through David. Was Rena all right? He wasn't sure how his jerking from her dream might affect her. No time to worry now. David scuttled backward while trying to get his feet under him. That cursed red ribbon held him prisoner, twirling around his foot like a live chain. The hooded figure kept coming, and a chill gripped David's chest. An overwhelming sense of dread took hold. His muscles twitched while his heart thundered so loud, he could scarcely hear himself think. Somehow, he pushed upward, but his fingers turned clumsy while attempting to free his ankle.

Damn, he had to wake. "Wake. Wake now!" he ordered himself. Nothing happened.

Chapter 11

Trouble in the Middle of the Night

Rena snapped awake, every muscle in her body tense. She bolted upright in bed, her pulse pounding as if she'd run one hundred meters. Her breaths came in harsh pants while her gaze jerked left and right, searching the corners of the bedroom. The smashing of glass had Rena leaping off the bed and running straight to Joanna's room.

Rena burst through the door, groaning with relief when she spied her niece still asleep despite the din. She grasped Joanna's arm and shook her. "Jo," she murmured. "Wake up."

Her niece groaned and fought waking.

More breaking glass.

"Joanna, please wake." God, if they stayed here, they'd end up trapped. She peered through the dim light and frowned at her niece. Why wasn't she waking? She shook Joanna again.

Footsteps coming from inside the house galvanized her to action. She scooped her niece off the bed, groaning at the added weight.

Although Joanna wasn't big or overweight, Rena would have difficulty carrying her far. Rena struggled through the open bedroom door while debating her chances. If she could make it back to her bedroom, she might escape via the window. That's if she could rouse Joanna.

Halfway back to her bedroom, the hall light switched on, and Rena froze in her steps.

"Going somewhere, Rena?" Tony asked, his tone as smug as his features. His curly black hair stuck up in tufts—not to his usual well-groomed standards—and he bore shadows beneath his blue eyes. Black stubble shaded his jaw, yet despite this, the man still looked as if he'd walked off the page of a magazine. Tall, dark, and handsome, even if that didn't show the accurate picture.

"What are you doing here? You can't break into my house."

He grinned, flashing white, white teeth. "Yeah? Been there. Done it again."

"Get out before I call the cops."

Tony prowled closer, a gun appearing in his right hand. "Make me."

Rena backed up, Joanna a dead weight in her arms. She spared a second to glance at her niece, worried because the girl still hadn't woken.

Jo's face appeared pale, and her breathing was ragged. Now and then, she twitched. "If you leave now, I won't press charges."

"Hand over my daughter," Tony snarled. "You can't keep her from me."

"No." Rena backed up until a wall halted her retreat. Her arms trembled to the point of pain, and she let Joanna's unconscious body slide down until her niece rested on the floor.

Rena scowled at Tony. How had he found them? Apart from the shopping trip, almost three days ago, they'd stayed close to the cottage, not even visiting the town because she hadn't wanted to tempt fate and run into a dragon.

"Stand over there." Tony gestured with his chin. "I'll be taking Joanna with me."

"The judge gave Liza custody."

"Temporary custody," Tony spat. "Where is my bitch of a wife, anyway? Shouldn't she be here watching over our daughter?"

Rena didn't reply but nudged Joanna with her foot, praying the girl would wake and give them a better chance of escape.

Joanna let out a tiny groan. She stretched and opened her eyes.

Knee-buckling relief poured through Rena as she met her niece's gaze.

"Aunt Rena, why am I on the floor?" Joanna mumbled.

"Joanna." Tony spoke harshly. "Come to me. *Now.*"

Joanna's eyes widened an instant before she let her gaze wander to her father. "*Uh-oh,*" she said in a tiny voice.

"Joanna, don't make me tell you again."

There was nothing Rena could do. Defeated, she gave a tiny nod to Joanna. Her phone was still in the bedroom because she hadn't grabbed it in her panic.

"How did you find us?" Rena demanded.

A grin chased the temper from Tony's face, taking him to movie star handsomeness. He didn't fool Rena. She understood the darkness behind the pretty facade.

"Planted a phone on you and used the GPS tracker to find you. I've always known your location."

Rena hung her head for a second, then blasted him with a glare. "How did you do that? I would've noticed."

"You take your handbag with you everywhere except—luckily for me—the day I visited your flat. I opened the lining and slid another phone inside."

She gaped at him, impressed with his ingenuity. If only he'd used his intelligence for good, instead of mooching off Liza. Hard on the heels of this thought came the knowledge she'd led the bastard straight to Joanna. This was *her* fault.

"Joanna," Tony snapped.

Joanna exchanged a glance with Rena before she stood and

walked one tiny step at a time to reach Tony. The man's smile of victory rubbed Rena the wrong way, and she ached to strike out with her fists. Take no prisoners. Instead, she remained frozen on the spot, aware Tony might hurt Joanna to get Rena to back off. At first, Rena had doubted Liza when she'd told her and their father about Tony. It hadn't taken them long to believe Liza. Tony had problems, but he didn't see it. The world owed him, and everyone had to pay or suffer the consequences. Now the bastard had Joanna, and Rena hesitated regarding the best course of action.

"Where are you taking Joanna?"

"None of your fucking business," Tony snapped.

He grabbed Joanna's upper arm and dragged her from the passage and around the corner until Rena couldn't see either of them.

"Don't follow us," Tony called. "Joanna is my daughter, and I have every right to have her with me. Liza isn't here to gainsay me. You want this fixed, then get Liza to contact me."

Rena closed her eyes, the sense of helplessness and guilt too much for her to bear. Liza would never forgive her. She'd failed Liza. She'd failed Cherry. And now she'd failed Joanna.

The sound of a vehicle starting up outside had Rena running to the front door. Tony must've seen her because he stuck his hand out the window and flipped her off. Seconds later, he and Joanna had disappeared.

What the devil should she do now? Liza and Cherry were missing while her father remained in the United States on business. She muttered a curse and stomped into her bedroom. First, she'd find that bloody phone, then she'd ring the cops. Even better, she'd photograph her handbag, and the foreign phone the smug bastard had hidden inside it. She'd place the phone in a plastic bag and make certain her fingerprints didn't get on the casing.

Heck, she didn't even know if they had a police station on Holy Island. She picked up her phone and did an internet search. One person on call. Rena dialed the number and waited for an answer.

"Hello," she said when the man on the other end introduced himself as a police constable.

Rena explained the situation and gave him the name of their police contact who'd dealt with Tony in the past. She informed the cop that Tony had kidnapped her niece against her will and at gunpoint.

"What type of vehicle is he driving?" the policeman asked.

"A range rover."

"Your brother-in-law won't be able to leave the island until tomorrow morning," the policeman said. "I'll keep watch for him and also have the police on the other side checking the traffic as it crosses the causeway."

"Thank you. Thank you so much."

"Do you think he'll hurt his daughter?"

"I'm not sure," Rena said. "He hasn't hurt her in the past,

although he has made threats."

"All right. I'll be there in half an hour to survey the scene."

"I'll be here." Once she ended the call, she attempted to contact her father. When she explained what had happened, he promised to contact his lawyer and to petition the court for full custody.

"The bastard. I'll throttle him myself," her father said with icy calmness.

"Do you think the judge will rule in our favor?" Rena bit her bottom lip, hesitating. Telling her father dragons existed wasn't the best idea. For Liza and Cherry's sake, Rena had to keep that bit of info to herself.

"Tony pulled a gun on you and kidnapped Joanna after a judge placed her in our custody. It doesn't matter if the order was short-term. Joanna is under our care until the judge says otherwise."

"Excellent." Rena sighed. "I'll talk to you later, Dad. Tony broke the window to gain entrance to the cottage. Ah, it sounds as if the cop is here. Once he's finished, I need to clear up the mess and inform the owner of the damage."

"Take photos of everything. We'll get the cops to charge Tony with breaking and entering."

"The cop told me the tide would keep Tony trapped on the island until tomorrow morning. Unless he has a boat... Oh, hell. He might have a boat. Tony has always enjoyed fishing and boating. Damn, why didn't I think of that earlier? Better go. I'll speak with the local policeman."

The policeman took photos and her statement. She mentioned Tony's prowess on the water, and the cop informed her he'd check the areas suitable for boats. Once he left, Rena cleared away the glass then made a pot of tea. There was no point waking the cottage owner until a decent hour. Neither of them could do much.

With a groan, she settled into a comfortable chair, her mind darting in all directions. *Please let Joanna be okay.* She didn't trust Tony as far as she could kick him.

Her phone rang, and she pounced on it. "Hello."

"Rena, darling," came Tony's smarmy voice. "Now that I have Joanna, tell your father he can have his grandchild back if he pays me the one million pounds I requested earlier."

"Piss off," she snarled. "You know my father will tell you to go to hell."

"Then you'll never see Joanna again."

Something about his tone—a hint of desperation—plucked at Rena. What was going on with him? "I *will* report this to the cops."

"I'm Joanna's father."

"Yeah, and you're treating her like a product to be packaged and sold at your leisure. She's your daughter. Why don't you act like it? Give her back. You know Liza wants nothing to do with you."

"Where is my shrew wife? Why isn't she ringing me?"

"None of your business."

"Tell Liza to call me, and we'll sort out transferring money then." He hung up.

Rena let rip with a curse. What the hell should she do? Liza wasn't handy, so it was up to her to fix this mess and discover a way to best Tony. She refused to let him get away with kidnapping. Rena straightened her shoulders and reached for her phone. The cops had the causeway covered, and Tony couldn't leave that way. She'd mentioned his ability with boats. Time for operation Rescue Joanna.

CHAPTER 12

Hunted

J ust as the robed man reached for him, David slithered free and ran. The dream ribbons twirled and danced, propelled by the unusual wind rustling through the dreamscape. They snatched at his limbs, forcing him to zigzag to elude capture. A sneaking suspicion had David glancing over his shoulder. He glimpsed the man's face this time and recognized one of the red robes. Instead of his typical red, the magic druid wore black to better blend.

Dizziness assailed David without warning. Weakness attacked his limbs and writhed through his body, slowing his retreat. His skin grew clammy, his breath bursting in and out of his mouth in mortifying pants. He shook his head, shook away his muddled thoughts, and forced his legs to move. The druid was doing something, had cast a spell to push dread and panic through him.

Abruptly, David tumbled forward. Head over foot until he crashed into a wall. He jerked away, heart hammering and that gut-clenching terror still wrapping around him like a traveling cloak. He sprang to his feet, ignoring the pounding of his heart and the throbbing of his head. The tension seeped from him when he took in the familiar surroundings of his cell. He relaxed for an instant before the truth struck him in the face.

A druid had attacked him on the dreamscape. He'd recognize David, which meant trouble. *Danger.* He grabbed his robe and tugged it over his head.

Next, he collected his few precious belongings and shoved them into a cloth bag. His spare robe. The info from Brother Jasper. The miniature painting of his wife and daughter.

Five minutes later, he slid from his cell and crept down the central corridor. When nothing louder than a few snores filled the air, he slipped from the building and into the shadows. During his lifetime, he'd faced the enemy at war, he'd found his wife and child murdered, and he'd seen fellow soldiers die gruesome deaths. He'd suffered dread and anxiety during those times, but nothing like this. His pulse thrummed, his breaths coming in harsh wheezes. If those red robes got hold of him, he'd end up in huge trouble—likely dead. He wouldn't be able to help Rena.

Horror blasted him, and his mind chased in circles as he

attempted to decide on his best course of action. A light flickered on the other side of the monastery grounds, close to the warehouse. It bobbed and wove around trees and gardens, heading in his way at speed.

David darted in the other direction, instinct telling him the approaching person meant him harm. He slipped from shadow to shadow, wincing each time he stepped on dried leaves and twigs. This wasn't the way to the grove, which meant he'd have to circle or strike out toward the mansion and town at the other end of Smoking Isle.

He glanced over his shoulder to see if the light followed him. It didn't, instead pausing in the junior druid's dormitory. Hell, they *were* after him.

David continued sliding through the darkness, setting a course for the mansion. Hopefully, the dragons there welcomed him. Not his best option because he was still within the same territory as the red robes. He wanted to join Rena to ensure her safety. If the red robe had watched him on previous nights, he'd know David often visited Rena.

He cursed softly. Damn it. He couldn't fail another woman.

He'd never live with his conscience if something happened to Rena.

Fatigue settled over his shoulders, but he kept moving, wanting to place distance between him and the druids. He couldn't trust any of them.

Not now.

David traveled throughout the night and the following day only, stopping to drink water. He still had an apple in his pocket, and he ate that on the move. When darkness fell, he kept moving until almost midnight. Shattered by then, he searched for a safe place to rest. He hadn't noticed signs of a chase, but the red robes held great power, and he couldn't relax until he reached the dragons. God, he prayed he'd find help because if he entered the dreamscape by mistake, he'd have someone to jolt him awake.

It was almost two days later when he stumbled out of a pine forest and spotted the mansion in the distance. As he neared, a red dragon took flight. It lifted to a high altitude before soaring on the breeze and disappearing over the hill.

David slowed. What if he was making a mistake by trying to get help here?

Damn, he wasn't usually this indecisive. Rena was counting on him.

He forced his legs to continue moving while his mind railed at him for not taking the correct option. *Return to the monastery since it was a haven for the brothers.* He'd healed at the monastery, had the support of his brothers. They'd forgive him and receive him with open arms.

Come home, a tiny voice whispered. *Come home.*

David frowned and came to a dead halt. His body turned without his permission, and he took two steps before he jerked up in horror. These weren't his thoughts. Someone was messing with him. A finding spell?

His legs took three more jerky shuffles before he halted them. It *was* a red robe spell.

A whoosh came from overhead, and in alarm, he snapped his gaze skyward.

The red dragon again. The massive creature settled in front of him, and terror of the sort he hadn't experienced for years flooded David. He trembled, and his breaths emerged in audible huffs. When the dragon opened its giant maw, and the sunlight reflected on sharp teeth, David thought he'd die without holding Rena again. Without kissing her. He attempted to move, but his feet rooted to the spot. For a second, he thought it was fear that held him in place, but his arms refused to obey his order. The bloody red robe must be near.

God's bones, if they got their hands on him, he'd die for sure.

While they hadn't caught him doing something he shouldn't, his disappearance from the monastery screamed guilty.

David found he could move his eyes, and he scanned his surroundings. He froze. The dragon was the least of his problems. Two red robes stood on the hilltop. One held his arms outstretched as if he was casting a spell. The other eyed David with determination.

"David, what are you doing here?"

David's attention jerked back to the dragon. Instead of a dragon, a naked and familiar man stood before him, his red dragon tattoo on full display, its gaze intent. It was Martinos, the dragon shifter who'd had his dragon bound. David had broken the red robes' binding spell and freed Martinos's dragon.

"David?" A faint breeze lifted Martinos's black curls, but the bearded shifter didn't appear to feel the cold.

"The red robes are after me," David gasped out. "They're using a spell to freeze me in position." His chin jerked a fraction to give Martinos a direction.

"I see them," Martinos said. "Why do they want you?"

"One of them spotted me in a place I shouldn't have been. A few of my other actions might've drawn their notice."

"I'll take you back to the mansion." Martinos shifted and scooped up David in his talons before he could argue. David gave a strangled shout as they rose into the air. More alert now, he turned his head and stared at the red robes. It was too far for him to see their expressions, but their forms gave off irritated vibes. As for David, relief swelled within him. Martinos's arrival had saved his skin.

Their determined pursuit of him begged the question: how many other druids had died because they didn't conform to the rules meted out by Brother Matthew?

Brothers had left the monastery before, and he hadn't queried their departure because it hadn't affected him. It was apparent now his questions should've been many and varied. The stench at the monastery grew riper and more disturbing with each fact he uncovered.

The building he'd seen in the distance grew closer. Martinos settled on the patch of flat land in front of the mansion and released David.

Cherry—Rena's best friend who he'd met while helping Martinos with his bound dragon—appeared at a trot, her red hair bright in the sunlight. Another couple trailed her—a slender woman with long, shiny brown hair and a dragon shifter with disheveled black hair, black stubble on his jaw, and piercing green eyes. Another man with shaggy light brown hair—dragon, judging by his immense height and breadth—emerged from the building.

"David, what are you doing here?" Cherry handed Martinos a pair of trews and a shirt.

"Cherry! I'm so glad you're safe." David paused to marshall his thoughts. "The druids suspect I'm causing trouble. My options were to flee here or to Holy Island. I didn't want to cause trouble for Rena, so I came here for help. I didn't know what had happened to you and Martinos, but I hoped I'd find you."

"Liza. Leo, come meet Rena's druid."

Unexpected heat coursed through David's face on seeing Cherry's impish grin. From what Rena had mentioned, her friend had bloomed since meeting the dragon, and it was obvious the pair were lovers.

"Liza?" His mind snapped into proper working order. "Are you

Joanna's mother? Rena's sister?"

Liza came forward and hugged David. The dragon at her side growled, and unconcerned, Liza rapped his knuckles. "This is David, my sister's...ah...man?"

"I am Rena's," David replied.

"You've seen Joanna? And Rena?" Eagerness shone in her eyes. "Is my daughter safe?"

David relaxed. "I spoke with Joanna last on the dreamscape, but I have met your daughter in person. She reminded me of my daughter—so bright and intelligent and curious about the world."

"The dreamscape?" Leo asked.

"Talk later," Martinos said. "We have a problem. David has two magical druids on his tail."

"I'm worried they'll hurt Rena. One spotted me on the dreamscape. I believe they killed Brother Jasper because he was interfering with the head druid's plans. I have other bits of information too, but right now, I must escape the red robes."

"We want to get to the mainland," Liza said. "The last time we tried, the red robes almost killed us. I want Joanna safe."

"The spell I used to travel through the yew portal should work," David said.

"Will the spell work for everyone?" Leo asked.

"Not sure." Tension tightened David's muscles. "Can we fly to the monastery yew grove? If we hurry, we might take the druids by surprise. They won't expect me to return so soon."

"Right," Martinos said. "The four of us will go with you plus Griffith. Blaze had to fly to Perfume Isle, but we're expecting him back soon. He'll want Griffith to search for their missing sister if he can't. If your number is limited, let Leo and Liza go to get Joanna. Cherry and I wish to return to the mainland, but we should be safe enough here. The druids leave us alone unless we get too close to the monastery."

"That might change once they realize you've given me shelter," David said in a grim voice.

Liza sent an imploring look at Leo. "We have to take that risk. Rena can only hold off Tony for so long."

Cherry scowled at the mention of Liza's ex. "She's right."

"Rena saw two dragons on Holy Island recently." David started to pace, unable to remain still. "Your ex-husband might not be a danger, but the dragons are trouble. Rena described an older dragon."

"Martinos mentioned he saw one of my brothers while he was on Holy Island," Leo said.

"He might've been the one we spotted while I was there to help Martinos." David shook his head. "We don't see many dragons at the monastery."

"Let's go," Leo ordered. "I see the red robes on the horizon. They're heading this way."

Martinos spoke to the brown-haired dragon—Griffith. Seconds later, three dragons shifted. Liza and Cherry clambered onto the dragon's backs, and the third dragon approached David. An instant later, David was astride the dragon and airborne. Instead of flying straight to the monastery, Leo, Martinos, and Griffith flew out to sea. Clever plan. The red robes would suspect they'd departed to Perfume Isle. After ten minutes, David realized they were flying around the island and approaching the monastery in that direction.

While it had taken him over two days to walk the distance, the flight took mere hours. Once they settled on the ground, David wiped insects from his face. It hadn't been a comfortable flight, but the fresh breeze had shaken the dullness from his brain. He'd used the time to sort the facts he'd learned and pondered the bits and pieces he'd discovered but didn't understand. If only he could've uncovered the purpose of the dragon's visits to Holy Island.

So much was a mystery still.

"Which way?" Leo asked in a terse voice on shifting.

"At the base of that hill." David gestured. "Follow me and keep out of sight as much as possible."

David strode from the forest clearing where the dragons had landed, not even waiting for the dragons to scramble into their clothes. The two women followed him, and the dragons hustled to catch them. The six of them walked in a careful line as they made their way deeper into the forest.

At the edge of a clearing, David halted to study the terrain.

"Do you see red robes?" Cherry asked, her gaze scanning the

open area with suspicion.

"No." But unease prickled the back of David's neck. "My gut says otherwise."

"Would they have left a guard?" Martinos murmured.

"Depends. If they're using the grove to travel to Holy Island, it's possible. I didn't see anyone when I traveled to unbind Martinos's dragon. Things might have changed."

Martinos nodded. "Let us go first. Walk in a V formation with us at the front and the three of you behind us since you're more vulnerable to magic."

"They placed an armband on you," David retorted.

"The guards held me down. I fought, believe me, and I inflicted pain before the druid imprisoned my dragon."

Leo started forward. "Let's move. David is right. This place is creepy, but we're out of options. We continue and fight should the druids attack. Liza. Cherry. Please take care."

Everyone fell into position. As they neared the yew grove, two druids wearing red robes appeared. A low chanting rode on the air. Immediate terror filled David, flickers of memory rushing in front of his eyes.

Another spell.

Keep moving forward. David forced himself to step into the memories. His hand curled as if he held his sword. In his mind, he parried an attack, an unkempt heathen trying to kill him. David fought, muscle memory allowing him to keep striding forward.

They were almost inside the yew grove when the recollections assailing David turned even more personal.

Helena ran toward him, her face covered with tears and panic.

"Help me! David, save me!" Although the memories didn't contain sound, he had no difficulty reading her words. Behind her, a Viking ran, his sword held high. Another Viking grasped his daughter—he hadn't noticed her earlier, his attention taken by Helena. The Viking caught Brianna by her hair. He lifted his sword, and an instant later, he held Brianna's head in his hand. David croaked out a sound of horror. He halted.

Cherry grasped his robe sleeve and hauled him onward. "It's not real. Look." She kicked the Viking, and he blinked from sight. "It's a magical spell. Keep moving, David. Please, we need your help. Rena and Joanna need us."

David blinked hard. He propelled his limbs to move, taking giant strides to catch up with Liza and the dragons. Cherry reached for his hand, her silent support doing much to help him regain his equilibrium. He forged onward, his determination bolstered by Cherry's confidence.

Once they burst into the center of the grove, David halted. "While I'm doing the spell, I can't watch for the red robes. The rest of you must keep them away while watching me closely. Once I open the portal, I can hold it for a short time."

"We understand," Martinos said. "You start, and we'll organize our strategy."

David inhaled and began the chant he'd learned to travel to Holy Island the first time. At first, the words tripped off his tongue, but as he continued, he struggled to recall them. Pressure built on his chest, his mind, his tongue. A moan squeezed free, pain taking over from his stress. The faint blue tattoos on his torso burned as he pushed out his spell word by unwilling word.

The dragons attacked the red robes with their flames while Cherry hovered at his side, her expression full of concern and anxiety. For him. When she noticed his struggle to continue, she wrapped her fingers around his forearm and squeezed in encouragement. The physical contact lessened the pain and grounded him, allowing David to return to his former rhythm. The chant took on the taste of sour apples on his tongue, and once again, he stumbled.

What were the red robes doing to him?

"Keep going," Cherry said. "Liza, take David's arm. The physical contact seems to ease his pain."

Liza stepped to his other side, her chilly fingers wrapping around his wrist. David sucked in a tremulous breath and continued to chant. The tattoos on his body flared with heat, and Cherry gasped. He wanted to tell her not to touch the blue lines that wove around his limbs, but if he interrupted his chant, he'd have to start over again.

No time.

Not with the red robes' determination. The dragons' fire didn't stop their magic.

David closed his eyes, embracing the way the words of the chant became easier. He continued with his eyes closed to halt the distractions. As he neared the end of his spell, magic prickled his skin. He heard one of the red robes shout a warning, and for an instant, the pressure became so much, he thought his knees might buckle.

"Steady," Cherry murmured. "Keep going. The portal is opening."

"You can do this," Liza whispered, her tone fierce. "Get me to my daughter, and I will bake you apple pies for a lifetime."

"She makes an excellent apple pie," Leo commented as if they weren't in the middle of a robe attack.

David pushed out the final words of his chant, shouting them for greater effect.

"Get ready," Martinos said.

"I'll stand guard and go through last," Griffith offered. "Quick! Move."

Leo continued spraying the red robes with flame, but it didn't halt their spells. One of them shouted power words, but their magic worked at odds with one another since the second had produced a shield to protect them from the dragon flame.

Liza disappeared, her hand reaching back to drag Cherry through the portal. Leo followed in his dragon form.

"Hurry, David. You're not safe here." Martinos spoke hurriedly.

"Come with us."

David had thought to stand with Griffith. While others had exited to Holy Island, Griffith had shifted, and while David hesitated, the dragon took to the air and attacked the red robes from above. One of the red robes screamed, flames catching his hair and igniting. The other one ceased his chant to go to the aid of his companion. Martinos shoved David through the portal, and an instant later, the glowing entrance blinked from sight. David found himself in pitch black. For a second panic overtook him, then his senses sprang to life.

It was nighttime on Holy Island. Probably for the best since Leo remained in his dragon form.

"Everyone okay?" Martinos asked.

"Yes," Liza said. "Are we on Holy Island? I'll get to see Joanna soon?"

Leo shifted to his human form and went to Liza. He drew her against his side and hugged her. "I can sense the barrier, my lodestone."

"David," Cherry said, her tone urgent. "Are you all right? They burned your robe, and you're glowing blue."

David blinked. "*God's bones.* That hasn't happened before."

"Are you in pain?" Martinos asked.

"No. I'm not sure." Even as he spoke the words, his knees buckled, and he fell. He struck the ground, and everything turned to black.

CHAPTER 13

Time for a Better Plan

David woke to lowered voices and a cool cloth on his forehead. His lids fluttered as he attempted to pry his eyes open.

"Water," he said in a hoarse voice.

"David! You're awake." Rena's beautiful face filled his vision, her brown eyes full of concern.

"Where am I? What happened?"

"You're at the cottage on Holy Island. David is awake," she called.

An instant later, Liza, Cherry, Leo, and Martinos filed into the room.

David pushed upright, surprised by the comfortable mattress cushioning his body.

"You created a portal, and we escaped the red robes," Cherry said.

"Griffith didn't make it through," David murmured, still unwilling to believe the dragon's sacrifice. "I pray he's okay."

"My ex-husband has kidnapped my daughter," Liza snapped out, her gaze fierce. "When I get my hands on him, he'll be sorry he ever met me. This time he has gone too far. Joanna is a child, not a— *Popsicles!* I want to swear so bad."

"I'll be right at your side, my lodestone," Leo muttered, his tone emphatic and promising punishment. "We'll get Joanna back."

"Here's your water," Rena said. "Does your chest hurt? Your tattoos are bright and more distinct than when I last saw you. Where does it hurt?"

David guzzled the water so fast he started coughing and spilled half on his bare chest.

Rena's fingers, cool and possessive, curled around his shoulder.

Cherry handed her a towel, and Rena patted David's torso dry. "Drink slowly. There is plenty of water. You can have more."

"Can those red robes travel through the barrier?" Leo demanded. "We need to know what we're facing. The last time we saw them, they almost killed us, and we haven't settled on a plan to get close to the monastery. By Lodar, I can't believe we made it to the portal and out the other side alive."

Cherry produced a pad and writing instrument. "We'll make a plan. We have so much to consider. Baddies are lobbing problems at us from every direction."

David sipped his water and emptied the glass.

Rena traced the whorl of a tattoo. "Do you want more?"

"Yes, please." A shudder sped through him at her touch, making him wish they were alone.

Rena disappeared through a doorway, giving David a chance to observe the room. Silky fabric in shades of blue covered the elegant and supremely comfortable bed currently cushioning his aching body. Striped blue-and-white curtains shielded the windows. Light shone from overhead, but it didn't come from a lantern. His gaze moved on to the other furnishings. A chest of drawers. A second door of glossy wood. A woolen carpet of cream with hints of brown covered the floor, a furnishing way too fancy for a simple druid.

He noticed Leo studied his surroundings with interest while Martinos appeared to take them in his stride. He'd spent time with Cherry, so none of this was new to him. Whenever he'd visited Rena on the dreamscape, their environment was immaterial. All he'd seen was darkness when his focus was on her—his key. His security. His sweet cynamone.

Rena arrived with more water. "If you're tired, we can leave you to sleep."

"No." Everything he'd learned told him to act with haste. "We take action now. Every instinct tells me this situation is coming to a head. We must investigate. Time is wasting."

"I agree," Liza said. "Tony will try to leave the island. Rena indicated the police would intercept him once the causeway opens, but what if he has another way off the island?"

"The druids must face the consequences for breaking the accord the clans signed when the barrier came into existence," Leo said. "They have allowed favored dragons to travel without restriction. They're endangering innocent humans. We've discussed the matter to death, but not one of us has any idea why the dragons come here. We know Nemyr was present before his death and probably Nandag."

"The brother next to you in age, too," Liza added. "He and Nan chased and attacked us."

"Which leaves Russays." Martinos shoved back his black curls and scowled. "He must be involved. I can't imagine him missing out on a power grab."

"That's the thing." Leo scratched at the stubble on his chin. "Even though Russays is the oldest and the next in line, I don't see him as the brains behind the scheme. I hate to sound disloyal, but not one of my brothers is a capable leader. They lack the skills to pull dragons and humans together, not that any of my brothers would try to unite the races. They're followers rather than leaders, although they do their fair share of issuing orders."

David sipped his water, listening to the group. "The head druid is involved. And the older dragon who visits him."

Rena wrinkled her brow. "Joanna and I saw an older dragon and a younger one in town. They saw us, and the younger dragon blew us a kiss."

"You mentioned that. Have you seen them since?" David asked, his tone sharp. God's bones, if those dragons tried to hurt Rena or the child, he'd join Leo in hunting them down.

"No, but they made me uneasy." Rena fiddled with her gold earring. "I brought Joanna straight home, and we've stayed close to the cottage since."

"Describe the older dragon," Leo said. "The one who meets with your head druid."

"He has a haughty attitude and kept his face turned away when I saw him in Brother Matthew's office. His hair is gray, and it's cropped close to his head. He's clean-shaven, and judging from his upright carriage, I'd say he keeps himself fit. He might appear older, but he's not someone to underestimate."

"That sounds like the dragon Joanna and I saw in town," Rena said.

Everyone fell silent, digesting the information.

"Leo, could your parents' butler—Telus—be behind this plot, whatever it is? You mentioned you saw him with one of your brothers when you were trying to break me out of the dungeon on Hissing Isle. He's intelligent enough to plan this. If David's head druid is of a similar mien, there you have your two leaders," Liza said. "What do you think? Telus personally delivered your summons to the castle, which you thought was out of character for him. That dragon your parents wanted you to marry—Nandag—or someone at her behest, visited your property and slaughtered those wolves because she wore wolf fur while at the castle."

"Telus?" Martinos whistled. "My parents always spoke of envy when discussing Hissing Isle. His organization skills are legendary, and your parents prospered because of his expertise. What would he gain by plotting to get dragons onto the mainland?"

"Power," Cherry said. "This entire plot has whispers of a power grab. Anyone who controls passage to Holy Island could make the rules and profit enormously."

"Greed too," Liza suggested. "From what I saw of Telus, he's at the top of the pile, and what he says goes at the castle. Leo's parents might have signed the proclamation to imprison me, but Telus instigated the arrest. He was in attendance at the initial meeting Leo and I had with Leo's parents."

Martinos nodded. "Liza makes an excellent argument. But if we assume Telus and Brother Matthew are the brains behind the scheme, why would Nan and Leo's brothers join forces with them?"

"Same thing. Power and greed," Cherry said. "I expect they'd have a second-level plan of taking over, eventually. Martinos, you know what they're like. They're backstabbers with no concept of loyalty."

Rena barked out a laugh, aiming it at her friend. "Why don't you say what you really think?"

"I did." Cherry leaned against Martinos.

Leo drew in a breath and eased it back out before speaking. "Maybe, although I can't figure out why my parents were so insistent that I become betrothed to Nandag. That part puzzles me."

David listened to the dragons and the humans discuss the topic, part of him surprised at the tight bonds between the two couples. But then, his growing friendship with Rena had shown him their strength of character. Their loyalty. He yawned, exhausted.

Rena caught his yawn. "Okay, everyone out. David needs to rest before he can join our merry band of detectives."

"No." David attempted to rise, but his body proved his downfall. His muscles failed to coordinate with his limbs. He toppled back on his pillows with a tired sigh.

Rena bent over him and straightened the covers. The unconscious caring and calm competence of her actions had his heart twisting. This woman was generous and brave, and he cared way too much about her. The future lay ahead like a murky pond, and he didn't want to lose his heart and later his woman. He'd fall apart if something happened to Rena.

"Whatever you're thinking, stop," Rena ordered as the others filed out of the bedroom. "Cherry and Martinos told me what Nan had done to her people, to her father. Together, we'll discover what is happening and put a stop to the skullduggery. If you can't sleep, consider this. Can you see a problem if dragons and humans travel between the worlds in a controlled manner? Life is different on the mainland, and humans no longer believe in dragons. The druids on this side are full of party tricks rather than true magic."

"And the humans?"

"Our technology is far advanced to yours. We have identification papers, but Cherry, Liza, and I can help those who wish to visit this side of the barrier. It won't be easy, but it's not impossible. Or, failing that, we might use our technology to help the humans on the Dragon Isles. If they wish to have our help, of course. In some things, the old ways are better."

"Is everyone on the mainland so considerate?"

Rena blinked. "We have humans of all degrees. Some kind and generous, while others are despots. The majority of humans sit in the middle of the scale. They care for their families and embrace life. They do the best they can."

David yawned again, his eyes fluttering closed as he fought fatigue. No time for sleep, not with the red robes' arrival looming.

"Don't fight it. We need your strength, and you're as weak as a kitten. We'll only win this battle if we work together." Rena kissed his temple, her familiar scent soothing his angst. He was asleep before she left.

Rena stalked out to join her sister and friend. "What's our plan? The clock is ticking."

"Leo and Martinos can follow his scent or perhaps Joanna's," Cherry said. "Liza and I thought we might drive around the town."

"Tony will stay in an expensive place. He hates to slum it." Liza rolled her eyes. "This time won't be any different."

Fear rushed through Rena. Guilt because she hadn't protected Joanna. "I'm sorry," she whispered, her voice breaking.

Liza stalked over to Rena and clapped her hands onto her sister's shoulders. "You are not to blame. It's all on Tony. Is he still harping on about money?"

Rena swallowed hard. "Yes."

"The minute I pay him will be the start of a nasty money pit. He'll demand more and more. I bet he's gambling again and is in trouble. He likes the best of everything and hasn't the first idea of how to save. He's a big one for instant gratification and the easy life."

Leo stalked into the lounge with Martinos on his heels. "We lost his scent at the..." He glanced at Martinos for help.

"At the garage," Martinos supplied.

"But it's possible to track the vehicle he drove here because it has a distinctive oily aroma." Leo wrinkled his nose. "The air here is full of strange smells."

"Do it," Liza said. "Follow the trail as best you can. I can't take standing around here, waiting for the tide to recede. Tony is smart, and he's clever enough to use a boat to escape."

Rena's phone rang, and she answered it absently, her mind still on the conversation. "Yes," she murmured.

"This is your last chance." Tony at his smarmy best.

Rena gestured to Liza and the others. "Where is Joanna? If you've hurt her, you'll never be safe, you bastard."

"I want my money. Five hundred thousand pounds will be enough to start. No money, then I'll spirit Joanna away and you'll never see her again."

Rena blinked. "Where would Liza get that much money? You bled her dry, stealing everything she had before she left you."

"Give me that phone," Liza snapped and grabbed it from Rena. "Tony, you give me back my daughter."

"Pay up and I will. You have until the morning and then I'll vanish with Joanna." Tony hung up.

"Give me my phone," Rena snapped. "I want to ring the cop and let him know Tony is still on the island and making his demands for money."

Liza handed over the phone. "If we hurry, there's still a few hours of darkness. Cherry and I will drive into town and do the rounds of the accommodation."

"No, my lodestone," Leo said. "That is too dangerous."

"I promise not to approach him," Liza said. "But we're better to split our resources. You and Martinos have a better sense of smell than us, but Cherry and I want to do our part. We'll be careful because we'd hate to place Joanna in greater danger."

"Liza and I can do this." Cherry's chin jutted up with the same determination Liza displayed.

"I'll stay and watch David," Rena said.

"We'll keep in contact with Rena," Liza promised.

"I'll give you my phone." Cherry plucked it from her pocket and handed it to Martinos. "Let me refresh your memory on how to use it."

"Aren't you shifting to dragon?" Liza asked in surprise.

"No, we'll follow on foot as much as possible. The last thing we want is to attract extra attention. Not even my brothers have taken their dragon form on this side of the barrier," Leo said.

"As far as we know," Rena said.

Liza fidgeted while Cherry gave Martinos a quick phone lesson. Finally, she handed over her phone and hustled over to Liza.

"Let's do this. We'll check in with you, Rena, and let you know what's happening."

Leo and Martinos departed, and Liza and Cherry drove away several minutes later. Without them, the cottage seemed way too empty. Rena filled the kettle to make a cup of tea and peeked in on David. He had curled up on his side and was asleep. She frowned, wondering if he'd be okay. He'd been exhausted and looked as if he hadn't slept for days.

An hour passed while she roamed the cottage and kept checking on David. Her phone finally rang, and she darted back to the kitchen to pluck it off the counter. "Yes."

"We've found him. He's staying at a luxury cottage on the outskirts of town, near the church." Cherry sounded jubilant. "Leo and Martinos beat us here by minutes. I've rung the local cop, and he's on his way."

"Damn," Rena muttered. "I wanted to be there when Tony got his comeuppance."

"Go," David murmured from behind her.

Rena jumped and whirled to face him. She patted her chest as her pulse jumped like a startled rabbit. "You gave me a fright."

"Go. I'll be okay on my own. For a short time," he added, slyness lurking in his slight smile. "I might have a relapse."

Rena laughed, reassured by his teasing. "Are you positive?"

"Go," he urged her.

"I'll grab my running shoes. If I run, I can be at the village in less than fifteen minutes." Rena laced up her shoes and took off. "Don't answer the door if anyone comes," she called over her shoulder. "We'll arrive back together. I hope we'll take care of Tony fast."

Urgency lent her wings, and she ran faster than her average jogging pace. She'd spotted a church when she'd first arrived in the village and knew the general direction she needed to head. Ten minutes later, she spied the church, and after another few minutes of jogging, she came across Martinos and Cherry, standing at the entrance to a driveway.

"That didn't take long," Cherry said.

"Seeing Tony in handcuffs was all the incentive I needed to sprint," Rena quipped. "Where's Liza?"

"She and Leo are hiding behind a tree and keeping watch on the place. They're not certain which room Tony is staying in and figured they'd do things right and wait for the cop to arrive."

Beside them, Martinos stiffened. "Quick, inside the vehicle. Get out of sight."

Rena dived into the rear of Cherry's car while Cherry and Martinos jumped into the front. "What's wrong?" she asked in a breathless whisper, her heartbeat picking up in pace again.

"Dragon." Martinos slouched to peer through the windshield.

"What? Flying?" Cherry spluttered. "That's not smart."

"No," Martinos said tersely. "It means they're taking things to the next level. Either that or they're reacting instead of using their brain."

"Do you recognize the dragon?" Cherry murmured, her gaze on the night sky.

Except it wasn't dark any longer. Rena stared in the direction Martinos and Cherry were looking and saw it.

Her first dragon.

It was a reddish color and immense. A dragon in a storybook bore little resemblance to the one flying through the sky in front of her—the spikes and scales and its regal head. The creature's giant wings propelled it forward effortlessly.

Martinos cursed. "The lawman is here."

"Has the cop noticed the dragon?" Rena asked in a terse voice.

"How could he not?" Cherry asked.

"Maybe he's a safe driver and keeps his gaze on the road," Rena offered. As she watched the cop car, it braked and skidded to a halt in the middle of the road. "Nope, he's spotted the dragon."

CHAPTER 14

Dragons Ahoy!

"**W**hat should we do?" Cherry whispered.

Rena peered out the window at the fearsome red dragon. *Holy frogs!* What big teeth. "Martinos, this is your area of expertise."

"Right," he said in a grim voice. "We'll distract the officer and focus him on rescuing Joanna."

"Plan." Rena brightened. "Let's do this."

"Cherry, sunbeam. Please sit in the driver's seat, ready for a quick getaway. You might need to escape with Joanna. She's a child, and her safety is the most important thing. Rena, watch the dragon and tell me if he's getting too close. I won't shift unless he attacks us."

With ground-eating strides, Martinos headed for the cop and gestured at the boutique hotel. "Tony is keeping Joanna in there."

The cop blinked. Once. Twice. Three times.

"What's wrong with you?" Rena asked, going on the offensive. She snapped her fingers in front of his long nose. "Have you been drinking? Aren't you responsible for the island's citizens? Should you drink this much when you're on duty?"

Martinos gave a huff of amusement and fell in with the plan.

The cop had his blue gaze skyward again. He closed his eyes, opened them. "I must be working too hard," he muttered. "I could've sworn I saw a dragon."

"You what?" Rena demanded and snapped her fingers again. "Concentrate, man. We need you to enter that building and get Joanna. Tony kidnapped her, and tonight he rang Liza and demanded money for their daughter. The man is a menace, and he belongs in jail. He's not even a British citizen. For all I know, he doesn't have the correct visa. He turned up in the UK and demanded money from Liza after refusing to give her a divorce. Please can you act like a cop and do something?" Rena held her breath because she'd crossed a line, blaming this poor policeman for this situation.

"Right." The cop stood taller, straightening his shoulders and his uniform jacket. "Wait here while I speak to Mr. Richards. If he's there, I will get your niece back." He strode to the door and rapped his knuckles on the wood.

Rena noticed a curtain twitching. Her phone rang, and she glanced at the screen. It came up *dickhead*. "What do you want, Tony?"

"I told you no cops," Tony didn't sound like himself, rather rattled and on the verge of panic.

"Send out Joanna, and we'll leave." Rena sounded calm but inwardly, her gut twisted and twerked, her breaths coming faster than average.

"Joanna is asleep."

"Wake her and send her out," Rena ordered.

"I can't wake her."

"She will want to see Liza," Rena pressed.

The cop rapped the knocker this time—a firm *rat-a-tat-tat* on the door.

"I said she won't wake," Tony repeated, freaked rather than his typical smarmy attitude. "She wouldn't shut up. Told me I'd be sorry when the dragons arrived. She told me I was a horrid man. I don't know what rubbish Liza has filled her head with. Dragons, indeed! I added a sleeping pill to her orange juice, but now she won't wake up."

"Moron," Rena said. "Why would you give a sleeping pill to a child? So help me, if you've hurt her, I'll murder you myself. Answer the door and let the cop inside. Joanna needs a doctor. Now, Tony."

"Not until Liza gives me the money."

"We owe you nothing," Rena spat. "Liza already walked away from your house in New Zealand, the one she worked her guts out to afford. All she took from your marriage was Joanna, and from what I hear, you didn't value your daughter. Not until you discovered my family has money."

"I need that money." Panic shaded his words. "You owe it to me."

"Because you want to go on a beach holiday and drink fruity cocktails?" she mocked.

"You know nothing about what I need," Tony retorted.

Rena decided to keep him talking. Liza and Leo needed to enter the building from the rear. Something was up with Tony, and she wasn't sure why he'd fallen off the deep end, but his terror set her on edge. Thankfully, he hadn't believed Joanna about the dragons, but each time he mentioned money, his tone shifted. Rena caught Martinos's gaze and jerked her head, indicating he should join Liza and Leo at the rear of the building.

"Get Joanna," she mouthed.

He backed away, his gaze divided between the sky and the cop.

"How about I give you half the money?" she asked.

The cop stiffened his broad shoulders and shot her a glare of disapproval, but she ignored him and kept talking.

"I need the full amount," Tony said.

"Give me reasons, and I might consider it." Rena eyed him with distaste.

The cop commandeered her phone. "Mr. Richards, this is Police Constable George. Open the door now, sir. Return the child to her mother, and the charges you face will not be as severe."

The crack of falling glass sounded in the background, and the cop straightened, piercing her with a stern gaze. "If your friends have broken into the building, I will charge them."

"They wouldn't take the law into their own hands." Rena attempted innocence and failed.

The policeman offered her a scathing glare and focused on Tony. "Open the door now, Mr. Richards."

"Not until I get money. Liza owes me, dammit," he screeched loud enough for Rena to hear without the aid of her phone. "Who the fuck are you?"

A crash sounded, and Rena backed toward the car. They'd need to make a fast getaway, and she figured they were in deep doo-doo with the cop for acting outside the law. Although, Tony would face charges too since he'd confessed to taking his daughter and drugging her.

Liza and Martinos ran around the corner of the building toward her.

Rena wanted to ask questions, but she figured Leo had Joanna or her sister wouldn't willingly leave.

"Did you enter the building?" the cop demanded.

"No," Martinos said. "We peeked through the window. Tony threw a book, and the glass smashed."

Liza didn't add anything further, but Rena's eyes opened wider when a green dragon lifted above the height of the building and flew away with something clutched in his talons. Luckily, the cop didn't notice.

"Can I have my phone back, please?" Rena asked in a polite voice.

"Why are you leaving?"

Yes, the cop had suspicions. "We found Tony for you. I expect you'll arrest him and take the next steps. We are superfluous." On that note, Rena hot-footed it to the car and climbed into the front seat. Seconds later, Liza and Martinos were in the rear, and Cherry drove away.

"Did you find Joanna?" Cherry asked in a tight voice, her gaze on the rear-vision mirror. "The cop is staring after us. He knows something is off."

"Yes, thankfully! Leo has Joanna. He'll meet us back at the cottage," Liza said.

"Tony was acting weird," Rena said. "Could he have a gambling problem?"

"Who knows," Liza muttered. "Tony used to visit the casino in Auckland, but he never bet more than he could afford. He's a skilled gambler from what I could see. I find gambling boring, and can think of more enjoyable ways to spend my disposable income."

"I'll call Dad and ask him if he could get a private investigator on the job," Rena said. "My gut says Tony owes money, and he's terrified of whoever holds his gambling chit. Of course, I could be wrong."

"I don't care about Tony. I just want to hold my daughter and make sure she's all right. Leo and I want to return to Smoking Isle. Joanna will be safer there. Martinos offered us the use of his home."

"You and Leo are doing me a huge favor. Besides, you've helped me so much already." Martinos spoke with sincerity.

"You treat our girl right, and we're all square," Rena piped up. "Holy crap. There's that red dragon again. I thought he'd gone."

"He's heading straight for us," Cherry said in a tight voice.

"Keep driving," Liza snapped from the rear.

"That's an enormous dragon, not a chicken, Liza!" Cherry shouted.

At her side, Rena grinned, and the stretch of her lips felt slightly maniacal. "Go, Cherry. Put your foot down. Play the chicken game. I dare you."

The small car hurtled down the gravel road, in the direct path of the dragon.

"What does he want?" Liza shouted.

Martinos gripped the seatback. "No idea."

"I'll try to make those trees. He'll be at a disadvantage if we reach shelter."

"That's my sunbeam," Martinos encouraged her.

Rena loved this dragon-man so much. If they weren't hurtling at a dangerous speed, she'd lean over and give him a big kiss for loving her friend. Past-Cherry would have never considered playing chicken with a big arse dragon.

"We're not going to make it," Cherry gritted out in a voice tight with banked terror. "Everyone have their seat belts on?"

"Wait." Liza peered out the window. "Slow, and we'll dive into those bushes. They're not big enough to cover the car, but we can each crawl underneath. At least that way, we'll have a chance."

"It will give me an opportunity to shift," Martinos said. "This red beast won't be so confident if I'm attacking him."

"Plan." Rena stared at the fast approaching dragon. "Let's do it."

Cherry slowed the car, her hands clenched on the wheel. "Get ready. Seat belts off."

"On. Off. Make up your mind, woman," Rena grumbled, hoping to lighten the tension.

"Shut up," Cherry snapped. "Everyone ready?"

"Let's do this." Liza's shoulders tensed. "Meet in that copse of trees."

Cherry screeched to a halt. Rena flung her door open and dived into the undergrowth just as the dragon swooped at them. The beast seized the car in its talons and rolled it. Windows shattered as the car thumped onto its side. Rena glanced back to make certain Liza, Cherry and Martinos had made it out of the vehicle. Her downfall because it slowed her escape.

One second she saw greenery and smelled the dust on the side of the road. The next moment red filled her vision before sharp claws curled around her body and lifted her into the air. Rena screamed and flailed but to no avail. The creature's talon curled tighter until she had difficulty breathing.

Martinos shifted to his dragon and lifted off as if he intended to attack. He let out an ungodly shriek and flew straight at them. The red dragon clutching her released a mouthful of flames. A second red dragon appeared, and Martinos backed off with a bugle of frustration.

Terror filled Rena as the dragon carried her through the sky. The wind whipped her hair, and she'd never felt so cold in all her life.

What did the dragon want, and where the devil was he taking her? If he wanted to kill her, that was easy. Open his talon and drop her. She'd never survive. Or he could fly higher, and she'd freeze to death.

The dragon kept flying, flanked by the second one. Rena gave up wondering why the dragons wanted her. Whatever it was, she didn't think she wanted to know because it couldn't be good.

CHAPTER 15

This is War

Rena gasped as the red dragon set her down. In the precious seconds where she might have made a run for it, her legs refused to cooperate.

The dragons shifted to their human forms, their dragon tattoos prominent on their chests, and, to Rena's dismay, they were large with fit bodies. Even the older dragon. She found her gaze dropping and shuddered in horror.

Eew! What was with the naked dragon men all the time? She much preferred human customs, although she'd sneaked a glance at Martinos and Leo before she'd realized she was oozing into rudeness. Not a great look to ogle her sister's dragon or her best friend's dragon when she had a sexy man of her own.

Hell. David. Was he still at the cottage, or had they captured him too?

The younger dragon grasped her upper arm and shoved her into motion. "Move it," he added for good measure.

"Why have you kidnapped me?" she spat.

While the younger dragon had the same black hair as Leo and a similar build, his face sported not a shred of humor. One glimpse of the older dragon told her he bore even less patience.

"I am Russays, The Magnificent," the younger dragon said with a touch of hauteur. "I am heir to Castle Caireall, and you will speak to me with the respect I deserve."

Rena curled her upper lip. "You haven't earned my civility."

"Don't speak at all," the older dragon snarled. "I am Telus, The Organized. You are a puny human with no rights." Ice coated his words, and another peek at the man—ah—dragon told her not to mess with the dude.

During the hasty flight, she'd been too terrified to watch the landmarks to discover their direction. But now, she recognized the yew tree grove. They were lucky they hadn't encountered the dragons earlier.

"Are you sure this plan will work?" Russays asked.

"It will." Telus radiated confidence.

Rena snorted. These dragons and their conceit. She slowed her steps, putting on a limp to crimp their plans. Sure, they were stronger, scarier, and in control, but no need to cave. She'd show them weak humans.

Russays entered the yew grove first, using his broad shoulders to forge through the trees. David had told them the trees were poisonous and not to touch any part of them if they could help it.

Rena hunched her shoulders and ducked her head while limping after the dragon. Telus followed in the rear, unconcerned with touching the yew branches. Did they not know or not care? Perhaps the yew poison didn't bother dragons.

"We're early," Russays muttered. "The portal isn't functioning yet."

"Matthew will arrive on time," Telus said.

"What do we do with her?"

"We will place her in the warehouse. No one will find her there." He barked out a laugh that held not a shred of humor. "Not by accident or on purpose."

Oh, joy. It sounded as if rescue would be like searching for a lost book in a library. If her sister's merry band couldn't locate her, she'd die here a crusty old woman. She required information, which meant asking questions. "If you're so disdainful of a weak human, then why did you bother to kidnap me?"

"We need the lock," Russays snapped.

Telus elbowed him, and Russays fell silent. Interesting. Russays might be the heir, but he took orders from Telus. More importantly, what was the lock? How did they expect her to help?

"Has Nan checked in yet?" Russays asked.

Rena listened, curious as to why they didn't know Liza had killed the dragon.

"No, but I'm not worried," Telus said. "Nan has a spine of steel. She'll follow through on her part of the bargain."

"What bargain?" Rena asked.

Telus lashed out and caught her cheek with his palm. He put power behind the blow, and she fell hard. Honest to goodness cartoon characters fluttered behind her eyes in full Technicolor. A pained gasp whistled through her teeth.

"Portal is forming," Russays said.

Telus poked her in the ribs. "Get up, human."

"Good luck with that," she murmured, a pained grunt emerging when he kicked her again. The man wore not a stitch, yet his feet jabbed like a pair of steel-cap boots.

Telus kicked her a third time.

"Don't break her," Russays ordered. "Kicking her won't make her move faster. Humans are weak. You can't strike her like you would one of your underlings."

"Thank you for the reminder," Telus said in a snide voice.

Ah, dissension in the ranks. Perhaps she could work with that once she regained her breath.

Russays picked her up and slung her over his shoulder as if she were a sack of vegetables. She groaned, her face throbbing and her ribs ringing out protests in an extravaganza of aches. The position Russays had placed her in made breathing difficult, and the blood rushed to her head, increasing the smarting of her noggin.

In front of them, sparkles of light formed in a ball and parted in a doorway.

Russays stepped through without hesitation, his shoulder jolting against her belly with each stride.

"Hurry," Telus ordered. "Matthew won't hold the portal for long.

Rena concentrated on breathing. Her stomach roiled while the *bang-bang-bang* of her head deafened her thoughts. Her stomach revolted, something about the portal upsetting her system. The cup of tea she'd drunk before they'd left the house made a return appearance.

Russays cursed, and Rena wanted to cheer at his outrage. She retched again, this time bringing up nothing. Russays released her without ceremony. Rena struck the ground, and everything went dark. When she revived, Russays and Telus were shouting at each other, and she was in a building of sorts.

"We need her alive," Telus snapped.

"You were the one who kicked her," Russays shot back.

Rena concentrated on breathing. Remaining still was a no-brainer because each time she moved every muscle, every tendon, every inch of her skin rebelled and cried surrender. Now, her throat was raw from vomiting.

"We'll assign a druid to care for her," Telus said. "Matthew can enchant a junior. They won't recall their actions or her."

"Works for me." Russays tossed his head like a show pony. "I refuse to nursemaid a human."

Bastard. She wasn't a mere human. Liza had bested these creeps, and Cherry had won the hearts of the dragons at Martinos's estate. She intended to do her bit for the cause.

"Do we need to feed her?" Russays continued.

"The junior druid will take care of it."

Rena's temper flared, and with it, her determination to kick butt. However, she bit her tongue and remained inert. It sounded as if the pair were leaving. She'd wait until they'd departed before she explored her prison. With her limited vision, she couldn't see much. The dragons retreated, although she didn't hear a door closing. Rena was about to move when a disgusted grunt echoed through the building interior.

"You better not have injured her too much to suit our purposes," Telus snarled. "I don't care what happens to her afterward, but we need her until we get our hands on the lock."

"I thought she was faking it."

"Evidently not," Telus said. "I'll organize a druid to fix her. You find Nan and your youngest brother. We must rework our plan to search for flaws."

The two dragons moved off, their murmurs drifting to her for long moments before fading. Still, Rena waited, her heart drumming in anxious beats. The pins and needles jabbing her calves became too much to bear, and she twisted until she lay on her back. A groan shoved up her throat, the harsh exhalation that followed coming from the depth of her lungs. Oh, god. She hurt so bad. Her legs. Each calf twitched in a gnawing throb that had her gritting her teeth. Her eyes fluttered open once she'd ridden out the cramp, and she stared at the ceiling. It wavered for long seconds until it came into focus.

A normal roof. *Nothing to see there.*

She rolled and forced her arms beneath her chest. In an awkward press-up, she came to her hands and knees, an entirely new set of muscle spasms freezing her in place. Her breath hissed in. Out. Her heart raced, and she realized if she didn't get a grip on her emotions, she'd drop back into old childhood habits and have a panic attack.

No! Rena screamed, panic pushing her deeper into her head. *Breathe. Breathe!*

Rena started the counting breathing exercise a friend had recommended. Her first effort hurt like hell and was half-arsed at best. *Focus, Rena.* But nothing helped, and she ended up tossed into a dark place where panic roared out of control.

She curled into a tight ball and rocked back and forth, both body and mind aching and numb.

"You let them take, Rena!" David sprang at Martinos and landed a fist on his jaw before Leo dragged David away.

Liza squeezed between them and placed her hands flat on David's chest. Tears shimmered in her eyes. "Don't you think we tried to keep out of their clutches? A dragon attacked the car. It's barely drivable. Instead of sniping, work out a plan to retrieve Rena. The dragons shouldn't be here on Holy Island. They shifted, and the local policeman saw them. They didn't seem to care. Whatever they're doing, they're escalating. Please, David. We need your help to beat back the dragons and close the portal between our worlds."

Liza's impassioned words finally got through to David. The tension eased from his shoulders. "I'm sorry," he said to Martinos. "This wasn't your fault."

"But you feel bad because you weren't there to protect her." Leo squeezed David's biceps. "Believe me, we understand. Rena is Liza's sister, and that makes her mine to protect too. I failed. We all failed. But we'll get her back."

Leo's determination squashed the last of David's angst. The tension seeped from his body. "At least you rescued Joanna," David said. "That's positive."

Cherry patted David's shoulder in sympathy, her expression holding approval. "I'll make tea and sandwiches."

"Yes, please, Aunt Cherry," Joanna shouted.

Liza whirled around, and David spotted the love on her face, the joy at seeing her daughter safe. "Joanna! I thought you were asleep." She gathered her daughter in her arms and hugged her hard. "I'm so pleased to see you. I've missed you, sweetheart."

"My tummy woke me up," Joanna shouted.

"Why are you shouting?" Liza asked, releasing her daughter enough to stare into her face.

David spotted the tears in Liza's eyes, and as he watched, one flowed down her cheek. He understood Liza's relief at seeing her daughter safe and at being able to hold her. Her love for her child was obvious as was her reluctance to surrender the physical contact. He massaged the tightness from his chest, the ball of pain. He comprehended Liza's emotions because he was in a similar position.

Those dragons had his Rena.

His sweet cynamone was in great danger.

"I'm in my boy disguise," Joanna shouted for the third time. She gestured at her jeans and her navy-blue T-shirt, which was inside out. She'd combed her hair back, so it appeared shorter.

Cherry and Martinos sported grins. "We did tell you," Cherry said.

"I didn't believe you," Liza confessed with a wobbly grin. "Joanna has always been such a girlie-girl with a preference for glitter and pretty colors."

Listening to his newfound friends calmed David further, pushing back his anxiety. He didn't understand why Telus and

Russays had taken Rena. "Are you positive it was Rena they wanted?"

"Yes," Cherry said. "After the dragon made my car roll, it went straight for Rena. He ignored the rest of us even though we were together. They came for Rena."

David swallowed hard. "Is it my fault? Did I cause this?" He couldn't be responsible for another woman dying. Not one he loved and respected.

"No," Leo snapped. "Don't take this on yourself. This plot has my brothers' hands all over it. Telus and my brothers are at fault here. We're the innocent bystanders they've dragged into their scheme."

Joanna's stomach rumbled, and she laughed. "Feed me," she chanted in a gruff voice.

Liza glanced at a giggling Cherry and rolled her eyes. She stood and gestured at Joanna, her smile still on the wobbly side. "Leo, deal with our son."

David watched the light blaze across Leo's face—a whoosh of open delight and emotion. *Love.* He picked up Joanna and carried her off, tossing the girl onto his shoulders. She shrieked with laughter, and David found himself smiling, savoring the innocent moment of joy. His daughter might have died, but his life had continued. He was selling his wife and daughter short by giving up.

No more.

Instead of feeling sorry for himself, it was time to go all-in with Rena and embrace the tentative friendship offered by this motley group.

"I had a thought," David said. "We know Telus and the others are visiting the mainland. What if they've decided the time is ripe to wreak vengeance on humans for forcing them into hiding?"

"How would taking over Leo's land help them do that?" Liza mused as she joined Cherry and placed bread and sandwich fillings on the counter.

"Hissing Isle is closest to the mainland of the three islands," Leo said. "My land is the nearest point. If Telus and his cohorts intend to take a fight to the humans, this would be the perfect strategy. They'd open a portal or take down the barrier and use my land as a base for their operations. It's more private. I bet that factored into their calculations. The residents from Castle Caireall and those of Perfume Isle and Smoking Isle are too far away to interrupt their operation or to demand answers."

"What about the differences in technology?" Cherry asked. "Humans have access to weapons that would decimate any dragons who attacked them."

"That's where the druids come into the equation. Magic," David said in disgust. "The dragons require the druids to give them an edge if they want to take a battle to the humans."

"If that's the case, we have to stop them," Liza said. "They're hurting innocent people. They didn't care about the policeman seeing them last night."

"How did he react?" David asked.

"He blinked a lot and rubbed his eyes," Cherry said. "Muttered that he needed a vacation, shook his head, and went off to deal with Tony."

"Did he see me take Joanna?" Leo asked.

"No, because you flew out over the sea and circled to our cottage." Cherry flashed him a grin of approval. "Smart move, mister."

"I can't take the credit for my flight plan. I was scared stiff I might injure Joanna. My dragon and I couldn't communicate with her to find out how she was doing." Leo shuddered. "I hope I haven't given her nightmares."

David grinned because Leo had forgotten Joanna was present. She was standing with Liza and Cherry, her small hand darting up to grab snacks before the two women noticed. The hand disappeared, and the girl stalked around the kitchen counter. She walked over to Leo.

"Are you a dragon like Uncle Martinos?"

"Yes," Leo said.

"I was asleep, I think. I dreamed of dragons. Did you help to rescue me?"

Leo's throat worked with visible emotion. "Yes."

"Can you draw dragons?"

"I think so."

Joanna clapped her hands together. "I'll get my sketchbook."

"After we eat. Leo makes jewelry. He made my ring." Liza held it out for Joanna to see.

"It's pretty. Will you make me one?" she asked Leo.

Before Leo could answer, Liza broke in. "You don't ask people for things, young lady. You earn items for yourself. Remember what I told you about deserving pocket money?"

"Yes." Joanna confirmed this with a nod.

"That ring is a Marquess," Martinos said, an odd note in his tone.

"Yes," Leo agreed.

Martinos assessed Leo and nodded as if he'd worked out a puzzle. "You're the jeweler behind the Marquess brand."

David gave a soundless whistle. "Even I've heard of the famous jeweler. No one knows the craftsman's identity."

Cherry grinned. "Until now."

Liza clapped her hand over her mouth. "Oh, Leo. I'm sorry. I didn't think."

"Not a problem," Leo said. "I'm among friends here. If Cherry and Martinos move to the mainland, Martinos might help me sell my jewelry."

"A gallery," Cherry whispered, her eyes wide. David could almost see Cherry's brain ticking over. She turned to Martinos. "If you started painting again, you'd have a place to sell your work and Leo's jewelry."

Leo nodded. "I wondered if this was possible. If you and Cherry can help, we can generate extra money for the humans from the villages. Many of them produce stunning products. We have weavers, woodworkers, and many other craftsmen."

"I wasn't certain I'd find a purpose on the mainland," Martinos said. "But if I went ahead with this enterprise, I could pay back the kindnesses given to me."

"What will you do for paperwork?" Liza asked. "Martinos won't have identification or official records." She paused, her brow crinkling as if she was thinking hard. "Wait! I'm certain we can obtain the relevant paperwork for Martinos if we pay the right people."

"What sort of money are we talking?" Cherry asked, shifting her weight from one foot to another. She only ceased when Martinos curled his arm around her waist and hauled her against his side.

"Getting a false driver's license, passport, and NHS numbers won't be cheap," Liza said. "But worth it, I think."

"Yes," Leo said. "Now that dragons have reached the mainland, we'll need someone to watch for trouble."

"Someone on Holy Island," Liza swept a brown lock off her cheek. "Cherry and Martinos have already mentioned Bamburgh is a more likely spot since the castle brings in tourists."

"Liza is right," Cherry said. "Martinos and others will need an official status here."

Seeing these humans and dragons interacting, their obvious care for one another lifted the weight bearing down on David. During his time at the monastery, he'd not let himself get close to the other brothers. The black robes at the same level as him had seemed younger while the more senior druids had constantly berated him for his lack of ambition. Rena and her friends, the two dragons, they cared about one another, and they were including him.

The little girl strode over to him. "Uncle David, I need you to draw more plants and flowers."

The fracture in his heart snapped together at that moment. The organ clenched as he replayed Joanna's words, and warmth filled him, a sense of belonging. He recalled his wife's face, the memory dimmed after the passing years, and sensed she'd hate the solitary life he'd led. She wouldn't have wanted him to close himself off from companionship. From love.

"Uncle David?"

"Sure, poppet."

"Once we eat," Liza said in a stern voice. "It's almost lunchtime. It will be naptime after lunch."

Despite Joanna's arguments and persuasive tactics, her mother held firm. As soon as Joanna settled, the adults sat on the deck with a pot of tea.

David allowed the peaceful setting to sweep over him. He sipped the tea from the china cup, his stomach full of unfamiliar but delicious food. "I could locate Rena on the dreamscape."

He frowned since the druids had noticed his power, and he

worried he might become trapped on the dreamscape. Until Rena, he hadn't actively tried to communicate with a particular person. During the crusades, he'd contacted his wife once, and her reaction had startled him. She'd accused him of witchcraft and begged him not to visit her in this manner less the local priest discover the practice.

"Why are you scowling?" Leo demanded.

"During my last visit to the dreamscape, I saw a hooded figure. It's difficult to explain the sense of eeriness. Every bad or impure thought I've ever had starts repeating over and over inside my head until I can barely concentrate. The dreamscape used to be a joyous place. I looked forward to visiting. I'd catch snatches of thoughts, and whenever I did, they were important. I knew to pass them on. Now, I worry I might lead them to Rena or worse, Joanna, since I've visited her once."

"If you're caught on the dreamscape or trapped there, will you die?" Cherry asked, empathy for his plight in her soothing tone. She reached out and squeezed his hand, and Martinos released a growl. "Oh, shush," she said and rolled her eyes. "I do so hold your hand."

Everyone stared at Cherry, and she blushed. "Martinos's dragon is having a hissy fit." She gave David's hand a final squeeze of sympathy then sat back to drag Martinos's hand into hers. "There! Remember this moment." Her blush deepened, and she pressed her lips together.

David smiled and was glad of the moment of levity. It appeared dragons spoke telepathically with their mates. Right now, he wished he had that power instead of the ability to connect via dreams.

"When you're on the dreamscape, what happens to your body? Are you asleep?" Cherry asked.

David shrugged. "I'm not certain. My cell at the monastery is a single, so no one has seen me dreamwalk. I haven't had a roommate for dozens of years because I used to wake screaming with nightmares."

"Girlfriends? Lovers?" Liza prompted.

"Liza!" Cherry protested. "That's personal."

"Not when Joanna might be in danger."

"Fair point," David said. "My wife hated it when I used my power. She worried I'd draw the priest's attention or worse, the devil's. I dreamwalked with her once, and she pleaded with me never to do it again."

"You're married," Liza snapped.

"You *have* dreamwalked again." Cherry spoke at the same time.

"Whoa, don't attack the man. Listen to him first. Give him a chance." Leo sent him a sympathetic glance. "Please forgive my mate for her rudeness. This is a trigger point for her because of her ex-husband."

"Sorry," Liza said, not chastened by her dragon's censure. "*Please* tell me you're not messing around with my sister while you're married to another woman."

"My wife and daughter died during a Viking raid on Iona Island hundreds of years ago while I was at war." His tone emerged flat and didn't invite questions.

"I... Sorry, how old are you?" Liza's eyes were big and wide as she exchanged a glance with Cherry.

"Older than you," David said.

"Off track here, people." Martinos pursed his lips. "If you can't dreamwalk, then we'll return to Smoking Isle and rescue Rena in person."

"It's a trap," Leo said.

"No doubt," David agreed. "But we're out of options. I've been racking my brain, trying to decide where they might have taken her."

"The monastery?"

David drummed his fingers on the tabletop. "No, the brothers, especially the younger ones, are a pack of old gossips. Any secret spreads like the plague." His brow crinkled. "Perhaps the new building near the vegetable gardens. The head druid—Brother Matthew—ordered the construction. Once the builders completed it, the red robes—those druids with magical powers—placed an invisibility spell on it. Either that or they placed a protective barrier around the building—much like the one screening the Dragon Isles. They might've placed her inside."

"Have you broken into the building?" Martinos asked.

"No. After my time working in the library, the senior druids watched me. I'm positive they added poison to my food, so I've antagonized the head druid."

"Can you help us return to Smoking Isle?" Leo asked. "We need to check out this building plus the monastery. I want to know my brothers' whereabouts at all times. On our return, I'll send a message to my friends on Perfume Isle. They need to learn what is happening at the monastery."

Martinos nodded. "I agree. Cherry, you and Liza can stay here with Joanna."

"No," Cherry snapped.

"No," Liza spoke at the same time. "Joanna and I are coming with you. We'll stay out of the way, but we're traveling to Smoking Isle where we're far, far away from Tony. I don't care what the law says about custody. Tony is frantic—so much so, I suspect he has gambling debts—and desperate men are dangerous."

"What Liza said." Cherry scowled at Martinos as if to dare him to argue.

"All right," David spoke before the two dragons mounted a counterargument. "We're all going. The druids will watch for us, so get prepared for a fight."

CHAPTER 16

Start Digging

It was about halfway through the day when her prison
door flew open. Too fast for Rena to pretend she was still
unconscious.

Two men wearing red robes dragged in a man and tossed him on
the floor before regarding her with interest.

"Brother Matthew will be pleased you're awake," one said.

Rena peered at them, attempting to see their features. It was
damn creepy the way they wore their hoods up all the time. "Take
down your hoods and let me see you."

"No."

"Why?" asked the other red robe a second later.

"I want to remember you and kick your butts at a later date," Rena snapped. "This is abduction. It's a crime."

The man they'd chucked on the floor groaned.

"I'm sure he'll want to kick your butt." Rena gifted the red robe with a broad smile. She wanted to rattle these arseholes. Get them to talk because information was power. Her father had drummed that into her from the time she could toddle. She'd joked she'd chisel the slogan onto his tombstone, and he'd grumbled. Thoughts of her businessman father lent steel to her spine. "What do you want with me?"

"Our purpose is not to question why," one said.

"We follow orders," the other chimed in.

"Follow whose orders?"

"Brother Matthew is in charge of the monastery. He has guided us to the light for hundreds of years now."

Hundreds of years? He sounded more like a despot to her. "Well, you tell this Matthew dude, I demand he frees us. It's against the law to imprison innocent people. Things to do, places to be."

"Ask him yourself." The red robe withdrew. He began a rapid chant as soon as the second red robe backed outside.

The doorway faded, and if Rena hadn't known of its presence, she would've assumed the structure lacked an exit or entrance.

"There must be a way out of this pickle," she muttered even as she pondered why they'd taken her. They didn't appear to value humans in this part of the world. Why kidnap her? If not for David and the things he'd told her, she'd be clueless like the mainland residents, never imagining the Dragon Isles lay off the coast of Holy Island.

The man imprisoned with her groaned again, and she approached him with caution. She crouched beside him and gingerly touched his shoulder. Before she could blink, the man had turned and grasped her arms, holding her captive with ease.

Idiot! Now what was she going to do?

As she always did when she became terrified, she tossed attitude at him. "Now you've grabbed me, what're you gonna do?"

"Who are you?"

The man was bigger, broader, and more muscular up close. His hair was a light brown and, like most dragons she'd met, he wore it long. A green dragon head peeked above his shirt collar.

"Are you a dragon?"

"Yes. Now answer. Who are you? Why are you imprisoned here?"

"Rena Carrington. I was on Holy Island with my friends when a red dragon grabbed me and brought me here. No one will tell me why. Who are you?"

"Griffith from Perfume Isle. I was with friends when the druid David opened a portal. I stopped the red robes from grabbing my friends, but they captured me."

"Leo and Martinos?"

"Yes, do you know them? Are they safe?"

"Liza is my sister, and Cherry is my friend. They made it to Holy Island."

Griffith released her and sprang to his feet. He began pacing. "Damn, I wish I understood what is going on with the barrier. The druids. The more I see, the less I fathom."

"You and me both. Any ideas on how to escape? The red robes made the door disappear. I've searched the interior, but the wall is seamless. Wait! Don't touch it," Rena warned. "It gives an unpleasant shock."

Griffith placed his palm against the smooth surface of the wall. Sparks flew. Big sparks and he removed his hand with a grunt.

"That all you got?" Rena mocked. "Why don't you try your fire?"

Griffith studied his palm and prodded what Rena assumed was a sore spot. "Where did you say the door is?"

"That spot over there, right where I marked the X on the dirt floor." Rena studied the interior wall for the *nth* time then lifted her head to check out the roof. The ceiling consisted of the same shiny material.

Without warning, a wall of heat seared her. Fire danced along the sleeves of her sweater. The acrid stench of burning hair galvanized her to action. Rena smacked at the flames with one palm while she slapped at her hair with the other. "Stop! Stop, you crazy dragon!"

The flames ceased.

"Sorry." Griffith bore a sheepish expression. His clothes had fared worse than hers, the front of his shirt burned through to his skin. "I never suspected that might happen."

"Well, now you know," Rena snapped. "Is my hair okay?" Her scalp still tingled with heat, but her arm was fine, despite the burn holes and scorch marks on her sweater.

Griffith winced. "It's sticking up."

"Thank you so much for the information," Rena said, her tone sweet—a warning to anyone who knew her well. "Tell me. My hair. What is the damage?"

"It's burned on one side." He wrinkled his nose. "It might look better if you cut it all the same length."

Rena rolled her eyes. "Great! Next time warn me before you use your fire, hotshot."

"I will," he promised. "Do you have a man? You intrigue my dragon."

Rena took a giant step back, accidentally touching the wall. She lurched forward with a curse. "Yes, I have a boyfriend."

His eyes glittered. "Who?"

"David," she said flatly. "A druid."

"Oh." His shoulders slumped. "I told you she was too old for us."

"Hey! Right here. Listening. It's rude to talk to your dragon in the company of others. Can't you just speak with your mind in silence and leave me right out of the equation."

"Yeah, She's smart. No, I'm not stupid." Griffith fell silent, and

Rena could've sworn his color deepened.

"Look, we need an escape plan. Did you see who grabbed you?"

"Yeah. Russays from Hissing Isle, and the butler, Telus, The Organized. I was holding my own against the two red robes, but the dragons overpowered me. One of them hit me and knocked me out. Before that, I kept the red robes away with my fire."

"Interesting. Does that mean it's possible to set the red robes on fire?"

Griffith shrugged one broad shoulder. "I think so, but if they know I'm awake, they'll take more care."

"If we have another visit from red robe druids, blast them with your fire. Take care with your aim and keep your fire away from me."

"I can do that. If we get that chance, the best place for you to stand is behind me. The flames won't burn me as badly as they do you." Griffith glanced at her hair and frowned. "Sorry."

"I guess it will grow back, but next time, tell me of your plan. We're a team and need to work together."

Griffith grinned. "My older brother is always telling me to think. Maybe you *should* hook up with me."

"For the last time, I'm David's girl."

"The druid." Griffith wrinkled his nose. "They're all about study and spells. Passive stuff. I bet he's pale and wobbly under his robe."

Rena let out a hoot of laughter, entertained by his irreverent humor. "As it happens, David used to be a knight. He fought in the Crusades and has scars from past wounds."

"The Crusades?" Griffith gave a soundless whistle.

"Yes, so stop talking him down and concentrate on a plan. If we can't find a door, and your flames won't burn through the material, what other options do we have?"

Instead of joking this time, Griffith remained silent, and his forehead puckered into a frown. He did a slow turn, his eyes narrowing while he studied their surroundings. Rena concealed her smile since she didn't want to start him off again, but the kid had a brain. She'd bet his older brothers didn't give him a chance to use it, so he fell back on jokes and humor.

Rena lifted her head to study the roof. No escape that way since the roof consisted of the same material as the walls.

"Down," they spoke at the same time.

Griffith nodded with enthusiasm. "The floor is hard clay, packed down. They may have spelled the floor to prevent an escape, but it's worth a try. Shush," Griffith warned. "Someone is coming."

Rena had mere seconds to throw herself on the ground and pretend to be asleep. She heard a low chant penetrate the wall before a black robe appeared carrying a tray of food. She also spied the hems of two red robes standing behind him, a tiny portion of their clothing visible through the screen of her hair.

"Why does it smell like smoke and soot in here?" a red robe demanded.

"I tried to burn my way out." Griffith sounded sheepish, and Rena imagined his smile backed up his words. "Didn't work," he added. "Singed my eyelashes."

"You can throw flames while in your human form?" a voice demanded, bossy and in charge.

"I can, but my control is nil as my eyelashes would attest, if they could speak. I won't be doing that again. Do you have food? I'm starving. She won't want food. She woke up briefly, told me she had a headache, and went back to sleep. Humans are weak creatures. Why do you bother with her?"

"Leave a portion for her, or you'll be sorry," the strident voice ordered. "We'll ask her when she wakes if she had food."

"Of course," Griffith said. "Have you sent a ransom demand to my family? I'd like to leave. I told you—I had no idea who those people were or what they were doing in the yew grove. Your red robes attacked, and I defended myself. When someone fires bolts of magic at me, I fire back."

"Cease your blather! Make sure she gets food when she wakes."

"What if she doesn't? You struck her hard. I've seen humans go to sleep and never wake."

"Cease or I shall remove your tongue," the red robe snarled.

Griffith fell silent, and Rena remained unmoving until Griffith murmured she could rise again.

"Why do you think they were so insistent we eat the food?" Griffith asked, eyeing the steaming bowls of soup and the slices of crusty bread.

"David told me he thinks the druids drug the food to make the younger druids pliable and obedient to orders."

Griffith's head snapped up, his gaze torn from the soup. "They've always done this?"

"No, this is a recent thing. Whatever they put in the food made him feel ill."

"This entire situation smells of putrid machinations."

He wasn't wrong.

"I vote we start digging," Rena said.

"We have no tools."

"We have our hands." Rena scowled at the sparkly pink polish on her nails.

"The shed is large enough to hold me if I shift to dragon. If you squeeze in the corner, I can use my talons to break the hard clay at the top. Hopefully, the earth is softer beneath that, and we can both dig."

"No point wasting energy if the druids have placed a spell on the floor too." Rena's gaze lit on the spoon that came with the soup. "Will the spoon be strong enough to use as a digging implement?"

Griffith grabbed a spoon and strode to the far end of the shed. He dug, grunting once. "It's working. The soil is softer underneath the top layer. Leo and Martinos are convinced dragons were the impetus behind this plot, but the druids are in this up to their necks."

"I'd say to the tips of their judgmental noses," Rena muttered.

Griffith's stomach rumbled, and he sent a longing glance at the soup. "I'm starving."

"Me too, but we can't risk eating."

Griffith took the first of the soup bowls from her and tipped it into the hole he'd made. The second bowl of soup and the bread fitted nicely, and he replaced the dirt and tamped it down by standing on it.

With that done, they returned the tray to the spot of the door's location. "We need a plan for when we escape."

"Yes." Rena nibbled her bottom lip while she weighed up the alternatives. "If we can break out, could we fly to your island and get reinforcements?"

"That's the most logical thing to do because we can't be certain your friends and the druid can return here. If I were the druids, I'd place guards at the yew grove. Getting anyone back through that portal will be hazardous."

"Let's dig. If someone comes, we'll hide the spot as best we can. Once the hole is big enough, you squeeze through first because you're stronger than me."

Griffith beamed at her, his golden gaze gleaming with humor. "Can I have that in writing?"

She rolled her eyes. "Lord, save me from smartarse men. No time for chatting, big guy. We're on a timeline. Start digging."

CHAPTER 17

To The Rescue

"This isn't working. I thought we'd decided the tide and the barrier are linked," Cherry said as she and Liza slid off their dragon's backs. "Every time we tried flying through it, the shock reverberated down my spine."

"At least riding on Leo's back left his talons free to absorb the pressure." Liza yawned. "And we stayed away from the red robes."

"They give me the creeps," Cherry agreed.

Leo tugged Liza in for a hug. "And there were no bugs, my lodestone. I enjoy myself more when you perch on my back."

David and Joanna had walked to the beach to join them, and David missed Rena so badly at that moment. He'd give anything to hear her sharp quips and see her bright smile. "We'll go to the yew tree grove this afternoon," David said to distract himself.

Liza shunted Joanna toward the cottage. "Let's help Cherry make lunch, then you can have a quick nap before we go on an adventure." She paused. "It might be dangerous, but Leo and I can protect her at the manor. Cherry and Martinos are heading there too. It makes sense to use the manor as our base."

Four hours later, they set off for the portal. Liza had received a phone call from the local policeman informing her of Tony's formal arrest and transport to the mainland. She'd spoken with her lawyer, and he'd told her they'd deport Tony back to his home country of New Zealand. Her lawyer intended to push for jail time then deportation. The policeman had requested her to come by his office later in the afternoon to make an official statement. She agreed, but once she'd ended the call, Liza announced she had no intention of attending the policeman.

"Everything will work today," she declared, her gaze moving from face to face, her chin held high. "I bested Nandag, and I believe we can beat Telus and Russays. We *will* save Rena."

David tensed as the motor vehicle sped toward the yew grove. He glanced at Joanna, who sat beside him in the rear. The child watched the scenery, unconcerned by their speed. No matter how often he traveled in this box with wheels, the rapid pace disconcerted him. He much preferred a simpler life where he traveled on foot or by horseback. From what he'd seen, Rena embraced all that her world offered. David cared for Rena, and he was confident she returned his sentiment, but what could he offer her? When he'd joined the druids, he'd donated his worldly possessions. He had no way to provide for her.

"What's wrong?" Cherry asked from the front passenger seat.

"Rena. Our worlds are so different. I won't fit into this modern world, and she won't want to stay in mine. I could travel on the dreamscape and visit her, but Rena deserves so much more."

"Martinos and I had the same problem, but Martinos has decided to use his existing skills to start again in my world. My advice is to ask Rena what she wants rather than making assumptions. That's the thing about modern women. We don't sit back and wait for our men to provide for us. We're equal partners with the right to make decisions with our lovers or husbands. Rena might have ideas you haven't considered, which is why you need to speak with her. Give her honesty. Give her a chance. Give her love."

"Is it that easy?"

"No," Cherry said as Liza halted the vehicle near the yew grove. "Martinos and I will have to keep working at our relationship. I guess we're in a mixed-race bond. Our expectations won't always match, so talking is necessary."

David sent her an incredulous stare. "When did you get so wise? My wife and I never had a conversation like this."

"Different times," Cherry stated. "You can't compare a couple from hundreds of years ago with one now."

David chuckled. "Are you telling me I'm old?"

"If the cap fits." Cherry winked.

"Cherry is right," Liza said. "Rena is strong, and she has enough confidence for five. Rena prefers a man willing to stand toe-to-toe with her, and she's not the type to accept orders. Speak with her and ask her what she wants. She might surprise you."

"Does that mean she'll never want flowers or gifts?" David asked, trying to understand. His wife had relied on him, and when he'd left to fight, she'd moved to a cottage nearer his parents on Iona. Until they'd died during a plague, she'd had the support she required.

"Most women, even Rena, love receiving flowers or small gifts. We enjoy having our meal cooked for us or going out for dinner. An invitation to walk on the beach and watch the stars twinkle. Breakfast in bed," Liza said. "The most romantic thing you can do for us, though, is to listen to our opinions and give them equal weight to yours. Ask us if you're unsure, or better yet, consult with Rena. You love my sister, right?"

"She challenges me. Meeting her on the dreamscape is the best thing that has ever happened to me. Rena brought me back to life, gave me a reason to live, to fight for what is right."

"Tell her that," Cherry said. "Kiss her, love her, and spend actual time with her rather than hours snatched on the dreamscape."

"You make it sound so easy," David murmured.

"I'd better hustle and pick up the boys." Liza checked her watch.

"They'll think something is wrong."

David, Cherry, and Joanna climbed out of the car.

"Won't be long," Liza said. "Take care of Joanna for me."

"With our lives," Cherry promised.

While they waited for the dragons, David thought about what he truly wanted. Rena's face formed in his mind, and she wore her characteristic lopsided smile, her eyes alight with mischief. He loved the way she offered her opinion and pulled him up if he made decisions on her behalf. They'd had a discussion one night on the dreamscape. Right now, he couldn't remember what they'd spoken of, but her answer had remained with him.

She'd said, "I'd rather make my own mistakes and fix them than rely on someone else. How else will I learn and mature?"

Her words had resonated because he'd spent his entire life either telling underlings what to do or receiving orders. During the crusades, others had commanded him and organized his life. Once he'd moved into the monastery, the senior druids had issued orders and expected him to follow them. No one had allowed him to make mistakes. He'd followed his rules, the blame filtered down to him even if he couldn't do a thing to correct the problem.

It struck him that he'd run from his blunders. The death of his wife. His daughter. Disillusioned from war and expecting a warm welcome, their fatalities had hit him hard. Instead of dealing with his grief, he'd buried it and given up on life.

Until Rena.

His shoulders straightened. "How difficult did Martinos find it to learn tasks here?"

Cherry gave him an understanding smile. "He enjoys learning, and this attitude makes him more successful."

He rolled that thought over in his mind and nodded. He reacted well to challenges. "What does Rena do?"

"She's studying to be a forensic scientist," Cherry said. "She'll be heading back to university soon to continue her studies."

"A forensic scientist?" He stumbled over the unfamiliar words. "I haven't heard of this. What does it mean?"

"We have crimes in our world. Murders. Theft. Assault and battery. Probably similar crimes to what you might have in your time, but on a more sophisticated level because of our advanced technology. We have policemen and lawyers and judges, but the job Rena is studying for helps these people catch the criminals. She looks at hair and fibers—the parts criminals leave behind after committing a crime. By studying these things, she and other people like her, allow our law to catch and punish those who commit the crimes."

"This job—if she lived in my world, she wouldn't be able to continue."

"No," Cherry said.

David pushed back the panic that speared him right through the heart. That made his decision cut and dried. He either made a life here, or he never saw Rena again.

CHAPTER 18

A Plan Revealed

R ena's stomach turned over as a door formed in the wall. "Can you squeeze through the hole?"

"No, but you could," Griffith said.

"Dig fast. I'll stall them."

Griffith hesitated, his expression torn.

"Dig," she hissed.

"I can't leave you," he whispered even as he used his hands to scoop soil.

"You have a better chance of eluding them. You can fly to get help. We need more dragons on our side."

"I'll do it, but I don't like it."

"Noted." Rena hated the idea too, but the way she saw it, they'd run out of options. She sucked in a breath and prepared to give the performance of her life.

When the door became visible, Rena grasped the handle, which thankfully didn't shock her. The wooden knob dug into her palm, and she smirked on hearing the consternation coming from outside. The pressure from the handle had her biting her lip to stem her cry of pain.

"Almost through," Griffith whispered.

"Less talk. More action," she gritted out. "Don't speak to me again until you're outside the shed."

"I can't believe this is working," Griffith said.

Rena couldn't either, but she didn't reply. She waited until the pressure came again and braced. Her eyes widened when a second door formed beside the first. "Well, that sucks."

A grunt sounded, and she glanced over her shoulder as Griffith attempted to shove himself through the gap. It didn't look as if he'd fit. Tension lines squeezed into Griffith's forehead as Rena feverishly pondered other ideas, discarding them all until she spotted a second handle forming. The knob tugged downward, mirroring the action on the other side. The first handle didn't move.

Her smartarse grin stretched from one side of her face to the other as she shoved open the first door and sprinted for freedom. An alarmed shout came from behind her. The smash of clay pottery hitting the ground propelled her to greater speed.

"Don't let her escape!" a druid hollered. "Watch the door, so the dragon doesn't flee. I'll grab the human."

Instead of running after her, he chanted. *Huh!* Like that would work. Instinct had Rena zigzagging through the clearing and heading for the trees. She was within spitting distance of the trees when she heard another alarmed cry.

"The dragon is loose. He's not inside the shed."

She couldn't let them recapture Griffith. As one of the red robes waved his hands and sparks shot in the direction where Griffith was ready to take off, Rena eluded capture by the second druid and dived at the spell-maker. The perfect rugby tackle. He toppled with the force of a beefy front-rower crashing under the opposition.

Rena and the druid struck the dirt. She released a rebel yell of success when she saw Griffith arrowing through the sky and over the hill.

"Take that." She pumped her fist in the air.

"You may celebrate all you want, human, but you're still here."

The older dragon she'd spotted on Holy Island stood before her. Once he ceased his speech, he pressed his lips into a tight line.

Sourpuss. Just because things weren't going his way.

"Get up," he ordered Rena. His gaze sliced to the right where the second of the red robes stood, his sandaled feet shuffling.

Rena suppressed her snort. These men came from an era that considered women inferior. *Boom. Take that!* A modern woman with smarts.

"You failed to subdue one dragon and a simple female," a second voice spat.

Rena tilted her head to view the arrival who wore a shimmering golden robe. His face contorted to a sour grimace. "Soon, we shall be overrun by Neanderthal beasts. I asked you to do one thing. A junior druid could've completed the task I set."

Rena rolled away from the red robe and pushed to her feet. "Now that I'm out, I'll be going." She took two steps before someone grasped her shoulder and hauled her back.

"Not so fast. The dragon doesn't matter. You, however, are a prize, and Telus and I won't be letting you go," the druid wearing the golden robe snapped.

"Little old me? A prize." Rena chuckled as if she thought the notion absurd. Meanwhile, her brain worked at speed. She needed answers. David needed answers. "I'm human. I thought you considered humans disposable. Useless creatures, only good to labor for the dragons."

Telus snorted. "Humans are weak, but some are handy."

"Me?"

The golden robe druid narrowed his eyes at Rena. "Did you eat?"

"Who me? Why yes, I did. I was hungry, so the snack you provided was much appreciated. Do you know Nandag?" She tacked on the end of her sentence.

"Matthew, she's immune," Telus growled. "Brother Jasper thought the youngster was the lock, and he was searching for his key. You told me that. If she is the key, she is necessary to our plans."

Anxiety bled in Rena since they were discussing plans in front of her. What did they intend to do with her? She'd need to eat soon, but she wasn't immune to their poison or drugs or whatever they were doing to contaminate the food.

Please, Griffith. Find help soon.

"Have you seen Nandag?" Telus asked, his gaze piercing. Shrewd. A little scary.

Interesting. "Yes, on Holy Island," she lied.

The two men shared a concerned glance.

Ah! That bothered them.

"When did you see her?" Brother Matthew asked.

"Three days ago. She was crossing the causeway to the mainland," Rena said without hesitation.

"I thought Nemyr and the younger brother were in charge of procuring a warehouse on the mainland," Brother Matthew said.

Huh! Telus had lost control of his coconspirators. He didn't know what they were doing or their location. *Interesting.* But Rena still had no clue of their purpose on the mainland. "What do you hope to gain by holding me prisoner?"

"Enough," Telus snapped.

Rena winked. "Spoilsport."

Telus slapped her, the crack of palm against skin loud and

startling. Rena's cheek stung, and she stared at the dragon, scorn twisting her mouth.

"Didn't anyone tell you to use your words?" she spat. "Hitting others is wrong."

"*Bah!*" Telus muttered. "Lock her up and set a guard on the door."

"They dug a hole for the dragon to escape," one of the red robes said.

"Fill in the hole and bespell the floor. Make it impossible to escape. Do I have to explain everything?" Brother Matthew thundered.

He wheeled and stalked away, his golden robe rustling with each step.

"I'll give you an incentive to do a better job." Telus spoke in an icy tone. "Any guard on duty who allows a mistake will die. Do you understand?" He turned to Rena. "Return to your prison."

"Gonna threaten me too?" she sassed. Maybe if he lost his temper, he'd reveal more.

"I don't have to beat you," Telus said in snooty disdain. "You are the key, and once we capture the lock, we will control these lands and beyond."

"What are you talking about?" Rena asked, her curiosity getting the better of her.

"You and the young druid. Since he met you on the dreamscape, he's become more powerful. His magic is stronger. With him under our control, no one will defeat us."

"One problem with your scheme," Rena said. "Neither David nor I will work with you."

"You have people you love." Telus eyes narrowed in warning. "Humans and dragons who matter to you. Do as we say or they'll die."

"What? You mean for the dragons to rule the mainland again?" Rena asked, scoffing at the idea.

"Yes." Telus stalked away, leaving Rena staring after him in shock.

An hour later, she was back in her prison. Instead of attempting to escape, Rena fumbled through the darkness for her jacket. Her phone didn't work. No surprise, but the torch was usable. She sorted through the pockets for anything to use as a weapon. Nothing apart from a crumpled tissue and half a chocolate bar. She unwrapped it and popped one square into her mouth before putting the rest back for later.

It was dark outside now, and Rena prayed Liza, Cherry, and the others were safe. They'd come for her—she knew that because she'd do the same for them. Would they come in the dark or wait? Had they traveled from Holy Island to Smoking Isle? Rena hated waiting, and this delay was doing her head. A yawn cracked her mouth wide open. Since she wasn't going anywhere, she might as well grab a few winks.

"Rena!" David's voice rang out.

"Where are you?"

"I'm on the dreamscape."

The next moment, David was with her. Rena sat up, her muscles sore and tight from lying on the cold ground.

"You shouldn't be here," Rena said. "It's too dangerous. Brother Matthew and Telus wish to capture you. They grabbed me to lure you here, and I heard them discussing a lock and a key."

"Brother Jasper told me the myth of the lock and key. I thought it was a tale to entertain me."

"Brother Matthew implied your magic has grown since you met me on the dreamscape. I'm not certain, but my best bet is they want to harness your magic for whatever plan they have in mind. Quick, listen to me. They captured Griffith with me, but he escaped. He's flying to Perfume Isle to get help."

"We're at Martinos's property. Do you know where they're holding you?" David glided toward her, his face paler than usual. Shadows lay beneath his eyes, underscoring his exhaustion.

"In an empty warehouse. The red robes chant to activate the door and make it visible. The walls deflect dragon fire. Griffith dug his way out, but they've fixed that now. The only way you'll release me is through magic."

"Soon," David promised. He shuddered as he settled her against his chest. "I've missed you so much."

Rena breathed in his masculine scent, relaxing against him. It felt like coming home, and she closed her eyes, savoring the comfort and the pleasure his presence brought her.

"I love you," she whispered. "I don't know what the future might bring, but I wanted to tell you. We've spent limited time together, yet I can't imagine my life without you in it. You're different from the men I've dated. You think of others instead of worrying about the latest clothes and hair products. Showing off the latest gadgets. You're capable of saving the world—the perfect man."

David's big body jerked against hers. "I'm not perfect."

"But you strive to be the best you can. To me, you're hero material, and that is the type of man I want to stand at my side."

"My wife and child died because I wasn't there to protect them," he murmured.

"You did the best you could. You didn't kill them. The Vikings did when they sacked Iona Island. If you'd been there, you would've died too, and I'd never have met you. You wouldn't be here to save the dragons and humans. It's time to forgive yourself. Instead, remember the precious moments. Your daughter's smile. A special dish your wife used to cook. A day you spent together. Share them with me if you want. Your wife and daughter are part of you. They've helped to shape the man I've come to love."

David remained silent, but his arms tightened around her. He nuzzled her neck. "Rena," he whispered, his words emerging thick as if they'd squeezed past gravel. "I want to make love to you, hold you in my arms, but I'm exhausted. It's hard to hold myself here on the dreamscape."

"We have time." Her heart was full, despite their situation. "Once this ends, we'll stay at an old castle with a four-poster bed and a thick, comfortable mattress. We'll stay in bed all day and only emerge when we're hungry. How does that sound?"

"It sounds fantastic," David said. "I'll get to undress you in person."

"I'll discover your tattoos," she countered.

A faint sound—a click—had her lifting her head. Every part of her froze as she stared at the robed man behind them.

David whirled, crouching in a defensive position at the same time he shoved Rena behind him. Something jerked her in the middle of her back, yanking her away from David. The robed man advanced on David, a chant speeding from his lips. David and the robed man dissolved in front of her, fading away to nothing.

Rena jerked upright, darkness surrounding her. Her heart thudded, adrenaline shooting through her. It took her long moments to realize she was back in the dark building.

She must've fallen asleep, and David had come to her.

Now he was in trouble, and she was helpless, locked in this bloody warehouse.

CHAPTER 19

Get Me a Pin!

R ena panicked, bounding to her feet and pacing through the darkness, her heart still thumping. She had to help David.

She pulled her phone out of her pocket and switched on the torch. Had they spoken the truth about the spell on the floor? Could she dig a second hole? She found a spot and started to dig. A shock leaped from the bare ground into her fingers. Her entire body twitched until she jerked her hand away from direct contact.

Rena picked up her phone and shone the torch at her throbbing hand. Blisters had formed on her fingertips, the pain from them turning her lightheaded. She blundered to the middle of the warehouse and dropped, her legs no longer able to hold her upright. A moan emerged as she cradled her hand to her chest. Damn, epic fail.

Tears formed in her eyes, her inability to help bringing her emotions to the fore. She hated injustice and those who mistreated others. Those who escaped punishment. This attitude had driven her to study forensics since she enjoyed puzzles and sifting through clues to make sense of a mystery. But her helplessness weighed her down and suppressed her ability to think outside of the box. Exhausted, she curled into a ball and closed her eyes. Inaction never suited her, but she'd run out of options. There was nothing she could do to help herself or David.

They'd played their cards and lost.

She fell asleep with her mind on David—the man who meant so much to her. The one she'd decided to keep instead of throwing away. She wasn't sure how they'd manage or if they even had a future, but oh, she wanted to merge her life with his, embrace his strength of character and the deep well of love he carried within his muscular body. If anyone had told her she'd fall for an older man, she would've laughed herself silly. A man from another time—even crazier—yet she was in love with David.

She wanted him so badly, wanted to save him, wanted to hold him in her arms, and plaster his face with kisses.

Where the devil was he?

She had to find him.

Without warning, Rena found herself in a murky world. A chill wind ruffled what remained of her hair. She stumbled forward on the uneven ground, fear drying her mouth. The cold penetrated her clothes, and a shiver ran through her body. She glanced behind her. More of the fog obscured her vision.

Rena's foot caught, and she tripped. She sprawled forward, catching her weight on her blistered fingers. Pain shot up her fingertips, and it took her long minutes to stagger to her feet.

A bright violet band undulated on the ground in front of her. She blinked, certain she imagined the color that attracted her like a signal fire. Every part of her wanted to reach out and grasp that violet ribbon. Rena froze, hesitating to follow her instincts.

When the ribbon remained, she took a cautious step forward. The mist twisted in the wind, and for an instant, she glimpsed a clump full of ribbons. Most were bright red with a few black.

As she stared at them, a golden ribbon blinked out of sight as did a beautiful turquoise one. Both disappeared, leaving the violet one amongst the host of red and black ribbons. She swallowed hard and took a halting step forward, every instinct in her urging her to touch. The instant her fingers skimmed the violet ribbon, a shock jerked her backbone straight. An electrical pulse zapped through her, not painful but not pleasant either.

Rena gulped, vacillating over her actions. *Popsicles!* This wasn't helping David. When she'd quizzed him on the danger he faced while he spent time on the dreamscape, he'd changed the subject. Now, irritation filled her because she hadn't pushed harder. She had no clue what to do—whether she followed the ribbon or she tried to wake up. Rena swallowed hard, the truth striking her with a one-two punch. Doing nothing wasn't her style.

"All righty, then," she muttered, and she clasped the vibrating violet ribbon more firmly, walking the length of it with tottering steps.

The closer she came to the clump where the ribbon started, the harder her hand vibrated. The hair on her arms and legs and the back of her neck stood to attention, and she had to force herself to continue. When she reached the base of the ribbon, a powerful force yanked her forward. Rena fell into darkness, her scream of terror tumbling after her. She struck the ground, a floor—*something*—and the impact shuddered through her for long seconds. A groan escaped, and she didn't care who heard. *Holy Frogs.* Every part of her ached and throbbed and jittered. Even her eyelashes, for goodness' sake.

"What are you doing in my bedroom?"

A familiar voice. Her sister. Proof she'd dived off the deep end. Rena forced her eyes open. It took a moment to focus, but she'd landed in a bedroom. It wasn't at the cottage, and from what she'd glimpsed in the moonlit room, it was old-fashioned, although luxurious. A four-poster bed containing a man and a woman. The woman sat up and stared at her.

"Rena! Where did you come from? Are you all right?"

"Liza, you're not wearing clothes," Rena croaked, her mind so muddled she muttered the first thing that came to mind.

Liza cocked her head, her brown eyes full of humor. "Do I have to explain marriage and relationships to you, little sister? I adore Leo, and we enjoy sex. Now, more importantly, where are you? We're coming for you, and narrowing the search would help."

Was she in Liza's dream? Wow, this seemed so real. "Ah... David visited me on the dreamscape. A hooded figure grabbed him. He blinked out of my dream, and I can't contact him. I can't find him." Her throat thickened to the point she was having trouble pushing out her words. A tear splashed onto her hand, and it ran onto her palm, stinging her blistered burns.

"He's here at the mansion. We'll check on him."

"Liza, if someone captures David on the dreamscape and he's separated from his body for too long, he'll die. Once the sun comes up, he'll weaken. If the sun comes up a second time, and he hasn't returned to his body, he'll never awaken."

"Rena, we will fix this. We're working on a plan to break the hold the druids have on the monastery and everyone in it. Where are you?"

"In a building at the monastery. I don't know the location."

"We'll find you," Liza promised, and the determination in her sister's voice told Rena she wasn't alone.

Her sister and friends would come for her, for David, and somehow, they'd kick the druid's butts. "David, first," Rena whispered. "Promise me. He's suffered so much. He needs to see we care for him. That we're willing to fight and understand his contribution."

"David is an honorable man. Even if I hadn't met him myself, I'd try to help because you love him."

"I didn't mean it to happen," Rena said in a small voice.

"Doesn't matter," Liza said. "Grab some sleep. *Kia kaha!*"

"Māori, right? That means to stay strong?"

"Yes. Battle like a Māori warrior, Rena. We're coming for you and David."

Rena nodded, a strange weakness pervading her limbs. She drooped, her muscles unable to keep her upright. A blink later, she found herself in the weird place full of colored ribbons.

Bed.

She wanted to sleep so badly. With a whoosh, she landed on the packed ground of her prison. She groaned, her body so bruised and battered she couldn't work out how to reposition with minimum torture. So she didn't. She lay on the chilly dirt floor and rested.

Liza bolted upright in bed.

"What is it?" Leo was instantly awake.

"David, he's in trouble. We must wake him." Liza rose and grabbed the first clothes to hand. By the time she was ready, Leo had dressed.

"How do you know David is in trouble?"

"I told you about the dreamwalking and how David and Rena communicate. They were together last night, and a hooded figure grabbed David. Rena is desperate. She thinks David is in acute danger, and she can't do anything to help."

"Where's Rena?" Leo asked.

"She told me she's in an empty building. The same one Griffith escaped. The druids improved security after Griffith absconded."

"Which room is David using?" Leo asked.

"This way." Liza sprinted along the passage and burst into the chamber at the end. She thrust open the curtains.

David lay on the bed, unmoving and non-responsive to the light. Liza hissed. "We have to wake him."

Leo crossed to the bed, grasped his arm, and shook hard. "David, it's Leo. Time to wake."

David didn't stir. He didn't react, but his tattoos pulsed blue.

Leo shook him harder, frowned at Liza. "Suggestions?"

"Try to get him to stand?"

Leo yanked David to a seated position, but the instant Leo released him, David flopped to the bed.

"Is he responsive in any way?" Liza nibbled her bottom lip. "What if we jab a pin into his big toe?"

"Torture him?" Leo's tone told of his disbelief.

"No, of course not," Liza said. "Doctors do it when they need to check a patient's response."

"If you say so." Leo's doubt came across clearly. "Just for the record, never poke my foot. My dragon won't like it. I won't either."

Liza rolled her eyes. "Wuss. I'll find something to check David's reactions."

"What's going on?" Cherry asked, rubbing the sleep from her eyes.

"It's David." Liza gestured at the open door. "Rena dreamwalked and told me David is in trouble. Leo and I can't wake him."

"Throw cold water over him," Cherry suggested.

"Truly?" Martinos asked in astonishment.

Cherry ignored him and sped away while Liza resumed her hunt for a needle.

When she returned, Leo and Martinos stood over a comatose David.

"Any luck?" Liza asked.

Leo gestured at David.

Liza didn't answer but brandished her needle and jabbed it into David's toe. He didn't react. "This is bad," she announced.

"Icy water from the well." Cherry hustled into the bedroom. "Stand back."

"Sunbeam, do you think this idea is feasible?"

"Do you have a better one? Out of the way, so I don't splash you."

Cherry tipped the contents of the bucket over David's face and chest.

For long seconds, nothing happened. The pulsing of his tattoos slowed, and without warning, he jerked upright, his breathing hoarse. He coughed and spluttered, his entire body quaking.

Cherry raced from the chamber and returned with a towel. "Let me dry you, David. Liza, a blanket, please."

Liza grinned at Cherry's bossiness. She loved this attitude Cherry exuded and couldn't wait to hear how Cherry's mother reacted to her new assertive daughter. Liza found a woolen blanket in the carved chest that sat at the foot of the bed.

"Martinos, he needs a warm drink." Cherry's brow puckered, then cleared. "A nip of the whisky we were drinking last night."

Martinos squeezed her shoulder as he went to do Cherry's bidding.

David's teeth chattered, and his shoulders shook as Leo wrapped the blanket around him. The brightness of his tattoos dimmed, and David regained his wits.

Martinos returned with a tankard of spiced ale and a nip of whiskey.

"What happened?" Leo asked once Martinos handed over the ale.

David sipped the scalding drink and gave another shudder. The ale sloshed over the tankard side.

"Let me hold it for you." Cherry removed the tankard from his grasp and held it to his lips, tipping the pewter mug gradually.

David swallowed, seeming to calm and become more alert. "T-the head d-druid captured me. O-on the dreamscape."

The two dragons exchanged a glance, and Liza thought they wanted to push David to spill his tale. Leo and Martinos remained silent, though, and waited for David to speak. He sipped from the tankard again with Cherry's help before cupping his hands around the base and taking control of his imbibing. He finished the ale and seemed far more alert when he surrendered the tankard to Cherry.

"David, why did they capture you? What did they want?" Leo asked.

"The head druid seems to think Rena and I can solve their problem, whatever it is. They've captured Rena, and now they want me."

"That's bad?" Martinos asked.

"I've been hearing whispers about dragons making a return to the mainland and things being different this time."

"We have to stop them," Leo said. "I don't disagree that change is necessary. Meeting Liza and Cherry has shown me the dragon race has stagnated. We've kept to the old ways while things on the mainland have progressed way beyond anything I could've imagined. When we start visiting the mainland, we need to do it with care. Liza says humans still won't react well to the reality of dragons. If we move to the mainland, we'll need to live in concealment. Brother Mathew and Telus have a takeover in mind."

"Leo, we need to return to Hissing Isle. Two reasons," Liza said. "One, you need to speak with your parents and your remaining brother. And two, you need to recruit dragons and humans to help us stop Brother Matthew and Telus. To rescue Rena. The moment they open the barrier—if that's what they intend to do—you'll have chaos. There will be dragons who want to travel to the mainland and plunder and others who will be dragged into the mess because they're trying to protect their families."

"Liza is right," Cherry said. "But what she's not saying is the bedlam that will erupt on the mainland. People will panic, and it won't be a pretty sight. Humans will die. Dragons will die. No one will win apart from Telus and Brother Matthew since they're carrying out their plan."

"What if telling others leads to unrest?" David asked.

"It's beyond that now," Martinos said. "The humans and younger dragons from Smoking Isle have vanished, and no one has an inkling of where they went. Nan might be dead, but the repercussions of her behavior are still rippling through Smoking Isle. We have no workforce. Only the children and the elderly remain. Perfume Isle isn't affected, but that's because Nan and your brothers didn't have contacts there."

Liza stalked over to Leo. "Hissing Isle needs investigation. It'd be interesting to learn if some of their residents have disappeared. Have you checked in with your village?"

"No," Leo said. "You're right. We require information. The

druids are expecting us to attack. We need to get help from the other isles." He scanned each of their faces, his expression impassive yet strong and that of a leader. "Unless you think we should walk away before the bloodshed begins."

"No," Liza snapped. "They have Rena for a start."

"No," Cherry seconded. "We suspect they're behind the vanishing humans and dragons. If we walk away, they win. The baddies win. No. *Just no.*"

"I agree with Cherry and Liza. We organize a force and fight for independence from the druids. For too long, they've exploited their control of the barrier. Our people haven't asked the questions we should've," Martinos said.

"We still require the barrier," David cautioned.

"We do." Leo sighed. "But one person shouldn't control the barrier. We've allowed the abuse of power. In the future, a committee of dragons and humans from all three isles should act as a countercheck to mishandling."

"Diplomacy," Cherry said. "With shared information and greater opportunities for residents to thrive. A few rule over the multitude. That must change."

"Blaze." Leo fixed his gaze on the brown-haired dragon from Perfume Isle. Blaze had returned briefly to his home to check if his missing sister had been found. After Griffith had escaped imprisonment and alerted his family of further trouble, Blaze had flown back to Smoking Isle to offer his aid. "You haven't contributed or stated your opinion."

Blaze glanced from Liza to Cherry before focusing on Leo. "Your mate and Martinos's mate have stated the salient points. We go to war. There are no other options. We tried approaching in peace, and the druids rebutted us. Their red robes almost killed us and now they've started imprisoning our people. I'll fly home to talk to our residents—dragons and humans."

"What will you tell them?" Cherry asked.

"It's time for the blunt truth." Blaze studied them in turn. "Our people should learn the facts."

"I'll fly to Hissing Isle," Leo volunteered. "Russays is part of this plot. If he's not at the castle, I'll approach my parents."

"You shouldn't go on your own," Martinos warned.

"We'll go with you," Cherry said. "All of us. If the humans see us working with the dragons, won't they be more likely to listen to you?"

Liza nodded. "Cherry is right. At present, it's best if we stick together. We should take David with us too. That way each race is represented in our group of warriors."

"What about Joanna?" Leo asked.

"Leave Joanna here with Alfred and Betty," Cherry suggested. "They're loyal and will look after her as if she was their own. Joanna likes them already, and I'm positive the feeling is mutual."

Liza bit her lip. "I don't want to disappear again since we've only just reunited." She frowned and issued a hearty sigh. "But you're right. She would be safer here. Cherry mentioned that Alfred and Betty visit the village or their friends stop by here. She'll have other children to play with."

"She'll blend with the other humans from the village," Cherry said.

"Alfred and Betty will protect her," Martinos agreed.

Leo reached for Liza's hand. "Liza? It's your decision."

Liza hesitated then straightened her shoulders. "I think it's best to leave her here at the mansion."

"All right. We depart in the morning." Leo pushed away from the wall. "David, will you be safe if you try to sleep again?"

"As long as I don't venture onto the dreamscape," David replied.

"Right. You fly with me on the morrow." Blaze paused in the doorway. "Rest well. We'll leave after we break our fast."

CHAPTER 20

A Chilling Threat

David managed a light sleep during the hours until dawn. Worry for Rena kept him from sinking into a restive slumber. He imagined she'd experience terror and frustration. Brother Matthew did not tolerate obstructions, and he'd try every trick to get her to lure David back to the monastery.

A lock and key.

He'd sensed the closeness between him and Rena from the first moment of their dreamscape meeting. He'd used the lock and key analogy himself, the sense of rightness whenever they touched, when they kissed or made love.

But even more worrying—what was the purpose of the lock and

key and why or how had Brother Matthew discovered he and Rena were the ones he sought?

A clatter and stomping in the passage outside his chamber told David it was time to rise. An attention-grabbing thump on his door emphasized his assumption.

"I'm awake," he called.

The door opened a fraction, and Martinos stuck his head inside the chamber. "I've brought you warmer clothes. Cherry and Liza told me to remind you riding on a dragon is cold and miserable without heavy clothes.

"Thank you." David accepted the clothes with gratitude.

Once he dressed in the trews, linen shirt, woolen vest, and a cloak, he felt stronger, which was weird. Clothes didn't make a man. It was the grit, honor, and a true heart that gave a man character. For long years, he'd sought refuge at the monastery, and it was obvious he'd outgrown his need for the peace and routine the druids offered. His was a soldier's heart, and it was time to fight for the Dragon Isles.

David exited his chamber and followed the voices he heard to the kitchen. Along with his friends and the child, Joanna, an elderly couple sat with them. A human woman bounded to her feet when she noticed him.

"I'll get you a mug of tea, sir."

"David." He smiled and took a seat beside Leo and Joanna.

"You look much better." Cherry gave an approving nod. "The

clothes are an improvement too. Every time I see a robe, it gives me the creeps."

David nodded. "I can understand your aversion to the red robes. From your account, you were lucky to escape."

Half an hour later, they took off. Joanna stood between Alfred and Betty and waved an enthusiastic farewell. For David, riding a dragon was a novel experience, and he soon came to appreciate the warmer clothes for it was mighty cold winging their way across the sea between Smoking and Perfume Isles. For a time, he amused himself by watching the scenery. Puffs of smoke emerged from the central volcano on Smoking Isle, while jungle and trees covered the slopes of the older cones. Closer to the sea, near to the mansion, the remnants of the old village stuck out. Farther along the coast, near a natural port, the new dwellings were underway, with several residents already living in their homes. Martinos and Leo had done an excellent job with the modern village plans, impressing David with the amount of work undertaken already.

From the corner of his eye, he glimpsed the monastery with its ordered gardens and the slate-gray buildings. The place had been home to him and his fellow druids. Anger, slow to build, now rippled through him. Those brothers were prisoners, the younger black robes, at least, as was Rena. David wondered what might have happened if he'd embraced the druid lifestyle instead of remaining in his bubble of misery.

Soon they were flying over the sea, and Blaze had told him

the flight would take around two hours, depending on the wind. David let his mind wander to the red robes and Brother Matthew. Their magic was strong, but still, they sought him and Rena, which meant what?

David frowned, filing through the possibilities. He thought back to when he'd first met Rena, and how his spells had worked faster and required less effort. He'd assumed his dedication to studies and additional research in the library had improved his skills, but what if it was Rena who amplified his power?

Why would Brother Matthew require them?

The barrier, perhaps?

If Brother Matthew had realized their spell was failing, or he and his cohorts required a new, more powerful spell... Yes, his hypothesis made sense, but it was still a guess. He prayed Rena remained safe and kept her feisty nature to herself. Brother Matthew was centuries old and had little respect for women. A plus for their side since he'd underestimate Rena.

Another question bothered him. How had Brother Matthew discovered David's dreamwalking skill? David hadn't noticed druids watching him closely, but it was apparent things he'd kept close to his chest were no longer secrets.

Finally, they arrived at Blaze's home on Perfume Isle. David's thighs throbbed from gripping the dragon's hide for so long, despite the thick pad he'd sat on during the journey. His legs gave out on hitting the ground, and he fell on his butt.

"I did that too." Liza didn't hide her amusement. "But believe me, riding on a dragon's back is much better than traveling clutched in a talon. Flying higher might be colder, but there are no bugs."

"Tell me I'll get used to that," David pleaded.

"You should focus on the benefits," Cherry said. "Few dragons allow humans to hitch a ride. You should be honored."

Behind David, the three dragons shifted, their brightly colored dragon tattoos visible on their torsos and shoulders. Liza and Cherry handed over clothes, but his limbs refused to function, his clumsy attempt to remove his backpack leading to frustration.

"I'll get it," Cherry offered. "You're still sluggish from when the druids caught you on the dreamscape. Luckily, we decided to rest the night here before heading to Hissing Isle. Will you sleep without dreaming?"

"I hope so. I can feel Rena's need for me. Her desperation. I suspect the druids have discovered a way to amplify her fear. They hope to entice me into a trap since their first capture failed."

"We will get her back," Liza said fiercely.

Blaze's brothers came to meet him, and he plus Leo and Martinos were busy issuing instructions. Leo stripped off his clothes again and left them in a pile.

Liza muttered under her breath and made a tsking sound of protest.

Cherry laughed as Martinos did the same. "We've inherited a

new task, although the view has improved."

Liza chortled and darted away to grab both sets of clothes while Cherry helped to support David. Liza appeared to communicate with Leo and stuffed the clothes into a bag before setting it at the dragon's feet.

"They're off to speak with the humans in the two villages here on Perfume Isle and to see the dragons at the training center. Leo trained here before he won his title," Liza added on her return. "Leo told me to organize food." She stepped onto David's other side.

David gratefully took advantage of the women's strength. "The last time I recall feeling this bad was when I first started training for the Crusades. I've become soft since I joined the monastery."

"You don't feel soft," Liza quipped.

"I'm going to tell Rena on you," Cherry singsonged. "You're feeling up Rena's man."

"I'd love to have her here to tell me off for cuddling up to her sister and best friend."

"We *will* free her soon." Liza's expression shone with determination. "My sister is strong. She managed to dreamwalk and warn me you were in trouble."

"She what?" David demanded. "How? When?"

"Oh, yeah. We didn't tell you that," Cherry said. "Rena saved you."

David's chest tightened, pride filling him along with a wave of love and longing. His woman was strong and full of surprises. Independent and feisty with opinions of her own.

"Tell me later," he suggested. "If I don't sit soon, I'll topple on my arse."

Liza directed them through a pair of carved wooden doors and up a flight of stairs that almost killed him. He was breathing heavily by the time Liza and Cherry showed him into a small chamber.

"Can you avoid the dreamscape when you're this fatigued?" Cherry asked, her brow puckered in concern.

"I can manage a protective rune." He fumbled with the borrowed pair of leather boots. "I hope."

Cherry brushed aside his inept hands. "Let me." She removed his boots in a trice and set them aside. "Do your rune now and sleep. We'll wake you in time for dinner."

"Thank you." David waited until the two women left before he slumped.

Rena was in trouble because of him. If he hadn't entered her dreams, she might be safe at home and preparing for university. He groaned and swallowed hard, his eyes stinging with an unfamiliar pain and heaviness.

His mind drifted, and his body jerked. He wasn't sure how long he'd wandered, but he'd almost fallen asleep. A dangerous slip since his subconscious would lead him to Rena. He forced himself to sit upright and centered his mind. Next, he sketched two protective runes, twisting them together with the special punch of power he'd practiced ever since he'd first started working with the medium.

He reclined, his pent-up breath easing out as he allowed himself to relax. David emptied his mind of everything, but Rena kept pushing back, stepping into his thoughts as if she belonged. Because she did belong, and once this was over—if they beat back those who quested for power, he'd talk with Rena. They'd work on a way to spend their lives together.

The lock and the key.

Rena groaned at the blast of light that shone into her face. A sandaled foot nudged her in the ribs. When she kept playing possum, the man kicked her. A pained grunt escaped as she curled into a protective ball. The kick had set off every one of her pain receptors, and they sang in a discordant chorus. Her blistered palms throbbed. Her scalp pulled where Griffith had singed her hair, and now, her ribs protested in outrage.

"I know you're awake," a masculine voice growled. "Start cooperating or I'll make you feel worse than you do now."

Rena blinked her eyes open, battling against the sun strike in her face. The floor smelled earthy, and the dampness had seeped deep into her muscles while she slept. Every inch of her ached.

"Girl, don't try my patience." It was the druid who wore the golden robe—the head honcho. A druid wearing a red robe stood beside him.

"What do you want?" Her voice emerged in a croak.

"Call the druid to you."

"I don't understand."

"Brother David."

Rena projected confusion. "I have no magic."

"You walk together on the dreamscape."

Okay. "He finds me—I don't have the first idea of how to find him."

"She's telling the truth." The red robe observed her with as much interest as she studied her forensic samples.

"We'll draw him in then," a third man said. "This has continued long enough. I've run out of patience. It's no matter to us whether she lives or dies."

Rena twisted her neck to see the man who spoke of her in such a dismissive tone. The older dragon. Arrogance filled his features while he carried himself with the confidence of a bully. He truly didn't care what happened to her.

"We leave for the mainland tomorrow. You have today to complete your part of the deal."

Rena sensed the consequences were terrible since the head druid's face blanched of color.

Brother Matthew remained calm, though. He bowed his head. "When have we ever failed you?"

"A warning," Telus said in his crisp tone. "I abhor failure." With that announcement, Telus stalked from sight.

"What next?" the red robe asked.

Brother Matthew eyed Rena with disfavor. "I was hoping she'd draw Brother David back to the monastery where we could capture him and force him to add his magic to ours. If the rest of us combine forces, we can summon enough power to attract humans to work in the factory. Once we've done that, Telus will ease off his pressure."

"Brother Jasper should've informed us of his untapped power."

Brother Matthew snorted, the tip of his bulbous nose turning red. "Jasper should've told us instead of hiding his suspicions. If I'd known David's presence powered the barrier rather than our spells, things might've happened differently."

"Will he come for her?"

Brother Matthew sent her a scornful glare. "He thinks he loves her." He aimed another kick at her. "If Brother David contacts you, tell him to return to the monastery. If he doesn't, you will suffer."

Rena bit her lip to suppress her groan. "What will you do with me?"

"Deliver you to the dragons on the mainland. They can use you in their factory. You'll join the other humans in the compound there."

"The dragons are holding humans prisoner?"

The head druid shrugged, his expression one of indifference. "I have no interest in the dragon's business operations. If Brother David communicates with you, point out that your safety depends on his actions."

A Plan of Confrontation

S leep had ushered the fogginess from David's mind, and
although his muscles protested, loud voices led him down a
set of stairs to a dining room.

"Come in, David," Leo said.

Martinos grabbed a spare chair and shifted over to make room.

"What have I missed?" David asked.

"The humans we spoke with told us they've had several residents
disappear. We're wondering if this ties up with whatever Nandag,
my brothers, and the monastery druids are up to," Leo said. "The
dragons at the school haven't noticed anything, but when they're
in training, they don't leave the premises."

269

David glanced at Martinos. "You mentioned most of the humans have disappeared from Smoking Isle."

"Most of the missing are younger and capable of working." Blaze wrinkled his brow before shaking his head. "Whatever they're doing, they require a labor force for their scheme."

"Are we flying to Hissing Isle tomorrow?" Liza asked.

"Yes," Leo said. "It's time to confront my parents and Russays. Telus, too, if he's there."

"You can't go alone," Liza protested.

"Already organized." Leo smiled at his mate. "I have volunteers from the training school. Six will travel to the castle, and six will fly with Martinos to the village."

"I'm going too," Liza stated. "I want to stand in front of your judgey parents and stare them down."

"Can I visit the village and thank Sam and Henry for looking after you?" Cherry asked Martinos. "Do you think the village residents will want to help us?"

"We'll ask them," Martinos said. "I'm hoping some of them might wish to move to Smoking Isle."

"I'll speak with more of our people. Tell them what is happening," Blaze said. "A few of the older dragons I visited earlier have no liking for Telus. Word of his scheming didn't surprise them."

"What's next? After we've gauged support?" Cherry asked.

"Martinos, Blaze, and I have discussed this. It's time to confront

the druids—this time with David at our side. You have the magic."
Leo indicated David. "We have the determination and firepower."

"The younger druids will buckle," David said. "I believe they've bespelled them with a food additive or the red robes have done a spell to cloud free will. My gut says the plans have been in place for a long time, although I don't understand the benefit to Brother Matthew."

"Blackmail," Liza suggested. "Telus is unscrupulous. He doesn't care about those he considers beneath him."

"We'll learn more tomorrow once we reach the castle," Leo said.

Liza grimaced. "As long as they don't arrest me again."

"Yet you still want to stare down my parents," Leo teased. "How can that be?"

"They were super snobby and disdainful," Liza said. "This time, we'll have more dragons on our side."

"Why don't my brothers and I come along too?" Blaze suggested. "I want to question Telus. If he knows anything about my sister's disappearance, I'll squeeze the info out of him."

The next morning, everyone rose early to prepare for their assignments. David decided to go with Leo and Martinos, and once again, Blaze was his ride.

"I'm glad you're coming with us," Leo said. "My parents are always difficult, and I'm not sure if my older brother will be present. We can't trust him."

Liza placed her hands on her hips and eyed Leo. "You forgot to mention Telus. The no-good two-faced snake."

Leo laughed, but David heard the note of strain.

"We must hurry," David said. "We're running out of time."

Not one dragon asked questions. They stripped and shifted to their dragon forms. David helped Cherry and Liza to collect clothes and stuffed the apparel inside bags. Each of them strapped a bag on their shoulders before clamoring aboard their respective dragons. Today, David had more time to enjoy the flight to Hissing Isle. He'd never visited the other isles, having spent his time on Smoking Isle at the monastery.

When he'd first arrived at the monastery, the isles had been visible from the mainland. Once the druids proposed the barrier, David hadn't cared because his guilt had been so profound. He'd mourned Helena's and his daughter's passing. The border closure had saved the remaining dragons, although he now understood the repercussions of the decision.

Dragon Isles' residents had clung to the past while the humans on the mainland had embraced change. The lack of advancement had allowed a core of rot to set in and permitted those in charge to prosper while those less fortunate had suffered.

As had the younger druids.

David dressed warmly again, and it was strange not to feel the air beneath his robe. As they took off from the courtyard, David experienced a surge of excitement. He recalled how he'd enjoyed traveling to different parts of the world. It had been the war and the fighting he'd abhorred.

Sweet spice and a floral scent floated on the air, then the tang of the sea. They flew over trees and jungle, and David spotted a waterfall and a lake before the salty brine aroma grew stronger.

Until the last two days, he hadn't realized how monastery life had constrained him. At first, the routine had helped. He'd needed it, but meeting Rena and her friends had changed and jolted him from the emotional prison he'd inhabited for hundreds of years.

Once they reached the sea, David surveyed the coast. They soared in formation. Leo, Martinos, and Blaze. Blaze's brothers flew behind them, along with six of the dragons Leo had called upon from the fighting school.

Leo had explained the trouble he and Liza had encountered before, and as well as enjoying the scenery and the peace as they soared through the air, David sorted through his protective rune spells. The freezing rune too. If anyone attacked, he could halt them for a brief time. Now, what else might come in handy? A blast spell. He'd experimented during his time at the monastery, but always in secret.

Brother Jasper had told him secrecy was imperative. David hadn't understood why, but now Brother Jasper's warnings and the reasoning behind them were apparent.

The two hours of the flight passed fast, and David spotted the coast of Hissing Isle.

It would be almost another hour before they reached the

castle, Martinos and Blaze's two brothers veered off, flying toward the human village on the other coastline—the one nearest the mainland where Leo had saved Liza from drowning. Their group continued toward the castle.

The castle reminded David of the ones around during his youth. The towers were square and like blocks rather than rounded as the ones in Europe. No one challenged their group as they flew closer, although a few dragons wheeled through the skies and soared on the fresh morning breeze. Still, David felt the tension in Blaze's dragon as they flew over the castle towers and landed in the battle training grounds.

Two sizeable men emerged from the shelter close to where they'd landed.

"Leo!" one man hailed him, and Leo waved back before accepting clothes from Liza. Several younger men, all of them curious, trailed the older men.

"Come on," Leo said, and they walked to meet the group.

"Leo, what are you doing here?" Jakab asked.

"Introductions first," Leo said. "You know your fellow trainers from Perfume Isle, but this is Blaze and David. You've met my mate, Liza, already."

"Not a snack," Liza said with a squinty-eyed glare at the redhead dragon who Leo introduced as Felix.

"Not a snack," Felix agreed. "I'd hate to upset Leo."

"Why are you here? It's not safe." Jakab scanned the sky for castle guards. "If they see you, they'll arrest you."

"It's imperative I visit my parents. First, I have much to tell you."

"In private?"

"No, gather your students and workers. We should make everyone aware of what is happening on the Dragon Isles," Leo said.

Once everyone assembled, Leo told them of his arranged betrothal to Nandag, Liza's incarceration, their escape, and meeting with Martinos. He spoke of David and their encounters with the druids. The dragons and humans from Smoking Isle who'd disappeared under mysterious circumstances and no one knew what had happened to them. He mentioned the red robe druids and Telus's part in the treachery. He mentioned the battles with two of his brothers who had died and Liza's role in Nandag's death.

Then, he moved on to the failing barrier and how Martinos had ended up on the mainland. He told them Liza and Martinos's mate came from beyond the barrier. The druids had imprisoned David's woman, and the way they'd attempted to capture David and had almost killed him.

"Our way of life needs to change," Leo said. "Those in charge are using us and abusing their powers."

"But the barrier is to protect us from the humans who live on the mainland," one trainee objected. "What happens if the barrier fails and the humans invade our lands?"

Excited voices rang out, and it took time for Leo to regain control.

"We must keep the barrier strong, but those dragons and humans who wish to venture forth and visit the mainland must have that option. Early days, though. First, we must stamp out the corruption invading our world. I intend to confront my parents and my older brother—if he is here. Anyone who sees Telus must consider him dangerous."

"They should arrest him," someone called.

David agreed, since Telus seemed to be the driving force behind the entire plot.

"First, I must face my parents. Each of you must speak with your friends and family. Decide the direction you wish those in the Dragon Isles to embrace. I have glimpsed a small part and can attest the outside world is very different to ours. We must prepare and approach this new-to-us world with caution rather than charging in like a thunder of castle guards."

"Why should we trust you?" someone called from the back.

David stood close enough to see Leo stiffen, yet he didn't hesitate in his reply.

"I understand many of you have little love for my family. All I can ask is that you judge me by my actions. I want to correct the wrongs here."

Liza pushed forward, indignation etching into her features. "Leo is an honest and hardworking dragon. He saved me from the dungeon. He saved a wrongly accused and falsely imprisoned Martinos. You know him as Leonidas, Champion of the Skies, and if you think he is dishonest, leave now. I don't want you here."

"Isn't she a human?" someone whispered.

David grinned. Liza was as forthright as his Rena. These dragons underestimated humans, and this flaw in Telus's thinking would be the downfall of his plan.

Leo grasped Liza's right hand in his and whispered to her. She laughed aloud and pressed against his side. As one, they fronted the group again.

"I'd like your support when we face Telus and the monastery druids. They're placing our families in danger. At worst, they're plotting to overthrow our way of life and intend to rule the Dragon Isles. Who is with me?"

"Aye," Jakab shouted without a blink.

"Yes," Felix said.

After their agreement, the youngsters followed suit. David eyed the group. Leo didn't realize it, but he was a born leader, and he'd summed up the situation without exaggerating the problem. He hadn't offered excuses for his family or become defensive. Instead, he'd offered a solution and told everyone what he intended to do to fix the problem.

The characteristics of an excellent leader.

Once the noise subsided, Leo suggested Felix and Jakab organize everyone who wished to help with the druids at the monastery.

Leo had discussed the red robe problem with David, and they had concluded there was strength in numbers. Given the number of red robes at the monastery, all they needed to do was overwhelm them with enough dragons to cause confusion. Brother Matthew would fight them, but once again, they hoped their numbers would keep the coup they intended peaceful.

"Ready?" Leo asked.

"Let's go kick some dragon butt." Liza winked at Leo when she caught his wince.

David concealed his grin by aiming his gaze at the ground. Yes, just like Rena. The idea sobered him. "I want to hurry and head back to Perfume Isle this evening, if possible. The longer I'm apart from Rena, the more danger she's in."

"Done," Leo said. "If I can't go back, Blaze will return you."

"Is that Martinos?" Liza asked, her gaze on the horizon. "Whoever it is, they're carrying a rider."

"Popsicles," Leo said. "This is bad news. He was meant to meet us at Perfume Isle after speaking with the villagers."

The tension rose within their group, and David sought to ease the fear wafting from Leo and Liza. "What is a popsicle?"

"It is a frozen sweet treat," Liza said. "Rena, Cherry, and I try not to curse in front of my daughter, however sometimes we require a special word. We chose to use the word *popsicles* instead of teaching my daughter awful habits."

Leo squeezed Liza's shoulder. "I am speaking in the same way since Joanna is now my daughter." He spoke with pride and a hint of challenge as if he expected the remaining dragons to take umbrage at his declaration.

"It's hard to imagine you have a daughter," Jakab said. "Perhaps I'll have a son one day who can court her."

Leo released a growl, and David chuckled, remembering how protective he'd felt toward his daughter. He recalled how she'd fallen one day when a boy had pushed her. He'd picked her up and glared at the offender. It was a pleasant memory—one of fatherhood and insignificant yet meaningful too. "I recall what it was like to have a daughter."

"You have a daughter?" Liza asked.

"No longer," David said, the familiar ache tinged with sadness for a little girl who had never known life. "Both she and my wife died during the Viking attack."

"I'm so sorry to hear that. I can't even..." She trailed off to close the distance between them to give him a swift hug. She stepped back. "That must've been so difficult." Then her eyes widened. "How old are you?"

"It was tough." David had never spoken of his pain at their loss and the consequences of their deaths for him. It had changed his path from returned soldier and probable farmer to druid. From there, he'd tapped unknown magical abilities, which had led him to Rena. He liked to think his wife and daughter had had a path in his reawakening. "Older than you. Once we enter the monastery, we age slowly."

"Does that mean you'll grow older now that you're outside the monastery?" Liza blurted.

"A druid trains constantly, and the founder of the monastery believed the training should not go to waste. He developed a spell to slow aging."

Martinos landed, and Cherry slipped off his back to join Leo and Liza. As she spoke, she extracted clothes from the bag she carried. Martinos started to dress.

"Martinos told me to report," Cherry said. "The elderly and children remain. They told us a group of castle guards arrived and rounded up the men and women of working age. It sounds as if they had red robes with them because Sam told us the dragon guards herded the people into a mass, then the men in robes began to chant. A few minutes later, every person disappeared."

"When did this happen?" Leo asked.

"Late yesterday," Martinos said.

"Apart from getting their loved ones back, do they need food or help?" Leo asked.

"They're running short of food," Cherry stated. "Sam has organized minders for the children, and his wife has organized food, but with no one to bake bread or milk the cows, supplies are becoming scarce."

Leo turned to Jakab. "Could you and your trainees drop food to the villagers before you head to Perfume Isle? How many adults are left? Around twenty?"

"Yes, with around fifty kids," Cherry said. "A wolf was defending the children at the church. A fierce creature that snarled at us. We didn't get too close but shouted to the children."

"Jenny!" Liza smiled at Leo. "I'm glad she's protecting them."

"I'd be happy to get supplies, but I don't have the money to purchase the quantity we'll need," Jakab said.

"Tell the merchants I will pay them," Leo declared. "I've dealt with them before, and they should recall my word is true."

"Done," Jakab said. "Are you certain you don't require an escort into the castle? I mean, the guards will arrest you on sight. I heard your parents were incandescent with rage after you broke Liza and Martinos out of the dungeon."

"David and Martinos will be with me."

"Cherry and I can kick butt too," Liza said, her tone fierce. "I want to stare your parents in the eye and give them a raspberry when they lift their snobby noses and reject me. I am Liza, The Fierce-Hearted Human. Last time, I was on my best behavior. This time, I'll roar."

Cherry nodded vigorously, her eyes flashing with passion. "What she said. No scared ninnies here. We are progressive humans from the mainland. We've got skills."

Amusement flooded David. Once they freed Rena, the trio could challenge the dragon world without pause. He'd stake his money on them emerging the victors.

CHAPTER 22

The Torture Begins

"*Are you nervous?*" Liza asked Leo on their private communication channel.

"*A little,*" Leo confessed.

"*That's an excellent thing,*" Leo's dragon added to the conversation.

"*Over-confidence is as bad as cowardice. But Cherry and Liza are right. It's time to kick dragon butt. Will we be strong enough with the druid's help? The castle guards will attempt to arrest us,*" Leo said.

"*Rena hasn't said much, but she and David have spent time together on the dreamscape. My sister isn't usually so close-mouthed, but she mentioned David is strong. Once he found Rena, he practiced his magic more with his mentor."*

Leo gave Jakab and Felix a few more instructions before they and their students left to purchase goods in the market. He glanced at Martinos, his feelings regarding the other dragon having shifted now that Leo and Liza were mates, and Martinos had his mate in Cherry. Martinos had changed, and Leo thought given time, they'd become even better friends. Not something he would've guessed after learning of Martinos's youth and the charges that had landed him in the dungeon.

"Let's go." Leo strode off the battlegrounds with Liza and Cherry walking behind him. Martinos and David brought up the rear. Contrary to their assumptions, no one barred them from entering the castle, although plenty of guards and less powerful dragons stopped to stare as they marched beneath the hanging gate and into the castle courtyard.

A lone guard standing beside a watch house near the castle entrance took one step toward them as if he meant to halt them, but then he scanned Leo's face. The guard gulped hard and withdrew his protest without uttering a word. Leo inclined his head and swept past.

"Where is Telus?" a feminine voice screeched.

Leo slowed to head for a stone staircase that led up to the next floor. "It seems Telus is away on other business," he commented.

Liza hustled to catch him. "Is that your mother? She sounds perturbed."

"Over the years, my parents have grown lazy and have lost sight of what makes them powerful—the dragons willing to toil for and alongside them. Telus no longer works for them. He has an agenda of his own."

The screeches rose to ear-piercing—a tantrum demanding attention. "Where is Telus? Fetch him. He will fix this."

"This way," Leo said, entering the throne room—a place steeped in bad memories since he'd received many punishments here.

Three dragons were present when Leo and his band of enforcers strode into the room. This was where an heir apparent became the leader of Caireall Castle. Russays, his oldest and sole remaining brother, sat on the golden throne at the far end of the room. His father hunched in a nearby chair while his mother paced back and forth, complaining, shrieking, and wringing her hands.

Russays's gaze lifted at their entrance, his black hair smooth and tidy unlike Leo's windswept mane. "Well, well. If it isn't Leonidas, The Youngest Son, and his band of humans and rapists."

"What are you doing here?" his mother snapped, her black hair streaked with more silver than Leo recalled. "You have a price on your head after you rescued this human and the rapist from our dungeon. You made us a laughingstock. Guard. Guard!"

"There are no guards on duty, Mother," Leo said.

His mother seemed older and smaller, even though a short time had passed since their last confrontation. Fine lines feathered from her mouth and around her bloodshot eyes. She tapped her feet and clicked her fingers, her constant jitters highly unusual. At least for her. In contrast, his father remained still and quiet.

Leo turned to Russays. "What is wrong with them?"

"Telus hasn't left them enough tonic." Sly amusement dug into Russays's mouth, giving it a cruel twist, and it was apparent he didn't care. "More to the point. Did you see Nemyr, Goticranth, or Nandag during your flight from the guards?"

Behind him, either Liza or Cherry snorted.

"They're dead." Leo didn't take his gaze off his brother.

"Who killed them?" Russays demanded, mottled red flooding his face.

Ah, so that bothered him.

Liza stepped forward. "I killed Nandag."

Martinos joined Liza, standing at her side. "I killed Nemyr."

"And I killed Goticranth." Leo stepped to Liza's other side.

"What of Telus? Have you seen Telus?" his mother asked with open desperation. "We require the tonic to extend our youth and regain our excellent health. Telus holds the supply."

"They look as if they're going through withdrawal," Cherry said.

David stepped forward. "I can offer them temporary relief."

"Who the hell are you?" Russays asked.

"Meet David," Leo said.

Russays drew himself up as if he intended to breathe fire. Before Leo could issue a warning, David sketched a rune in the air. His older brother froze, his jaw gritting as he tried to move. Nothing happened, and Russays issued a guttural grunt of displeasure.

Once David had rendered Russays ineffective, he turned to Leo's mother.

"Stay away from me," she shrieked, scuttling backward like a beetle. "Leave me be. I order you."

"You can't order me around, Mother," Leo said. "Tell me what has happened."

"You happened," his mother snapped. "You and your sainted father and your grandparents. Every time you stall our plans. If you'd accepted the betrothal to Nandag, you would've died as planned. Finally, we would've been rid of you. Russays could've inherited the castle and secured our future without you hovering in the background like a cancer."

"Mother," Russays gritted out, his glare full of warning.

"Let her speak." Leo's gut twisted at the mention of his grandparents.

Although he hadn't been old, he recalled the day rebels had attacked their party. His grandmother had hidden him in bushes by the roadside and told him to remain quiet. She'd told him she'd come for him once it was over. Except, his grandparents and his beloved uncle had died that day along with their servants. He'd been the sole survivor.

"Why do you hate me so much?" he asked. "I'm your son, but you treat me like the enemy."

"You are not my son," she hissed, saliva spraying his face as she advanced on him. "You are not of my flesh, you hellspawn. We should've killed you when we found you after the attack. I wanted to, but Tudoarreo got an attack of the guilts and said stealing your birthright was punishment enough."

"Mother," Russays howled.

"Wait, you're not fully related to these horrid people?" Liza asked. "Hallelujah!"

"My uncle was the heir to the castle." Leo recalled everything he knew of the past. "You succeeded to the title after he and my grandparents died. That would mean..." His uncle was really his father. His brow furrowed. Why the secrets? He'd never known. It had never been discussed. He'd always been the youngest son of Tudoarreo and Qille. *Always.* He'd never heard gossip to the contrary.

"Yay! You're not their son," Liza repeated, her smile so full it almost ran out of face. "I worried Joanna and I would need to be polite to them for the rest of our lives."

"You killed my uncle—no, my father—and my grandparents to grab the title for you and your sons," Leo said, so much making sense now. It was why his brothers had hated him, treated him like an inconvenience, and bullied him mercilessly during his childhood. They were his cousins, not his brothers.

"Why does everyone accept I'm your son?" Leo asked, that part not making sense.

"Tudoarreo's parents forced us to bring up Leonidas as our son. Your sainted father had an affair with a married woman. You could never have inherited the castle, yet your grandparents wanted you to enjoy a privileged life without nasty gossip. Your mother didn't want you, so they foisted you on us."

"Leo, don't listen to her poison. You have great value to Joanna and to me. Your friends love you. Do not listen to her spiteful words. You are the only one here capable of running this castle with fairness." Liza's words rang with conviction.

He'd loved his uncle and remembered his regular visits and small gifts. His uncle—father—had played with him, and in hindsight, it was easy for Leo to see the man, although fallible, had loved him.

"Who is my mother?"

"No one of consequence," Qille, The Taker of Life, spat. A shudder passed through her, and she coughed. Blood dribbled from her mouth and down her chin. She didn't notice.

"What was in the tonic?" Cherry asked.

"A slow-acting poison. One that is much favored by Telus since it makes the eventual death seem natural." Russays's voice held unconcern and the smugness of one pleased to impart bad news. His muscles strained as he fought the freezing spell David had blasted him with. "Release me. You have no power here. No say. I shall rule this island and soon, the other Dragon Isles. Nothing will stop me."

"We have stopped you. You might have murdered your parents

with Telus's help," Liza said, "but you're a fool if you think Telus is helping you. The butler is playing his own game. You can bet he'll be working hard to finish whatever he has started. You're all his minions, but you're too stupid to see past your nose. Telus is the dragon in charge."

"What's a minion?" Martinos whispered to Cherry.

David had wondered that himself, and he listened for the answer,

"A yellow cartoon character," Cherry whispered back. "I'll explain more later."

"David, can you help my parents? My uncle and aunt?" Leo asked.

Froth formed on Tudoarreo's lips while Qille was still bleeding from the mouth.

"When was the tonic last administered?" David asked.

Martinos poked his childhood friend in the ribs. "Answer him."

"Five days ago. The last time we saw Telus," Russays said, his voice sullen.

"Did you expect him to return?" Leo asked.

"Two days ago," Russays said.

"Or so he told you," Liza taunted. "You trust the dragon, or have you started to worry because he has disappeared?"

David approached the older couple. The man trembled in massive body-twisting shudders while the woman never ceased her twitching.

"Keep away from me," she snarled.

David turned to the man. As David reached him, the man shrieked. He slouched forward and fell off the chair on which he was sitting. The man seized, then froze. David had never witnessed the like, and he leaned closer to listen for breathing.

"David, I'll check his pulse. That will tell us if he's still alive." Cherry crouched beside him and lifted the man's wrist.

David watched her press her finger to the veins showing there, then the vein under the jawline.

Finally, she moved back and stood with a shake of her head. "He's gone. Do you have anything you could give her?"

"Only a tisane to deal with the pain," David said. "Without knowing the poison used, treatment is difficult."

"Do your best," Leo said. "Martinos, will you help me deliver Russays to the dungeon?"

Martinos stepped closer. "With pleasure."

David formed a different rune and flicked the power he created at Russays. "You should be able to walk him to the dungeon now. You'll find him pliable and able to move freely. Escape, however, will be difficult for him."

"Poor Leo," Cherry said once Leo and Martinos left. "It must be horrid to learn the people you considered your parents are, in fact, your wicked aunt and uncle."

"From the little Leo has told me, his brothers bullied him. At least now, he understands why. He told me he left and traveled to Perfume Isle because of his brothers. His brothers' bullying set him on the path to success. He's a self-made dragon and is wealthy, although he doesn't flaunt his prosperity. I'd say Nandag discovered the identity of Leo's true parents and decided to use the information for her purposes. That's a guess, but I'd say if she didn't know, then she was after Leo's land. The barrier runs close to Leo's holding."

"Hissing Isle sits closer to the mainland than the other islands," David confirmed.

Liza nodded. "Leo told me an anonymous someone attempted to purchase his land. Just after I arrived, Leo discovered one of his herd butchered, and he found two dead wolves. I'm wondering if that was the start of subtle pressure to make Leo sell."

Leo and Martinos stalked back to the room where David and the women waited.

"I've placed Russays in the dungeon, but whether he'll be there on our return is another story. I'm uncertain as to the soldiers' loyalty. Word is they haven't received wages this month. I promised to see them paid, but their trust is paper thin. I've placed Kalab—the guard who helped Liza and Martinos escape the dungeon—in charge and sent a message to my banker to pay the guards the funds they're owed. Kalab will hold the castle and make certain no one loots or steals supplies." Leo turned to Liza, and then his gaze dropped to his aunt.

David witnessed the grudging sympathy in the dragon even though from Liza's accounts, Leo's childhood had been miserable, and he'd escaped at the first opportunity.

"Can you do anything for her?"

"I refuse to let your friends touch me," she screamed. "Leave me be, you miserable bastard."

Leo swallowed and turned away. Even then, he didn't show anger, but instead, compassion and sorrow filled his gaze. In their way, each of them had been Telus's victims.

A jolt of fear tore through David without warning. The hair at the back of his neck stood on end, and that sensation continued through his body, making his arms and legs sting. He froze, his gaze traveling the room in which they stood. Nothing appeared out of place. Portraits of stern dragons from earlier generations scowled at them. Harmless, but still intimidating. No one hid behind the oak furniture or prepared to toss a figurine at their heads.

David backed to the nearest wall to allow himself a better view of the room. Qille was too sick to offer danger. Tudoarreo was dead. David centered his mind in the way Brother Jasper had taught him. He forced each of his muscles to relax while his mind slid into the tranquil state he used while dreamwalking.

"David," a familiar voice whispered.

"Rena?" David spoke louder than he'd intended.

"Is Rena there?" Liza asked.

"Need to concentrate," David said.

Liza fell silent.

"Rena?" David whispered and placed a magical rune of *oomph* behind his speech. "Are you there?"

"Danger," she whispered, the word floating through his mind along with fear. *"Come soon. Torture."*

Dread engulfed David. *Torture.* "We're coming for you," he promised, meaning it with every particle of his being. He might have failed Helena and his daughter, but history would not repeat. "Stay strong, my sweet cynamone. We're coming." He maintained a positive air for her, concerned because she sounded nothing like her usual feisty self.

The link between them broke as suddenly as it had begun, and David snapped from his calm state. "We have to leave now. Rena's life is in danger."

To the Rescue

When the two red robe druids returned Rena to her prison, she could barely stand. One of them had ordered the other to take her arm. The red robe who'd issued the command had eyed her with suspicion the entire time. *Idiot.* As if she could run with the burns Brother Matthew had inflicted on her feet.

At least she'd contacted David during the brief time when Brother Matthew had assumed she'd fainted from the pain of his torture. She still wasn't sure how she'd accomplished this feat under the scrutiny of the flinty-eyed druid, but she had—a win in a shitty day.

With the aid of the stolid red robe gripping her arm, Rena

teetered her way to the warehouse. Once there, she balanced against the wall, each breath emerging with a harsh whistle. Heat radiated from her right cheek, where Brother Matthew had slapped her.

After she'd collapsed with her pretend faint, he'd waited until she emerged from her swoon and told her to reconsider her responses. She could repeat them tomorrow if she wanted, and her resistance would garner a greater punishment. Tomorrow, if she didn't answer his questions, she'd lose her right arm. The next day, she'd lose her left leg. The fourth and final day, which she'd learned was when Telus, The Organized, arrived, she'd die if she ignored Brother Matthew's questions.

Two red robes chanted their spell, but Rena no longer tried to recall the words. There were too many tongue-twisting terms and only ended in her frustration.

The door formed and opened at a push from one red robe's hand.

"Get in," he instructed.

Rena took half a step, and a foreign cry had her stilling.

"Inside." A red robe shoved her into the dim interior. "Nothing to fret over."

With every sense hyperaware, Rena limped into the warehouse, tears filling her eyes with each painful step. During her absence, they'd filled the place with others. Rena halted three teetering steps inside, but it was enough for the druids to work their closing spell.

"Who are you? Where did you come from?" Rena asked once the door sealed.

"Prisoners," a man snarled, echoes of his fury bouncing at her. "Bloody dragons. You can't trust any of them."

"That's untrue," Rena stated, her voice quiet but defiant. "Leonidas, Champion of the Skies, is an honorable dragon. He is my sister's mate. Martinos, The Changed Dragon," she began, making up a more prestigious title for him.

"You know Leo?" a man wearing a minister's collar asked. A slim woman clung to him, and in the dim light the druids had arranged for the occupants, it was easy to see she'd been crying.

"Liza, his mate, is my sister," Rena said. "Cherry, our friend, is Martinos's mate."

The minister frowned. "Do you know why the dragons and druids rounded us up and brought us here?"

"Not the exact reason, although I know Leo and his friends are coming to our rescue." Rena wavered, and the minister reached out to grab her arm. She yelped.

"You poor thing. What did they do to you?" the minister's wife asked.

"Brother Matthew wants to get his grubby hands on David, one of his younger druids. Look, can I sit? My feet are killing me." An understatement since they were burning and throbbing like the fires of hell.

"Let me see your feet," the minister's wife said. "Sit here against the wall."

Rena had no trouble following the order. She dropped onto her butt and released a groan. Damn, she'd thought she had enough fat on her arse to cushion the poke the red robe had inflicted to make her hustle. Apparently not.

"What happened to your hair?" another woman asked. Once Rena had started chatting with the minister and his wife, several of the women sidled closer, braver now that they'd established her a non-threat.

"When Brother Matthew first captured me, a dragon from Perfume Isle was here. Griffith tried to burn his way out, and his fire bounced back and burned my hair." She winced when one woman prodded her heel.

"That looks right nasty. Who did this? A dragon?" the woman asked, her tone hard and disapproving.

"Not a dragon. The head druid. Brother Matthew."

"But they're nonviolent and refuse to get involved in the squabbles and skirmishes between the island rulers," a man said from the background.

"They're happy to ensure their profit and comfort," Rena snapped. Holy frogs, her feet were killing her, and she hadn't even had the pleasure of wearing a pair of pretty, impractical shoes.

"Where's the dragon who was locked in here with you?" a different male demanded. His voice also bore an edge of frustration, but along with it came suspicion and fear.

"After we discovered we couldn't break through the wall, we tried digging underneath. The two of us dug a hole, but the druids came before we could escape. I told Griffith to leave because he could fly. Help is on the way."

"I don't trust dragons," another male stated.

"You were happy to take Leo's money when he spent it at your bakery," the minister's wife said coolly.

Impatience rose in Rena. "None of that matters right now. Whatever their plan, it's speeding up because the head druid is on a timeline. Instead of arguing, we need to work together. When the druids or dragons come, we must be ready to counteract. Escape."

"Running is fine," a man declared. "But where? We're on a different island. This is my first visit to Smoking Isle."

"Head south to the dragon mansion. The people are allies," Rena said.

"Dragons will help us?" the man scoffed.

"Would you rather leave our children alone for longer or fight to return to them?" the minister's wife spoke into the silence. She turned to Rena. "Are you positive Leo is working to stop whatever the druids are up to?"

Rena winced again when the minister's wife cleaned one of her burns. "Yes. Nandag, Nemyr, and Goticranth are dead. They were part of the plot. We believe Brother Matthew and Telus, The Organized, are in cahoots. The dragons are on their way. You must believe me."

Rena caught the doubt on several faces, the expressions of disbelief, and outright hatred. The dragons hadn't treated humans well, and their merry band of rescuers was now reaping the reward—apathy, mistrust, and doubt.

"All right," a man called. "Say we believe you. How can we escape the druids? Their magic froze us so we couldn't protect ourselves. Their second spell made us behave like docile sheep. They herded us together and brought us here. My mind was active, but my body refused to obey any of my instructions. We put up no fight, and now our children and the elderly are alone."

Rena's lip curled upward, and she balled her fists as her anger at the druids grew. How had David not noticed this activity? "Will they be okay?"

"We're hoping the elderly and the fishermen who were at sea will protect our children," the minister said.

"You mentioned a plan," a woman said. "What did you have in mind?"

"The druids arrive in pairs and use their magic to create a door on the side of the building. They bring food and water that way. First, we need to take care because they've drugged their younger druids to make them more pliable. The best idea is to nominate a food taster, and the rest of you to eat and drink later."

"How do you know this? And why haven't they drugged you?" a woman asked.

Rena screwed up her face in partial answer. "They've tried.

They're using me as bait to draw my friend here."

"Wot's so important 'bout yer friend?" a burly man with shorn hair asked.

"He has the magical powers they need to succeed with whatever plan they've hatched."

"You talk funny," the burly man said.

Rena shrugged, not about to tell them she came from the mainland. "I suggest we split into two groups. When the two druids come to remove us, we should use every weapon at our disposal to take them out."

"What weapons?" a man demanded in a dismissive tone. "We have one penknife between the lot of us."

"Check the floor for tiny stones. Scrape up dirt to throw in their faces to blind them and give one of us a chance to jump them. Throw boots or shoes at their heads. Anything to distract them."

Several women nodded.

"If you divide into groups and each group focuses on one druid, we might get lucky," Rena suggested.

"If there are many druids?" a short, rotund man asked. "What then?"

Rena barely refrained from rolling her eyes, and luckily another woman spoke up before Rena could.

"Then, we improvise. If we want to save our children, we do our best," the woman said. "We take them by surprise instead of following their orders."

Rena's jaw widened in a yawn. She covered her mouth. "I'm so sorry. I can't keep my eyes open."

"You sleep, dear, while you have the opportunity," the minister's wife said. "I'm afraid we can't do much more to help your poor feet."

Rena hesitated, then nodded. She had to sleep sometime, and she doubted David and the others would rest. He'd promised they were coming, and the determination in his words made her believe him.

They arrived at Blaze's home on Perfume Isle three hours later. David shivered with the cold as he slid off Blaze's back. The force of the wind had slowed their journey and frustratingly added to the travel time.

"We'll eat here and rest for an hour before we fly to Smoking Isle," Leo said. "Will that be long enough?"

"What's our plan?" Blaze asked.

"We'll meet the remainder of the dragons at Martinos's mansion. Then we'll fly en masse to the monastery."

"What if they fire rocks at us again?" Cherry asked, handing over clothes to Martinos.

"How many red robes live at the monastery?" Leo asked David.

"Sixteen. No, fifteen now that Brother Jasper is dead."

"Does Brother Matthew have magic?" Martinos asked.

"He possesses some magic and excellent leadership qualities. When I arrived at the monastery, he was assistant to the head druid. Once the head druid died, Brother Matthew took over his duties."

"We'd better assume he's as dangerous as the red robes," Leo said. "Just in case."

"They sent their entire force to repel us then," Cherry said. "That makes our plan easier. If a group of us approaches the monastery and engages with them, another part of our group can mount a rear attack."

Blaze disappeared through a doorway and returned in a few minutes to usher everyone out of the cold wind. The warmth hit David as soon as he strode into what turned out to be a kitchen. A fire crackled in a hearth, and a dragon woman—one who resembled Blaze with his light brown hair—turned a half side of beef on a spit. A stout wooden table stood in the middle of the room while smaller shelves lined the walls. The scent of cooking meat and hot bread had David groaning under his breath. It had been hours since they'd last eaten.

"Welcome," she called. "It's most irregular to entertain in the kitchen, but Blaze assures me none of you will mind, and you require food and rest. Take a seat."

David sat with the others, exhausted in mind and body. Blaze's mother set a massive bowl of a meaty stew on the table and directed a servant to serve dishes for them. She placed a plate of fresh bread near him and another of bright yellow butter. David's stomach let out a loud rumble, and Cherry and Liza, who were sitting either side of him, laughed. Cherry pushed a bowl of stew at him while Liza slapped a hunk of bread on another plate and shoved the butter in his direction.

"Eat," Liza said. "Rena needs you strong for what is to come."

David nodded, seeing sense in this. He wasn't sure what he'd do once he faced the head druid or which runes he should use, but he had to fashion a loose plan of attack. No matter how determined the dragons and humans were, retrieving Rena wouldn't be easy.

David spooned up a mouthful and gave a low groan of pleasure as the rich, meaty flavor coated his tongue. "This is tasty. Thank you."

"You're welcome. We enjoy feeding men who appreciate a meal and the time that goes into preparing it," Blaze's mother said with a twinkle in her eyes.

"I made the bread," the servant said with a sassy smile in his direction.

"If the scent is anything to judge by, I'm positive I'll enjoy the bread as much as the stew," David said.

Blaze chuckled, his golden eyes gleaming. "Spoken like a tactful man who wishes to eat his meal in peace."

"I have to eat with care at the monastery. They doctor the food. Whatever they place in the meals makes the younger, less experienced druids more biddable. They follow commands, even if the orders make no sense."

"How did you discover they were adding to the food?" Liza's bright smile and the way she cocked her head reminded him of Rena, and a pang of urgency struck him. They were eating a pleasant meal and were safe while Rena remained in captivity. Scared and alone now that Griffith had escaped.

"David?" Cherry prompted.

"I'm sorry. I was thinking of Rena. The other brothers stopped their usual laughing and joking, their practical jokes. They were deferential toward the senior druids and followed every order. The food made me ill. I have no explanation, but I took notice, and after that, I ate fresh fruit that I stole from the orchard or vegetables from the garden. I was careful about what I drank. That's why I'm enjoying this meal so much."

Liza grasped David's forearm and squeezed in sympathy and with concern for the woman they both loved. A faint growl had David raising his head to stare at Leo.

"I love Liza's sister, Rena," David said slowly and clearly. "Liza is my sister."

Leo gave a clipped nod, but his dragon flickered behind his eyes. Dragons were a possessive race, but David understood.

Liza and Rena were worth fighting for, and he'd do anything to restore Rena to his arms. Finding her had been the jolt he'd required to live again. Brother Jasper had told him it would happen once he released his guilt. David hadn't believed his mentor until now.

The flight to Smoking Isle took four hours since, once again, they faced a headwind.

David spent the flight planning the runes and practicing the steps in his mind. Since joining the monastery, he'd taken his vows seriously. To save Rena, he'd break hundreds of years of passive behavior without a second thought. It'd be up to him to block the red robes' magic. The dragons needed to blunt Telus's power and halt the plan the dragons and Brother Matthew had set in place.

It was dark when their party settled in front of Martinos's mansion.

The welcome scent of tasty food—something meaty—floated from the kitchen. Loud and ribald masculine laughter came from the mansion, and servants rushed to and from the kitchen with platters of food.

Jakab came forward to greet them, as did Blaze's younger brothers.

"We set a watch on the monastery," Jakab said. "We believe they're holding other prisoners with Rena. A group of red robes and several druids wearing black robes delivered food. Whoever is inside gave fight and were driven back inside without the food getting delivered."

"Rena." Cherry puffed out her chest. "If she's in that warehouse, she'll be fighting."

"If the druids had arrived ten minutes later, she would've escaped with me," Griffith said with approval. "She is a warrior woman."

"She is." Liza smiled with pride. "We move tonight, as soon as we come up with a solid plan."

"I agree," David said. "My gut tells me we're running on borrowed time."

"Right." Leo sucked in a deep breath. "This is what we'll do. Jakab, you arrange a group to keep watch and a runner to come back and report if something dire happens that means we shouldn't dawdle. The rest of us will eat and relax for one hour."

David made a sound of protest even as he understood the requirement for a respite. These dragons had flown long hours without complaint. Ideally, they should have several hours of slumber before they attacked the monastery. "Sorry, I understand, but I'm worried about Rena. I wish I could contact her and find out if she's all right."

"Why don't you try?" Cherry suggested. "Liza and I can watch while you sleep and make sure you wake again."

Liza rose. "I'm willing to help, but first, I intend to check on Joanna. Betty said she's sleeping. I'll feel happier once I see my daughter."

"Isn't dreamwalking a risk right now?" Martinos asked. "You're our most important weapon. If they grab you on the dreamscape, that will be the end for us. We can't fight their magic."

"But what if David can contact Rena? That will give us the inside knowledge. An edge," Liza suggested.

"I'll do it," David said. "There is a danger of capture. I wasn't prepared last time. This time I am. I've designed a rune I can use as a weapon."

"That sounds risky," Cherry warned. "David, take care and skulk rather than going in on the attack."

"I promise to use stealth." David rose. "Is there somewhere I can stretch out?"

"We'll use the bedroom you had before," Cherry said. "Liza and I can sleep afterward."

A few minutes later, David reclined on the bed and closed his eyes. Exhaustion already weighed him down, and it didn't take much for him to drop off to sleep. As soon as he entered a restful state, he slipped from his body and floated toward the dream zone. Now, he needed Rena to cooperate. He wasn't sure what he'd do if he couldn't find Rena.

Disappointment drooped Rena's shoulders after the failure of their surprise attack. Regret filled her because they wouldn't get a second chance. While the others ate, she tried to grab sleep. Every muscle in her body throbbed, and she suspected the wounds on the soles of her feet might've become infected because arrows of pain darted up her calves. Although she should eat, she couldn't summon the energy. Her eyes closed, and she sank into deep rest.

"Rena."

David's soft voice whispered through her mind the second she nodded off.

"David?" She sat up, and when she stared downward, she discovered she'd slipped from her body. Peculiar. That hadn't happened before. "How is this possible?"

"I'm not certain." David strode toward her, halting millimeters away. "You're glowing," he said, his voice full of wonder.

Rena lifted one arm and stared at the writhing electric-blue tattoos shimmering on her arms. "They haven't done this before. The marks formed after I arrived on Smoking Isle. I figured it was a rash."

"The druids are still holding you in the shed."

"Yes, along with men and women they captured from Hissing Isle. Most of these people know Leo."

"Ah. Leo worries about their welfare. Tell them their children and elderly are fine, and Leo has organized food supplies for them."

"Are you coming?"

"Soon. We have a large party of dragons coming to the rescue. Do you know where they're taking the humans?"

"I'm not sure, but I get the sense Telus and his cohorts have set up a business on the mainland. Others have gone before them. Other villagers, I mean."

"Any idea where on the mainland?"

"I'll try to find out."

"Don't put yourself in the firing line." David cupped her cheek, tenderness shining in his eyes. "Do everything you can to stay alive and believe this. I am coming for you, my sweet cynamone. We will be together soon."

Rena sighed. He hadn't witnessed the determination in Brother Matthew. The head druid balanced on the cusp between desperation and madness. He was determined to capture David and use him for gods knew what. She mentioned none of this, however. Instead, she pressed her lips against his and sank into the maelstrom their kiss created. Heat and power and a vivid blue flash that preceded a solid click. Like a key turning with a lock.

Their lips parted, and David held her, the embrace bringing tears to her eyes. She blinked them away and savored his closeness. If only it were in person.

Finally, David freed her and lifted a hand in farewell. He faded in front of her eyes. Rena wandered over to where she lay on the ground and scowled. How the devil did she return to her body?

She kneeled beside her still form and touched a fingertip to her arm. A whooshing sensation zapped her, and it felt as if someone was sucking her organs from her body. Her mind blanked, or she blacked out—she wasn't certain which—and she awoke with a shout.

"Are you all right, dear?" the minister's wife asked.

Rena struggled to sit upright. A moan escaped without her permission as every muscle in her body protested the abrupt move.

The minister's wife frowned and placed a cool hand on her forehead. "You're burning up. You didn't eat or drink anything."

"No." Rena swallowed, heat sweeping her body. She needed water, but she didn't trust those druids. "I have news."

"How? You've been asleep."

Rena didn't have time for explanations. "Please, you must listen."

"Dear really. You need to drink and rest. Unfortunately, we have no medical supplies, but perhaps we can obtain some when they feed us again."

Rena wanted to scream. The minister's wife sounded compliant already. Rena crawled to the nearest wall and used it to claw her way to her feet. "Listen to me," she called above the chatter and murmurs.

Silence fell as gazes turned in her direction.

"Leo has assembled a group of dragons to rescue us. He'll be here soon, and we must be ready."

"Why do we need rescuing?" a tiny woman asked. "We are not in danger."

"Eloise!" a mountain of a man snapped. "We are being held against our will." He glared at Rena. "How do you know they are coming?"

"You wouldn't believe me if I tried to tell you." Rena leaned against the wall, breathing hard. "You need to prepare for a second escape attempt. Grab anything you can use as a weapon."

"Why would the dragons rescue us?" someone called.

Rena gritted her teeth at the need to repeat this reassurance. *Again.* "Leo is a decent man. I mean dragon. If you don't want to accept the dragon's help, fine. But they are coming for me. Also, you should know Leo has sent food and help for your children and elders."

"How...why didn't..." A woman standing near Rena shook her head.

"She's deluded. Look at her face. She's sweating with a fever when it's icy cold in here. Her mind is going."

"Fine, don't believe me," Rena said. "I don't care."

A thump and a clatter came from outside the shed. A door formed in the wall, and Brother Matthew stood there flanked by four red robes. He waved a hand, and the interior brightened. His gaze locked on her.

"You. Come with me. We don't have time to waste."

Rena pushed away from the wall and focused on staying upright. Despite everything, her steps wobbled, and she fell.

"You," Brother Matthew pointed at Mountain Man. "Help her back to her feet. You can come with us."

"No!" a woman wailed.

Mountain Man ignored the woman's protest and stalked to where Rena lay in a heap on the dirt floor. He scooped her up and cradled her in his arms, gentle despite his gruff demeanor.

Brother Matthew backed away, his face impassive while the red robes remained watchful. Rena didn't give them trouble, lying passively in Mountain Man's arms because every part of her hurt so much.

Later, once Leo and David came—that's when she'd exert herself and create trouble for this arrogant Brother Matthew.

CHAPTER 24

Brother Matthew's Confession

D avid's eyes flew open, and he gasped as he sat bolt upright. His heart was beating faster than normal, and he swallowed hard. Rena was hurting, and it was his fault. He paused, took a series of quick breaths, and tried to calm his fear for the woman who meant everything to him.

No, dammit. This wasn't his fault. This entire situation had come about because Brother Matthew and his dragon cohorts were greedy. He still didn't know what they were trying to achieve—Brother Matthew and Telus—but whatever it was, the achievement came to the detriment of the humans they'd kidnapped.

"David." Cherry knocked on the door and stuck her head into his bedroom. "We're getting ready to leave."

"Coming." David slid off the bed and pulled on the pair of borrowed trews. He donned a shirt and a thick woolen jacket before he hurried to join the dragons.

Cherry and Liza had dressed, ready to go, while Joanna stood with Betty.

"Are you sure you should come with us?" David asked, catching Liza's torn glance at her daughter. "It will be hazardous."

"Rena is there, and she's in danger. The druids hurt her. We're going," Liza said, her tone not brooking refusal.

"What she said," Cherry added, her jaw set in determination. "Rena needs us. She'd do the same for either of us."

David glanced at their mates. He could see neither Leo nor Martinos were keen on their mates flying to the monastery, but they weren't willing to order them to remain.

"Are we all clear on the plan?" Leo called to the assembled dragons.

"Yes!" they chorused.

Several of the dragons nodded.

"All right," Leo said. "Off you go with your team leaders. Remember, the red robes and Brother Matthew are dangerous. Approach the other druids with caution. The younger ones who wear the black robes are most likely innocent, but once again, approach with care. Any questions?"

When no one spoke up, their leaders signaled their groups to move.

The thunders flew away in formation. There were four groups, and each one was advancing on the monastery from a different direction. David, Leo, and Martinos intended to land near the new warehouse.

David wasn't sure how this confrontation would go, but he'd do his best to free Rena along with the younger druids who had no part in this fight.

Once Blaze shifted, David clambered up on Blaze's back and settled for the short ride to the monastery. As always before a battle, David's nerves simmered. His mind grew calm, and he centered on what he needed to do. Save Rena from the monsters and help to free the captive humans.

He refused to fail her.

Each of their group bristled with determination, and they had greater numbers. As long as he could hold the red robes at bay, the dragons should handle the rest.

The monastery came into view, and David's instincts picked up a disturbance in the air. Things had worsened since his departure, the imbalance a blight on the hardworking brothers at the monastery.

Everything appeared silent, and that worried him. The kitchen seemed empty. The druids responsible for milking the six cows weren't in the shed. Someone should've released the hens to scratch for bugs in the orchard.

Instead, the cows stood at the gate leading to the milking shed, their low moos of complaint riding on the breeze. The hens clucked in their cage.

David slapped his hand twice on Blaze's neck—a pre-arranged signal for him to land in a different place to that which they'd discussed. David pointed to the orchard, and Leo and Martinos must've communicated back to Blaze because the dragons wheeled in that direction.

Once they landed, David, Liza, and Cherry dismounted from their respective dragons.

"What's wrong?" Liza asked.

"None of the normal activities are taking place." David indicated the restive cows. The enclosed hens. "Something has happened."

"They know we're coming?" Cherry said.

"Yes." David considered their options and straightened his shoulders. "First, let's release anyone held captive in the warehouse. This way." He gestured and skulked through the orchard to the building on the other side. Unlike the last time he'd been here, the warehouse was visible. They approached from the rear and circled the building. It didn't have a door.

"How will we get inside?" Liza asked. "Leo can hear someone within."

David closed his eyes and focused, his hands drawing a series of runes, each one successively faster. When he completed the series, there was absolute silence.

"Wow," Cherry breathed beside him.

David opened his eyes and allowed himself a burst of satisfaction. The entire building had disappeared, leaving only the contents behind.

"By God," a man said, gaping at the dragons. "She told us you'd come, but I didn't believe her."

"Gwenyth." The minister and his wife stepped forward.

Liza darted forward and embraced them. "We don't have much time. We need you to follow Gregorious here. He will lead you to a group of dragons who will help you get to the mansion at the other end of Smoking Isle. You'll be safe there since we have left guards in case of an attack. Did anyone see my sister, Rena?"

"The fierce lass," the minister's wife said. "Yes, the druid in charge took her. She couldn't walk on her own, so he ordered one of our men to carry her."

While they spoke, Leo, Martinos, and Blaze shifted and pulled on clothes.

David stepped forward, and his tattoos sparked to life beneath his clothing. "Do you know where they took her?" He must've looked scary because the woman retreated behind her husband.

"Somewhere inside the monastery. They didn't tell us much," the minister said. "Rena warned us against eating the food or drinking. Most of us followed her advice, so we are in our full state of mind. Those who did eat and drank appear compliant. They will be safe if we stay together."

"Thank you," David said. "Go with Gregorious."

"What do we do now?" Cherry asked. "We need the dragons as backup."

"If Brother Matthew and the red robes think to hide inside the monastery, they should think again." Anger pumped through David. Rena hadn't been able to walk by herself. He tamped down his fury and reversed his rune to return the warehouse to its previous state. "I have a plan. This way."

As David moved toward the main monastery hall, a tingle began at his breastbone. He allowed the sensation to guide him, and as he neared the side of the monastery that housed Brother Matthew's office, his tattoos shimmered brighter and hotter.

"Rena is in Brother Matthew's office." David pictured the walls and rooms and let his hands form the same runes he'd used to dismantle the shed to free the captured humans.

"Wow, David," Liza whispered at his side as a wall dissolved, but the rest of the structure remained intact. "That's a handy trick."

An understatement. His magic seemed much more robust on his return to the monastery. He had his suspicions, and as he came closer to Rena, the answer became clearer. The old myth told to him by Brother Jasper when David first arrived at the monastery held basis in truth. Rena truly was the key to everything, and somehow, Brother Matthew knew this too.

Somehow, Brother Matthew believed he had a way to harness their combined power.

The one thing Brother Matthew hadn't factored into his sneak attack was that David loved Rena. He'd do anything for her. *Anything.* He'd die to save her life, and this time, he had friends at his back who intended to stop the plan the dragons and Brother Matthew had put into motion.

David continued to take down the monastery wall by wall, startling the brothers working in the various offices and partaking in the morning meal. When he reached the communal dining hall, he found the youngest black robes sitting at the tables and staring at their plates. The brown robes and a few yellow robes sat with them. Not one moved on their arrival. David paused and used his senses to search for the source of their predicament. It couldn't be poison since these druids were in a trance. But even as he tried to think what he should do to free them, Rena's presence drew him onward.

"Keep going," Leo murmured at his side. "I'll allocate men to get them to safety. You are certain they're innocent in this scheme?"

"As positive as I can be," David murmured.

"Wait a sec while I issue orders to our team. I don't want you to face the head druid alone," Leo said.

"I'll organize help," Blaze offered. "You go with David as backup."

"Done," Leo said. "Let's move."

Warmth grew in David's chest. Until this moment, he hadn't realized how much he'd missed having friends to talk with and share burdens. Once he moved into the monastery, he hadn't cared about anything except his grief and guilt. Gradually, the harshest of the feelings had faded. Brother Jasper had taken David under his wing, and he'd ended up with a mentor rather than a friend.

Now he had Rena, her sister, and her friend, and by extension, their mates. A team to challenge the head druid.

"This way," David murmured. "I'll dismantle the walls as I go so the dragons can follow us."

Leo trailed him. "Won't the building collapse?"

"Magic at work," David said. "You don't need to know how it works. All you need is confidence."

"Do you sense them?" Leo asked.

"Yes." David raised his hand for quiet. He glided on silent feet, taking care not to kick any pieces of furniture or the like. A door opened at the end of the passage, and Brother Matthew appeared with two red robes at his side. The man carried himself stiffly, tension in the creases on his brow. He appeared years older than when David had last seen him. His expression cleared on seeing David.

"Ah, you're here. Splendid. I thought you'd take action once I captured your key. You always did expose your soft underbelly." He flung out a hand, and a jagged spear of white energy crackled toward David.

David blocked the bolt, freezing the bright light in a jagged shape mid-air. It dropped to the ground and smashed into tiny bits.

His action seemed to please Brother Matthew because the man beamed. "Leave your followers there or I'll take more expansive action."

No. David needed his friends at his back. He ignored Brother Matthew's request and stepped closer. His tattoos flared to life, stronger and hotter than ever before. It was Rena, or rather the two of them together that increased his power. It made him wonder if Rena possessed latent magic, ignited by her visit to Smoking Isle.

Perhaps that was the reason he'd chosen her on the dreamscape—because she possessed the same magic.

An amended plan sprang to life. He'd keep Brother Matthew talking and try to communicate with her incognito.

"I'm here now," David said.

The red robes stood on alert, yet their faces were without expression. Drugged? He wondered where the remaining red robes were lurking.

"What do you want of me?"

"You and the woman will help Telus to power the factory we've established on the mainland."

"What sort of factory?" David asked.

"We manufacture pottery and other useful items, but we imbue them with magic to make those using them susceptible to suggestion. It also aids us in controlling the workforce. They're productive and can work for longer."

David stared at Brother Matthew, shocked by the man's offhanded explanation. His lack of empathy. "Why would you control the workforce?"

"It was Telus's plan. Once we have a foothold on the mainland, we can expand. It's time for the dragons to defeat the humans for the way they treated us."

"You're not a dragon," David said.

"No." Brother Matthew's mind seemed to drift, then he shrugged, determination sliding over his features.

The man was insane. "The humans have weapons. You'll never beat them once they mobilize their armies."

"We have weapons," Brother Matthew warned. "Tell your tame dragons to back off. They can't help you."

"Where's Rena?"

Brother Matthew gestured at the door of his office.

David stalked past the silent red robes and spotted Rena lying on a mat on the floor. He started to go to her, but the red robes barred his progress.

"You will eat this," Brother Matthew stated.

Like hell. "No, I won't."

"I refused too," Rena said. "They forced it down my throat."

Brother Matthew spun around to stare at her, astonishment making him gape. "How is this possible?"

"Check your pot plant. I made myself vomit." Rena twisted her body and pushed to her hands and knees. Slowly, she shoved to her feet and stood. She wavered, but her shoulders were straight, and her raised chin signaled contempt. She radiated challenge.

Brother Matthew snarled, "Stop her."

Anger burned in David as the red robes raised their hands, ready to power a combat spell. The druids were shadows of their former selves, and he sensed they'd lost their humanity. Brother Matthew had transformed them into soldiers who questioned nothing. David dragged in a breath, and magic swirled through him stronger than before.

Rena gasped, and one glance at her told him she felt the power swelling within him. An echo arced back to him, and he smiled, glad his suspicions were correct. Together, he and Rena could control this situation.

"Help me." He sent the message silently to Rena without taking his gaze off the druids. *"Take the right red robe. Make him freeze in position."*

The red robes hurled their magic at them. Since he wasn't certain Rena could do spells, he targeted both red robes. The red robe on the left froze with his hands extended. Halfway through his rune, the lack of completion allowed the red robe's magic to trickle free and disperse.

The second red robe froze too. *Literally.* His entire body turned white as ice crawled over his skin. His face was the final part of him to whiten. A horrendous cracking filled the office, and exclamations of surprise came from behind him. Shock filled David too. Rena possessed as much power as him, and once she refined her control, they'd be a formidable weapon. He knocked aside the concern at so much concentrated power and turned to Brother Matthew.

Rena spoke first. "What else have you got?"

"How did you do that?" Brother Matthew rubbed his eyes and blinked.

"We will not be helping with your crazy plan," Rena snapped, her mouth twisted as she stabbed her finger in the head druid's direction. Fierce and determined even though she teetered unsteadily. Half of her hair was missing, and a bruise covered her swollen jaw. Blue tattoos glowed on her bare arms.

Brother Matthew rocked in place, his eyes shiny and wet. "You must help me," he pleaded.

"Why?" David asked, scrutinizing him.

Sweat beaded on Brother Matthew's face. He released a pained cry. It was as if someone had pushed him, and he took a rapid step forward, his arms flailing. He groaned again, and David took half a step toward him. Rena advanced too. David cried out as a warning filled him. A preternatural sense of danger.

Brother Matthew grabbed Rena and shifted position. An instant later, Brother Matthew held a knife to Rena's throat.

David froze. "You can't escape. You're surrounded. Let Rena

go."

"I'll slit her throat. I have nothing to lose," Brother Matthew spat. His eyes rolled left and right, never coming to a rest on one spot.

"What has Telus got over you?" David stalled for time as he played the angles. "Why are you frightened of him?"

"He has my s-sister. He learned Garnet was my sister after he followed me when I visited her one day. A few weeks later, he came to the monastery and presented me with a proposition." Brother Matthew's hand trembled, and a bead of red appeared at Rena's throat.

David's gaze met Rena's, and she showed no fear or panic. "What was the proposition?"

"He told me he and a group of dragons wanted to explore the opportunities on the mainland, ultimately to take back the freedom we lost when we retreated to the Dragon Isles."

"What did he expect you to do?" The conversation seemed to center the druid, so David continued with his questions.

"Let him and others through the barrier. We'd left a portal because the original dragon families wished an escape route if the isolation didn't work as they'd envisaged."

"The yew grove portal?" David asked.

"Yes," Brother Matthew said.

"Why didn't you refuse?"

"He threatened me. I didn't believe he'd kidnap my s-sister and leave her two young children alone."

Yes, the dialog was calming the man. Perhaps it wasn't too late to talk him down. He'd acted against their principles, but he wasn't happy with his predicament.

"Where is your sister?"

"She's not on Smoking Isle. Telus laughed and told me unless I cooperated, I'd never see her again."

"What happened to the children?"

"I sent them to the other end of Smoking Isle with a servant and her husband. They were happy to visit family and didn't mind taking my n-niece and nephew with them."

"And the red robes. How did you cajole their cooperation?"

"I created the spell to add to the food. It's the same spell I've used on the brothers to cover my actions."

"You've only used it recently, though," David said. "After Brother Jasper died."

"Telus ordered him killed when Jasper refused to do his bidding."

"Did it ever occur to you to ask for help?" Rena gritted out. She twisted and jerked her elbows back into Brother Matthew's ribs. She did it with enough force that he instinctively bent forward. In a flurry of movement, Rena stomped on the top of his foot.

Brother Matthew slashed with the knife and nicked her arm before David jumped the druid. Leo leaped forward to help restrain the man, and once they had possession of the blade, Liza and Cherry darted over to check on Rena. In a trick David had learned during his fighting days, he rendered Brother Matthew unconscious by pinching nerves at the neck. The man crumpled, and David caught him and set him on the floor in a heap.

"How bad is the knife wound?" David asked in a terse voice.

"I'll live, but I feel as if I could sleep for a week."

"I can organize that for you." David had never taken time for himself and his lady, romance and courtship, but retreating to the mainland with Rena sounded like a grand idea.

"What should we do with him?" Leo asked. "And what of the missing red robes? They're powerful and dangerous."

"I'll bind his magic, and we'll lock him in one of the druid's cells until the senior druids decide on his punishment," David said. "As for the red robes, once we find and capture them, we'll detain them until the magical effects subside. When they're clear-headed, the senior brothers will determine the correct reaction."

"Telus forced Brother Matthew to do this," Leo said.

Fury rose in David. "Brother Matthew had options. He could've informed the senior brothers, and they might've stopped this together. He didn't. Instead, his lack of action caused suffering. We saved the village residents in Hissing Isle, but what about those still missing from Smoking Isle? There should be repercussions."

"He was worried about his sister," Rena said. "Give the man a break."

David glared at her, although he didn't put much of his ire

behind the glower. His woman had suffered because of this man, and David wasn't ready to forgive the head druid, no matter his excuses. "Instead of thinking about his fellow druids, the villagers, and the dragons, Brother Matthew put his needs first when he should've done the right thing." He spoke his mind, angry all over again.

There was strength in numbers. If Brother Matthew had shared his problem, this situation might never have occurred. David might've never met Rena. David paused, considering. No, he didn't believe that. Before he'd known of the barrier problem, Rena's pure and enticing turquoise dreamscape strand had drawn him.

Leo nodded at David, his gaze flashing understanding. "You're right. What should we do with the druids?"

"I'm hoping once they eat non-doctored food and drink, they'll regain their normal personalities." David's gaze drifted to Rena. She needed to eat and rest in that order. He strode to her and pressed a gentle kiss to her forehead. Up close, it was easier to see her injuries, and rage pumped through him yet again. Brother Matthew had tortured Rena to save his sister and his own skin. David scooped her into his arms. She relaxed against his chest, and her eyes fluttered closed. A faint smile curved her full lips.

"My hero," she whispered.

"Always," he said gruffly. "I'll always be there when you need me, my sweet cynamone. Your brilliant turquoise ribbon led me to you, and now that I've found you, I'm not letting go."

"But our worlds are so different," she murmured.

"We could straddle two worlds and enjoy the best of both. Rena, cynamone, we have magical powers that combine to create incredible supremacy. I understood tonight what Brother Jasper's hints meant. We are the mythical lock and key, which is part of druid legends. If you want, we can leave here and start a life together in your world, but we are honor-bound to help the druids and, by extension, those who make the Dragon Isles their home. The dragons need the protection of the barrier. You've said it yourself—your world fears what they don't understand. We must protect the innocent and help Leo, Martinos, Blaze and the others to create a better world for the dragons and humans."

"Yes," Rena said simply.

"It would mean we'd need to spend most of our time here on Smoking Isle at first. Once trusted druids take charge, we could spend more time in your world, so you can continue your studies."

Rena chuckled. "I've already agreed. Spending time with you is no hardship, David. You entranced me from the first moment you slipped into my dreams. Our days together in person are a gift. Waking up and cuddling before we start our day. Going to sleep together."

"Making love," he teased.

"All of that." She reached up to stroke his jaw. "I've fallen for my dream man."

"We'll make our plans later," he promised. "Once this is over."

"It's a deal."

A faint tingling zapped through him from their physical connection, not unpleasant but different.

When they left the office, his Rena gasped. He grinned at her astonishment.

"You did this?"

"I did."

"Are you intending to fix Brother Matthew's office?" Rena asked. "Can you repair the building, so it has walls again?"

"Cynamone, that sounds like a challenge." David smiled at her because he could. She was on the same physical plane, and the weight of her in his arms thrilled him.

"Can you do it?"

The teasing in her heartened him. His Rena possessed a powerful spirit, along with courage. "If I construct the correct rune. I am confident since I've practiced this in my days as Brother Jasper's pupil."

"All righty then. Make it so," she instructed with a wave of her hand.

Leo and Martinos guided Brother Matthew from the building, and Cherry and Liza walked either side of the docile red robe.

Still smiling, David set her on her feet. When everyone was clear, he traced the reversal rune with his two hands and fingers, and Rena clapped her hands together on seeing the solid walls form again.

"Neat trick. Are there limitations to your magic?"

"Yes," David said. "Brother Jasper worked with me to write out a series of boundaries. I promised not to do magic to harm or kill another being unless they were trying to kill me. I try to help others. My specialty is medicine and herbs, but since I contacted you, the power behind my magic has increased. Brother Jasper told me the tale of a key and a lock—two who come together for the greater good. I think we are the two chosen."

"I...chosen. Did I kill that red robe?"

"I'm afraid so. He was frozen solid."

"I didn't mean to do it," Rena said. "What if I can't do this? No one asked me if I wanted the role."

"You'll learn to finesse the power. I'll teach you everything I know."

"Incoming dragon," Leo said as a shriek rippled through the sky.

"Who is it?" Martinos asked as they studied the green form arrowing toward them.

Blaze strode outdoors with two other dragons. "All done. Everyone is on their way to Martinos's mansion." He stopped speaking when the dragon roared another ear-splitting bugle. "That's Griffith. What's he doing here?"

CHAPTER 25

That Weasel Dragon

G riffith landed and shifted almost in one action. Something in the younger dragon's expression told David he bore bad news.

"What is it?" Blaze asked.

"Telus, six other dragons, and the red robes hit the village on Smoking Isle again. Before we arrived, the dragons snatched the children and any adults they could find." Griffith turned to Liza and Leo. "Betty took Joanna with her to the village when she went to visit her friends. Betty assumed it would be safe."

"Telus took Joanna?" Liza screeched.

Leo went to her and drew her into his arms.

"Did they hurt anyone?" Rena asked.

"No, the red robes helped the dragons," Griffith said. "At least there was no bloodshed."

"How do you know this?" David asked.

"Two of the boys were playing by the stream and watched the dragons fly over and land. The boys hid, and we found them when Betty didn't arrive back at the mansion as expected."

"Telus has Joanna," Liza whispered. "I hoped she'd be safer here."

"We *will* get her back," Rena said.

"Yeah," Cherry added. "We didn't go through the drama with Tony for some weasel dragon to kidnap her."

David smothered a laugh at Cherry's description. Having seen Telus, he agreed with her assessment.

"Where do we search for her?" Martinos asked. "How do they shift those they capture from here to the mainland? If that's where they've taken them."

"Is anyone guarding the shed?" David asked.

"No," Blaze said. "We didn't think it was necessary."

"Stake out the shed. They might already be there," David said.

"Approach stealthily," Leo instructed when Liza started to hustle. "If they're in the building, we want to take them by surprise."

"They'll be expecting the other humans to be there," Blaze pointed out. "They'll know something has interrupted their plan."

"Not necessarily," Liza commented. "You don't have the easy communication we have on the mainland. If they're working in teams, they might believe everything is going to plan."

"Liza is right. The red robes are necessary to transport humans to the mainland. Split up," David said. "Rena and I will take the front of the building. Martinos, you and Cherry approach from the right side. Blaze, you and Griffith advance from the rear, and Leo and Liza approach from the left."

"They won't have had time to give them food or drink to subdue them," Rena said.

"She's right," Blaze said. "We tipped out the entire water supply and destroyed the leftover food. If they need their captives pliable, they'll have to delay the journey to the mainland."

"If the kids are young, they'll be frightened," Cherry cautioned. "They'll cry and whine. Telus has taken adults thus far, but it's obvious he requires more workers. Some of the children will create problems."

Liza frowned. "I hope Joanna doesn't annoy the dragons with her questions. You know what she's like since she arrived here. She's curious about everything."

"Rena and I should cope with Telus on our own," David said. "You'll hear if we're in trouble. Rena, we'll take out the red robes first. We'll freeze them without turning them to ice."

"What if I muck up?" Rena asked, her voice troubled. "I can barely stand on my own."

Concern flooded David. He wasn't thinking. She needed treatment and rest to heal. "You're right. I wasn't thinking. We can detour to my cell. You can relax there."

"No way. I'm coming with you even if I have to crawl."

"Stubborn woman."

"You should learn this early," Rena said, catching and holding his gaze.

"To me, you are perfect. It's true you're different from my wife and other women I've met in the past, but your bravery, your determination, and the way you protect those you love is inspiring. I believe in you, cynamone. You can do this," David whispered as the others left. "The children are in danger. We can save them if we work together. You are our surprise weapon. Brother Matthew might have warned Telus about me, but he has no idea of your abilities. Let's go." He clasped her hand, the physical touch calming the obvious tension in her and bringing him a wash of contentment. "I'll carry you until we reach a vantage point." He swung her into his arms.

Rena fluttered her lashes at him, a mischievous grin on her lips. "My hero." Her smile faded, her expression turning pensive. "This lock and key thing. Are you positive? You've studied magic for years. Hundreds of years. I'm twenty-three, and although I'm clued in on technology and modern events, magic isn't something I've ever considered. People in my world don't believe in magic. They used to, but times have changed."

"It's true. I've mentioned it before, although now I'm positive. You *are* my key." David reached a small clump of trees bearing bright red flowers and set Rena on her feet.

"Well, I hope you're an excellent teacher, because I need all the help I can get." She shuffled closer to peer around a tree. "No action yet."

"My gut says this location makes the most sense for the dragons' base. They'll be here."

"You know this because of your magic?"

"No, my experience in battle. One, they've brought their captives here before, and two, it's close to the portal."

Rena frowned. "I've been thinking about that. My question is, how do they get the people from Holy Island to the mainland?"

"Perhaps they don't. Have any of you considered that?"

"Excellent point. Smaller population on Holy Island to observe strange comings and goings."

"And it would account for Cherry and Martinos seeing the dragons on Holy—"

A thunder of dragons flew over the hill, and Rena fell silent. David watched the dragons land, and an instant later, six red robes blinked into sight, and with them a group of terrified children and elderly men and women.

Rena took half a step forward before David stayed her.

"Wait until they herd the children and adults inside. If they're contained, they're less likely to get in the way or injured."

Rena peered out from their hiding spot. "Should've given Liza the memo."

"Joanna!" Liza screamed.

"Move, Rena. Just imagine the red robes freezing like a statue. Not quite that firm, though," he added. "Take the three on the right."

"If you say so," Rena said, doubt clear in her tone.

"Cynamone, you can do this. Focus and imagine the outcome you require, and our joint power will work for you."

"Joanna!" Liza screamed again.

David and Rena darted from cover, and David was pleased to see Rena wasn't limping at present. A soldier's exhilaration at the start of a battle. The red robes were watching Telus as he shifted to sneer at Liza. Leo was holding her back, his mouth close to her ear and issuing instructions. The dragons who'd flown in with Telus bore smirks. They were enjoying the entertainment.

Perfect distraction. "Now," David whispered, his fingers rapidly sketching the runes to freeze the red robes. Before he'd even finished the spell, Rena seized the raw power they created together. This time, she managed a light casing of frost around the red robes and two of the dragons, He winced but focused on completing his rune.

The remaining dragon took to the air and headed straight for them. It opened its massive maw and spat a sheet of flames at him and Rena.

She released a startled squeak before focusing her ire on the dragon. Rena muttered something inaudible under her breath and pointed her fingers at the dragon. "Hiyah!"

David made sure the druids on his side had frozen before turning his attention to Rena. His eyes widened as the dragon froze with flames roaring from its mouth. The giant beast was still alive because its eyes blinked, but with its wings out of action, the creature dropped and thumped to the ground. The terrain shook beneath their feet, and an apple tree flattened beneath the creature's weight.

"Holy f-frogs," Rena muttered. "I did not see that coming."

"Me neither." David had doubted he had enough power to contain a dragon, yet Rena had done it without difficulty. It made him realize if Brother Matthew had captured David and Rena and discovered a way to control them, they'd become an effective weapon. Scary thought. He refused to become anyone's deterrent. He and Rena needed to take care of whom they trusted.

"Mummy!" a child shouted, an edge of panic to the shriek.

David's head snapped around to watch Joanna, Rena's niece, race from the warehouse. Before she could reach her mother, Telus seized the child. Joanna wriggled and screamed.

"I want Mum—"

Telus's hard slap stopped Joanna mid-sentence. David sucked in a hasty breath, every muscle tensing.

Rena swore under her breath, unfamiliar words uttered in a

vicious tone. "She's a child."

Triumph filled Telus as he smirked at them. "Ah! The lock and key. You'll be coming with me."

"When hell freezes over," Rena muttered.

David agreed with her sentiment.

"I'll have no trouble in killing a human child," Telus said.

Telus wasn't a dragon who made threats. David believed he'd kill Joanna without raising a sweat.

"Release the child, and Rena and I will obey you."

"Do you think I'm stupid? The pair of you will come with me. Unfreeze my convoy."

"Don't trust him," Liza shouted.

David tensed, and he sensed Rena's fury along with the acrid anger wafting off Leo and Martinos. The two dragons were poised to act the instant Telus let down his guard. As David waited, Blaze landed on the warehouse with a thump and scanned the scene.

"You're surrounded. You can't go anywhere, and your red robes and dragons can't help you," David called.

In reply, Telus yanked Joanna's hair. Joanna yelled and wrenched free from Telus's grip. Then she whirled and struck Telus in the balls with her fists, putting all her force behind the punch. He gave a pained shout and fell to his knees.

Joanna kicked him in the ribs. "You're a mean dragon, and I don't like you."

Leo was there in a flash, scooping up Joanna before she could assault Telus again, and taking her to Liza. Blaze flew down from the rooftop and stood over Telus as he writhed on the ground.

Martinos sprang to help Blaze with Telus while Cherry and Rena rushed to Liza.

David called for everyone to exit the warehouse. "It's safe now. We'll take you home."

"Are the dragons and red robes dead, or can you bring them back to life?" Leo murmured.

"Some are dead. The others, I can revive. I think. Wait until the captives are safe, and I'll see what I can do." David stood back as the children poured from the warehouse. Several elderly men and women hobbled after them, their expressions wary.

"Is it safe?" one man called in a rusty voice.

"It is," David promised.

The man glanced around, apprehension digging into his craggy features. "I don't even understand how we're here. We were in the village, and the next, we were here."

"We'll get you home soon," David promised.

"I'm hungry," a little boy whined.

"We can fix that." David waited until Blaze, Martinos, and Leo escorted Telus away before smiling at the children. "Come to the dining room. We'll ask the cooks to give us bread and cheese."

"Yay!" another little boy cried.

"Follow me." David herded the children and the older villagers toward the dining room.

David wasn't sure what he'd find when he entered the dining room. Soft chatter and a rich chuckle greeted him, and he relaxed. It appeared the food they were serving was hearty fare and no longer caused side effects.

"Brother David. Well met," Brother Peter hailed him. "Are you collecting waifs and strays?"

"Not exactly. Brother Peter, could you arrange food for these children and their minders? They inform me they're hungry."

"Of course, I will," Brother Peter said with a broad grin of welcome. His friendly wave relaxed the more cautious amongst them.

As David ushered the children and the elderly villagers toward the dining room, Rena approached a red robe. His skin was a weird white color. She shuddered and averted her gaze, almost tripping over the tail of the dragon she'd frozen. Guilt swept through her. This strange power she and David generated between them was scary and not to be taken lightly. She didn't want to hurt others. Perhaps she could get rid of it...

"Who taught Joanna to do that?" Liza planted her hands on her hips, her glower fixed on her. Her sister bared her teeth, and a vein twitched in her jaw.

Uh-oh. Rena hustled over to join her sister and Cherry. "Ah, it was me. But in my defense, I told her only to do it if her life was in danger. I explained she mustn't do it to the boys at school, but she could do it if someone attacked her."

Liza's expression didn't shift, so Rena continued to talk fast.

"I suggested if a man grabbed her, she had to act decisively and do it right the first time. She wouldn't get another chance. I'm sorry, okay? It never occurred to me she'd do that to a dragon."

"He pulled my hair." Joanna placed her hands on her hips, mirroring her mother.

Liza's entire posture softened. "Thank you." She hugged Rena hard. "You helped her to save herself. You and Cherry have gone beyond the friend and sister code with Joanna. If it weren't for you, Tony would have her or that disgusting weasel dragon."

"See," Cherry said. "I told you Telus resembled a weasel."

Joanna's stomach grumbled loudly enough to stop the conversation. "I'm hungry," she announced.

Liza laughed. "Just this once I excuse your appalling manners. Come on. We'll find the others and feed you."

David returned, pausing to speak with Liza and Joanna, before continuing to join Rena. Leo strolled over to them.

"Telus?" Rena asked.

"We locked him in the cell next to Brother Matthew while we discuss what to do with them," Leo said. "Telus informed us we need him to find the humans they'd taken."

"No, we don't." David turned toward the dining room.

Rena limped after him. "Wait for me."

He backtracked to join her. Before he spoke, he scooped her into his arms. "Sorry, my cynamone. I'm so angry with Telus, I stopped considering you."

"Why didn't you make a deal with him? We're only guessing the missing humans are on Holy Island. They could be anywhere."

"My gut says they are there. If they're not, we'll widen our search until we can save them." David sighed and bent his head to kiss the tip of her nose. Affection filled the action, and she grinned at him, her heart beating a little faster.

"Excellent. I hate the notion of them suffering more under Telus's tyranny. We must locate them as soon as possible."

"We will. I promise."

Rena cuddled against his chest. "You know, I thought I was going crazy when you kept popping into my dreams. I fell for you then with your silken caresses and sexy kisses. Making love with you in my dreams seemed so real."

"It was. Everything about us is genuine. My feelings for you—certainly. Meeting you, Rena, shoved me out of the despondent rut I'd fallen into. You've made me appreciate the small things too. These days when I walk through the garden, I get a whiff of the peppery herbs and the sweet scent of the flowers and spices. I smell your sweet perfume." He nuzzled her cheek. "I feel your weight in my arms, and it makes me happy. Happier than I've been for years."

"Me too, but I'm scared as hell about what I can do by focusing my mind and pointing my fingers. To have that much power—the ability to kill someone scares the bejeebers out of me."

"I will help you to understand and control your magic. This, too, is a promise."

Rena frowned as she considered the possibilities. "I do want to continue my studies."

"I understand," David said instantly. "I want you to, but I'm needed here, at least for a short time. Brother Matthew has created a colossal problem by overextending and abusing his position as teacher and mentor."

"Aren't you a junior druid?"

David laughed. "I am a junior, but I can't walk away from this mess. It wouldn't be right."

Rena considered his words and nodded. "I want to stay with you, but your life is different. I don't expect a frantic nightlife." She held up her hand when he started to speak. "But this is like a foreign country. Holy frogs, it *is* a strange place. I still can't get my head around how you age so slowly here."

David sat Rena on a chair and squatted to examine her feet. He hissed as he surveyed the soles. "How are you even standing? Who did this? One of the dragons?"

"Brother Matthew wanted me to call you here," Rena said.

"Selfish bastard. He could've done the right thing. The other brothers would have aided him. I would've helped him, but he threw in his lot with Telus. Wait here while I gather medical supplies. I need to check on our frozen dragons and druids too."

Rena grimaced at the reminder of what they'd done, guilt popping to life again. She hoped she hadn't killed that dragon even though it had tried to murder her.

Liza and Cherry arrived while David was away.

"Where's David?" Liza asked.

"He's gone to get supplies to treat my feet, and he's inspecting the druids and dragons we froze."

Cherry brushed back Rena's hair. "Would you like me to trim your hair and even it up for you?"

"How bad is it? I haven't seen a mirror for days."

Liza wrinkled her nose. "It's not your best look. Is your scalp burned?"

"It was tender at first, but it feels fine now."

"I wonder if David has a pair of scissors," Cherry said. "I can't get over the fact life here is like something I read in the pages of one of my history novels."

David strode back into the room and grinned at Rena. "Yes, we have scissors. I'll ask Brother Peter if he'll mind retrieving a pair for us when he arrives with the bowl of warm water. A warning, he's excited to meet you, and he'll head back to his friends for a gossip session."

Rena patted her chest. She grinned and fluttered her lashes at David. "What? You have gossip here? Never say it's so."

David rolled his eyes. "You wait until you meet the brothers. Ah! Brother Peter. Come and meet Rena, her sister, and their friend."

A slender man with a bird's nest of hair walked toward them with eager steps and curiosity blazing in his narrow face. Once he was nearer, Rena saw he was young with several pimples on his chin.

"Brother Peter, this is Rena, her sister, Liza, and their friend, Cherry," David said. "Please set the water bowl here." Once Brother Peter followed David's instructions, David lifted her feet and positioned the bowl under them. He indicated she should set her feet in the warm water, and she hissed at the surge of pain on contact. A medicinal scent wafted upward, and she noted a few green leaves floating on the surface.

"Thank you, Brother Peter. Can you ask the brother in charge of the kitchen today to save food for us, please? Tell him we'll be around half an hour. Oh, and could you bring us a pair of scissors before you dine?"

"I have a pair with my tools." Brother Peter pulled out a black pouch and opened it to reveal a variety of tools.

"Awesome." Cherry held out her hand.

Brother Peter stared at her as if she was an exotic bird.

"Brother Peter?" Cherry asked.

"You have red hair," he blurted. His face flushed. "I've never seen red hair before. It looks as if you're kissed by sunshine."

"Thank you," Cherry said. "That's a lovely thing to say."

"Are you flirting with my mate?" Martinos asked from the doorway.

"No. No, I wouldn't," Brother Peter said. "S-she has red hair. It's pretty."

The expression on Martinos's face softened, and Rena hid her smile.

Martinos loved her friend. It was easy to read his expression, and Rena was so pleased for Cherry. Her gaze went to Leo and Liza, who were murmuring together. Joanna's hand was clutched firmly in Leo's. She tugged at it, and Leo crouched to listen to her. He glanced at Liza, and she nodded and escorted Joanna from the room. Her sister had found a wonderful man too. They were taking the changes in their stride, and that's what she should also do. Returning to the mainland with little to no control over her magic made no sense. It could be dangerous, but she hated to disappoint her father when he'd helped to pay for her university course.

"Liza," Rena said on her sister's return. "Do you think Dad would be angry with me if I stayed here? I need to learn to control my magic, and I can't do that if I return to university."

"Could you do your course via correspondence?" Cherry asked. "One of my customers studied by correspondence because they had to travel so much for their job. They did their lessons online, and once a year, they went to the university for in-person workshops. That's an option if your computer works here."

"If I can't do that here, I could on Holy Island, and that's just a short hop away," Rena said, her smile broad now that an answer had presented itself. "Thank you, Cherry. I was struggling with what to do. I should be able to transfer from the university in Edinburgh to one that allows an online course."

"Let me doctor those feet again," David said. "I intend to meet with the senior druids and explain the situation. Apart from the red robes, none of them understand what has been happening under their noses."

"Will they listen to you?" Rena asked.

David made a huffing sound. "They're about to discover the junior brother they accused of lacking ambition is more capable and talented than most of them. It will also surprise them to learn the myth of the lock and the key holds elements of truth."

Rena jerked, the sudden move sending a wave of water over the lip of the bowl. "You're dragging me into druid politics?"

"Hell, yes," David said. "It'll be necessary because they won't believe me. We'll have to give them proof before I can win them over."

"What do you intend to do?" Cherry asked.

"Brother Colin, the second-in-command, is a decent man, and the others respect him."

Rena winced when David washed a tender portion of her heel.

"Can't you magic them better?" Liza asked.

"I can treat the symptoms, but it's better if they heal naturally.

I use magic in conjunction with normal actions, but we should never rely solely on magic. It's why the junior druids toil in the gardens and kitchens and serve the senior druids," David said. "Brother Jasper always told me there is value in honest work."

"My mother taught me that." Liza smiled, her grin misty and full of memories. "It's something I try to instill in my daughter. I teach her to keep her shoes clean and pick up her clothes. Small things, but as she gets older, I'll add more chores."

"Back to the whole lock and key thing," Rena said. "Surely you don't expect me to perform magic for the druids' benefit? You saw what happened to those poor red robes and the dragons I froze."

"Ah, I have a plan for that," David said. "For the demonstration and proving to them you are the key to my lock, I'll light something on fire, and you can freeze it with your magic. Simple."

"Huh." Doubt tugged at Rena. "Don't get too cocky. There is nothing simple about this. And another thing—how do your brothers feel about women invading their home?"

"Rena has a point." Liza gazed left and right, her eyes wide and curious. "I haven't noticed a surplus of women around here."

"We need change," David said without a blink. "The brothers need a shakeup before we move into the future. I think part of the problem is we have changed little in hundreds of years. Not since we druids formed the barrier to protect the Dragon Isles."

"David is right," Leo said as he and Martinos entered the room.

"We dragons haven't changed. We continue to do the same

things as our parents and grandparents," Martinos said. "Perhaps that is why Telus and his followers sought to break the barrier."

"I've said it before, and I'll say it again," Rena warned. "Humans on the mainland are not ready to deal with dragons. They will destroy the Dragon Isles if those in charge learn of their existence. You must move slowly and with caution. Involve everyone here with your decisions and explain the reasoning behind them, so you don't end up with dissent. Maybe improve life for those here by introducing labor-saving ways and improving the lot of humans."

Blaze and Griffith had joined them while Rena was having her rant, and when she finished, each of the dragons bore thoughtful expressions.

"We will heed your advice," Leo said.

Blaze grimaced. "I hope Sasha is safe."

"Despite Mother and Father treating Sasha as a child, our sister is clever and adaptable," Griffith said. "We shouldn't worry."

Blaze shrugged. "I pray you're right."

"All done," David lifted her feet out of the bowl one at a time and dried them carefully. "I have salve to place on your wounds before I wrap your feet."

"Thank you," Rena said. "Who is guarding Brother Matthew and Telus?"

"I left four of my men," Blaze said. "But I'd feel better once we can bind Telus's dragon. I don't trust him."

"I'll check the red robes to see if they've regathered their wits.

They'll have the spell at their fingertips, while if I do the binding, it will take me time to research." David finished wrapping Rena's feet and stood. "I'll check on the red robes and the other druids now."

Before he could leave, shouts came from outside. A dragon shifter burst through the door.

"Fire!" he shouted. "That bloody dragon set the place on fire before we could stop him."

"Stay here," David said to Rena, his gaze going to Cherry and Liza. When Rena didn't move, David and the dragons sprinted outside.

Liza sniffed. "I presume they're running to the fire instead of away from it."

"I hate not knowing what is going on," Cherry muttered.

The three women shared a glance, and without speaking, Cherry and Liza went to Rena's sides. They helped Rena hobble from the room and outside.

A vast cloud of smoke rose from the buildings to their right. Flames licked along the roof of a low squat building.

"My guess is that way," Liza said, tongue-in-cheek.

Liza and Cherry helped Rena to limp along the footpath toward the burning building. Dragons and druids worked together with a bucket line to put out the fire.

"Don't they have hoses here?" Rena asked, shocked by the inefficient firefighting.

Liza shrugged. "I guess not. You'd think dragons would know better."

"We should help," Cherry said. "They're short of people on the second line.

As one, the women stepped forward. The druids hesitated when they joined the line, but each of the women showed they wanted to pull their weight.

It was over half an hour later when the flames died back and the smoke dispersed. Rena's eyes were tired and gritty, and she suspected she looked as bad as Liza and Cherry. Her feet were throbbing anew, and her face and arms felt gritty while fatigue had her longing for a flat surface.

Up ahead, David, Leo, Martinos, and Blaze threw their last buckets of water before disappearing inside the building.

"What happened?" Liza asked the dragon in front of her in the waterline.

"Brother Matthew shouted he'd tell David what he wanted to know. Telus told him to shut up, but when the druid continued shouting for David, Telus lost his temper. Before we could stop him, he breathed flames over Brother Matthew. I was outside, getting the two prisoners a bucket of water each. I could hear the shouts and what they were saying."

Cherry stepped closer, leaving Rena to wobble until Cherry grabbed her arm in support.

"What happened next?" Rena asked.

"Telus set Brother Matthew on fire. His robe caught, and flames covered him before we could unlock the door and put out the fire. The next thing, the entire building caught, and Telus cackled like a madman the entire time. The dragon is a loose cannon with no morals. He disgusts me. He heard Brother Matthew's screams and didn't care."

"Is Brother Matthew all right?" Rena asked. The druid was a moron, but that didn't mean he deserved to suffer at Telus's hands.

"He's dead. The other druid—the young one in the black robe spoke to him before he passed."

Shouts came from the half-burned building, followed by a maniacal chortle that made the hair at the back of Rena's neck stand on end.

Two red robes rushed into the building while Leo, Martinos, and Blaze exited.

"What's happened?" Cherry asked.

"Telus is crazy," Leo said. "He set Brother Matthew alight and laughed while the druid burned." He shuddered, lines of distress digging into his features. "I've never seen..." He trailed off, unable to vocalize his feelings.

"He wanted to rule the Dragon Isles," Liza said.

"No, his actual plan was to claw back the position the dragons used to have on the mainland. What he didn't consider was the progress of the human race. He envisioned snapping his fingers and everything falling into place for him," Leo said. "When I was a child, I tried to avoid him. He was cruel to the servants, and those he considered inferior. The best thing I ever did was listen to the castle cook and the old dragon who taught me to create beautiful jewelry. They told me to leave and seek my way in the world, to be accountable to no one but myself. I shudder to think what might have happened if I'd stayed at the castle."

Liza went to Leo and squeezed his hand. Rena didn't have to see her sister to know she had tears in her eyes because emotion welled up in her too. Leo was an exceptional dragon, given those who'd had a hand in his upbringing.

"I want to see Brother Matthew." Rena had no liking for the man or the way he'd tortured her, but she wanted to see him.

"Rena, I don't think—" Blaze started.

"I want to spit in Telus's face," Liza said.

The three women, as one, stepped forward.

"We'll all go," Cherry said. "I'm lining up behind Liza. I want to see the boogie ghost standing behind bars."

Without a word, Leo stepped back to allow them to pass before falling in behind.

Martinos ushered Cherry forward, his protective hand on her shoulder. "I understand what Liza means. Telus sidetracked my fate too. I have no sympathy for him."

The smell as they entered the cells was indescribable. Smoke, charred wood, and another stench that Rena didn't want to identify.

David stood in front of Telus's cell. His hands were on his hips while Telus wore a smug grin.

"What's wrong?" Rena asked, going straight to David.

Tension radiated from him while the two red robes standing nearby were relaxed and serene. Rena did a double-take since every time she'd spotted a red robe, their features had been scarily blank. These two gave off more friendly vibes. Liza and Cherry were whispering with Martinos and Leo, their gazes also on the red robes. David had reversed whatever Brother Matthew had done to control the druids.

"Telus is refusing to tell me where he has hidden the missing villagers. He informs me they have lowborn dragons too." Without taking his gaze off Telus, David said, "The truth spell, if you please."

Immediately, the two red robes began a chant. Telus stiffened, and his eyes rolled. Rena found it interesting the red robes never hesitated to follow David's order. He had no power over them, but they appeared happy with the status quo.

Several minutes later, Telus stopped twitching, and the stiffness leached from his muscles. He glared at David as if daring him to do his worst.

CHAPTER 26

The Truth at Last

David took a deep breath. He had to do this interrogation right since Telus had hurt many—humans and dragons. The dragon had murdered Brother Matthew to stop the man from blabbing, but Telus had made a mistake. He'd never fathomed a truth spell since they seldom used them at the monastery. They'd had no need. Until now.

David straightened his shoulders and channeled the soldier he'd tucked away in a hidden corner of his mind. "What is your name?"

"Telus Caireall, the oldest son of Percius Caireall. Telus, The Organized. Telus, The Instigator."

"Who is Percius Caireall?" David ignored the whispers from

behind him and focused on Telus. This spell didn't always treat the recipients favorably, which was why the druids seldom used it.

"A distant cousin to the ruling clan. The current ruler's ancestors robbed my branch of the family of the wealth and standing that should've been theirs. They cheated me of my birthright."

So Telus had played the long game and allowed his family's bitterness to set him on the path of revenge. David had met knights of a similar caliber during the Crusades, and he hadn't had much sympathy for them either.

"Who did you involve in your plan?"

"Nandag, The Strongminded. Russays, The Magnificent. Nemyr, The Scary. Goticranth, Eater of Bunnies. Qille, The Taker of Life. Qille and her family didn't see my end goal." Telus continued listing names, many of whom were lesser nobles on Hissing and Smoking Isles. They'd stayed away from recruiting on Perfume Isle, or they'd received a rebuff.

When Telus finished, David asked, "Where are the others?"

"On Holy Island. We took over a farm and established our base there." Telus pursed his lips. He paused, and his eyes rolled back to give David a glimpse of his dragon. He was fighting the spell.

David hurriedly continued his questioning. "What do you have your prisoners doing on Holy Island?"

Telus firmed his lips, but words burst from him without his volition. "Some are making drinking vessels while others are making more of the drug we developed with Brother Matthew's help."

David frowned. "What is your plan for the drinking vessels and the drug?"

"We doctor the drinking vessels with the drug to make humans pliable. We intended to take over one sector at a time."

"What would happen if the humans washed the drinking vessels before they used them?"

"Nothing," Telus said a trifle smugly. "The drug coats the surface and remains for months. Any human who drinks from them receives a dose. A single vessel infects many humans, so we focused our efforts on pubs and the food industry."

Not an awful plan. It was a peaceful and surefire way of spreading the drug and gaining control. "How do you distribute the drinking vessels?"

"We have a team of twenty dragons. At each place they visit, they leave a complimentary box of vessels. They inform the business owners if they're interested in obtaining more, they can call the number on the card inside the box. Otherwise, they are welcome to keep the goods for free. It has worked well. We have received dozens of orders to date."

"What did you intend to do after the drug wore off in six months?"

"We have developed an addictive sweet since the dwellers on the mainland hunger for sugar. We intend to issue complimentary packets. Dissenters will fall for another of our plans. It won't matter. We will overcome the humans and rule the land again. Imagine dragons soaring over our homelands once more. Free. Unfettered. In charge." His golden eyes glittered with triumph and malice and a hint of dragon. "It's time for our revenge to come to pass."

Disgust filled David. Telus hadn't hesitated to use innocents or corrupt those weak-minded fools who'd thrown in their lot with him.

"Why did you want my land?" Leo asked.

"Ah yes, Leonidas, Champion of the Skies, and pain in my arse. Your land sits closest to the mainland. If you'd accepted our agent's offer to sell your land, the monastery wouldn't have become involved in my plan."

"You would've needed the barrier to come down," David said.

"Oh, didn't Brother Matthew tell you? His ability to control the barrier has become fickle. Your red robes managed to maintain the barrier for *most* of the time, and their repelling spell kept away the curious humans. He was most frustrated. Only a few days ago, he discovered Brother Jasper had developed a way to divert your magic to the barrier. Once Brother Jasper died, Brother Matthew's problems worsened while making our way easier." Telus's gaze went to Rena, and he sneered. "Brother Matthew intended to control you and the human. He called you the lock and key and was confident his kingdom would become secure once he had you in his grasp."

David tried to hide his reaction and suspected he failed because Telus cackled.

"Brother Jasper wrote of his plans in the diary Brother Matthew found in the library."

"How did you blackmail Brother Matthew?"

"I have his wife. He'd hustled his children to safety, but their location was no secret. I could've grabbed them on a whim."

His wife and children. While the druids didn't forbid marriage, it wasn't typical either. Some more conservative senior druids might have voted Brother Matthew out of his position.

"You can't stop my plan," Telus said. "We've distributed hundreds, nay, thousands of the drinking vessels to the mainland. Our agents have supplies of the sweets and intend to give them to charities. I believe charities search for ways to collect money, and humans enjoy making donations."

"Do we have other questions?" David asked, sickened by the dragon.

"My brothers," Leo said.

"Don't you mean cousins?" Telus asked with a sickly sweet smile.

"My cousins," Leo gritted out. "What were your intentions for them?"

"Kill them off one by one. I do enjoy a stealthy poisoning. So delicious watching the gradual decline and the recipient's suffering. My direct family line is the true heirs of Hissing Island," Telus boomed. Spittle flew from his mouth, and his eyes flashed dragon. "Not the heir apparent Russays and not you, the deposed bastard."

As David listened, his anger grew. This dragon had caused pain for many people, and he held not a shred of regret for the lives lost, the humans he'd placed in slavery. He'd killed Brother Matthew, but not before Brother Matthew had whispered his apologies and begged David to help his family. He would because Brother Matthew's wife and children were the innocents in this travesty. Besides, Brother Matthew had given David the whereabouts of his diary and Brother Jasper's missing one. Once he'd found himself out of his depth, Brother Matthew had recorded everything.

David liked to think Brother Matthew had wanted to atone for his sins.

"What will you do with me?" Telus asked, his crazy-tinged smile, giving David the creeps. "With me gone, my plan won't stop. Not immediately. That is the beauty of it. Russays will continue because he's greedy for power. He knows Leonidas could issue a challenge and win, but he'll go down fighting or lose face."

"No, he won't," Leo said in a hard voice. "Russays is in the dungeon, and we will try him for his crimes, as we will you."

David lashed Telus with a glare rather than the whip of magic that tingled for freedom. "We will bind your dragon, as you arranged for the druids to restrict Martinos's beast, and you will spend the rest of your life in the dungeon."

"No." Telus projected confidence. "That won't happen."

David stared, attempting to read the dragon's mind. How did he think he'd escape punishment? Murdering Brother Matthew was only his latest crime. To get to his goal, hundreds of others had suffered, and those who stood in his way had died. As David opened his mouth to tell Telus he was deluded, the man yanked a tiny dressing off his arm. David glimpsed a bright orange pill before Telus shoved it into his mouth.

Telus straightened his shoulders and eyed David with amusement. "I truly thought it was my time to move, but I hadn't considered Leo might find a group who'd help him. S-should have c-consid-considered that. I w-win," he slurred.

Telus's body rocked from side to side, and orange froth poured from his mouth. It dribbled down his chin and plopped to the floor, sizzling on contact.

"God's bones," David shouted. When he couldn't find the cell keys, he cried for the guards. Telus fell, his body convulsing, and even more of that orange foam ran from his mouth. David studied the lock and formed a rune. He wasn't sure if it'd work but was gratified when the lock clicked and the door opened at his touch.

"What happened?" Martinos asked.

"Poison." David kicked himself for not searching Telus. The dragons had hunted for weapons, but none of them would've imagined poison. God's bones, he hadn't either. "I assumed him too arrogant to commit suicide."

Telus cackled, the sharp sound raising goosebumps on David's arms. "I w-win."

"Dying isn't winning, old dragon," Leo snarled, showing a flash of sharp teeth. "Where's the antidote? You always have a plan."

"T-too late." Telus convulsed, his sharp shriek of pain resounding in the cell. His body bowed. He issued a groan and stilled, his mouth falling slack.

"What did he use?" Martinos asked. "And what's that smell?"

"I believe it's the composition of death," David said. "From memory, Brother Jasper told me of a man who died from the death poison. It's rare, but then Telus seems to have perfected the art of poisoning."

"Is he dead?" Leo asked.

David stooped beside Telus and pressed a finger to the man's neck, just below his jawline. No pulse. David wrinkled his nose at the stench. It was the orange froth that reeked. He rose. "He's dead. I'll ask the junior druids to clear the cell."

"OMG," Rena cried. "What is the gross smell?"

"What happened?" Cherry asked.

Liza stared at Telus. "Is he dead?"

"Yes," David said. "He took poison, which is the smell."

"What do you do with your dead?" Rena asked.

"We build a funeral pyre and burn them," Leo replied.

David spared a glance for Telus and felt no pity at the dragon's death. "Burning him seems the best solution."

"A recommendation," Rena said. "Since the dormitory has already suffered at Telus's hand, why don't you set him on fire here, then clear the area later and build a more modern structure for the younger druids?"

"The block is far enough away from the main part of the monastery," Leo said. "You could use the warehouse as temporary accommodation for your youngest druids. I can help with the design of the new building."

"You should see his home in the mountains." Liza beamed. "It's gorgeous with running water and a few mod cons."

David nodded in agreement. "That sounds perfect. The junior druids would appreciate new quarters. It's cold sleeping in the current cells."

A red robe appeared in the doorway, and Rena and his friends froze.

"Are they safe now?" Leo asked in an urgent undertone.

"I have interviewed each of the red robes. There are two unaccounted for, and I believe they are on Holy Island. Brother Herbert," David said to the new arrival. "We intend to destroy the dormitory and burn Telus. Could you and your fellow red robes power a protective barrier between here and the community rooms and do a cleansing of the site once the fire is out?"

"Certainly, Brother David," Brother Herbert said in a pleasant voice. "I shall arrange it posthaste."

Once Brother Herbert had departed, Rena pulled a face. "Those red robes give me the willies."

"Right there with you." Liza stared in the direction the red robe had departed.

"Brother Matthew bespelled them," David said. "They weren't to blame for their behavior."

"Huh!" Cherry said, full of indignation. "You didn't have roots wriggling from the ground to capture you or enormous boulders attempting to crush you. I reserve judgment on those red robes."

David laughed, the sound coming from deep in his belly. It felt satisfying to share amusement because he hadn't had much to cheer him since he'd arrived at the monastery.

"Who will run the monastery now?" Martinos asked.

"The brothers will vote," David said. "I assume Brother Colin, the current second-in-command, will take over leadership. Tomorrow, we will start our search for the missing. Holy Island is small. I doubt the search will take long. Other than that, my next task is to ensure the barrier works correctly. Once we sort ourselves out at the monastery, I believe we should meet with the head dragons from each island. It's time to set up safeguards to enable all our residents to prosper. Together, we'll decide on rules for crossing the barrier and under what conditions."

"What of Telus's men who are hawking the drinking vessels and sweets?" Leo asked.

"Once we locate the premises, I'm hoping we'll be able to pick off Telus's salespeople as they return to base," David said.

"That makes sense," Martinos agreed. "Better to let them come to us."

"Exactly. We'll investigate the extent of the problem on the mainland later. Cherry, Rena, and Liza can guide us there while I'll attempt to find a spell to reverse the vessels' effects," David said.

Rena rubbed her tummy. "It's getting late, and I'm starving."

"You shouldn't be standing on your injured feet," David chided.

"I don't know what was in the ointment you used, but my feet feel much better," Rena said.

As always, her irrepressible spirit drew him, and David gravitated to her. He slung his arm around her shoulders and savored her weight at his side. "We can eat as soon as we set the funeral pyre."

"We have to tote wood?" Rena asked in clear dismay.

"No." David gestured at his friends. "Please stand back." He closed his eyes to center his mind and sketched a rune with his fingers. An instant later, firewood blinked into sight. Small combustible branches first, then more substantial pieces on the outside.

Once the stack was high enough, David gestured at Leo and Martinos. "Would you do the honors?"

"One side each," Leo said to Martinos.

With a nod, both men positioned themselves.

Leo gestured everyone outside. "Martinos and I don't want

anyone to get hurt."

The fire lighting took seconds, and they didn't even bother to shift. Soon the two dragons strode from the burning dormitory. Their group stood in silence as the fire expanded and engulfed the entire building. Sparks shot into the sky, and puffs of black smoke drifted away in the breeze.

"It's a sad ending to Brother Matthew," Liza said.

David didn't reply, his opinion unchanged. Brother Matthew should've confessed to the senior brothers. While some brothers might've disapproved of a wife and children, the head druid would still be alive with his loved ones, which brought David to the next point. He refused to part from Rena, so he needed to follow his own advice and front up to the seniors.

Several of the junior druids remained in situ in case of problems or wind shifts.

David guided Rena away from the burning building. "We'll organize sleeping quarters for everyone, then I must speak with Brother Colin, the second-in-command. I won't be long."

With the bedrooms allocated, David paused to kiss Rena, and he took his time, his lips moving slowly against hers. His eyes fluttered closed as he fell into the kiss. He caressed her back and slid his hands down to cup her buttocks, drawing her close enough for her to experience his need.

"This is so much better when we're truly together," she whispered.

"Yes." He dived in for another taste, savoring the press of her breasts against his chest. Her softness. "I wish I didn't have to go."

"I'll be here waiting for you."

David leaned his forehead against hers. "I've missed you when you're not with me. Worried, especially after the dragons abducted you."

"I've missed you, too." Rena's smile brightened the room and radiated her joy in his company. She made him feel ten-foot-tall and capable of anything. Rena never tried to sway him with feminine tears, and although a hint of disloyalty crept into him, he enjoyed this difference between Rena and his wife. Tearful farewells and hand-wringing had never sat well with him. Part of his guilt, he realized, had been because his wife's protestations had come true. During their last parting, she'd wailed they'd never see each other again. The truth.

"Rest," he urged, shaking himself free of the past. It was time he focused on the future. Their future. "I suspect the older druids will eject me from the monastery once they learn I want to stay with you."

"If they do, they're short-sighted," Rena said. "You've saved a lot of people and helped to capture Telus and Brother Matthew. There's no telling how things would've ended if we hadn't stopped them. Do the other brothers understand this? The fact that Brother Matthew used them to do his dirty work. He drugged them until they were zombies."

"Do I want to hear of zombies?"

"Mainland culture. I can't wait to show you and experience my world through your eyes." Rena chuckled, her hearty laughter drawing an answering lightness in David.

"I don't think the druids understand the lengths Brother Matthew went to in order to protect his secrets. His wife and children and his lucrative position at the monastery." David paused in the doorway. "Before you go to sleep, take the bindings off your feet and apply more of the ointment." He produced the jar from his pocket and handed it to her. "See you later."

Unwilling to leave her, but knowing he had to, he stole another quick kiss before he departed the guest room.

David found the senior druids in the private room where they relaxed between duties. Actually, their furious shouts and squabbling rippled from the room in greeting. For a shocked moment, he watched a red robe and a blue robe grapple together.

Brother Colin, the second-in-command, tried to tear them apart and ended up falling on his arse for his trouble.

David's brows rose. *Idiots.* They needed someone to shake them from their stupor, and he was the man for the task.

"What is this kafuffle?" he thundered.

Silence fell, and such was the brothers' agitation, not one of them questioned him or demanded to learn why he, a junior druid, dared to enter their private room.

Chaos at the Monastery

David advanced in long strides. "Please take a seat. I wish to inform you of everything that has happened at the monastery."

"Is it true Brother Matthew is dead?" a blue robe asked.

"Yes." David explained what had happened to Brother Matthew, the mess he'd involved himself and the red robes, and by default, the entire monastery. He told them of his part, how he'd met Rena, how something about her had increased his power, and he'd gained knowledge of the future. Brother Jasper's suspicious death had concerned him, and David had combined forces with the dragons. He reminded them two red robes were still missing and presumably under the influence of Brother Matthew's drugs.

"Treat them as dangerous until they go through detoxification."

Finally, he told the brothers about his tattoos and how Rena had developed matching ones.

"Prove it," one of the white robes called.

David opened his robe and tugged it back from his shoulders. His tattoos glowed an unearthly electric blue, and strangely, this time, he experienced an answering pulse as if Rena was close.

The brothers whispered to each other. Several exchanged glances before Brother Colin stood.

"Brother Jasper spoke to me several months ago and told me he suspected you were the lock, and you would soon find your key. The woman—her tattoos mirror yours?"

"Yes," David said. "I love her and want to be with her. I realize this means I must leave the monastery."

"No!" Brother Colin thundered, his loud voice drawing attention. He swallowed hard, his gaze darting around the faces of the other druids. "The truth is we're not sure how we've powered the barrier these last six months. Brother Matthew was most concerned because the barrier kept failing, for short bursts. We couldn't work out why our magic wasn't remaining constant. We managed to keep the failure secret since, as I mentioned, the downtime was minimal, and the situation rectified itself. This puzzled us. Brother Jasper insisted you were powering the barrier. Unfortunately, we didn't believe him." He bowed his head, but not before David glimpsed shame creeping into his expression. "I was one who sided with Brother Matthew against Brother Jasper."

If he had, in fact, powered the barrier, he'd no idea how he'd managed the feat. "Could it have failed when I was on the dreamscape?" he asked.

"It's possible. Brother Jasper opined we drew our power from you. He always deemed you special even though most of us wondered why he bothered with your lack of ambition. He told me and Brother Matthew, you would mature when you were ready, when we needed you. Brother Matthew pooh-poohed the theory, but I have never forgotten Jasper's words. Brother Jasper was an experienced man. He was correct to hold faith in you."

"I don't understand," David said. "Who will power the barrier once I leave the monastery as per the rules?"

"We're not asking you to leave," Brother Colin emphasized. "We require your expertise to help us rebuild and carve a path going forward. Your key is welcome to stay with you. We need her too."

"But you've never had a woman living here and working alongside us."

"I believe it is time to start. We require every advantage while we rebuild. From what you've told us, your key has suffered much at the hands of Brother Matthew. She has courage and dignity, and she is wise if she found you."

"You mean this?" David asked. "I want to help to rebuild, but my Rena requires time on the mainland. She is smart and is studying to help catch criminals, thieves, and murderers in her world. I applaud her drive and ambition and wish to make her happy. She won't be if I must stay to power the barrier."

"What say you brothers?" Brother Colin asked. "It's time to vote. Brother David and his lady key should remain at the monastery while we rebuild. They should have our permission to travel through the barrier and spend time on the mainland to ensure their happy union. In return, they will help us regain control of the barrier."

"I agree, but at the same time, I believe we should offer accommodation for travelers and sell our produce. Our reliance on the dragons helped us into this mess," a blue robe said.

"Aye," the brother beside Brother Colin said. "I agree with the proposition and believe we should allow limited numbers through the barrier to grow our communities. Change is important. Adaptability. In our long years hidden behind the barrier, we have remained at a standstill."

Astonishment filled David at the druids' words, and at the way the vote continued at breakneck speed.

"Will you stay?" Brother Colin asked. "Now that you understand, we are in favor of you staying."

"I wish to consult with Rena, but I believe that will be acceptable. Rena's friend and Rena's sister are both mated to dragons. She is close to the women and wishes to have regular contact."

"While we are gathered, I would like to suggest we promote Brother David to senior druid status. I believe that as the lock, he will be suitable to begin a new training regime for the junior druids," Brother Colin announced.

"I could help train," David said cautiously.

"Not simply train but start a new program. We should offer kitchen and garden work to humans. While we'd have to pay wages, this would free up time for study and proper training. During the last years, we have treated the youngsters as our slaves. There is little laughter or enjoyment in our days. While we should be serious at times, there is a place for frivolity and happiness." Brother Colin said.

"I agree," one of the blue robes said. "I volunteer to work with the community to offer medical aid. We should use our knowledge to help humans and dragons."

"Yes," a red robe corroborated. "A complete upheaval of our routines. Our lives. We should become more open, and I believe this would stop the situation with Brother Matthew from reoccurring."

"Aye."

"Yes!"

Several brothers nodded to add their agreement to the monastery reorganization.

"Excellent," Brother Colin said. "I suggest we go away and ponder the changes we believe would help the entire monastery.

We will reconvene our meeting tomorrow at the same time. Please bring your ideas, and we will choose the best one. Brother David, you and your key, Rena, should attend, since you will live here for part of the time."

"Rena and I are traveling to Holy Island on the morn with our friends. We wish to locate the missing humans."

Brother Colin nodded thoughtfully. "You think that is where the missing red robes are at present?"

"Yes," David said.

"Take red robes with you," one suggested. "Brother Jerrard and Brother Jerome won't know we are no longer under the influence of Brother Matthew's drug."

David hesitated, debating the pros and cons. "No offense, but we're wary of red robes at present. While I understand you weren't aware of your actions, several of you attacked my friends and almost killed them. We will be happier if the only red robes we come into contact with are the missing ones. If we hesitate to attack, assuming they are part of our group, we might die."

"Brother David is correct," a red robe said. "We have much to atone for since we allowed Brother Matthew to turn us into weapons, but you mustn't underestimate Brother Jerrard and Brother Jerome. Of all of us, they are the strongest and most experienced with their magic, and their identical twin status gives them an extra boost of power. Take great care, and if you require our aid, you know where to find us."

"I don't believe Brother David requires your help," Brother Colin said. "Between him and his key, they have more power than two red robes. They will deal with the two missing should they come across them. Remember, bring your ideas to our next meeting."

The brothers dispersed, leaving David with Brother Colin.

"Jasper would be proud of you." Brother Colin beamed in approval. "He always saw your latent talent and your possibilities."

David frowned. "You say I have power. Aren't you worried I could hunger for more and take over the monastery?"

"No," Brother Colin said without hesitation. "You have integrity. You care for others. Also, I believe the monastery is the seat of your power. If you do not intend to stay here full time, that will be a form of a check on your magical powers."

"That makes sense. It's a relief. I find myself eager to experience more than life at the monastery."

"Brother Jasper and I discussed you leaving at some stage. Everything is happening as it should. As he predicted."

"I miss him," David said.

"Remember him with fondness," Brother Colin said. "He could not wish for more. Off you go, lad. Join your lady. Tell her I look forward to meeting her. Tell her she and her friends will always be welcome here."

"Thank you."

"No, thank you. Change is important, and none of this

would've happened without you and your friends."

David left the meeting, feeling positive regarding the coming changes. Brother Colin was a virtuous man who was always willing to listen to others' opinions and suggestions. That boded well for the monastery's future.

CHAPTER 28

Love, Happiness, and Crushing Evil Dragons

"Why didn't you wake me on your return?" Rena asked the next morning.

David smiled, enjoying her soft body against his and the warmth they generated together. He dropped a kiss on her naked shoulder. "You were exhausted and needed sleep. You scarcely moved when I slid into bed."

"I can't believe we're together," Rena said.

Her hips undulated, and David bit back a groan. This...being together...every sensation magnified. So much better than on the dreamscape. He ran his hand down her back, his fingers skimming her silky skin.

"I want to spend time with you. Be with you now. Always. I love you, Rena Carrington. From the moment I followed your ribbon on the dreamscape, and you awakened and said hello, I wanted you."

Rena grinned. "You seduced me pretty damn quick."

"You enticed me. Once I laid eyes on you, I saw no one else." David kissed her shoulder, her neck, and the corner of her mouth.

Rena turned into the kiss. She swept her tongue over the seam of his lips and swallowed his groan of enjoyment. When their lips parted, he rubbed his nose against hers and grinned. "I believe we have plenty of time before we must break our fast."

"What are you saying?"

"We can make love at a leisurely pace. Don't you think we should savor each other?

Rena gave a solemn nod. "Let's do this." She rolled until she sprawled on top of his big, naked body. The blue tattoos on his chest brightened and glowed. To his astonishment, the faint tattoos on Rena's body glittered in the same shade. He traced a whorl of blue on her ribs and followed the flowing lines up toward one of her breasts. With each of his delicate touches, her tattoos glowed brighter and radiated more heat beneath his exploring fingertips.

Curious, he leaned down and traced one of the spiral curves with his tongue. She gasped, her upper body arching.

"Steady, my sweet cynamone," he whispered. He traced a circle around her nipple and sighed with pleasure. "You taste so sweet." Wanting another taste, he cupped her breast and drew her peak between his lips.

Her soft sigh pleased him, and he set out to draw more murmurs from her.

More pleasure.

She gripped his shoulders, baring the cords of her neck to his explorations. Enticed, he nuzzled her neck before drawing on her flesh. She shivered, her groan telling him she delighted in his touch.

"Please kiss me again." She offered her mouth, and her eyes shut as she waited.

"Any time," David said and claimed her lips.

Rena couldn't believe she was touching David. Kissing him. Every part of her shimmered with pleasure, his hands and mouth stirring her nerve endings to life and bringing joy. So much joy. His big hands, callused from working at the monastery, slid over her back and drew her closer.

Each touch generated more blue light from their tattoos until they both glowed. His cock slid across her hip, leaving a wet trail. She parted her legs, and without warning, he twisted and loomed over her. He grinned down at her, pleased with himself for taking control. Their lips met again, and Rena drifted into a world of sensation.

She'd thought that, despite his words of a leisurely loving, he'd hurry, as eager as her to consummate their love. Instead, he kissed his way down her rib cage, twirled his tongue around her navel. Moisture gathered at her sex with each of his touches, the strokes of his talented fingers. He paid attention to each shiver and tremble, the caresses that drove her pleasure higher. The curve of her hip. The tender skin of her inner thigh, and the more he stroked and petted her, the brighter those weird tattoos glowed.

Instead of lying back and selfishly enjoying his touch without reciprocating, she explored the lines of his tattoos. He shuddered as her finger followed the curving sweep of one across his chest.

"No," he said, clutching at her hand. "I can't concentrate when you're doing that. Flames engulf my skin, and the power and heat of it sinks to my groin. I fear I will have no control if I allow your hands to wander. Please, for this first time, can you let me taste you before we give in to the magic between us?"

"This isn't our first time," Rena whispered.

"It feels brand new." David cocked his head, his brown gaze intense. "We both have tattoos that shine an unearthly blue and power pulses between us. My entire body feels more alive than I've ever been."

"Yes," Rena said, understanding what he meant. "Making love had never been like this. Do your worst," she whispered. "If the urgency takes me over and I jump you before you're ready, you have only yourself to blame."

David laughed in delight, and Rena found herself joining in the hilarity. Except she wasn't joking. Her skin sizzled, and already her orgasm loomed. He'd yet to start licking and teasing her sex. She wasn't sure her heart could stand the low-level power that zapped through her veins.

When he moved farther down her body, she splayed her legs for him, flashing her folds without shame. His mouth tightened, and hunger blazed in his gaze. He gripped her upper thighs and licked her flesh with faint, barely-there pressure. The current racing around her body centered, sinking to one achy spot. She lifted her hips, silently asking—no, demanding—more.

David obliged with his lips, tongue, and fingers. He feasted on her flesh and ran his tongue up and down her slit, then pushed one finger into her, banishing the empty sensation. Her tattoos brightened, seemed to pulsate, yet she remained balanced between falling into pleasure and dropping into pain. David's mouth closed over her clit, the tiny nubbin vibrating beneath his touch.

"David," she gasped. She felt empty, the single finger not enough.

As if he could read her mind, he slipped two more fingers inside her, curling them with each stroke while he carefully suckled on her clit.

The magic cascaded through her, growing bigger and bigger. She gasped, each breath a harsh saw of desperation at her inability to cross from the promise of pleasure to ecstasy. David seemed to understand, and he gave her more pressure while simultaneously stroking her internally. The ripples grew faster. Stronger until she thrashed beneath him. One final suck, along with a hint of teeth to introduce the new sensation of pain, was all it took.

She exploded.

Imploded.

The pleasure had her shuddering. Gasping. Her tattoos shone such a bright blue, she had to close her eyes, and then she was falling, falling, falling. Throughout it all, David held her safe in his arms. When the ripples faded, she clutched his shoulders.

"Fill me," she said, her tone insistent. "I need you. Want you. Crave you. David, please."

He notched his cock to her entrance and slipped inside her heat.

"No gentleness," she insisted. "Take me. I want you to claim me." Where the guttural words came from, she had no idea. All she knew was she desperately required him to dominate her. But equally, she wanted to return the pleasure he'd given her.

David grazed his mouth against hers before he thrust. Each pump of his hips filled her, rubbed her in the perfect spot, and intensified the passion between them. Their room was awash with an electric blue light that came from their tattoos while heat gathered within Rena anew. David's strokes became faster, harder, and she gloried in the exchange. She shuddered as a flash of blissful sensation raced from her clit and streaked down to her toes. Another wave of pleasure blasted upward, hitting every heavenly spot on the way. Her mind narrowed, focused on the wonder and the man who loved her.

He groaned, and she sensed the waves of magic were bombarding him too and doing their damnedest to undo and annihilate him in the same way they were destroying her.

"I love you, Rena," he whispered against her ear. Then he took her lips, and they kissed seconds before the fever claimed them both.

"Wow," Rena whispered long moments later.

"Yes, my sweet cynamone." David parted their bodies and fitted her into his arms. "We should move soon."

"I don't think I can." Her mind still whirled from their lovemaking. "That was beyond anything I've ever experienced."

"Yes," David said, accepting the miracle in his stride.

"I'm not certain my heart can handle that much excitement each time."

He laughed then, caressed her cheek, and planted a kiss on her shoulder. "You are my one."

"Yes," she agreed with a yawn. "As you are mine."

Rena must've napped, and she woke, invigorated, and ready to face the day. Even better, David remained at her side, the warmth of his naked body shielding and protective even when he was in slumber. This was happiness, she realized. Despite the craziness and the danger, they had found each other, and she never wanted to leave his arms. She expected there might be difficulties ahead, but they'd face them together.

"You're awake," David said.

"Yes. I guess we should get moving. Rescues to carry out. Baddies to catch. Adventures to enjoy."

"Right." David kissed her forehead before rolling away. "Let's do this."

Blaze had arrived overnight with a thunder of his trusted men. Liza entrusted Joanna to two of the black robes who David vouched for, and Brother Colin promised to check on her throughout the day.

Their group set off on foot, and the portal crossing was without danger this day since Brother Colin and several of the senior druids aided them. The sun hadn't risen when they exited the Holy Island side of the portal.

"Split up into groups of two. We'll cover this side of the island since it has fewer tourists and inhabitants," David said. "We'll meet in an hour. Remember, if you discover the property, don't engage. Fall back and reconvene to share notes. It's better to join forces once we've located the property."

"Will an hour be long enough?" Leo asked.

"Yes," David said.

Without further discussion, they split into pairs, leaving David with Rena. "Shall we go?"

Rena grinned and held out her hand. Her skin glowed, a picture of health. A newly formed blue tattoo curved down her cheek, over her chin, and down her neck to disappear beneath the tunic Liza had given her. A matching tattoo marked his cheek, jawline, and neck too. The blue tattoo didn't glow as brightly as it had during their lovemaking, and he guessed it would fade soon, especially when they left Smoking Isle.

There had been questions, more curious than nosy, and Rena had blushed, much to her sister's and friend's astonishment. David had informed them it was because they shared magic and left it at that. But it was much more. The lock and key had a duty to protect those who were weaker.

The area they checked lacked buildings, so it didn't take their allocated hour. They arrived back at their meeting point first.

"Any luck?" Leo asked as he and Liza strode into the clearing near the portal.

"No, nothing," Rena said.

Gradually, their remaining groups arrived back.

"We think we've found them," Blaze said. "We didn't see anyone one, but I caught a whiff of dragon." He described the building where he thought the dragons had imprisoned the humans. "The property is isolated with no close neighbors. They've planted trees along the boundary and have done their best to disguise the building. I felt a faint sense of repulsion so my guess is magic at work."

"Can you break through the magic they've used?" Liza asked, her gaze on David.

"I believe so, but we have to remember the red robes' warnings about their missing druids. The dragons have planned well, and it would make sense to place their strongest druids where they have the most at stake," David said.

"Do you have a plan?" Leo asked, his brow furrowed in deep thought.

"We have the element of surprise," David said. "I'll attempt to break the magic wards to let everyone inside the boundaries they've established. Once we're through, we need to capture any dragons and druids and release their captives."

"Remember some captives might be dragons," Martinos said. "Many of our people are missing—those who worked at the mansion. They didn't go with Nan to Hissing Isle. It's as if they've fallen off the face of the Dragon Isles."

"So once we get past the magic, we're wingin' it." Cherry forced a grin. Her eyes were enormous in her pale face, yet she'd fought Martinos's suggestion for her to remain at the monastery.

"I'm afraid so," David said. "Once the magical protection fails, they'll know someone is outside. Stealth is impossible."

Cherry gave a curt nod. "Let's do this."

Their group of twenty moved off with purpose. Once they reached the property, David's skin prickled with the magic in the air.

"This is it," he said when they stopped in a cluster. "I suggest we split up and circle the property. Give the building a wide berth until you hear the commotion at the front. We'll give you ten minutes to get into position."

"Make certain of your targets," Leo said. "We don't want friendly fire. If in doubt, use your fists and cunning instead of your fire."

With nods, everyone split off in their pairs, melting into the early morning light. David stood with Rena and observed the property.

"There are no obvious guards," Rena said.

"Because they think they're safe. There will be guards inside because the human and dragon workers aren't doing this willingly."

"They might be if the dragons have fed them a load of lies or drugs," Rena said.

"But they won't let them wander. That must make their captives suspicious."

Rena glanced at her watch. "Any last instructions for me?"

"You've frozen people in position before. Use that skill since you have an intuitive understanding of what to do. Leave the red robes for me and target the dragons."

"I'm terrified."

"So am I," David confessed. "But we're here since we believe in the cause. Work with your fear and embrace right."

Battle had always scared David. An understatement, but he'd done his duty and walked from the skirmishes with little more than scratches. Now, when the outcome was so important, he prayed they could work with their friends to apprehend these rebel dragons. His gut tingled in a mysterious warning. Something told him this mightn't be as easy as they hoped.

"Ten minutes is up," Rena whispered. "What are we going to do?"

David sent her a grin, and it felt devilish and daredevil on his lips. "We'll blast through their magical wall and create a ruckus. Hopefully, the others will sneak into the rear while we're causing a distraction."

"Oh." Rena's brows rose. "I presumed we were gonna be sneaky."

"Nope. We want to grab the cat by the tail and make it shriek in anger."

"Distraction. Why didn't you say?"

David strode forward until the faint tickles of magic increased. Fear rode up and down his spine, and he reached for Rena's hand, squeezing it in silent comfort.

"I don't think I can do this," Rena pushed the words out, the fear racing through her so intense she could barely think. Her knees trembled and struggled to hold her body weight. Her muscles tensed, and a silent scream formed deep in her chest.

"It's the magic," David whispered in a soothing voice, although she could see the tension in his jaw. "See the building where we think they're holding the humans? Concentrate on the outline or pick a point on which to focus. Let the fear roll through you, and hold on to the thought that I will face monsters to keep you safe, and together, we are stronger. We are the lock and key, and those who live in Dragon Isles need us to survive."

"Hell of a pep talk," Rena managed. "No pressure at all."

David chuckled, and she stared, arrested by the humor echoing in his beautiful brown eyes.

Rena sucked in a deep breath, puffed it out, and repeated the process until she felt steadier. "I'm ready. Let's kick these dragons' butts."

"Right. We'll blast that tree by the shed door. Once we have everyone scurrying around, we'll have a better idea of what we're facing. I'll set it on fire, and you blast it with cold if the fire spreads toward the shed."

"That's your plan? It sucks, you know."

David grinned, and her heart did a little pitter-patter. This man blew her mind. As she watched, his smile faded, and concentration took over. He lifted his right hand and drew a complicated rune in the air. Purple sparks shot from his fingers, and he directed them toward a spindly tree—the sole one in the dusty area outside the shed. A sharp crack exploded from the tree, and the trunk split into two as the flames caught.

The shed door flew open, and a tall, beefy man strode two steps. He didn't see them at first, the fire in the tree catching his attention. Three men raced outdoors at his warning shout.

"Freeze the two on the right, Rena. Don't kill them because we want to ask questions."

Rena hesitated, recalling what had happened the last time she'd attempted to use the powers she'd somehow inherited.

"Rena," David said in a sharp voice.

She jolted from her hesitation and focused on the outcome she required. With the picture planted in her mind, she raised her hands and pointed them at the two huge men on the right. Dragons, her mind supplied. The nearest one came to an abrupt halt while the second kept coming fast. Rena scuttled backward, her concentration fracturing.

David fought at her side, his attentiveness total while her heart almost beat out of her chest. The dragon she'd tried to freeze sprang at her, his smirk telling her he thought he'd won. *Freeze. Please freeze.* The man stilled mid-air with his determined gaze on her. Then, he fell, the ground shaking when he struck dirt. She eyed him, adrenaline rushing through her, and wondered if he would spring to his feet again.

A racket erupted from the rear. Rena figured the team had discovered an entry point. A furious roar sounded, and a red dragon took to the air. Another red dragon flew after it with a triumphant scream.

Martinos and Cherry sprinted around the edge of the shed. Liza trailed them.

"What's going on?" David asked.

"That's Nemyr, The Scary," Cherry gasped. "I don't get it. Martinos killed Nemyr. He fell into the North Sea and didn't surface. I saw him with my own eyes."

Two more figures stalked outdoors.

"What are you doing?" a woman demanded.

"Nandag, The Strongminded," Liza whispered, shock and horror in her words. "I killed her. She was dead."

Meanwhile, David stared at an older man, and Rena recognized him straightaway. Telus, The Organized. What the hell was happening here? They'd all seen Telus die by his own hand.

Martinos and Blaze shifted as one, clothes ripping as their dragons exploded from them. They attacked Telus and Nandag without hesitation. Talons struck flesh and flames speared through the air. The screams of fury were deafening.

The sight of two red robes exiting the building jerked Rena from her shock.

"Now," David shouted.

Liza and Cherry dived for cover while David grasped her fingers and started chanting and tracing runes in the air with his free hand. More dragons appeared from behind the shed, and Rena prayed they were on their side. Flames pierced the morning and sizzled on connecting with the dew-damp grass.

Shouts filled the air, the accent different from the voices Rena commonly heard. Somewhere, a woman sobbed as people fled the shed.

David squeezed her hand so hard she winced. Guilt flooded her as she realized her mind had wandered. Rena swallowed hard and imagined Nandag freezing in position. A rock flew, whistling past her head. More rocks flew and annoyed shouts of complaint added to the cacophony.

"Not her. The red robes," David ordered.

Rena gulped as magic filled the air. It wasn't coming from her, nor was it coming from David.

Martinos and the other dragons fired on Telus and Nandag. Rena couldn't wrap her mind around the fact they were dead, yet they were here.

"Rena, *now.*"

She jerked, aware her mind had wandered again. Holy frogs. *Holy fuck!* She'd get them killed if she didn't snap out of this stupor. Action now. Answers later. She squeezed David's hand and focused on the two red robes. Neither bore an expression, but their hands waved through the air, and their mouths moved in a chant.

A tiny flame of heat ignited deep in Rena's mind. She stoked the fire, and instinct had her directing it outward. The warmth darted through her chest and along her arms until bright blue sparks sizzled on her fingertips. More fire banked behind it, and with it came a wave of fear because no one should have this power.

No one. *And definitely not her.*

Beside her, sparks shot off David's fingers as he sketched a rune.

Their magic and the red robes' magic met in the area between them.

A scream built in Rena's throat as yet more blue flames shot from her hands. One struck a red robe mid-chest. His look of surprise came a second before he shrieked. Seconds later, the blue fire engulfed him.

Rena shuddered as his unearthly screams filled the air.

A flash of red snapped her from her trance. Pain followed on the heels, and her knees buckled, ripping her grasp from David's.

"Rena!" Liza shouted.

An instant later, Liza and Cherry stood at her sides, holding her upright while they pelted the remaining red robe with rocks. The red robe hollered and raised his hands. The roots of the spindly tree stirred to life.

"No way," Cherry muttered. She and Liza kept tossing rocks at the red robe, and it was working, distracting him from his magic. At least the tree roots ceased growing and merely vibrated in the air as if they awaited instructions.

The red robe sneered at David, the druid's jaw firming with determination and disgust. He rattled off a guttural charm and fired a blast of magic at David.

David groaned, his right arm twitching as he attempted to trace another magical rune.

Anger built in Rena. While Cherry and Liza sent a renewed hail of stones and rocks at the druid, she centered her thoughts and pushed away every erroneous thought. With her mind scrubbed clear, she concentrated on attacking the red robe. Instead of fire and blue sparks coming from her fingertips, a storm of hail erupted. The icy balls zapped through the air and tore a hole in the red robe's chest. For an instant, the druid continued chanting, then he crumpled.

Rena gaped at the man, shocked at the damage she'd inflicted. Silence fell, and several of the dragons landed. Rena rubbernecked, unable to tell one dragon from the next. To her, they appeared similar while in dragon form.

David groaned, and Rena scrutinized the man she loved.

The red robe had burned his arm, and his skin blistered beneath the charred cloth of the shirt he'd been wearing. While Leo, Martinos, and Blaze took stock of the situation, Rena stripped off David's shirt, peeling it away from his injuries with care.

"Place your fingers on the wound," David murmured to her. "Your fingers are still cool from spitting hail. Neat trick, by the way."

"I never want a repeat," Rena said. "I doubt even one of my forensic tutors could explain the hole in the red robe's chest."

"Do not feel guilty. He would've killed us without a care. We are on the side of right."

"We've captured or killed everyone," Leo said as he joined them.

"Everyone all right?"

David hissed as Rena placed her fingers on his arm. "Give me a little more of your chill. I will heal. I have had worse."

"Any idea how Telus, Nandag, and Nemyr returned to life?" Leo asked.

"More importantly, can they do it again?" Liza chimed in. "They are dead, right?"

David released a sigh when Rena increased the coolness of her fingertips. She focused, hating to worsen his injury. Yet instinct guided her, and the angry redness left his skin.

David coughed to clear his throat. "I wish I'd considered the possibilities earlier. Brother Jerrard and Brother Jerome were identical twins. That must've given them the idea to duplicate our leading players."

"They didn't fight as fiercely," Cherry said. "They appeared weaker."

"Which points at these being the doppelgangers. The drive and compulsion to complete their plan weren't as strong."

"This Nemyr was my true brother," Leo said in a harsh voice. "Cousin, I mean. He taunted me with something that no one else would know."

"But that also makes sense," Liza said. "Mixing their personnel to make stronger teams."

"Is everyone okay?" Cherry asked.

"The captives look tired and underweight, but I think they'll be fine once we return them to Smoking Isle," Leo said.

"Are they strong enough to walk to the portal?" David asked.

"My car is still there," Cherry said. "I can drive the older ones and any injured.

It took almost two hours to round up the scared humans and demoralized dragons Telus and his cohorts had kept captive. Some of those they rescued cried while terror still shook others who found it difficult to believe they were going home. Cherry kept busy driving humans to the portal while David and Rena got them back to the monastery. The druids fed them and treated wounds and injuries.

Finally, only Leo, Liza, Martinos, Cherry, and Blaze remained at the factory shed. David and Rena arrived to find them staring at the deserted building.

Leo gestured at the place. "The dead dragons and druids are inside."

"We deemed it best to hide the bodies from curious eyes," Martinos added.

"I think we should burn the building," Rena said. "But we'll need to do something extra because if the humans sift through the remains, we don't want them to discover bodies."

"What do you suggest?" David asked.

"Freeze the bodies with my haphazard magic until the remains shatter. The transformation to ice changes the body composition, and I think that even the experts will assume the building contained statues." Rena turned to Liza and Cherry. "Do you see any flaws?"

"No," Cherry said. "That guy you iced did look like a statue, and when he cracked, he was like a broken vase."

"Excellent idea," Liza approved.

"Let's do this then." David claimed Rena's hand.

"Is our magical power finite?" Rena asked.

"Let's find out," David said. "If we've only enough power to do this, then we've done a stellar job. I don't care about the influence of the lock and the key. All I care about is you."

"*Aww*," Liza said.

Cherry grinned. "That is so romantic."

After the event-filled morning, lethargy filled Rena, and she forced herself to move. This was to save the dragons and the druids, and to protect the humans who'd suffered at this place.

"Are you as tired as I feel?" Rena murmured to David.

"Yes, which is why I wondered if this power we have is limited to one act."

"I'd be okay with that," Rena said.

"Me too," David said, and she could tell he meant every word.

"I met you because of the key and lock thing," she said. "A man who completes me and accepts me with my mouthy attitude and ambition."

"You are a treasure beyond price, my sweet cynamone."

"You sweet talker, you."

They strode forward and stopped a few feet from two human figures and the remains of the two red robes. Three other bodies lay close to the red robes.

"I didn't realize the dragons change to their human forms when they die," Rena said.

"In this case, it makes this easier," David said. "Ready?"

"I feel as if we should utter a few respectful words, even though they tried to kill us." Rena bit her bottom lip.

David rubbed the back of his neck. "How about this? May your spirits soar upward, and when you begin your next life, go with peace and goodness and atone for all that you have done wrong in this life."

"Amen," Rena said.

With that, Rena cleared her thoughts and centered on the task at hand. A chill streamed through her exiting in a *splat, splat, splat* of icy rain. While her magic wasn't refined and tidy like David's chilling fog, she took care of half of the bodies before her hail faded to an intermittent splatter. Her head bowed, fatigue almost taking her out by the knees.

David's good arm curled around her waist, and they watched together as the bodies shattered into china-like pieces that no longer resembled their original forms.

"Done," David said.

Together, they walked outside, their silent watchers following them.

"Cherry, can you drive David and me to the yew grove?" Rena asked. "I'm so tired, I doubt I can walk that far."

"Go," Liza said. "Leo and I can walk. I want to call Dad while I'm here."

Half an hour later, they met up at the monastery. Brother Colin had fed and doctored the wounded, and tomorrow, they'd organize transportation to their home islands.

"I have news about Tony," Liza said once they'd gathered. "Since I disappeared with Joanna, the cops decided to deport Tony for visa deficiencies instead of charging him for kidnapping. They put him on a plane to New Zealand, and he's not allowed to return. Dad told me Tony seemed broken when he last saw him and terrified. My bet is he's actually pleased to get deported."

"If he owes a debt, his creditor will pursue him, especially if he's the illegal type." Cherry said.

Liza shrugged. "His problem. He brought this on himself."

Joanna ran into the dining room with a young boy, and both children clambered up beside Liza.

"Did you enjoy playing with Harold?" Leo asked.

"Yes. Harold and I helped Brother Colin pick strawberries." Joanna grinned. "It was fun. Later we helped make potions to fix sores. I like it here."

Liza rolled her eyes at her daughter. "Mystery solved. The strawberries account for the red smeared around your mouth."

Joanna giggled along with the more reticent Harold.

"We'll wash faces later," Leo said. "I'm starving. Let's eat."

Rena and David ate with the others and retired early. She checked David's arm and applied more of his healing balm.

"This is amazing stuff. What is in it?"

"Several healing herbs boosted by magic," David said.

"Not a drug to market on the mainland then."

"No," he agreed.

"I can feel a faint echo of magic still," Rena said. "I didn't feel it until we returned to the monastery."

David sighed. "I suspected the magic ties to the monastery, but I wasn't sure. I need to do more research and read the book Brother Matthew confiscated from me."

"You want to stay at the monastery," Rena said.

"No, I want to be with you," David said. "But I believe we should spend time here, so we can study this new power and also make certain the monastery proceeds as it should."

"That is a compromise I'm happy to make. Cherry and I will want to visit Liza and Joanna. We can live here for part of the time and perhaps Edinburgh. I believe you'd feel at home there. Plus, maybe a base on Holy Island."

"As long as I stand by your side. You are my heart, my sweet cynamone." He stretched out beside Rena and tugged her into his arms. Despite the fatigue that tugged at him, he wanted to kiss his lady. "I want to marry you, Rena. Will you marry me?"

No sooner had he asked than the blue tattoos on his body pulsed with light.

"I will care for you, support you in your ambitions, and even more, I will love you until the end of our days."

"Yes." Rena didn't hesitate—she who'd never wanted to wed. She'd thought it before and reflected on it again now. David was a gentleman, yet he was no pushover, either. He believed a man should care for his woman and protect her. But he understood she didn't need the same level of protection as his wife. "What if we argue?"

"Most married couples do at some stage. It doesn't mean they don't love each other. You and I have much in common. We want to help others and do the best we can. I help you here at the monastery, and you help me on the mainland. Throughout it all, we will love each other and demonstrate that love as often as we can."

"I thought you were tired."

"Not that exhausted," David said, and he kissed her. Slowly. Tenderly. Gradually, the kiss deepened, and Rena clung to him. Silken sighs and soft caresses filled the moonlight streaming through the monastery window. As he slipped into her heat, they made unhurried love, savoring the peace, the rightness, and the passion soaring between them. Rena closed her eyes to enjoy the sensations coursing through her. The licks of heat. The warmth encasing her entire body.

David gasped, and her eyes flew open when he stilled. "What's wrong?"

"We're glowing again," he whispered. He withdrew a fraction and slid slowly and firmly into her heat. A soft pulse of blue radiated around them.

Weirdly, every one of her senses heightened. Rena smelled the lemon soap they'd used to cleanse their bodies. She tasted the red wine on his breath, and somewhere in the distance, a night bird sang a sweet lullaby.

"This proves we're right for each other," she whispered. "Our bodies know."

"You still have doubts? We can wait. That would give me time to court you. I'd enjoy that."

"We can court each other when we're married."

"We could. I hadn't thought of that." David sought her mouth, and the slow buildup of their lovemaking turned to something with more urgency. The blue lights glowed brighter, and a faint hum began as they reached for their pleasure together.

Rena gasped as she shattered, the carnal thrill taking her by storm. David stroked into her then stilled, his breathing labored. Another mini-series of spasms prolonged the sweet gratification in Rena, and she held David tight. A loud click had them both snapping their eyes open and staring at the door. No intruder, but the entire room glowed an electric blue.

Slowly, she and David separated, and she gasped on seeing the intricate tattoo on his chest instead of random blue whorls. It reminded her of a Celtic pattern, and it covered half of his torso.

She opened her mouth to say something, but he was staring at her. When she glanced down, she spotted a mirror image tattoo on her upper body.

"The legend says if the lock and the key are worthy, the gods will gift them with long and fruitful lives," David said. "Brother Jasper told me if a man and woman did not abuse the power offered to them, the gods also favored them with a tattoo. *Mates.* We are mates, and the gods have shown their appreciation."

It sounded farfetched, yet she could hardly dispute the evidence. "I love you, David."

"And I return the sentiment a hundred-fold, my sweet cynamone."

Rena kissed David and put everything she felt into that kiss. Their room glowed a beautiful electric blue into the early hours of the morning.

Want More Rena?

Not quite ready to let David and Rena go? Yeah. Me neither. Get a glimpse of their first Christmas together in the bonus epilogue!

Visit Here (https://dl.bookfunnel.com/7ysovppzda) for your free bonus scene

Are you ready to read about Sasha, Blaze's and Griffith's missing sister, next? This feisty "Lionhearted" dragon is about to become the main character of her own real-life adventure story...

Visit (https://shelleymunro.com/books/sasha/) to check out *Sasha, Dragon Isles 4,* and read this standalone romance today! Learn what happens to Sasha when she goes missing off the coast of Perfume Isle.

Afterword

So now you know.

The butler did it!

LOL. I've always wanted to say that because the butler often commits a crime in mysteries, or at the very least, he's a creditable suspect. In fact, the butler is such an obvious baddie he's become a bit of a cliché. *Too bad.* I refused to forsake my butler character and gave him my own evil twist. After all, not many butlers are dragons as well!

I hope you loved David and Rena as much as I do. If you did, please feel free to leave an enthusiastic review for **RENA** and rave about my brilliance at your favored online bookstore. *grin*

Don't want to miss a new book? The next book? Sign up for my entertaining newsletter at my website (https://shelleymunro.com/newsletter/).

Thanks for reading!
Shelley

About Shelley

USA Today bestselling author Shelley Munro lives in Auckland, the City of Sails, with her husband and a cheeky Jack Russell/mystery breed dog.

Typical New Zealanders, Shelley and her husband left home for their big OE soon after they married (translation of New Zealand speak - big overseas experience). A twelve-month-long adventure lengthened to six years of roaming the world. Enduring memories include being almost sat on by a mountain gorilla in Rwanda, lazing on white sandy beaches in India, whale watching in Alaska, searching for leprechauns in Ireland, and dealing with ghosts in an English pub.

While travel is still a big attraction, these days Shelley is most likely found in front of her computer following another love - that of writing stories of contemporary and paranormal romance and adventure. Other interests include watching rugby (strictly for research purposes), cycling, playing croquet and the ukelele, and curling up with an enjoyable book.

Visit Shelley at her Website

https://shelleymunro.com

Join Shelley's Newsletter

https://shelleymunro.com/newsletter

Also By Shelley

My Precious Gift
My Grumpy Wolf

Middlemarch Gathering
My Highland Mate
My Highland Fling
My Elusive Mate
My Valiant Princess
My Highland Wedding
My Highland Billionaire

Dragon Investigators
Blue Moon Dragon
Blood Moon Dragon
Black Moon Dragon
Snow Moon Dragon

Dragon Isles
Liza
Cherry
Rena
Sasha